Family Lies

Doug Booth

Family Lies

To Davidson and Emily,

Now looking down and, I hope, pleased.

Family Lies

Part One

1940 – 1945

1

The bold print of the Reuter's headline robbed young Emily Ashton of her breath and many more months would pass before she would know the truth. The thin daily paper dropped from her hands and she walked away from it, knowing inwardly she would already have felt the horror of his death. She knew deep in her heart he was still alive. The baby was crying and she forced the dread of recurring thoughts from her mind. She loved Davidson desperately. She also knew he would only love her for as long as he stayed away. Her ascetic and severe mother glanced down indifferently at the alarming black print, her mouth twisting into a heartless smirk as she clasped her hands in solemn prayer, knowing all would be for the best if he were never to come back.

Emily left the room to suckle her baby beyond the puritanical attitude of her mother. She murmured soothing lullabies and wiped warm tears from her breast and Noëlyn's delicate pink face. Another Christmas Eve had come, and Christmas Day would be a day like any other.

2

The night air over the Mediterranean coast of Algiers was black and the turbulent water, blacker. The bright and silent orange halo of death illuminating the horizon had seemed like a beautiful midnight sun. Suddenly the glow was gone and to a man they feared the worst.

Crushed together, those in the back rows dragged heavily on the cheap French cigarettes they cupped in near-frozen hands and spit flecks of wet tobacco from the tips of their tongues that had long ago lost all sensation. Some prayed they would not be next and looked toward heaven for German war planes, not a God in whom many had ceased to believe. Others no longer cared. Little else beyond survival mattered to them. They just wanted to go home, if that home they dreamt of still existed other than in their hearts and dreams. Their faces had been painted with the grimness of death and the loss of their own souls for three years, they were old before their time, and for many their greatest fear was not of their own death, but of what they had become.

The commanding voice was sharp and clear even though the weather was not and the ominous words travelled the crowded length of the stark grey warship faster than the driving rain, cloaking each man with an even deeper gloom. The beautiful midnight sun was the Santa Elena, a former luxury liner operated by the Grace Line. She had taken a direct hit from a German torpedo plane and had begun her unconditional surrender to the sea with seventeen hundred soldiers and a crew of merchant seamen onboard.

The SS Monterey came about suddenly, the ship's steel prow and churning engines turning the black water to white froth as soaked and weary bodies scrambled away from the precarious angle of the portside deck. The biggest and the fittest who stood closest to the starboard railing were pressed into service by the ship's crew who were under orders of their captain. All others were ordered below deck. No one spoke. They all just looked out toward the invisible shore and waited. Their ETA was 0130.

Rain-soaked woollen gloves smeared their sore and roughened faces and their bodies shivered against the third day of cutting and relentless rain. Their khaki serge uniforms were wet through, their bones ached and their skin clammy and chafed, but no one seemed to care about that. Their waterproof ponchos were useless protection against apparent gale force winds and the cutting white foam that flew across the deck and away from the peaks of twenty-foot waves that bashed against the pitching bow. They were meant for water-filled trenches, or staunching cold moisture that would seep through their threadbare ground sheets, not racing against time at twenty-six knots, and most of the rubber-lined capes lay dry in the quarters below deck.

As though swept away by a single hand the 300 soldiers stood smartly back from the rail as the captain's voice pierced the wind and his own merchant crew made ready to come alongside the stricken vessel. The Santa Elena was off the starboard bow and listing to port. There was no option. They had each heard the order, though no one had bothered to obey it, one amongst them thinking aloud with a snigger that he was already half-drowned and the bloody hindrance would do nothing more than keep him fresh for the sharks. "The captain be buggered this one time…with all due respect," he said above a whisper.

Metal scraped and banged violently against metal,

shrieking and screeching as the heavily burdened ships repeatedly collided together and tore apart in a frightful cacophony of howling wind and human screams. The crew stood ready to heave heavy braided lines over the gunwales to the foundering ship as the bubbling sea beneath them spewed up blinding curtains of frigid water and oil. Coarse rope ladders made of hemp were flung recklessly upwards and down as the ships yawed and pitched beyond their masters' control and one man yelled through the din and wall of thickening smoke: "We'll not stay long if you've got no booze for us. We've not just come to save you ladies." The ribald answer came back quickly: "We'll keep the whiskey for ourselves, if you don't mind, sweet cheeks, but would you catch the butter?"

The determined soldiers rushed forward to the waist-high gunwales in an uneven and raucous chorus line as though they had practiced the manoeuvre a hundred times. Some were immediately hurled forward, forced to stare downward into the sinister black sea beckoning them to the mythical locker of Davy Jones, while others were flung carelessly backwards like broken dolls onto the slippery decks of the Monterey. Undeterred, the ranks of both ships rushed forward again and again, trying desperately to maintain their slippery stations for as long as they could, grabbing at each other's harnesses and belts as men were catapulted unceremoniously from their unsure footing onto the unforgiving yet welcome steel deck. Others leaped back onto their own deck to avoid being crushed between the violently surging ships until the once proud Santa Elena again towered over the Monterey and its men could rain down over their stalwart and cowering rescuers.

The rescued men were tersely ordered below as the frantic work continued and steel helmets clashed together; men driven by fear and warmed by adrenaline fought against the unconquerable and encroaching black sea. As the damaged rails of both ships continued to crash and shudder together, as one was thrown up and the other down into the sea, the brave men of the Monterey were determined in their resolve until all had been saved, except for a single man who had lost a leg to the indifferent ferocity of the two ships.

"Stand by me, Little Brother. Be ready for me and clear the deck for me," was all the huge Cree spoke before he turned his back on a stunned Davidson. Then, with every one of his muscles as taut as the string of a perfect bow and as the mighty steel frame of the Santa Elena came up to meet the Monterey, Big Earl threw himself over the grinding gunwales and landed on the Santa Elena's deck with perfect balance. The big Indian scooped the delirious man into his arms as he would an empty knapsack. He waited, poised, until the very moment the abandoned Santa Elena, pushed by a mountainous wave, rose up like a threatening grey colossus high above the gaping crew of the Monterey.

At that moment, Big Earl leaped with a high-pitched scream, making all but one man turn and scurry from the hideous scene of faces grimaced with agony and effort while the torn pant leg of the crippled man flapped wickedly behind them and sprayed sticky dark blood into the wet air. He landed on his toes and fell to his knees, swinging his pitiable charge around so that the tattered leg was in the air. He grabbed the stump almost viciously, keeping it held high as the soldier cried uncontrollably and looked on helplessly with wide-eyed terror, biting through the flesh of his own arm, as a ready Davidson staunched the bloodied stump with one urgent wrap of his belt. He swept the man away from Big Earl, forcing the severed limb into the air, and hurried away with all speed. No one stood in his way.

Not thirty minutes had yet passed and not a man had been lost to the sea. As the SS Monterey manoeuvred to a safe distance before surging away under maximum revolutions from the smouldering carcass of the Santa Elena no one remained topside. There would soon be nothing to see. From the darkened pilot station the two captains looked on with quiet reverence as the stern of the defeated ship rose up from the agitated sea in a final salute, vanishing beneath the surface with an almost deliberate slowness.

With calmer seas the SS Monterey would reach Naples by 2400, they were told, albeit wishful thinking in the mind of each soldier onboard. There would then be two days to drink and dry their clothes before the long march to Ortona and another chance to die. The troops and crew of the Santa Elena disembarked the Monterey the moment the first gangplank was secured. The Fifth Armoured Division had already been instructed to remain onboard until 0800 the following morning, by which time Father Darius Cicero had visited with each of the Canadian troops to deliver a gift from the U.S. War Department. No one felt the need for prayer. The old man's simple benediction over the ship's intercom had sufficed before the voice of a company commander boomed throughout the ship authorizing shore leave and freedom.

Davidson stayed swinging in his hammock, filling in the blank spaces of his new prayer book after reading the inside front cover which instructed him, by special order of the U.S. military and naval authorities, against writing anything more than his name on the fly leaf. To do so might afford valuable information to the enemy, the message threatened, and he wondered what Hitler would do once it was known he had come from Montreal and had joined the war to earn more money than a clerk at Morgan's Department Store.

The empty bunk below belonged to Big Earl: 6'6", built in the shape of a V from the waist to his shoulders and with powerful legs to support his trim 300 pounds. Even the officers who, one or two years before, had been teachers or office managers or cops treated him with obvious deference. That evening, though, he had better things to do than read pagan verses and bemoan a distant lover.

Davidson pondered what to write, despite the threat. He had sailed from Liverpool, England five days earlier, November 02, and his name was Davidson Alexander. That would have to do for now, he thought. Then he noted the padre's name because he felt the need to write more. He wrote to Emily every night, in his mind, and at least once a month on clean white parchment which was his most precious possession. He wanted to write more often, yet he knew that to miss one expected letter would worry her, perhaps with reason, making her believe he was dead when he wasn't.

He had not seen his young fiancée in more than three years and waited eagerly to receive her weekly letters, several months after she had written them. He kissed Emily's yellowed and sweat-stained photograph with his eyes closed, trying hard to remember the soft touch of her lips. He whispered his promise to her, the last words he had called out to her at the train station in Nova Scotia as the train's momentum all too soon pulled their desperate fingertips apart. He would never let her down, he would never betray her, and he would make something of himself.

Now his words and the touch of her hand seemed so long ago and unreal.

3

0500, November 09, 1943 came all too quickly for most of the men who were sprawled this way and that in their bunks or hammocks, some trying hard to remember fragmented pieces of their weekend, others not caring at all. The ear-piercing shrill stopped abruptly, leaving fifteen hundred men to exchange the usual empty grins and lethargic shrugs. By 0900 they would be marching to Ortona and could expect to be there throughout the winter. That's all they knew. There was nothing else to know. They were office clerks and tradesmen, taxi drivers and salesmen, cops and crooks with nothing in common beyond their continued frail mortality and the realization that eventually the man standing by their side would be dead. And many believed that would be the lesser of two evils.

He did not want to die; not then, not ever. He hadn't thought much about dying before the war; now he did and he knew he didn't want to die with them or without Emily. He was not like them. He was twenty-five and, unlike his craven father, he had everything going for him. He certainly did not need to be reminded that a dead German was better than a dead Davidson Alexander, a belief which, thus far, the Germans seemed to embrace.

His favourite hymn had always been Nearer My God to Thee, and he had sung the psalm for the platoon one evening in the mess during their Atlantic crossing. When he had finished someone yelled out: "Let the bloody Germans have as much of bloody heaven as they bloody well want, lad, if they can find it, or hell for what it matters, whichever is best suited to the buggers in our sights. Just let's make bloody certain they get there before any of us."

His kit was burdensome, much too heavy for war, though he never complained. None of them did, especially him. He stood six-foot-five and had the strength of any two men in the company, if not three, except for Earl who seemed to tower over him. He was always good natured and the others looked up to him for any of a dozen reasons, though to him their admiration was another heavy burden to conceal when all he wanted was to go home to be with Emily.

Much of what was in the kit was useless, particularly the entrenching tool many of the men had discarded in favour of pickaxes and shovels given to them by their English sweethearts in Liverpool. The standard issue barely made holes deep enough for them to squat over, let alone lie in. Their new equipment allowed them to dig suitable accommodations for two in less than an hour. On longer marches their Lee-Enfield's would be their walking sticks and grenades were thought to be problematic only by those who had none. The lucky ones had Bren machine guns that were light and obviated the need for precision aiming.

Most had long ago discarded their steel water bottles. What was in them never lasted long and weighed them down. Toiletries were a straight-edge razor to be used dry or wet, often with cold rainwater, and a precious bar of soap was always kept with special care for their next sweetheart. A ground sheet was just that and their poncho was often their blanket. The compass was thought to be good, though the gas mask was thought not to be because no one had been told how long it would last. The singular piece of useful equipment, they all agreed, was the web and the woven canvas pouches that hung from it. The pouches held ammunition, cigarettes, personal items, and the New

Testament for those who believed. Those who did not believe had taken the prayer book from Father Cicero anyway to barter at some later date for more cigarettes or soap.

The march to Ortona had taken several weeks over steep hills and narrow roads made muddy by heavy rains. The men were seldom much cleaner than the roads. Vehicles were constantly bogged down and weary soldiers in uniforms already mud-caked often slipped and fell trying to free them. At night, for as long as they could, many of them slept sitting up, wrapped in their ground sheets and ponchos for warmth while their feet, calloused with ancient blisters, were tucked into the palms of their gloves.

Davidson had given up counting the days. He had enlisted one year into the war, before being called to register, and had spent the extra incentive money on a ring for Emily. They had said the war would last three years, that he would be home in two, yet he was into his fourth. Emily was nineteen when they had first met and not yet twenty when he had left her. She had promised to wait. Now she was twenty-three and still the letters came. He loved her and he knew she loved him.

That past spring, and again in the summer, he wrote to her asking that she send another picture of herself in time for Christmas. Now Christmas Eve had come and all he had was the little tattered sepia cached in the pages of his prayer book. He squeezed his left eye shut. Seeing the solitary head two hundred feet to his left he pulled back on the trigger. He had given up counting them also.

Ortona was a city divided. Half was owned by well-rested German fanatics who were being air-dropped into the battle to maintain their numbers, the other half by beleaguered Allied Forces who bore the brunt of landmines, crude time bombs, and malicious booby-traps. Narrow streets were blocked with the rubble of battered family homes. Blackened windows in the light of day framed unknown dangers while rooftops were the preferred playground of the fierce German 1st Parachute Division.

Short range six-pounder guns and mortars were aimed at those blackened windows and rooftops, causing more rubble and destruction, while men were ordered away from the perilous streets and into the buildings to search room to room, smashing their way through centuries-old walls and down steep archaic stairways. Davidson had never killed a man, staring into his face, and hoped he never would.

Tanks delivered munitions, but there was no water or food, and no relief. Men urinated while on their knees or standing in the tight corners of buildings while comrades watched their backs. Christmas was everywhere except Ortona, a simple coastal village where hundreds of men, friend and foe, had gone to die. The scourge ended on the 28th, when, on their knees, the living prayed for the dead still scattered about them.

Slowly the narrow streets came alive with women and children whose husbands and fathers would never walk them again. The soldiers were invited into devastated homes to share modest meals and to luxuriate in cold showers, or to bathe in colder brooks and ponds. The older women of the town pounded sopping bundles of clothing against rocks made smooth from decades of the daily chore, seeming not to look. Nevertheless, they smiled and chattered while the younger women danced at the shore, teasing the naked men with bare thighs and kisses sent into the air.

No one in the division had used their soap, the one gift they had to give the women in return, beyond the lives of their fallen comrades.

Even Big Earl had parted with his precious bar, certain that by doing so he had forfeited a sweetheart wherever they would be marching to next. He had been with Davidson from their first day of the war and was constantly after him to enjoy what he repeatedly called life's sweetest honey. On more than one occasion he had traded a half-full bottle of questionable scotch for Davidson's soap bar. "Our women expect it of us, Little Brother," he would say. "It's what we do best, and what they desire most. We have no right to disappoint any lovely woman, or these lovely ladies." Yet, throughout it all, Davidson was adamant. There would forever be but one woman for him, and she was waiting.

The division would remain one week longer before marching north to Ravenna where they would join with the 1st Infantry and 1st Armoured Brigade to train as the newly formed 1 Corps. The men were rested. They were clean, well-fed and the hard floors of the ravaged homes were a comfort they would remember for weeks. Goodbyes were tearful as women walked arm in arm with the men along crumpled roads to the barricaded village limits; children clung to the arms of soldiers as they stood on the running boards of trucks or sat on the fuel tanks of motorbikes.

The men squeezed the women hard and kissed their cheeks without missing a step. Gently pushed away, the women turned back, saddened and suddenly empty again, but no longer afraid. Big Earl seemed to be marching ahead of the others. In fact, they were all marching quickly, for different reasons. Most were anxious for the mail they had been told would be waiting for them at the port city. More importantly, Big Earl had a new bar of soap.

4

Still there was no photograph, though to Davidson Emily's words were sweeter than any honey Big Earl would ever taste. He read each word as slowly as he could, savouring the chocolates and the warmth of his new socks and leather gloves she had sent him for Christmas.

She always began the same way, so he could do more than merely picture her in his mind:

*

My dearest and darling Davidson, I am sitting alone with you in my room, ready for bed and listening to the radio, hoping as always not to hear terrible news. It's September, my darling, and it's late, yet I can't sleep for thinking of where you are and if you are well. How strange it is to write such words to a man I know so little about, yet whom I love so much. I read your letters each and every night and wish you could write more often, even though I know you cannot. I am well, and mother is well, though she still doesn't understand how we feel and tells me so whenever she can. I don't care. I know you will be with me soon, to start our lives together.

There are still no guests in the boarding house, except a hobo who has fallen on hard times like the rest of us and does odd jobs for mother. Nevertheless we are still doing better than most. Mother and I continue to work at the textile plant, however this summer, my darling, I lost my other position at the munitions plant, which I didn't like anyway, so I'm not very…

*

If there had been a knock at the door her thoughts had blocked it out. Emily's fountain pen scratched a thin trail of blue across the paper and she looked up. The house was still her mother's and the old woman's unexpected interruptions were only one way she preserved her dominance.

"Did he send you anything?" she asked in her typically haughty manner.

"Yes, mother. He sent me silk stockings, which I won't wear until my birthday. They're too exquisite. Sometimes he can be so rash, but he means well."

The old woman pinched her lips together and shook her head disapprovingly. "Just like him to be so frivolous when others can barely make ends meet. Are you telling him in the letter?"

"No, mother, I'm not. I'm not ready."

"There are plenty of good men around who wouldn't mind. You know that for yourself. They'll overlook it to be with a pretty young girl. It's not like others haven't shown interest. He'll mind, though. Mark my words. It's his way and he'll not take long to be gone. You know that for a fact."

Emily knew her mother was right. She had made a promise to Davidson which she had broken, and no one could rebuke her or think any less of her than she already did herself. He would never forgive her, she knew, but until that moment she would be his and she would not stop loving him.

"Interest in what, mother? I don't care about any of them and I know what it is they're interested in."

"And why shouldn't they be. Let one dirty thing under your dress and there'll soon be a long enough line of them ready to poke and prod."

"That's enough, mother. I know what I've done, and I

know what I have to do when the time comes."

"I know very well what you're thinking, daughter, and it will come to no good, just like him. He's the devil's own son and no better than your own ne'er-do-well father. Mark my words: he's trouble and he'll do the same to you one day."

"Davidson isn't the one who did this to me."

"No, you did it to yourself. No matter. They're all cut from the same cloth and they'll do what they want when there's no one to see. That I know. And don't believe he's been away three years and not paid for it or taken it for free. It's not your name he calls out from behind some barn or some whore's mattress, to be sure. It's his nature, daughter, as much as it's yours to be swayed by silly dreams and his one letter to your dozen."

"Believe what you want, mother. I know in my heart he would never do that. I'm the one who's disappointed him."

"And you'll pay the price. It's best you tell him in your next shallow letter and let it be done with. I can write the words if you lack the strength."

"I love him terribly" Emily protested, "and you can't possibly know what it is I'm thinking."

"I do know, and it's best done now. I know he won't want what's not his to brag about. You must know that much, if you know anything at all."

Emily didn't want to believe her mother's hateful words, as much as she knew they were true. Each night in her room she would lay awake, resisting the overwhelming need to sleep. Awake she could be with him and let him love her; asleep she would tremble and cry into her pillow. The doorbell rang.

"The taxi's here." Her mother's tone was harsh and impatient. "Don't be a stupid girl about it. There's still time and he'll never have to know. He won't marry you once he knows you've been soiled by another."

Emily eased slowly from the edge of her bed.

"And if he dies? What then, mother? Isn't that what you keep saying, that he would be much better off not coming back to me, killed by a German bullet or trapped by a bastard son?"

5

The march to Ravenna was not an overly arduous one. The men were in better form than they had been for quite some time and spirits were high at the thought of pretty young girls, mail and several weeks of relative quiet. The training would be difficult and exhausting for new recruits. Though the men of 1 Corps were seasoned and hardened; for them training was a welcome furlough

By May 23, '44, Emily had received two more letters and a gift that happened to come to her on Valentine's Day: a painting done on the lid of a wooden cigar box. The intricate work had cost Davidson the contents of the box, not to mention one of Big Earl's priceless bottles, which meant he was severely in debt; money well-spent to see his one portrait of Emily against a backdrop of idle sailboats and stormy November skies in the Port of Naples.

Davidson lay in the damp earth of a shallow ditch, his rifle flat in front of him and the dome of his steel helmet not much higher, waiting for a stray German, though not hoping for one. The Allies were battering the Germans with everything from mortars at close range to 25-pounders positioned a thousand yards to the rear. They had the easy job, and the trucks, but the Germans were not giving away the Adolph Hitler Line. 1 Corps had been expected days in advance and what Davidson thought about most were the mines and going home without his feet.

He could barely see, camouflaged as much by flying dirt and debris as the heavy early morning mist. He was almost twenty-six, going on sixty-six and knew she wouldn't need a cripple coming home to her. He would go home in one piece or not at all. He promised Big Earl the same and they spit into each other's hand, leaving no time to think and barely enough to fix their bayonets and rush into the oncoming horde of determined and screaming men.

By nightfall the once pastoral setting was a palette of blood and fragmented bodies: Those who had died and those who still wanted to die. Forty-five dead Allies lay alongside 120 dead Germans. The injured were countless and the prisoners lay on their fronts with their hands behind their backs. They were the fortunate ones, their war was over. Davidson lay on his side and bummed a smoke. In five days 1 Corps would take Frosinone after a slow and nerve-racking march along roads and barren fields littered with German mines, but he didn't know that, or anything else. Neither did he know that three days after Frosinone they would be ordered back to the Adriatic coast where they could once again smell the brilliant blue and pristine water before marching north to the Gothic Line. Not knowing was the worst: never knowing what would come next, simply doing whatever did come next or feeling the cold steel of a captain's gun pressed against his head. He swore that one day all that would change, the way he had promised Emily.

The Gothic Line was savage and he knew then the war would never end. For as long as he had stayed in school he had always sat at the back of the class. Now, it seemed since his war had begun, he was always at the front. His turn would soon come, then others would follow, leaving the generals to kill one another. And about bloody time, he thought. Infantry tactics were for the classroom and well-fed generals who leaned over obsolete maps while they swirled French brandy, smoked British cigars and soldiers died. When two-hundred pound shells rained down on them from deadly five and ten-barrel German Nebelwerfers, exploding the ground around them or blasting men from their trenches and ditches, all that theory went to hell pretty fast. The Moaning Minnies were intended to wantonly terrify, kill and maim, doing both with an indiscriminate lack of precision and high-pitched screeching emanating from all directions. The Germans knew precision was inconsequential when they had so many available targets. What mattered to them was maintaining a barrier of black smoke and dust, hearing the shrill of human screams above the cacophony.

No one heard the orders because no one shouted them. They all just sat crouched and tense behind the relative safety of trees, their next defence already in sight as they waited to see their platoon sergeant scurry or crawl a few precious yards closer to their objective.

Davidson stood several inches taller than the other men in his troop. Big Earl was the one man he had to look up to, which made them both easier targets. At first the others in the company had thought Big Earl was a man possessed, hearing his blood-curdling war cry as he ran a zigzag path amongst them. Davidson had once thought the sight comical as well, if not maniacal. Until that first night when, crouched together in a narrow ditch and knee-deep runoff, catching their breath, the big Cree explained how he and his tribal brothers got away from the Mounties back home whenever they were caught drinking. The nightly sport was a ritual more than a crime. There was nothing else to do in the remoteness of the north and somehow the cops never caught them. They would always wait until the boys had downed a few before going into to the bar to arrest them and the game always changed to catch me if you can. Then Big Earl had pointed out how the naval convoy had crossed the Atlantic, doing the very same manoeuvre, and when they had jumped from the trench all the others thought Davidson was no less crazy.

For some time after, when they ran, they ran together, albeit in different directions. Though with much more effort as Davidson soon discovered and he quickly decided that crawling had several distinct advantages. Crawling was easier on his feet, easier to aim, easier not be targeted or hit and sliding into holes was always faster and took less effort than jumping. The downside was the mines.

The advance was slow and costly. Ironically, the ear-shattering twenty-five pound guns had eventually quieted the battlefield. Another Allied victory came shortly after midnight for those still living and Davidson sat leaning against his Enfield with its bayonet buried deep into the ground. He was exhausted and grateful. He had not moved from his last position and strained to nod his head toward his friend who was walking a slow serpentine path towards him, too weary to shake his head in disbelief at the contorted bodies strewn around him. The scene was eerie and surreal to them as they sat amongst so many dead and injured under a moonlit sky muted by thin clouds. Rustling leaves were silent. All Davidson could hear were the frenzied shouts of medics and the wailing screams of the wounded amidst a horrible vista of spectres and shadows, one of the worst he had witnessed as he struggled to erase the reckless slaughter. Throughout the night sporadic muffled shots would halt the aftermath for mere seconds, when those who did believe crossed themselves and those who did not clasped their hands together as though they did.

He had not had a decent bath since Ortona and he shaved much less often to avoid seeing his face that had become an incongruous and leathery brown mask atop a pasty white likeness of a man. He had begun to plug his ears with cotton, to save the one that was still good and his coughing had become a wicked thing. Like everyone else, he wanted out.

At some point he had simply stopped talking and had slipped into a deep sleep, too tired to dream. His wristwatch read 0700 when Big Earl joined him with the news from Field Command, handing Davidson his own tin cup filled with something amber. The Division had been put on reserve status. They were marching to France and Big Earl had already bartered several more bars of soap. What was in their cups would be their last for a while.

6

The hundred miles back across the peninsula to Livorno on the Lingurian Sea were long. More so in anticipation of one full day of sitting, laying or sleeping onboard the transport ship that would take them to Marseille, France. The sea was calm and the day was bright. Local fishermen cast their nets from double-enders or mended them along the rocky shoreline. Onboard was a complex scene of soldiers strewn everywhere who soon bared themselves to the waist to soak up the sun as much as be burnt by the wind. They were lean and trim and some had stripped to their khaki shorts. Davidson just stood looking down at the tongue of his belt still stained with the blood of the man whose life Big Earl had saved. He wondered how much more to cut off and who would take in his trousers, which fell quickly once released.

Drinking onboard was strictly forbidden, though the men were content to do nothing at all with the memories of their last battle vividly etched in their minds. By dusk many of them were twisting this way and that, some thinking it wise to splash saltwater on themselves for relief while others gingerly eased into their shirts. Big Earl sat beside Little Brother snickering, asking why white men always wanted to be red, when being red had always got him into a piss pot of trouble. There was no answer, other than a satisfied smile and a snort as Davidson reached into his sack. The warm night air was clear; the sky was free of German planes. He poured the dubiously acquired and very precious scotch quietly so that no one would be the wiser, although the next morning he and Big Earl were not alone in reacting slowly to loud shouts and piercing whistles reminding them of a war they wanted to forget. They were a few miles off Le Port de Marseille with 300 miles ahead of them before reaching Dijon. Along the way there would be minor skirmishes, crap shoots of death and survival and no one would ever know with any certainty where or when anyone had died, or even if they had.

He missed Emily and would sing to her during marches and cold showers or when he thought he was alone, when he wasn't. No one cared. He sang like an angel and many a man had a girl back home, so it was as though he was singing to all of them. Increasingly his silent letters to Emily became quiet whispers as the others slept. He would speak with her as they were dining, or dancing, or making love, even though he had not yet felt her in his arms the way he longed to hold her.

Each night he would cry the silent tears of a soldier. He was running out of words to write and his letters to her were less frequent. He was going home with his feet. That's all he knew or cared about. He had left her during an age of innocence and would return to her jaded by death and feeling old before his time. How could he tell her that? How could he warn her to not be there for him, as much as he loved her? He could not, and for that he felt all the more cowardly.

This time he asked differently:
*

My darling Emily, I have recently discovered I am a coward. Better you should know the truth now, and that my feet are of primary importance to me, for without them I will not come back to you. I am alive, though I no longer pray as there is sufficient evidence around me to suggest the two are very much unrelated. Many of us with Bibles have either traded them for smokes or bars of soap. Mine serves primarily to protect my single and fading image of you.

I am tired most mornings because at night, when I should be dreaming of you, I am invaded by horrible thoughts of those who will never again see their menfolk whom I have killed. You are young, Emily. I am not and I doubt I will ever be again. You need not feel any obligation towards me. It's been so very long and I fear I shall die here. I love you, and have from the very first moment. If, my darling, you still love me, then send me a photo so I might have something more than my dreams. I will fight with renewed strength and come home to you as soon as the bloody Germans let me. If not, I shall know I am free to remain here and die with a beautiful young girl imprisoned in my heart.

I am yours, my darling. I always will be, even in death, although that is certainly not my immediate preference.

Yours most sincerely, the newest Sergeant Davidson Alexander.

*

"Little Brother, you've got to listen up." Big Earl's clear voice was stern. "You're pissing from your eyes again and that's not good, neither is talking to yourself until all hours. You've been gone too long to expect anything other than someone else's sweetheart when you go back. The girl's been on her own four years and she's probably been to a party or two, and don't try to tell me differently. Damn it. She only ever sends us food, socks and underwear. We get the same from my sister, which should tell you something. A man needs more, and so do they. Jesus, man, we're in France. If you don't know about Frenchwomen you can be bloody sure your Emily does. I'm telling you, she'll expect it of you and you shouldn't disappoint her, or be disappointed yourself if you ever find your way home from this hell hole. Expect the worst and be pleased if I'm wrong, but I'm not, Little Brother. So find yourself a little French girl and do your best to break her heart."

Davidson stood slowly and smiled, looking up at the huge Cree. Bringing his right foot up behind the Indian's left knee he pushed hard. "I love her, and she loves me." He kicked dirt into the face of the grinning man lying sprawled on the ground. "That's all you need know, you pathetic red-faced totem and I'm writing her not to bother sending any more extra-large for your fat Indian arse because I'm about to kick the sagging flesh from your britches."

The wrestling match went on for thirty minutes or more, and not for the first time a crowd had gathered for what had become a nightly event. Though Davidson had never been inclined to fight his best friend in a loin cloth and smeared with grease, despite Big Earl's constant assertion that doing so would please his honoured ancestors very much.

Davidson was Scottish by virtue of his dead parents, or at least by virtue of his dead mother. When he did remember his father his thoughts were generally of finding the despicable old man and smashing a fist into his face. He had not seen his father in thirteen years, not since the man had left home to look for work one morning. He never came back and Davidson thought that might be a good enough reason to not die, so that he might find the old man one day and tell him how his wife had suffered for so long before dying in misery and abject poverty.

He looked down, a mocking smile spreading across his face to remind Big Earl that Scots did not do well unclothed, save in the dark. Then he was looking up and doing his best to manoeuvre against his massive opponent only to lose again. Anyone who would dare speak against Big Earl had a big man to go against if Davidson were to hear the words. And to Big Earl, Davidson was Little Brother. The duo was inseparable, other than those times when Big Earl deemed the company of a beautiful woman better suited his immediate purpose.

7

Gabrielle de-Saint-Valéry stood leaning into the window frame of a bedroom she had not been in since her flight to safety fifty months earlier. All day she had thought how excited and happy she would be, yet she was inexplicably sad. There was nothing to be happy about and she was solemn. Nothing left behind in the small apartment was hers, or his. Nothing was there to remind her of him other than the few most cherished possessions she had carried with her for two years: the gold filigree locket around her neck and too few pages she had quickly torn from a picture album before escaping. He would never again walk through the door the way he once did to hold her and squeeze her and whisper torrid words to make her slap his cheek and kiss him tenderly. He was gone from her and her life without him would never be the same. Jean-Philippe was dead, buried in the desolation of North Africa and she had already forgotten the strength and reassuring warmth of his arms.

Throwing out everything that was no longer hers would not be difficult or painful and she would sleep on the floor until she could afford a new bed. Peering out from the window at the final contingent of routed Germans hurrying to evacuate her street and the city of Paris, she knew her apartment would never again be hers. The squared panes of glass were thick with caked-on dust and her eyes began to blur with a flood of unexpected and confused emotions, making the Germans appear as one grey and fluid entity with thousands of booted feet hammering the ground. She looked at the revolver in her hands, wanting to kill the thing for what it had stolen from her and the vivid memories of her parents' torn bodies dancing like frightened puppets against the brick wall, held there by machinegun fire as she lay concealed in a filthy gutter watching them die.

The auberge was her home, her auberge, and her once-popular bistro downstairs would be popular once more. The Free French were on the fringes of the city and the German officers who had commandeered her small establishment had thought more of their lives than the contents of the wine cellar. France would soon be free, apart from the lingering and haunting memories of war.

The Free French took back their depleted city on September 26th. The night before Gabrielle's auberge was full to capacity and she had applied a strict ration to each patron so others would not be disappointed. There was no distinction between vin de table and grand cru. The choice was red or white and the price was whatever anyone could afford, even if that meant cleaning dishes or sweeping a floor. By the end of October she had made modest gains and all history of the German squatters had been washed away or removed from L'Auberge-de-la-Plus-Belle-Gitane. The inn was to have been their life together and Jean-Philippe had wanted every passer-by to know that inside was the most beautiful woman in Paris with the heart and soul of a gypsy.

The locals called it La Plus Belle and she was the most beautiful woman then and now, until she chanced to see the door open late one cold October night when her face contorted and she blurted out a blood-chilling shriek, letting the tray she was carrying crash to the floor.

Seconds later Big Earl was none the wiser when he came in behind Davidson. He just assumed the little Frenchmen seated around the bar were staring in awe at the big red man and that the women were openly fantasizing being ravaged by the biggest and the bravest of the Cree Nation. Davidson rushed to help her with the spillage, somehow thinking he was to blame.

"Did I frighten you, miss. You looked straight at me as though I had come to rob you or do you harm. I've only come to taste your fine wine. A glass, mind you, for I'm no more than a poor foot soldier and my friend behind me is in the same miserly condition."

Gabrielle ignored him completely, clearly flustered, snapping her fingers and calling firm commands he did not understand. Davidson looked back at Big Earl who stood shrugging his shoulders and summing up the male patrons.

Davidson reached into a pocket and held out a hand to her. "Clearly it was I who startled you, miss. Please, may I pay for the damages?"

Gabrielle stood quickly and rushed away, calling out more orders that preceded a flurry of activity behind the bar. Many of the men at the surrounding tables had also stood, arms by their side, sending a very clear message.

"Little Brother, this place is not for us. We're not wanted here. Perhaps they still have the sour taste of foreigners in their mouths. Let's bugger off, as your wise ancestors in their thick skirts would say."

"They're not skirts, you stupid heathen. They're kilts, kilts for the hundredth bloody time and nothing your savage folk could bear the weight of."

Big Earl's voice was firm. "We have to leave. I'm starting to feel a little like Gulliver. Do you know the story, Little Brother?" There was a disparaging look in lieu of any clever reply. "It doesn't matter. What does matter is that we're not wanted here."

"Aye, I know the story, Earl, and you're right. Let's bugger off. There's no point in being where we're not wanted. It's not as though we look like the bloody Germans. I'm far more handsome."

They left, Big Earl gently slapping more than one Frenchman's shoulder to make a point on his way to the door. The clamour of excited voices began when they stood outside and they stayed to listen.

"Do you speak much French, Earl?"

"Do you speak much Cree, Davy?"

"Cretin. I know they're talking about us."

"I didn't see it happen, but it seems to me you scared the crap out of her, Little Brother. The girl turned whiter than your arse." Big Earl paused. "It doesn't matter. We're here for no more than a week, maybe two if we're lucky. Let's make the best of it. Forget her. There's more to think about than one little girl. They've had a rough time and so have we. It's also our time to forget."

"I did it to her. I scared her, Earl."

"Little Brother, if you even think of going back in there I'll carry you back to base camp on my shoulder like a disobedient squaw."

"You're not that bloody big, you ugly coot, but you're right. We're not wanted. That's clear enough. They've had a rough time and want to be alone with their own." He looked up at Big Earl, disturbed by what had happened. "You go your way, Earl, and I'll go mine back to camp. I've no mind to party after spoiling the sweet girl's evening."

"You're right to feel that way, Little Sister. Look over there." Davidson had barely processed the words or turned before he was bouncing along la ruelle de la Falaise atop Big Earl's shoulders, not even knowing how he had gotten there. "One more white word and we go this way to camp. It's your choice, Little Brother."

8

It was one of the few mornings there was no sergeant screaming in their ears. In fact, for some months Davidson had been the sergeant doing the screaming. Despite the difference in rank he had not forgotten Earl: with one went the other.

The barracks were subdued. Most of the men were sleeping, oblivious to the muffled sounds of snoring and other relaxed expulsions breaking the peace and quiet of early morning. The two had come back late, barely meeting curfew; neither one better than the other. Both men had fallen asleep as they were.

What made Davidson wake as early as he did he would never know. What he did know was that he had to see her again. He had to see the little black-haired waitress who had seen him walk in and had changed instantly from a girl so beautiful and young to a wretched creature he had seen all too often on the battlefield. He stole quietly from the barracks, leaving Big Earl snoring contentedly.

The simple breakfast menu was scrawled with thick white chalk on the chipped and fissured black slate: Eggs and bacon with coffee and toast. No wine until 4:00 PM. When he walked through the doors the place was empty except for two old men sitting by the windows. They turned to study him, smiling and waving before calling out a slew of slurred words across an empty room. The loud rattle of dishes lasted until the doors of the kitchen swung back. The uncertainty they shared of one another lasted much longer. She was beautiful, even in the thick cardigan sweater with her hair pulled tightly back and dabs of baking flour spotting her cheeks.

"Is there a particular table you wish me to occupy, miss?"

She remained still, mere seconds seeming an eternity and very aware of the ancient cronies at the windows grinning toothless smiles and exchanging mischievous whispers. The energy in the room was palpable.

"Do you not speak English, young lady? Did you not understand me last night when I tried to help you?"

"I do speak English." She reached onto the bar for a mug and a coffee urn and came towards him haltingly. "Where is your big friend? Will he join you?"

"The brute's still snoring in his bed, if you can call the thing a bed. I think we'd be better off on the cold floor, but I hope I won't have to eat alone. Will you join me?"

Her brow furrowed as her cheeks tightened and glowed bright pink.

"No. I am busy," she answered curtly. "There is much I must do before the afternoon and I am not hungry."

"Then for a coffee. I must know how it was I offended you last night, how I frightened you so. I've not slept a wink thinking about it," he exaggerated. "Surely you would not want me injured or dead on the battlefield because of it."

She called out to the kitchen.

"I am sorry. It was not you who made me scream. You do not understand and I cannot explain. The story is complicated and personal. Please eat your breakfast and go." She looked into his eyes as though searching beyond him. "The wine here is of very poor quality and not much is left. There is another bar at the end of the street if you need somewhere to go tonight."

"Aye, I know the place. Though I doubt my big friend

will have much memory of it."

"Then you must take him back. Thank you for coming. I will tell the kitchen to hurry with your order."

She stopped, slowly, as he called out behind her.

"Then may I speak with the old gypsy lady. I suspect she'll want me to pay for the damage I caused last night. I know it was me. I saw it in your eyes and I feel the need to make things right. I don't want you to suffer for it or lose any part of your wages."

"I am the old gypsy and you owe me nothing. The breakfast is in the house."

She walked away without looking back.

He ate as slowly as he could. He poured three cups of coffee and still she had not come out. He left ten times what the breakfast was worth on the counter. Then he left feeling confused, not seeing the tiny shadows move away from the doors. He would tell Big Earl he had needed to go for a walk to clear his head, knowing full-well the big Indian would see through him. He tried to sing, though his heart was not in it and when he tried to whistle nothing more than muffled puffs of air blew from between his lips.

Big Earl had said nothing at all. He knew his friend's melancholy moods too well. It was not a time for humour; it was a time for distraction and by noon there was plenty of it along the Champs Élysées and La Place de l'Étoile. By mid-afternoon Earl was whistling for both of them and begging Davidson for his extra bar of soap, being that his friend had no real use for it other than bathing. That's when Davidson smiled for the first time all day. Big Earl could have the soap, free of debt, if he could find Davidson any kind of pretty ribbon by day's end. They agreed to meet back at the barracks to make the exchange. If there was no ribbon, there would be no soap.

L'Auberge-de-la-Plus-Belle-Gitane was crowded and noisy. Women sat lounging on narrow wooden chairs and men stood shoulder to shoulder around them or with one elbow glued to the bar as they argued or laughed with the one beside them. Everyone held their wine glasses with great care and sipped the wine as though tasting the last drop of a magical elixir. No one paid attention to him.

The man behind the bar stopped what he was doing and stared at him, motionless, as Davidson wedged his way into a space barely wide enough for his arm and pointed to the cask labelled Bordeaux. The barman's hand went blindly to a goblet and the ivory spigot. He filled the goblet with red wine and pink foam, putting it in front of Davidson without a word and opening his palm. Davidson dropped in a single franc and signalled the man in closer.

"The gitane. Moi," he pointed to himself before opening and closing his fingers against his thumb like a duck's bill, "parler with the gitane. Understand?"

The barman seemed annoyed.

"I am not deaf, monsieur. There is no need to scream at me. Who are you? Mademoiselle is very busy this evening. What is your business with her?"

"I have a gift for her." He reached into his pocket for another coin. "And I'll thank you for another tankard of your fine wine, whichever one the young lady prefers."

The barman walked away after taking the second franc. Moments later he was back with a second goblet filled from the same cask.

"You are the one from this morning? I know who you are."

"Yes, I am."

"She does not want to see you, monsieur. Let her be."

"I have a small gift for her, nothing more. Tell her I'll leave as soon as she has it, if she wants me to."

"You will leave very soon, monsieur. She is the one who has friends here, not you. Do not expect to finish your wine. Follow me."

The barman came out from behind the bar and went to a corner table without looking back, summarily ordering the young occupants to the windowsill behind it. He thrashed the surface with his towel, removed the ashtray and walked away. Davidson sat, acknowledging the younger couple at the window. He was a head taller than the tallest man in the bar and already felt awkward enough. He stared at the goblet, not wanting to touch it for fear he would spill the wine. His mouth was dry, making him feel all the more ill at ease not knowing how long she would make him wait.

She came towards him matter-of-factly, making it very clear she wanted him gone. She was unbelievably attractive with billowy jet-black hair that swayed as she walked. Her skin was creamy white and her white peasant blouse lined with red rosettes was untied for affect under a black bodice that was laced tightly up the front. Her red knife-pleat skirt was a simple A-line and her shoes were low-heeled black leather pumps. Her legs were bare. She let him pull out her chair and sat without looking at him as she took her first sip.

"What do you want? Is my English so bad that you did not understand me? Or are you lost?"

"No, I'm not lost. I have a gift for you, nothing more."

"A soldier with a gift and who wants nothing." She moved a closed hand across the table, letting the coins drop quietly. "You paid for your wine this morning, sergeant, and the broken dishes. I need no more gifts."

"You're very beautiful. I wanted to tell you this morning, but then you walked away."

"I was busy. I am still busy."

Davidson reached awkwardly into his jacket, really wanting to reach for his glass and slid the crushed soap box towards her.

"I hope you can forgive the poor condition of the box. It's been with me for a while. Do you like the ribbon? My friend could think of no better use for it, though, had I the choice, I would have chosen a colour more like the green of your eyes."

Gabrielle looked at the box, already smelling the freshness. She could have auctioned the contents instantly to any one of the dozen women who were already eying the coveted luxury.

"The ribbon is very pretty. Where did he find it in Paris? It must be the only one."

"My big friend has he ways. It was very expensive, I might add." He smiled. "He charged me my other bar of soap. I fear I shall be filthy for quite some time."

"It is very kind, monsieur," She frowned, handing him back the bar. "I cannot give you what you want in return. Perhaps your soap and your ribbon will have better success at the end of the street."

"What I want in return is to enjoy our wine together and to know your name. I haven't been with a pretty girl since I left the one who's been waiting for me back home these four long years. Believe me, I want nothing else. Your face has haunted me since last night and not because of your remarkable beauty. It's the shock and the fear I saw in your eyes and on your face: a horrible mask like none other and I need to know what it was about me that terrified you so."

Gabrielle sipped her wine. "I accept your gift, and now I must go…and you must go."

"Will you tell me if I promise never to come back, never to bother you again?" He paused, his hands folded in his lap. "Or I can sit outside until you do. We're here for ten more days."

She sighed deeply, looking around forlornly for any excuse. "My name is Gabrielle."

Davidson held out his hand. "It's a pleasure to meet you, Gabrielle. It's a very pretty name, much better than 'her' or 'the gypsy'. I'm Davidson, and I'm sorry for calling you old this morning. It was stupid of me. You're anything but."

"I am not a gypsy. It is what they call me." Gabrielle brought her hands to the nape of her neck, unhooking and kissing the locket. She locked the clasp before holding it out to him protectively in her cupped hand. "This, monsieur, is the reason that I screamed."

Davidson had not taken his eyes from hers, afraid that whatever else might capture his attention would make matters worse. As though on cue his thin smile disappeared as he glanced down at the open locket. He looked back at her, then at the locket not realizing how closely he had leaned into the table.

"Now you do wear a horrible mask, monsieur. Now you do understand?"

"Who is he?"

"His name was Jean-Philippe de Montparnasse. We were to be married, but then the Germans came. When our families ran from the city I joined la Résistance with my parents and his, he went to North Africa to fight with the Free French. It is where he died, unless he has come back to me in you."

Davidson was stunned, hearing her words, unable to look away from the miniature sepia that was his exact likeness. Every detail, every feature was his. He swallowed his wine in one gulp and slumped back.

"It's uncanny, Gabrielle. It can't be so."

"I do not know that word, nevertheless it is so and why I did not want you to stay. Now when I will think of him I will also think of you. When I will try to remember his voice, I will also hear your strange voice." Gabrielle replaced the locket and stood. "The next glass is in the house, monsieur. Then you must go as you have promised." She took up her soap and held it to her nose, inhaling deeply. "Thank you. I am very sorry that you will be filthy because of me."

He tried not to look at every inch of her, failing miserably and absorbing all of her unabashedly as she strode away. When the barman came with the wine Davidson stood and returned the table to its rightful occupants. Then he took their place and squeezed sideways onto the windowsill. It was 10:00 by the time he stared down into an empty glass, questioning why he was still there and eleven when the bar began to clear. One by one he watched the patrons leave, envious of couples holding hands. It was midnight and one minute past curfew when the barman yelled at him, telling him the bar was closed.

Arriving at base camp after dawn would not be an issue; arriving after curfew would be. The night air was not yet uncomfortably cold, though a heavy and penetrating dampness would soon glaze the cobblestone road and chill the bones. During the day la ruelle de la Falaise was picturesque with bakers, butchers and merchants' shops lining both sides of the steep and winding road that was no wider than an alley. At midnight, when everyone had gone, the road dark and quiet, devoid of life, and behind the patchwork of windows dotting the stone façades of historic and uneven buildings was nothing but more darkness.

Davidson looked in both directions, listening for the footfalls of military police assigned to protect as well as arrest those who had ignored the hour. Most of the doorways were flush with the outer walls, the others were no better than shallow recesses. The best he could hope for was that the MPs would scan the street from either corner and choose another street to walk down.

He chose the closest door, not seeing the need to measure or compare. He leaned into the corner of the doorway as tightly as he could and struck the match so near the tip of the cigarette that he drew in as much sulphur as smoke. He hacked once into the sleeve of his jacket, turning to lean against the frame with the cigarette in his mouth and his hands in his pockets.

9

Gabrielle saw him leave from her apartment window. She knew he had not gone as he had promised and she hated him for it, as though Jean-Philippe had come back to her. Yet she could not run to him to love him, to drown him in hot tears and smother him with passionate kisses. He was dead, buried in a foreign land, and yet he was so close she could smell the pungent smoke of his cigarette wafting past her open window.

"What is he doing?" she asked herself, speaking the words aloud. With each deep breath his face was dimly lit behind the glowing ember, a face she had always seen in her dreams and always would. Why had he stayed when he had promised he would not? What did he think he would gain? She closed the window and hugged herself warm through her cotton chemise and woollen robe. She knew what he wanted. If the bribe had not been soap he would have brought stockings or chocolates or perfume. She knew what the foreign soldier wanted.

She kissed her locket and spoke to him, asking him why, why he had not come back to her when he had promised nothing would ever keep them apart. He had lied to her and she would never forgive him. She would always love him, and him alone, though she would never forgive him.

It was a horrible trick and from then on his beautiful face and sweet voice would always be shared with someone whose young face seemed years older and whose strange accent she barely understood. She wondered how old Jean-Philippe had looked the day he died. What was he doing there? Why had he waited so long to leave the bistro? There was never a reason good enough to satisfy the patrols. She knew that and so should he. She wiped her eyes and stood at the window lost in time, watching him flick his crushed butts into the street and not waiting too long before turning away to light another. Every so often she would see him shudder from the dampness and finally he eased onto the narrow landing and melded into the shadows.

She turned and walked to her apartment door almost without thinking, other than to stop at her dresser for her revolver. She knew every square inch of the bistro and the lights remained off. When she opened the door to the street she shivered and tried not to think of him as she walked towards the shallow doorway.

"What is it that you think you are doing, you stupid man?" she whispered forcefully. There was no answer. She found a pebble on the street and threw it at his face. When he jerked awake she was standing at the curb. "What are you doing here? They will arrest you, you stupid man."

His smile was sheepish. "I'm afraid I have no answer for you, Gabrielle. I can say nothing more in my defence than I lost track of time and found myself here. The hour was much too late to report back to camp, though I'm very comfortable and the nightly rate suits my budget."

"You cannot stay here. I have called the police and have told them who you are. You have to leave. They will arrive very soon to arrest you."

"Aye, you're right. I should have walked a wee bit further, but it's been awhile since walking has been a favoured activity of mine."

She backed away. "They will arrest you. Please go."

He nodded, pursing his lips tightly as he stood. "Consider it done. I'm gone and I'll not bother you again. I meant no harm and I certainly did not mean to scare you or stir your memories of Jean-Philippe. Good night, Gabrielle."

She watched him walk away as though window shopping with her on a beautiful Sunday afternoon. She should have expected as much. Nothing had changed. Whenever he walked away from her he would always turn and wave. Then he would blow her a kiss and yell out how much he loved her, not caring who heard.

She stayed as she was, watching until he was no more than a vague outline. Then he did the cruellest thing of all. He turned to wave his final goodbye and a streak of frigid cold jerked her from the road and she crashed onto her knees. She looked at him from so far away for as long as she could before her shoulders sagged and she burst into tears, her body convulsing in the middle of the narrow street. Davidson hurried to her, half running and half sliding on the slippery cobbles.

He swept her up like a feather and she let him. Then he saw the gun. He hugged her close to him with one hand and pressed her head against his shoulder with the other.

"Come, Gabrielle. Come, sweet thing. I'll take you back in and then I'll leave you. This time I really do promise. It's bad enough the bloody Germans want me dead. I'll not see myself killed by a wee thing like you."

He eased her gently into a chair and went to the bar to search for a light. Then he searched for brandy. There was none and he poured her a glass of wine which he held out to her until she took it in her trembling hands. Then he went for a towel and a bowl of hot water. She had not looked at him all the while, not even when he tenderly washed her scraped hands and touched each of her knees with a single fingertip to check for bruising or worse. She winced and he had no idea what to do about it, so he did nothing. He wrung the towel once more and left it by her elbow. Her head was turned away when he lightly stroked her hair and walked to the door.

"You are still such a stupid man. You cannot leave. They will arrest you." There was no sound. There was nothing he could say. "The room number nine is empty. You can stay in there until morning."

"Gabrielle, that's very kind. How much..."

She blocked him out and walked to the stairs with her wine and the steaming towel. When she closed the door to her apartment behind her she slumped against it and gulped her wine, depleted. Before she curled onto the blanket on the floor she turned the key.

Davidson filled a glass for himself, left a franc by the cask and climbed the stairs. He heard the clicks from down the hall and frowned. He felt cruel and no better than a cheat. He had no idea what he was doing in Gabrielle's home when he should be at the barracks writing letters in his mind or talking out loud to annoy Earl. And how could he be so cruel as to torment such a sweet and sad young woman when he knew he should let her be? He was gone at first light.

When Gabrielle's help knocked at the door and looked in later that morning the bed had not been slept in.

10

"So, tell me Little Brother, are you sticky with honey from the hive?"

Davidson's face was grim. "I think she would have killed me if I hadn't been so charming. The wee girl has a gun and I believe she knows how to use the thing. I've hurt her, Earl, and you'll not believe how. I can't believe it myself." Big Earl rolled from the top bunk, more curious than concerned. "I'm the spitting image of the man she was betrothed to. He's dead, killed in Africa, or he was dead until I walked in on her the other night. I saw his picture, Earl. It's me in every way."

Big Earl sat on the bunk facing Davidson. The rightful occupant huddled into the covers had nothing to say about the intrusion into his space and neither did Earl. It was his time to listen. His friend spoke for an hour or more, rambling as much as confessing. He was not talking about a girl he had hurt as much as a girl he wanted to see again, or of a dead man as much as a man whose place he wanted to take.

Better she should know the real Davidson, rather than supposing the worst about him for however long, he argued with himself. He could take her to lunch away from her bistro and tell her about himself. He could tell her about Emily and whatever else would make her think well of him.

Earl grunted out simple words of advice before springing back onto his bunk. "Don't do it, Little Brother.

Let her be. She'll forget both of you in time. You'll just make things worse for yourself and for her. Let her go."

When Davidson replied, Big Earl ignored him. It was midmorning when he left the base on his own. By noon he had bought a single red rose and had paid a dirty-faced street urchin in need of spare change to deliver the deep-red blossom and return with a full description of the woman's reaction. When the boy did come back very soon after there was nothing he said that Davidson understood and all he could think to do was lean against a wall and wait.

A few hours later he paid the same boy to go into the bistro to buy whatever he wanted for himself, pointing to each of their stomachs and moving his open hand in a circular motion to make the point. He hoped for the best when, an hour later, the boy still had not come out. When the boy finally did he had rosier cheeks and was speaking excitedly. Gabrielle was with him, carrying a plate and a tapered pewter mug.

"Give the boy his money, monsieur."

"Did he think I wouldn't? I gave him enough for a meal as well, which I believe he's had time enough to pass while I've been out here in the cold."

"He ate inside where he can be warm. Please pay him. He has work to do. He is my new table boy."

Davidson flipped the coin into the boy's hand, shooing him away with a smirk.

"Thank you, Gabrielle, for not killing me last night." He looked at the small baguette filled with ham and cheese, then at the mug. "Or should I call the boy back to taste the food and the wine."

"It is not four o'clock. I have brought only water." Her face was expressionless. "The air is too cold for tables outside, so you will eat your food standing here."

"Thank you, I will." He took the meal from her. "And what am I to do with the dishes? Will the little nipper come back for them?"

"Leave them by the door when you are finished. No one will take them."

"I have nine more days, Gabrielle. I spoke this morning with my friend, Big Earl. He let me ramble on and when I was finished he warned me not to come here. He was right, I know. Still, here I am. I told him about Jean-Philippe, though it didn't mean much to him. Anyone would have to see the picture to understand. I told him what you said about never being able to erase me from your thoughts of him, but, again, he's not seen the picture. I told him I wanted you to know me for the man that I am: that I'm good and honest for the most part and would never want to hurt you in any way. Would that not be better than imagining me as some horrible creature who's stolen your dreams and tainted your fond memories? For my part, I don't want to remember you alone on your knees in the middle of the street, shaking, and knowing I was the reason." He looked at her knees that were scraped raw and looked sore. "How are they? You shouldn't be standing."

"Do you remember all the women who have washed with your soap, monsieur? Do you remember their names?"

"There's been one, if there's a need to keep count and, yes, I do remember very well," he replied with a teasing smile and a dreamy look in his eyes. There was no reaction, not even a look of disgust. She simply turned and walked away. "Her name is Earl, Gabrielle. She's big and she's ugly, as you've already seen for yourself. What he does with his soap is no concern of mine, though I've noticed he never seems to be very sad." Her pace slowed. "I swear, Gabrielle, Earl's the only one and don't think for a moment it's been very easy."

She glanced over her shoulder without slowing. "It is not far from four o'clock. Bring your wine inside where it is warm, if you must. You will sit alone and leave when you are finished."

He looked into the mug, smiling. When he got to the

doors with both his hands full, they had already closed behind her. She had not looked his way once and he had been about to leave when he finished. However that was after he ordered dinner and his second ration of wine. By that time the bistro had begun to fill and people were sitting at whichever of the intimately small tables had available seats. By 10:00 there had been more than one Frenchman who had shared his second ration with the lonely soldier, disregarding his apparently sincere need to leave. They had no other way to say thank you for giving them back their homeland. They also knew his war was not yet over. He left at 11:00, feeling content that she had understood him well enough not to shoot or poison him. His happy whistle pierced the cool autumn air.

He would have heard any man, but the boy was the runt of someone's litter and came up from behind without the slightest warning. "Pour vous, monsieur. Ça provient de la gitane." The boy raised both hands, holding up the baguette rolled in plain brown paper.

"What is it you said, lad?"

Gérard shook his head, not understanding. "De la mademoiselle."

"Thank you, lad, and thank the mademoiselle for me."

Davidson reached into his pocket for a few centimes and dropped them into the boy's hand. He looked up and along the row of darkened windows, seeing nothing as the boy tugged at his sleeve. He knelt down to follow the boy's line of sight without comprehending a word of his eager chatter. He told the boy to go back with a slight push to his small back and waited for the door to close. When he stood he waved discreetly at the window and walked away singing a gleeful song that would have sounded like gibberish to anyone who might be awake to listen.

Saturday the sky was bright, the air was finally warm for however brief a time and he had eight more days. Not enough time had elapsed to write another letter to Emily,

Big Earl had not come back by curfew and Davidson found himself sulking alone on his cot at the far end of an empty barrack.

He had no friend other than Big Earl and wanted no others whom he would have to bid farewell to on the battlefield. He had no wish to chase local girls, no more than he wanted someone back home to chase Emily and he had no reason to bother Gabrielle more than he had already. He wondered about her knees, whether she worked weekends and whether she would be there when he arrived. Mostly he wondered what he would say to her when he did.

The tables had been set up for hours and crowded with patrons except for the one squeezed up against the door. He looked ridiculous balancing himself on the wrought-iron antique chair. When he went to cross his legs he almost toppled over, taking the table and his baguette with him. He felt his face flush in response to the giggles he knew were meant for him and what he assumed were sympathetic comments from equally uncomfortable men. The afternoon sun was in perfect alignment with the narrow street and very few people were wearing their coats or jackets.

The first to come out was the freckle-faced young boy dressed in a clean white shirt, an apron that reached his new shoes and a beret that sat atop his small head to give him a look not much different from a speckled mushroom. When he saw Davidson his face lit up and he dashed back in. Not long after he came back out alone with a small goblet of wine and set it down once the table had been cleaned to his satisfaction. Then he stood staring at Davidson who must have seemed like a mountain to him.

"Thank you, lad, and where might your mistress be? Where's the gitane?"

"You are welcome, sir."

"So she's teaching you the King's English. And where is she, lad? Is she loading her gun?"

"You are welcome, sir."

"Somehow I think not, lad, though I do thank you for the sentiment."

The boy held out his hand and Davidson put a coin in it. But the coin was dropped to the table and the boy held out his hand again, this time trying comically to take the much bigger one in his. He said "merci, monsieur," then he ran away.

"He wants to say thank you. His name is Gérard. His parents were killed by Germans and he thinks you are someone special. He believes it is you who brought him to me and he wants to pay for your wine. He has already instructed me to deduct the amount from his salary. He is seven."

"Is it you who scrubbed him so pink?"

"You did not eat your sandwich."

"I had no wine to go with it, a situation happily corrected. And by the way, the boy's already told me I'm welcome to stay. Though I won't stay long, I've come merely to enquire as to the condition of your legs. I would have asked yesterday, if you hadn't ignored me." He stood to pull out a chair. "Were you spying on me from the window again?"

"No," she lied.

He took her hands in his, turning each one over and stepping back to look at her knees. "You heal well. I'm glad I've not hurt you more than I have."

"Will you come here for eight more days?" She shrugged her shoulders, putting her hands in her lap as he pushed in the chair. "I have nothing to give you."

"There's nothing I want."

"Then why are you here, when you know what is in my heart?"

"Perhaps I want you to know what is in mine, Gabrielle. Perhaps I want to know more about the man who looked so much like me." Gérard reappeared, clutching another glass of wine and set it down in front of his new boss. "Will you disappoint the young lad, Gabrielle? Will you at least share my sandwich? It's bigger than my arm."

"I thought it would last the week, so that you would not come back."

"And it will, unless you help me with it."

She sipped her wine, staring deep into his eyes and then she seemed to study every detail of his face.

"I am sorry. I cannot. One of my people is sick and we are all very tired. I have no time." She stood, taking up her wine without looking down at him. This time she didn't walk away. Instead she sighed deeply with her head lowered, resigned or defeated with tears in her eyes. "I eat my supper at ten. I have not walked alone at night for so long because of the danger. It is something I would like to do. Goodbye, Davidson."

11

When he arrived the tables had been cleared and the chairs had been turned over. Inside the bistro was crowded with men and women who had come to forget the war everyone had underestimated and to talk of better times to come. The air was pungent with thick, grey-blue smoke and the smell of cheap or water-downed perfumes. The bistro was a place for locals, with little opportunity for lonesome soldiers who had come to prefer the more convivial bounty at the top of the hill, most of them ready with soap or stockings if things went well.

Her legs had been bare each time he had seen her and he was once again in serious debt to Big Earl who had been ill-disposed to part with what he saw as the difference between an excellent evening and an ordinary night. If the barman had put the glass in front of him with any more disdain there would have been precious little left to drink. He ignored the spillage and he ignored Davidson. He knew what dumb meant, but 'bugger' was a new term and when he disappeared behind the kitchen door Davidson was still muttering to himself. He had intended to have the man deliver the package to Gabrielle, but it was too late. She would see the gesture as an afterthought and he tucked it into his jacket.

The barman came out looking quite distressed, apparently having discovered a new word and crossed eyes with Davidson as he walked by with a thermos which he thrust swiftly into the air. Gabrielle was right behind him and barked out an order as she stopped in front of Davidson to hand him a wicker satchel. The barman stopped at the red wine cask, filled the thermos and said something that made Gabrielle grimace and walk over for it as he shuffled off to the other end of the bar to continue his tirade.

"He does not like you."

"What was it he said to me?"

"It was nothing, something about a bayonet."

"You don't say. Then perhaps he'd like to learn a few more words. I'm thinking up the arse would do particularly well, though I suspect he's already acquainted with the feeling."

"He thinks he is my brother. That is why he does not like you. Take the bag, and this. We do not have much time before the curfew."

Davidson took the bag and bottle in one hand, already knowing she would not be the one to open the door. The night air was pleasant without the slightest breeze and they were the only couple not holding hands or kissing. He said nothing as they walked. He just looked down at her and enjoyed a feeling he had missed for more than four years.

He had never been to La Falaise, which was no more than a vertical rock wall to the winding roadway below where couples went to be couples or to sit and dream amidst the darkness that made the backdrop of the Paris skyline so singularly spectacular. He put the wine and the bag between them, and still he said nothing. To speak would have spoiled the moment. When he poured the wine into the silver goblets he held one out to her so that their hands would not touch. When he looked into the satchel there were ragouts, bread rolls and a linen table cloth he laid out on the bench.

"I thought you might have eaten without me. I was thinking I should even come later. I wasn't sure."

"It is nothing, the remainders from the day. It is more

important for my guests to eat."

"I think you mean leftovers, though I don't believe anything leftover could smell as grand as this. It looks delicious, Gabrielle."

It was all either of them said. He reached to the bottom of the bag for the spoons and laid one beside her bowl. When they finished he placed the bag on the ground and stared out over the city, calculating how long he could remain with her if he ran as fast as he could back to base camp. Being with her was easy. She was beautiful and well-suited to her nickname, though he would have preferred to see her in her serving outfit to the woollen sweater and long gored skirt. She had her hair twisted in a way he thought must hurt and he could smell the soap he had given her. She was too far away and would never be closer. It was just nice to be with her.

Eleven-thirty came too soon and he thought back to how nervous he was the first time he had thought to touch Emily's breasts. There was no more wine and his mouth would have been no less parched had it been filled with grains of hot sand. He wanted to ask her, but she sat there as though she were alone.

As he went to stand she shivered and only then did he realize how the night air had changed. He cursed, talking more to himself than to her as he unbelted and pulled off his jacket. When the package fell to the ground he called himself a bloody fool as she watched him stoop with nowhere to put it and looking at it as though it was foreign to him.

She shivered again with the warmth from his jacket, seeming in no hurry to leave. "Is it for me?"

He snorted, exasperated with himself. "Aye, it's for you. I meant to give it to your hired help before he snubbed me and damn near changed the colour of my jacket with his clumsiness; something the colonel would not regard with much humour."

"My rooms are full."

"Now you see, that's why I hid it from you. I knew your suspicious mind would go there. It's not where mine is. And, by the way, we say a drink is on the house, not in the house. Saying the other might be construed as an invitation by someone who doesn't understand your loose affiliation with the language."

He looked at his watch.

"My English is perfect," she argued, but really she pouted.

"No, it's not. It's your high opinion of yourself that's perfect." He looked out over the cliff. Then he glanced at his watch, cursing the time. "It's time to go, Gabrielle."

She stood without saying a word, clutching the thin package like a purse and walked away. When he caught up to her she slowed and let a dangling arm of his jacket touch his side. She shrugged it off when they came to the doors of the bistro and took back her satchel.

"You do not have enough time to walk back," she said, doing her best to sound indifferent. "Take my bicycle and bring it back tomorrow. Besides, Benoit is still sick and I have no one to carry my bags from the market tomorrow morning."

"I'm afraid I can't do that, Gabrielle. The other day I promised the padre over at your wee kirk that I'd sing for his flock. It's not quite the opera, though I suppose beggars can't be choosers."

She showed absolutely no interest, pointing to the bike. "Then return it when you can."

"It's a girl's bike, with a basket."

"Then you should be able to ride it."

"I'll be a bloody laughing stock. Is there no limit to your dislike for me?"

"No."

She gave him the key to the lock and walked inside without saying goodnight. He fiddled with the lock in the dark, cursing in whispers and hating that Big Earl had been right all along.

12

Sunday morning Big Earl declined Davidson's offer of atonement. Heaven was no place for an Indian, he explained. His ancestors were waiting for him in a far greater place, a place of plenty: plenty of liquor and young maidens. Heaven was better suited to Scots and other old women in their drab, woollen skirts.

The church bells were silent. The deafening blast of a direct hit had silenced their final chimes years earlier. The diminutive priest spoke no English and had not quite known how to react when Davidson, shortly after his arrival in Paris, had gone in for a few moments of quiet reflection without feeling any particular need to speak with God aloud or in prayer, or with any of his earthly messengers. Thinking himself alone he had stood in the second row of pews and filled the empty cavern with reverberating verses of Ave Maria in faultless Italian. He practically caused the confused cleric to fall from his simple bench that was hidden behind a portiere between his pulpit and the first row of pews. People, who normally never would, filtered in: soldiers and civilians alike, the pure and the impure sitting together, mesmerized by the voice of the young man who had assumed he was alone.

The applause was thunderous. Even the little padre had clapped his frail and veined hands together as he scurried over to Davidson delighted to be able to speak his mother tongue, though he was soon disappointed by the English response.

"He wants another, lad. Don't let the old man down, or us," is what Davidson heard. "Belt out another, lad, or you'll certainly cause a riot and that's no lie." There was a second, this one from alongside the pulpit with a voice that would have drowned out the organ had there been one to play.

That first day the little man had looked like a spindly and impoverished monk, though on the Sunday he had doubled in size by virtue of his ornate robes and he carried himself with quiet and pious dignity. When Davidson walked in the priest waved like an excited schoolboy. People had heard about the big Canadian and his flock had not been as full in years. No one looked at their watch, no one cared that they had not been saved or preached to on the evils of fornication and frivolous abandonment. They were at the opera or their favourite theatre, or wherever they had to be to find peace and salvation with standing room only and the padre seemed to have floated up to heaven.

The concert-like service ended too soon and no one seemed to know what to do, or what was proper until the little priest began clapping and jumping up and down. Much later the church was slow to empty and Davidson was the last to leave, not understanding why the priest had engaged the help of a parishioner to tell him to wait outside without telling him why.

The following moments were difficult for the young woman dressed completely in black, and perplexing for the priest because he knew. He knew the girl and he had known her young man. He knew how she had loved him and how gladly she would have died in his place. To do so would have been selfish, he had once chastised her, condemning the one man she had ever loved to a life of bitter loneliness. The priest was old, yet he had never thought of a hair shirt as a suitable part of his ecclesiastical wardrobe and he saw no good reason for such a beautiful young woman to live the rest of her life in misery. He understood and he told her so without saying the words. When Gabrielle left her face was streaked with blue-black tears. The priest remained in the confessional. His tears were clear.

She already knew he would be on the right and she turned to the left, hoping she would hear anxious footsteps behind her. There was none and she knew why, happy to be alone, happy he had not waited for her to come out. She had treated him badly when all he seemed to want was not to be alone. By the time she reached the market she had forgotten him. There would be other women for him to be with, to give him what he had said he did not want. The war was far from over and in another week she would have been no more than a wasted bar of soap and a pair of ill-spent stockings to him. To her the week would have been one of stirred memories and aroused emotions that had once made her smile and laugh, despite her deep sorrow. Now all she could do was to think of him leaving her again and again. Each time he left her she remembered the words. She remembered how they had told her of his death, and how each time she cried. Strangely, she would no longer have to and she felt sad relief.

"I'm very flattered, Gabrielle, that such a beauty as you would make herself even lovelier for no other reason than to come hear me sing." She twisted so quickly that her basket banged into the side of his leg. "Is there nothing you won't use as a weapon against me? I suppose it's a good thing I wasn't on my knees. You would have bashed my head."

"It is not too late." She turned away. "I am busy. There is nothing left of quality and I did not hear you. I arrived late, to speak with the priest."

"No, you didn't. You arrived early and told him to make me wait outside while you had your little chitchat with him. If you weren't so lovely I'd give you a good spanking, but I daresay it would excite me and God forbid that should happen."

Davidson reached out and took the basket, smiling as she filled it nonchalantly while humming one of the hymns he had sung and pretended she was alone. The second basket was filled to overflowing as slowly as the first and more than once on the way to the auberge he had to jostle them to prevent dropping them as she walked quietly beside him. When they arrived she told him to wait. The next person he saw was Henri the barman who yelled through the doors for someone to open them after Davidson had pushed the baskets into his unsuspecting arms before stepping back to be entertained. Not a moment too soon Gabrielle came to the man's rescue.

"Now he will never like you," she scolded Davidson.

"The man walks like a girl. I'm sure he'd soon be a favourite back at the barracks."

"He is very brave. Many times he risked his life for France. Do not be so rude to him."

"I'm truly sorry, Gabrielle. Why don't we go to the cliff? You can shove me off and listen to me shouting my sincere regrets on my way down. Would you like that?"

She had no expression on her face when she took his hand without looking up. He was the one who seemed shocked. "Where are we going? Is there something else for me to carry?"

"We are going to La Falaise," she said, flatly.

"I was joking, Gabrielle. Do you want me gone that badly, girl?"

"Yes, I want you to go, but you are too stupid to understand why. So instead I will tell you a story that even you will understand." Near the top of the hill she said. "The priest did not tell me what I wanted to hear."

"What was it you wanted to hear from a priest, Gabrielle, if I can know?"

"That I am wrong not to hate you."

He said nothing as they strolled together. The only other woman he had touched in four years was the widow who had opened her house to him and Earl, when he had hugged her goodbye. Now Gabrielle was holding his hand as lightly as a feather and he suddenly felt as though he should leap from the cliff.

Her story was long and he hung on her every word, too intrigued to know what to say, especially anything trite. The slim picture album held all that remained of her parents and Jean-Philippe, other than her locket, and with each photo Davidson came to know more about the man whose life he would perforce always share with her. When she finished she closed the album and placed it on the bench beside her. She lowered her head and pulled the hem of her skirt to her knees as she crossed one over the other.

"Thank you, Davidson. I put them on very carefully so that I would not ruin them. They are very fine."

"You've made them very fine, Gabrielle. Thank you, and forgive me for playing the fool."

"You are not a fool, Davidson. You are a man, which is not the same thing most of the time."

"Thank you for that. Does it mean you'll stop trying to injure me, or kill me? Can we be friends, Gabrielle?"

She nodded. "It is too late to say no."

He watched silently as her tears splashed onto her folded hands. He pulled her in close, kissing the side of her head and stroking her hair.

"If you promise not to be killed when you leave me next week I will let you take me for a dinner tonight. There is a little place that I know which is very quiet and not very expensive. I will make myself very pretty for you."

She nestled close to him, and he wondered sadly to which of them she had spoken. Darkness had fallen when they left La Falaise. Soon after, when she came down the steps from her apartment, more than one head turned and more than one man called out her name to make her blush with words that were foreign to him. Henri ignored them all, fluttering around the taps, pretending to polish them while admonishing her girlish naiveté and cautioning her to not surrender anymore of France to the bigheaded and very homely barbarian than she already had. It caused a chorus of "Vive La France!" followed by lively fists thumping the bar in rhythm to chants of "Gabrielle! Gabrielle!" whose face flushed from pink to deep crimson very quickly.

The night air was unseasonably warm, yet felt cool against her heated cheeks. After she rebuked him for his suggestion that he put the irritating little Frenchman into a bag and carry him to the barracks, she reached for the cigarette in his mouth and crushed it under the ball of her shoe. She ignored his comment about needing a friend, not a mother or a nurse, and so did he when she slipped both her arms through his.

She knew the owner of the charming café, apparently very well, he thought. They kissed and hugged and Davidson was shocked twice in one day when the young woman reached up to kiss his cheeks. She was Jean-Philippe's sister, Marie-Claude de Montparnasse. She gave them the most secluded table, alone on a tiny mezzanine three steps up from the main floor and he didn't take long to dislike not sitting beside her or not seeing more of her, at least not seeing what everyone else could see. Men and women were looking at her legs at eye-level, some admiringly, others enviously.

"She's a lovely girl and very kind, Gabrielle. Why did she not scream the way you did when you first saw me?"

"Because she has seen you each day since you made me drop my dishes. We have cried together in my rooms. Today she went to the church to hear you sing; even though she does not understand the strange way you talk. To see you was like seeing her brother again."

"And you, Gabrielle?"

"I know who you are, and I know why you look so angry. My Jean-Philippe would also try to be angry with them, but he never sat so far from me. They are looking at my legs because they are beautiful in my new stockings. Also, my skirt is short. Any French man would be proud of me. You are not. So you should not care. It must be that Scottish men do not like to be proud of the women on their arms?"

"Aye, they do. Like any other man we're proud of the pretty ones. We prefer that our sisters be the ugly ones, not our wives or girlfriends. And I am proud to be with you, Gabrielle, very proud. Though I would like to see a bit more of what's making everyone else so damned happy." He waited for the waiter to leave after pouring the wine, indicating politely with his hand and Gabrielle's help to forego the niceties. It would be time not spent with her. "Why didn't you tell me, Gabrielle, about Mary-Claude? She's such a sweet young girl."

"To tell you would have spoiled her evening. I told her this morning that we would be here tonight, if I did not kill you before." She didn't smile. "You would have come in to this café differently, not the way you did or the way we did so many times before, Jean-Philippe and I. You would have been afraid to meet her and Jean-Philippe was never afraid. She would have seen the difference. She would have known that you were afraid to meet her and that is maybe what she would have remembered. I did not what that for her."

"So you knew this morning, you wild-eyed vixen. And what made you so certain I would follow you from the kirk? You're not the only French loaf to be found on the shelf. There are plenty of others for the picking."

"Not for you. You are too fuzzy."

Davidson chortled. "Now there you go again with own interpretation of God's first language and your complete and unabashed appreciation of yourself. It's fussy, not fuzzy and, aye, it's true: I want nothing more."

The wine was a special reserve, though Davidson didn't know. Gabrielle knew. Before the war he would not have afforded it, however Marie-Claude had the same policy as

Gabrielle for most patrons who would order red wine no matter what the label indicated. The meal was very special, he could tell that much, though he would have preferred a more filling steak and kidney pie or a pile of hot mashed potatoes soaked in gravy with beef hash to be followed with a generous slice of sugar pie.

They spoke about everything and nothing. It was enough for him that she smiled once or twice and when he asked if he could sit closer to her she wriggled in her seat to make him believe she had pushed down the hem of her skirt. When he feigned disappointment, she showed complete indifference. He called her heartless and cold. She retorted easily that the one time he had touched her she had been cold because he had waited too long to be gallant. So how would he know? She was infuriating. No, she was French and she could only seem infuriating to him because he was British and had no idea how to be with a real woman. Was that so, he argued? She shrugged, and he thought to ask her how she could keep her eyes open for so long a time without blinking. It was disconcerting, if not unearthly: a terrible weapon and he had seen it work on him more than once over the past week.

When he sat beside her he eclipsed her body from everyone's view. Her hands were warm and fragile in his and suddenly she was not infuriating. She was wonderful and soft and she was his for as long as he could hold onto her. When their cappuccinos came she took a sip and left him to sit alone at the table without saying why. She went towards Marie-Claude and both women hugged before walking away together. It was eleven o'clock and thirty minutes later when Gabrielle came back.

Marie-Claude approved of him and Gabrielle remembered what the ancient priest had told her. There was no check. The evening was on the house, though Gabrielle whispered discreetly what he should leave for the waiter. Marie-Claude met them at the door. She was crying when she kissed them both and told Davidson through Gabrielle that she would pray for him. She reached up, touching his face with her open hand, thanking him for one last chance to see and touch her brother and then she quickly walked away.

Though they had not exhausted their conversation, not talking seemed right on the way back to the auberge. He refused the bicycle, preferring to end his perfect evening by walking straight on his feet and not zigzagging around amused or angry pedestrians on a bike several sizes too small for him. The hour was late and he had promised himself all evening he would not falter. He would act decisively. She would expect nothing less of him, he told himself. She had twice taken his hand and twice had let him take hers at the café. She was expecting it and waiting a moment longer would certainly make them more uncomfortable.

Her body came away from the sidewalk like a young girl's doll and the grip that held her close to him was as gentle as it was firm. When their lips pressed together there was no urgency or passion, no reluctance or regret. What he felt was a lingering softness and warmth and all too soon the time had come for him to go. There was nothing more to say or do that would make his day more perfect, or hers more filled with divergent emotions.

By the time Gabrielle stood by her window he was nowhere to be seen and she sank to the floor to ease off her stockings and to be with the one she loved. Monday morning she stayed as she was, curled on the floor under a blanket with one thin pillow under her head and another cuddled to her chest. She knew he would not be coming for her and she hated that she had been so weak the night before.

The day would be cold and the weather too furious with black smouldering clouds and deafening thunder. Crooked bolts of lightning were all that lit the sky to show a horizontal rain slashing at all things and flowing in deep irregular rivulets from the top of her window to the bottom, diffusing her view. The weather was too violent for anyone to brave for a coffee or a newsreel. It would be the same the next day, and then it would be Wednesday and then Sunday. Her soft shoulder shrugged against the hard floor and she cried into one of her pillows as she crushed the other.

There was no need for her to hurry. Henri could easily manage breakfast for their guests and it was unlikely very many others would come for their midday meal, if at all.

13

"Earl," Davidson whispered, close to his friend's ear so others would not hear. "I need a favour. Are you up to it, lad?"

Big Earl yawned and turned his head, bursting into a laugh. "Yes, father. I'm up to it. What do you need this time for the girl, soap or perfume?"

"I need you, you big brute. The devil's pissing a century's worth of beer and blowing foul winds from his arse worse than you ever have. I've been to see the lieutenant and he's agreed as long as we're back by curfew. You'll have to hurry. We may have to make more than one stop. I'll treat you to a lunch, if we make it in time, and your beers to boot."

"Slow down, Little Brother. What's happening with the lieutenant?"

"He's allowed us the truck. We've got the thing for the whole day. I've got the papers."

"Do you need me to drive, Little Brother? Are you afraid of a little rain?"

"That's the second time in two days someone's called me afraid and I don't much care for the sentiment. Listen to me you big, listless thing. The wee girl's got no bed. She sleeps on the floor each night when we're in here nice and cozy. Some German bugger slept in her bed for four years, no doubt with innocent girls who had no say in the matter.

She had no choice. She had to throw out the filthy thing. It would never be clean enough for her."

"Or for you, Little Brother. Is that what this is all about?"

"Listen to me, you big, senseless oaf. She's replacing each one as she can and hers will be the last to go. She eats leftovers at the end of the day, for pity sake, after everyone else, though she's not crying about it. I need a new bed for her, Earl, and if I try to carry it on my own I'll get blown halfway back to your bloody ancestors and the damn thing'll be soaking before she gets to use it. I need to do this one little thing for her, Earl. I need one that's wrapped and clean, one she can lie on and dream on in peace without hurting herself. Is it not worth a lunch, Earl, a grand lunch fit for a grand tribal chieftain and a superior warrior? Would you have me beg any more than I have?"

Earl swung himself over and off the bunk, landing like a feather in booted feet.

"I get the truck after lunch. Deal?"

"Aye, it's a deal and I'll wait till we're in the truck to kiss you, you lovely big man."

Big Earl feigned a solid blow with one hand and pushed Davidson to the floor with the other to a chorus of cheers and exaggerated kissing sounds from most of the rowdy ninety-man rifle company who had missed the nightly scuffle of late. When they were outside they pushed each other sideways, each one aiming for a puddle and missing before giving their attention to the weather and running full speed toward the truck to spring onto the running board and into the cab. They were drenched to their knees and laughing convulsively. They hadn't been together for a while and it felt good.

The rain showed no sign of letting up and the worn down wipers were more annoying than useful: they lifted and slapped against the flat and cracked windshield and Davidson's head was more out of the cab than in. Most of the shops were open, though they soon learned that did not mean much. Over the past week the war-weary Allied Forces had depleted most of their stock to be used in gainful bartering and very little of anything remained.

By late morning they were no further ahead until, by a stroke of luck, Big Earl had chanced to look out his side window. They had been to the department store an hour earlier without success, where now there was an animated stage scene of men and women dressing the storefront window and Big Earl was quick to smack his friend's arm.

The manager wanted nothing to do with them and was insolent in a way particular to Frenchmen. He had seen them come and go earlier, leaving his store empty handed. With customers like that, he sneered, how could he possibly be expected to give the immaculate centre-piece of his window display to someone who had stupidly discarded a perfectly good bed? He turned his back to them and began jabbering in French. Big Earl responded in kind, half talking and half chanting in his native Cree as he pulled Davidson beyond earshot.

A very short time later they were back, their arms filled with what they had both agreed would be appropriate ladies' wear for the boudoir, as well as stockings Big Earl had taken from a mannequin while ignoring certain ribald comments. It was more than the store would hope to sell over the next two days, considering the weather forecast, plus whatever the bed would cost, or nothing at all. He would also want everything gift wrapped for a very special lady, and the biggest ribbon possible for the mattress.

Big Earl was certain the manager had been influenced by the mystical powers of his departed forefathers who had heard his plea. Davidson argued it must have been his own determination and charm, though they both really knew the sudden and jovial acquiescing had more to do with his suddenly very empty pockets. The ribbon turned out to be several small rolls of coloured crepe paper taped and twisted together, and the decorative gift boxes, once wrapped, were more than an armful for either man.

The well-intended conspiracy had all taken much too long and they were much too late to do anything about it. What was done was done and if she would have anything to say about it, well, then, let her say so to their backs. They were agreed. They would give her a show and when the truck rattled and screeched to a stop outside the bistro they were still all puffed up with bravado and gusto for the task ahead.

One o'clock, the rain had not relented and the narrow sloping road had become a serpentine sluice made worse by the channelled wind that worked hard to blow the rushing torrent in all directions. They closely inspected the doors, then the sky, then the other side of the road and it was thumbs up. There was nothing and no one to be seen in either direction. And no wonder. They couldn't imagine who would want to struggle against such a tempest for a mere bowl of soup and a glass of wine, though they had not thought to wonder why the windows of the La Plus Belle were fogged or why they were painted with the muted orange-yellow glow of flickering flames.

The truck shrieked backward, then forward to the other side of the road, then back in a perfect arc that put its canvas-covered tailgate perfectly in line with the doors to the bistro. Big Earl jumped out from the leeward side, water instantly gushing up over the tops of his boots as he cursed ancient words. At the end of the canvas top he bent into the wind, first opening one door then the other, holding one back from slamming into the wall and pushing the other into a locked position before he banged the tailgate with his fist and screamed out a blood curdling war cry.

Davidson jerked to a stop a hair's width from the doorframe and scurried into the storm to lift the windward canvas and squirm under it before crawling on all fours to the back to the truck and tumbling out beside his friend.

They slapped each other heartily on the shoulders, turning as one to see the stunned expressions of a few dozen patrons and Henri doing his best to hold back a furious Gabrielle.

They looked frightful with their windblown hair dripping from every direction, their greatcoats sodden with rain and hanging from them like heavily weighted cloaks and their trousers half out of their boots. They stood in their own puddle of water with nowhere to run. The best of the best had blocked their own retreat and the enemy had broken free.

The thunderous weather that raged on suddenly seemed calm and inviting to them. Big Earl was suddenly Little Squirrel and if the once brave Scot had been wearing a kilt he would have shrunk down into it for her to step on and squash before throwing him into the trash barrel.

"I have no idea what she's saying, Earl. Normally she speaks to me in something closely resembling English."

"She's not giving us the menu, Little Brother. She wants us out of here, right now. She's hollering at the little fellow at the bar to bring her the kitchen knife. That's how long we've got to leave. She means it, Little Brother. This little maiden of yours is righteously pissed."

"Now am I supposed to believe you speak French, Earl?"

"I do speak French, Little Brother. I learned it from the trappers and traders in the north when I translated for The Company. Some were even smart enough to learn a bit of Cree and many of them came from here."

"And what was it you screamed out before I backed in? I thought you were about to rip someone's scalp from their head."

"I was telling you to back up."

Davidson laughed, not really meaning to, transfixed by the glare of Gabrielle's deep emerald eyes and rapid movement of her lips. "And what was it you said to the storekeeper?"

"That if he didn't sell us the bed I'd be having Frogs' legs for my supper."

He laughed again. "What else don't I know about you, Earl?"

"Little Brother, you're not making things any better for us. We've made a mistake by coming here this way. She wants us to leave and she's making no bones about it. Tell her about the bed."

Davidson looked down at Gabrielle who was livid with rage. "I don't speak your medieval tongue, madame, which I must assume is sadly deficient in words because they all sound the same to me. Please do me the courtesy as a patron of your fine establishment to greet me in my own language, such as you speak it."

"Don't push it, Little Brother. She's saying we've acted no better than the bloody Germans, that we've terrorized her guests. She's right, look at them. If you're going to make this right, do it now and do it without that smirk on your face before she slits your throat and, worse, mine."

"Aye, you're right, Earl. For some reason I've come to talk this way with her. I suppose it's my defences. I don't know. Look at her, Earl. She belongs in the universe on a dark summer's eve for the entire world to see. Have you ever seen any woman more beautiful?" Davidson dropped his heavy coat to the floor and stepped away from it, running his hands through thick black hair and pushing the wetness to his collar. "Ladies and gentlemen, I'm sorry to have disturbed your meals with our stupid and inconsiderate antics. It was merely my ardent desire to see this beautiful young woman once more and to bring her a birthday gift which I will not be able to give her at the proper time because I don't know when it is and I'm marching from Paris in less than a week's time. I will likely never see her again, so can any of you blame me for wanting to fill my eyes and my heart with her for as long as I can?" There was no reaction other than an unsure silence and he turned to

Big Earl. "Let's do it, Earl, and be gone with our skins."
Then he turned to Gabrielle who stood behind him, her lips
were quivering with what he thought was rage. "I know
what you're thinking. You don't have to say it. You don't
need my gift and you have nothing to give me. I'm truly
sorry, again, and if you can kindly show us where to put
your package we'll be out of your hair and you'll not see
me again. It's too easy for me to be the fool around you,
Gabrielle."

Big Earl had already dropped his coat and had pulled the
six-foot mattress to the rear of the truck, neither man
listening or caring what was being said behind them. An
older man sitting in the corner had stood to tell the others
what Davidson had said to them and suddenly they were all
standing and either clapping or walking over to the truck to
see what was going on. Gabrielle dropped into a chair and
hated him, still quivering with emotion or shivering with the
cold seeping in between the truck and the doorframe.

There were too many hands, though none of the men
cared. They all wanted to be part of the event. They all
looked down at her, waiting, holding the mattress for her to
see all the pretty paper ribbons and bows. She yelled
directly at him, blaming him for all the men in Paris seeing
her private bedroom and they all cheered, excepting
Davidson who stepped away from the crowd and snapped
his fingers at the smiling and excited Gérard. Her room was
number fourteen and the crowd of men rushed to the stairs.
Earl jumped into the truck. Davidson threw in their coats
and jumped up behind him asking what all the commotion
was about.

"The women are shouting at them not to go into her
room, that you can do it for her later. And the time's come
for me to go and for you to get out of my truck. A deal's a
deal, so bugger off, Little Brother."

"You can't leave me here alone with her, Earl. The
woman thinks I'm a complete ass. Besides, I owe you your

lunch and don't forget your beers."

Earl was halfway under the canvas covering, shaking his head. "It's time to be a man, Little Brother. That's what she wants."

"Wait! What about the bloody gifts? If she sees them now I might as well shoot myself. It'll be a damn sight better than a kitchen knife sticking from my back. Five minutes, Earl, no more."

"Get off my truck and close the doors when I pull away. Don't waste time or I'll come back in and show her where to stick it in your ribs." His head disappeared under the canvas and he yelled for anyone close enough to hear. "By the way, Little Brother, the Royal has a show at three…and you've got that many minutes to get off my truck."

Davidson bounced from his knees to a sitting position with his feet hanging over the lowered gate. "Gabrielle, would you think to go to the movies with me. We'll go Dutch, of course, and I'll sit anywhere you want me to." Every eye was on her, waiting. The gears shifted to neutral and the truck jerked. "Gabrielle, he's not a warm-hearted man like me. I've mere seconds left before he drives off and I'll not sit here begging you in front of half the world."

She looked across to the red brake lights, avoiding his eyes. She was not giving in. She wanted him to go. She had spent the entire morning knowing he would not come to see her and he had even managed to ruin that for her. What was the point? The bistro was still, even the wine on Henri's tray was perfectly still in the goblets.

The truck rocked slightly as Big Earl turned the wheels to face the downward slope. The motion made Davidson's legs suddenly sway and Gabrielle unconsciously mimicked the motion. There was less than a minute, she knew, and she tried to count in seconds. Then he would be gone and she could forget him and his warm kiss.

Then suddenly he was gone and the doors were closed. Davidson had jumped out when Big Earl began to coast downhill and had run as quickly as he could to catch up and dive into the rear of the truck, completely drenched. He cursed when he saw one of the bistro's doors fly open, thinking she must have invented something else to hate him for, either a broken door or a wet blouse. She would find some reason, he knew, and he let himself fall back against the cold steel of the side panel.

Whether it was what he thought he heard, or what he did hear, he glanced up to see Henri shouting and waving a fist in the middle of the road. Davidson's first thought was to give him the finger, though he knew there was no real reason. It was his own fault and nothing to do with the rude little bugger from behind the bar. Henri became smaller and smaller, waving his white apron clenched in both fists and, without warning the truck ground noisily to a stop and began to climb backwards uphill sounding more like a freight train. When the truck stopped Henri clambered onto the tailgate Davidson had not raised. He looked down, shivering with cold and exhibiting a boldness he showed more than felt.

"You are a big man, but not so much a brave man. You are not so much a brave soldier. You are a coward and a deserter. Yes, a deserter. All this morning our petite Gabrielle has been mopping around like a miserable little girl because of you, because of your stupid ways, thinking maybe that you can be for her what you can never be. She does not need you, so do not come back here with your stupid ideas if all you want is to hurt her. Go away from her, she does not need you. Or, you will go to her this very moment and wait for her. She is in her appartement and I will tell her." He paused, looking towards the front to see Big Earl's eyes peering through a small square of glass. "So, what do I tell her, that she must wear a pretty dress or that you have run away from her with your big stupid friend like the coward that you are?"

"Tell her to wear a pretty dress, Henry. I'll not run

away."

Henri eyed the boxes. "And are they also for her birthday?"

"Aye, they are."

"I will bring you a table cover to keep them dry."

"They're a surprise, Henry. I'd prefer she doesn't see them."

Henri jumped out with nothing more to say. When he came back he carried one tablecloth in his hands and had another wrapped around his head and shoulders. A few moments later he was back out holding open a door to a gauntlet of raised glasses and approving masculine smiles that were balanced with unforgiving feminine frowns. No one noticed the truck rumble away, though they did notice the gifts and one-by-one the frowns evaporated.

He was given a glass of wine and ushered unceremoniously into a vacant room where he was able to shower and spend the better part of the next hour pacing the floor in a towel. His laundered clothes were brought back to him by Gérard, neatly pressed and ready for any parade inspection, with instructions to dress quickly and to go downstairs to the bistro.

None of the guests had gone. They needed closure, meaning the women would not leave and because it was a slow day Henri had allowed a third ration of wine, meaning the men would not leave. For Davidson it was like descending into a funeral salon, not knowing Henri had instructed them to remain quiet after explaining that Gabrielle did not know the soldier had come back.

After taking care of the ignorant Scot, Henri had gone to her apartment to scold her like the schoolgirl he told her she was. She had a business and guests to attend to, and she was not to come down until she looked the part. He told her what to wear and how to wear it, and that he would let her know when the mood of her disgruntled guests had settled. She was not to come down before. Did she understand?

Yes, she did. Would she accept the ogre's gift, he asked? No, she would not. Henri said nothing. He simply placed a little green bag wrapped with ribbons beside her on the floor and walked out mumbling with her coat in his hands.

It was time, and when she opened her door she thought she could scold him back for being insolent, but Frenchmen cannot be scolded and he told her to wait at the top of the stairs until she could no longer see him. She was very put out, very flustered, and made a note to talk to him about it. She was the boss, not him, and that was all. When she stepped into view the men stood cheering and clapping as the women leaned into one another with nods and whispers of approval.

Gabrielle's cheeks flushed a deep crimson, which suited her. She was indeed a vision. She wore a dark grey V-neck knit dress that hugged her every curve and the black low-heeled Spanish pumps strapped across her feet barely raised her to 5'3". A deep burgundy sash encircled her small waist and a matching burgundy beret crowned luscious black hair she had pulled into a ponytail. She stopped at the bottom landing, facing her guests and Henri, feeling like a beautiful woman for the first time in years. She posed sideways, bringing one knee slightly up over the other and with one hand raised her dress to mid-thigh where tiny white silk ribbons showed against her second pair of new stockings.

She blew Henri a thank you kiss, knowing how much they would have cost him. He smiled in return and shook his head no, redirecting her gaze with a slight tilt of his head and raised eyebrows. Her beautiful green eyes turned black and she pushed down her hem, leering at Henri with contempt, but Henri was unshaken and nonchalantly tapped his watch that showed ten minutes shy of three o'clock.

"I think he likes me a bit more now, Gabrielle, possibly more than you do. He's even loaned me the money for a cab and a picture show, but that's another story and, if you don't mind, we'll have our supper here with a promissory note if that's alright with you."

Henri gave her a curt nod, conveying the message better than any words. She scowled back at him sending a silent and clear message of her own before walking down the few remaining steps, snubbing Davidson as she passed him by and waiting at the double doors for Henri to bring her coat and help her on with it.

"Run to her, monsieur," another patron yelled out. "You are her slave. Enjoy every moment. There are many here who would trade places with you, were it not for certain encumbrances. We salute you."

"Vive La France!" the male patrons sang out in unison, before the men were pulled into their seats and the women began. Davidson understood none of it, other than her extended elbow and the seemingly approving smiles of the female contingent. His greatcoat would have taken triple the time to dry. When they ran to the taxi his makeshift protection was chequered and made of plastic.

She said nothing at all during the ride to the Royal, too intrigued as she listened intently and openly surprised when the taxi driver drove onto the sidewalk and stopped under the overhang to help Davidson's clothing predicament. He waved away the fare with tears in his eyes, saying in an uneven voice that he had recently discovered his family was alive and safe. They lived in Ortona and had welcomed in some Allied soldiers whose names he had since forgotten. He would hear no more about the fare and shooed them both from the car.

Inside the theatre his money was no good. As much as he argued that he deserved no special treatment, the usher refused, smiling at Gabrielle and telling her in French how lucky she was. He did pay for the popcorn and Coca Cola, although he would have preferred a cigarette at any cost.

Gabrielle's mind had been a veritable whirlwind of confused thoughts and memories throughout the day, now she simply did not know, other than she hated him as much as she loved him. But who did she love and who did she hate, and why? Her thoughts drifted to North Africa and to what she had heard about Ortona. Then she understood that the man sitting beside her, so much like a brother or a cousin, could die in seven days and she would never know, or the big Indian who had helped him with her new bed. How cruel she had been to him and to his friend. When she looked up at him he did not look down.

She pulled herself up to kiss his cheek, she adjusted her hem to a little above her knees, she wrapped her arms into his and she closed her eyes. When she woke her eyes were damp, her face was streaked with colour and she was the most beautiful woman in the world. He had not moved, nor had he seen most of the newsreel or movie, not that he would have understood either. She looked up at him and smiled, then she closed her eyes with a rock-hard arm around her shoulders and placed a small white hand on his chest, counting the rapid beats.

The taxi ride home was just as quiet, the storm continued to rage and the bistro was empty with the exception of a few lingering guests who preferred the warm ambiance to their empty rooms. Their table was waiting for them and Henri was prancing around like a prima donna when they arrived. She excused herself to Davidson first, then to Henri with a very tight embrace while she whispered something in his ear. She would not be long, she promised. She wanted to re-do her make-up and was invoking feminine prerogative. She never came back.

"Monsieur, please understand. Mademoiselle is sleeping." Henri dropped into Gabrielle's chair, facing Davidson and poured them each a glass of wine. "I love her like my very own sister. For the last two years she has been a wreak without her Jean-Philippe. They were one together and nothing apart. Vous comprenez?" Davidson nodded. "When he died, he did not come back to her. He was left there without any closing for her and in a way she still hopes. Then you came here like an apparition, like a ghost. That is why I do not like you, or why I did not like you. Perhaps I can, if I try."

"Henry…"

"Monsieur, let us not pretend. You will soon go and perhaps you will soon die. I hope not, but maybe it will be so. She does not love you. She loves the thought of you. When I first saw you my body went to ice. Can you image how she felt?" He sipped his wine. "Now she is sleeping and you are sorry for yourself. Monsieur, you think that for weeks she has slept on the floor. This is not so true. For weeks she has been awake on the floor, waiting for him, and last week he came to her. She does not sleep, not ever. I did look into her room. She is sleeping now, like an angel, on the top of your new bed and in her hands are your beautiful new gifts that I did put into her rooms when you were gone. Her face is coloured with sadness, monsieur, and it is your culpability. I hate you for that, and I salute you for that."

He raised his glass.

"So what do I do?"

"Monsieur, we are in France, n'est pas? We will eat this fine meal that I have prepared and we will get drunk as we wait for your big Indian friend. As we do that I will tell you more about Gabrielle and you will tell me something about you." He snapped his fingers for more wine and he listened.

When Gabrielle woke and found her way downstairs the bistro was dark. She stayed where she was and prayed silently. She was strangely happy, strangely at peace. She knew no matter what the weather, she would see him in the morning.

14

A few short hours later Gabrielle woke to the familiar smells of Henri's cooking and the quiet murmurs of her guests in the hallway greeting one another on their way to breakfast. She was in no hurry to get out from her bed. She lay there running her hands over the thick, down-filled comforter and let her head rest on a billowy pillow that seemed to her more like a fluffy summer cloud. When she had come back to her room from the darkened bistro she had fought the urge to wear her new lingerie. Doing so would have been too much too soon and she wanted to savour her gifts for as long as she could. She was angry with him for making such a scene and she would tell him as much after she made him something special for supper to make up for falling asleep in her rooms.

She had pulled off her dress and kicked off her shoes, which was all she could manage. The need to jump between those fresh sheets and pull them up to her chin was too overwhelming. She sat up, almost reluctantly, easing herself away from the warmth to pull her camisole over her head and very carefully unclasp her stockings from her garters before pushing them down her legs as slowly as she could. When her bare feet touched the floor she unclasped the slim belt, letting it fall over her dress. She pushed her laced panties to her ankles, stepped out of them and stopped to gather up each piece and lay them out on the bed. It was her best dress and her best underwear. She patted the comforter dreamily before crawling back onto the bed and falling face down to make invisible arcs with her arms and legs. No one would ever touch her new bed. She hated the thought of getting wet, her shower could wait a while longer and she wiggled her little body deeper into the plush fabric.

Eventually she padded to the bathroom, stopping suddenly in front of the mirror. What she saw was strange to her. She no longer looked tired, or like the person she had come to despise. She was Gabrielle, Jean-Philippe's Gabrielle and she was smiling.

She would wear her black straight skirt with her big red belt and her peasant blouse. She would tie her hair in a French braid and she would wear her stockings, after she made her bed and sat on it for a while longer. Had she known she might have been more inclined to hurry, though Henri had instructed the auberge staff not to disturb her. Henri's breakfast menu had not wafted into her room; the lunch menu had permeated the auberge.

Henri was bent over the bar with his face buried in his folded arms. La Plus Belle was full and even though it was dark outside it was a gloomy midday darkness. She scanned the room not knowing what to expect, so she expected nothing. Davidson was not there, which was fine as long as he came for dinner. She leaned over the banister, staring at Henri and wondered how long she would have to wait before he moved.

"Henri?" she called. "Henri, dors-tu?"

Henri was sleeping, politely and without any noise that might disturb the guests. She poked him in the ribs thinking she would startle him. When that failed she put an ice cube under the collar of his shirt. The reaction was slow and when he did move his head towards her and open his eyes his face was blotched with patches of green and grey and his eyes were streaked with red.

"Henri, you are drunk."

"No, I am not drunk. I am suffering with terrible pain."

The effort to stand straight was agonizing, the torment showing on his face. "Look at what they have done to me, Gabrielle."

"Who?"

"Your big stupid friend and his bigger stupid friend."

"Davidson and Earl did this to you? They made you drink so much that you look like rotten meat?"

He rocked his head in his arms. "Yes, until almost midnight. It was horrible, Gabrielle. You would not believe me if I were to tell you. It is too horrible."

"You drank for six hours? And what did you drink?"

"They drank your wine, but it is paid for in full."

"Stand up straight, this very instant and I hope you fall and hurt yourself." She poured him a glass of wine. "Was he very angry with me when he left?"

"No, he was happy that you were sleeping in your new bed. I told him how tired you have been."

"I did not sleep in his stupid bed and I never will. Why would you invent such a ridiculous story? When I have time I will throw it out."

Henri leaned back for support. His shoulders drooped at the same angle as his head that was pounding and spinning. He looked at her over the rims of his glasses.

"I saw you on top of it. I saw you holding your new gifts so close to you. Do not lie to me. Lie to Davidson if you must, but not to me. He is not so bad, you know. Neither is the big Indian."

"So, now he is Davidson. How nice that you have a new friend." She tried to look furious. "You are lying to me. How did you see me on the bed when I was not on it?"

"I went to your room when you were late for my special supper. I saw you. When I told him how you looked he was so happy. Now you cannot lie to him. He knows that you like your new gifts very much. I saw your face, and I see now. You have not been so beautiful in two years. He has made you young again. Do not pretend with me."

"And I can see your face. It is a good thing that you cannot. I hope that you feel as bad as you look. I should make you eat your own cooking, imbecile. Go to the back and clean yourself. You are disgusting and do not think for one moment that I will be any easier on him if comes back to bother me." She glanced over to the doors. "Is he coming, Henri?"

"I forget. It could be that he said yes...or maybe not. I am not sure."

"Get away from me you pathetic excuse for life. When you are clean you will work in the kitchen where it is noisy and I do not have to see you."

He eased past her, bringing an open palm to his creased forehead that seemed quite fine at its current altitude, not seeming to mind the ice water was dripping down the back of his trousers. When he had disappeared behind the swinging doors she took up his glass and sipped, feeling very content with herself and trying hard not to look at the clock.

By 3:00 the two old men who were fixtures more than patrons sat alone by the window, arguing as much with their hands as with their mouths about whatever news story they were reading, their attention broken when the door swung open. It was something for them to do, perhaps something for them to talk about. Everyone on the street knew him. He stood out. They were still talking about his singing in the church and very few had not heard about the bed and the animated scene that had followed.

He was putting on a good front, she thought, and if she hadn't considered the old men she would have begun banging steel pots together. He was pale and his wide smile came to his bluish lips with great effort. His eyes were red and tearing. His wet face and hair making them appear all the redder. She waited until he was right in front of her.

"Bonjour, monsieur. Vous désirez un verre de vin, possiblement?"

"I've learned a bit since our last encounter, Gabrielle. To say such a thing tells me a lot about you. It tells me you're a cruel and heartless woman. No, I don't want any of your coarse wine. I believe a coffee would be better suited to my condition."

"Would you like a baguette, thick with rôti de boeuf and a bowl of spicy jus to dip it in? Or would you prefer a late breakfast of bacon and eggs with toast and thick marmalade?"

"Just coffee, please, you spiteful woman, or I'll take my business elsewhere."

"You cannot, you wasted all your money on me." She reached under the counter for the urn. "Do you want it black or with thick cream?" She pushed it towards him, not hearing the answer. "Do you want a slice of sweet pecan pie, or perhaps sour lemon meringue?" she persisted.

He pushed the empty cup back. "May I have another, you horrible shrew?"

She poured. "You should not drink it so quickly, monsieur. It is not good for your stomach. Instead you should drink the yokes of some eggs. I can ask Henri to prepare it for you."

"How is poor Henry?"

"He is very much like you, monsieur. He is stupid."

"You look beautiful, Gabrielle. It's as though I'm seeing a different woman."

"I know. That is why I did not come back last night, because I was too ugly for you."

"It's not what I meant and you know it. Henry told me how you looked last night. It was all I could do not to run upstairs and see you for myself."

"He lied to make you feel good about your stupid bed."

"So, you didn't sleep in it." He finished the second bitter cappuccino, reluctantly. "He told me he stood a while in the doorway watching you, that he hadn't seen you look so peaceful in a very long time. I see the difference as well and

I like it."

"How is your friend Earl?"

"He could drink me under the table, had he a mind to do so. He's got an enviable constitution, but it's just as well there were no constables along the way."

She walked away from him without excusing herself to call out instructions from the kitchen doors, moments later Henri appeared with a large bowl of steaming broth. She stood in the corner, watching the two exchange defeated shrugs and sorrowful facial expressions. Henri retreated before he was told to and Davidson did his best not to deliver empty spoons to his lips.

"Do you feel better?"

"Aye, I do."

"You do not look so good, especially beside me. I do look beautiful, it is true. And I feel beautiful, which is more important, no? I chose my clothes for you, to look like a gypsy. How unfortunate that you cannot see me because your eyes are so filled with my expensive wine."

"We got a wee bit carried away, I'll admit. We were talking about you all the while and then Henry wanted to know about Indians and cowboys and tomahawks and if they wore knickers under their cowhide leggings and their wee flaps. We wanted to leave, truly we did. So if there's a finger to point, you'd best look to your curious barkeep."

She inhaled deeply through flared nostrils, squeezing her lips tightly together. She wanted to appear annoyed, but she couldn't help herself. She smiled. "Do they?"

"Do they what?"

"Wear knickers."

"I'll never know. I left to relieve myself. I have very little interest in the subject matter."

"And the Scottish men, under their dresses?"

"They're not bloody dresses. They're kilts, girl. Why does no one know that?" He copied her smile. "And you'll have to see me in one to know yea or nay."

Gabrielle's forehead crinkled at the strange words.

"I fell asleep in my dress. When I came down everything was black. I am sorry that I missed Henri's special supper, but I will not admit that to him. I want him to suffer very badly. This morning I opened my eyes and did not believe that I could feel so good as I did. It took a very long time for me to leave my new bed. Merci, Davidson. That is why I wanted to dress like this for you. You told me that you like me like this. I have nothing else to give you."

"Aye, and it's more than enough. There's not a man in France who doesn't envy me at this very moment." He pushed away the broth. "Tell me, did I choose the right colours and the right sizes?"

"They are beautiful, yes. I did not wear them, but I will very soon. It has been so long since I have received a gift. Thank you. However you must stop. It is too much and anything more will make me angry with you."

"I thought you liked being angry with me."

"I am angry with you, and my stupid Henri. I wanted to hit his head with a pot. I did not do so only because it was clean."

Davidson snorted.

"Room number four is empty. Go to bed to rest and to look better. You can stay for supper if you want. It is not necessary that you do."

"I'll stay, of course I will, because I know you want me to and you're too stubborn to say how much you like me. I know you do. Who wouldn't?"

Gabrielle pulled over a milk crate that she stood on to reach over the bar. She looked at him eye to eye, moistening her lips, letting him smell her and listen to her deep breaths. Then she slapped his cheek, stepped down and walked away humming to herself. When he was locked in his room she hurried from the bistro and was gone three hours.

15

Henri's skeletal body was in the final stages of a slow recovery, though still very humble in his demeanour and in no way consoled by the fact Davidson was feeling much better. He knew the preferred way to feel better was for someone else to feel worse, but he was the one who felt worse and he grimaced pathetically when told that Earl had gone out again drinking with the boys. He had done his best to make things right and to placate the woman who had shown him no compassion throughout the afternoon. He had planned each detail down to the candles and very rare Belgium chocolates and all was ready when Gabrielle sidestepped down the stairs.

She went to each table to greet her guests, knowing many of them by name, including those who were staying at the auberge. Davidson slid from the banquette, not at all surprised when she ignored him. She was drop-dead gorgeous. Gabrielle and Marie-Claude had decided it would be more practical to wear each other's clothes for special occasions than to spend money on new outfits until conditions improved for both their establishments; something Davidson would not have to know. Her shoes were bright red leather pumps; her three-quarter sheath skirt was pale mauve and hugged her from her waist to her calves. The matching silk blouse was unbuttoned to she shallow swell between her breasts and a bright red silk neckerchief was knotted to one side of her neck and positioned to accentuate more than conceal. Her lustrous black hair flowed over her shoulders and her lipstick completed the classic look.

When she finally came to where they stood, she looked up at Henri in a way that showed she was really looking down at him. Then she looked at the intimate setting in the private banquette and all was forgiven with a loving squeeze. She slipped in first, knowing Davidson was watching every curve and she tugged at the hem of her skirt with innocent coquettishness after crossing her legs and before patting the seat beside her.

Henri poured the wine and left them alone, coming back as though on cue to remove dishes and be obtrusive until each of his courses received appropriate praise. Anyone seeing them saw lovers. She blushed when he laughed and she laughed when he seemed confused by something she had said. Hurtful barbs became playful teasing and they held each other's hands. They spoke about Wednesday, Thursday and Friday. No matter what the weather they would climb the Eiffel Tower and later stroll along the Champs Élysées to discover other little bistros and maybe go to the movies or perhaps have a picnic on a blanket by La Falaise.

Neither one spoke about Saturday, which was too close to Sunday and intuitively taboo. Neither wanted the evening to end, nor did Henri who stood for his final assessment as he placed a crêpe Suzette between them with snifters of Rémy Martin VSOP he had brought from his modest home where he lived alone.

Gabrielle wanted Davidson to stay. If he stayed he could have room number four. His clothes would be clean by morning and they could talk for as long as they wanted and maybe they could dance. It had been so long since she had danced. She knew he was lying when he said he could not, and she knew why. She knew he wanted to stay, to be with her, yet she knew he could not. She knew already she would not lock her door, that she would wear her new lingerie for him and how she would be sitting on the edge of her new bed when he came through the door.

He wanted to. With all his heart he wanted to stay and be with her. Then what? What of tomorrow and the next day and the next? He had four more days and as many nights. He wanted to be with her, but whose name would she call out and whose would he forget?

What he could do was dance as well as he could sing. He snapped his fingers and called out to their private garçon who had the perfect music. The bistro had emptied by then and Henri poured the couple their final ration of his prized VSOP. He kissed Gabrielle on both cheeks and squeezed her, saying something Davidson understood by tone, if not by the words. Then he kissed Davidson on both cheeks and slapped his back. He put the scratchy long playing seventy-eight on the monophonic record player and he left, grinning from ear to ear and feeling quite self-satisfied. It was 10:15. They had one hour to cry, to dream and perhaps to regret.

At first it seemed like such a long time, until the hour had disappeared and now seemed like nothing at all. When he left she ran to her apartment to watch from the window and wave to him. He waved back, smiling, unable to see the tears glistening on her cheeks or to hear her whispered words.

He lay awake on his bunk all night, sorting mixed emotions. He had not seen Emily in over four years and every man knew the worst battles of the war were too few days away. The orders everyone had been expecting had not been confirmed to the lower ranks, those most likely to die, but that was a matter of a day or two, if not hours. The Germans had been squeezed into northern Europe and that's where the war would end if he lived long enough to see the day.

He didn't have to wait long. Wednesday he was sombre, almost despondent and a late-morning beer with Big Earl did nothing to improve his humour. The orders had been posted: 1 Corps was marching north Sunday at 0900. There would be no Saturday with Gabrielle and suddenly he needed to be with her.

Henri waved him to the bar, pointing to the empty stool with the full glass of red wine in front of it. His condition had much improved and he asked about Earl.

"You are sad, my friend, for which we cannot blame the weather. The day is so beautiful and certainly the wine cannot be the reason. It is from the cellar, not the cask. However do not tell her. She is still unhappy with me a little."

"She'd be in difficult straights without you, Henry. Make certain nothing ever happens to her when I'm gone."

"So," Henri nodded, "the time has come for you to leave her, mon ami? I can tell by your sad face that you know."

"Friday, Henry. We're marching Sunday and we're ordered to be at the base from noon on Saturday. So there it is. It's a proper bugger and there's not a blessed thing to be done about it."

"Then you must tell her immediately. Do not lie to her or let her believe. To wait longer would be wrong. She must have time to prepare herself to lose what you have brought to her in so few days. At this time she feels inside that you will be here forever and I must tell you that she has planned for you a very exceptional Saturday. The news will hurt her very much, though she will not show it. Sometimes she is a foolish young girl." He leaned onto the bar. "She has lived a very bad life, Davidson. You know this. If she discovers what I told you while drinking our wine, that together she and I saw her parents being slaughtered by men with smiles on their faces, she will kill me. It is good that she is happy now. She begins slowly to heal, though she will never forget those faces. It is her time to be happy. It is what she mérite. I am not in a very big hurry to see her sad again and I will not leave her alone. Never will I leave her."

"Go get her, Henry. Tell the sweet thing I'm here. There's no point to put it off." He expelled a deep breath. "She'll forget me soon enough, Henry. It won't take someone very long to sweep her off her little feet after this bloody war's over and done with."

"The day she will die is when she will forget, Davidson. Until then she will know that somewhere on this miserable earth her Jean-Philippe still lives. When I see you I see him. You still have no idea. Nor will you ever. Even now, all that is lacking is your French. You have brought to her very much happiness," Henri shrugged, "and when you go you will take it with you. This I do know."

Davidson pushed an envelope under Henri's folded arms. "Thank you, Henry. Though I can't say I remember very much of the movie. I was too busy watching her. And can you blame me?"

Henri pushed the money back. "Do you think I cannot afford a few francs to see my little angel be happy and not so miserable? I do not need it, you do. It is true that you have only two short days. However you have many more hours than that. Do not waste one of them on me. Think like a Frenchman for once." He raised his glass in a toast. "She is upstairs, mon ami. Go to her. The time has come to stop being a visitor and become a friend to her. Allez! Vite!"

Davidson downed the rest of his wine in a single swallow, incurring a raised eyebrow and a series of tsks as Henri swept away the empty glass. He had no idea what to say or do. He had never been into Emily's bedroom, or any other woman's for that matter. He was barely twenty-two when he had registered for the war and had become much more proficient in killing the Germans than loving the French.

He tapped his knuckles on the door and stepped back. She opened the door slowly, smiling up at him without a word. She was wearing tight black leotards, and with them a black cable-knit sweater and ebony-coloured link chain that hung loosely from her waist. It was like seeing her naked from her hips to her toes and she giggled at his obvious shock. She leaned seductively into the doorframe, crossing her arms.

"Please put your long tongue into your head or I will put on a long skirt and thick shoes like a British woman."

"If there's one thing you'll never be it's British, Gabrielle. Not to say they're all ugly, mind you. You're just so beautiful." He was transfixed, staring down at her legs. "Do you walk around like that all the time?"

"Yes, of course. Why not? It is my place."

"You're practically naked. It's a bit brash, don't you think?"

"If you do not like it, do not look at me. Go downstairs to be with your new friend and I will join you when I can. I am busy."

"Busy doing what? I thought we were off to the tower and a wee bit of lunch."

"I was on my new bed. I have something that I must complete by the end of the week. Or, you can come in if you want. It is okay with Henri. He trusts you, even if I do not."

"I can't come into your bedroom, Gabrielle. I'll wait here for you."

"It is an apartment. I told you that, unless you are too afraid." Then suddenly she was over his shoulder, squealing, with no idea Henri was at the bottom of the stairway with his second glass held high in a salute.

"Another word, girl, and I'll take my hand to your wee bum. It'll be pink for a week or more. I'll make sure of that."

He plopped her down on the bed, not believing how lucky he was to see her dressed so seductively and he walked away from the bed forming a wide 'O' with his mouth and rolling his eyes. Her silky gifts were neatly strewn over a brocade and mahogany récamier meant for lounging and her new satin ballerina slippers were side by side underneath it. He peered down to the street from the window and thought back to the night before when he had been looking up.

"Henry made me feel much better than I did when I first walked in."

"It is good that you like each other. Now that you have been drunk together you must feel like brothers. Do you like me as much?"

"One more cheeky word from you and I'll carry out my threat. Don't think I won't." He turned, sitting on the window ledge with his arms crossed. She was sitting on the bed, scribbling notes. "Gabrielle, if that's our special Saturday you're working on, you'd best change the date to Friday. I'll not be here Saturday, sweet thing. The Division's marching early Sunday. I can't tell you where."

Her face blanched and she dropped her pen. "It is not your business what I am writing. Henri is a pig to tell you anything and I am going to scald him for it."

"I'm sure you could with that fiery tongue of yours." He approximated a chortle. "I'm sorry, sweet thing. Listen, what we have is a meagre two days, Gabrielle, a full forty-eight hours and a bit more. I have until Saturday at noon. So I won't be leaving you until late on Friday and as late as I can each night before."

She took up her notes in her arms and fell forward onto her front and elbows, pensive, not seeing his eyes shift to the perfect roundness of her buttocks.

"If you're trying to tempt me or tease me, you're doing a damn fine job of it. I'm sure my hand could cover all of it if you don't soon put on your britches or a skirt. I'm a man, you know, not a bloody eunuch."

"Be quiet, Davidson. Come to sit beside me and be quiet. Do not talk to say things you do not mean."

Moments later she felt the bed shift under his weight. Her eyes were closed and her head was resting sideways on her folded arms and voluptuous black hair. Her sweater had travelled to her waist and Davidson was content not to speak. His mouth was bone dry and his heart was palpitating wildly. There was no need for him to imagine, the difficulty was in concentrating as she spoke.

"He was killed two years ago, Davidson, and he left me more than two years before that when the Germans invaded the city and our homes. I was twenty years old and I never knew real love with him. He never saw me the way a man longs to see his own woman and I never felt him or saw him the way that I always saw him and felt him in my dreams, which was so perfect and so wonderful for me and for him."

She felt his hand wrap lightly around her thigh that was closest to him, squeezing gently. "Gabrielle…"

"No. I am not finished." A single tear trickled from each deep emerald eye. "I do not know whether it is you that I want, or Jean-Philippe, because what I have said would happen to me has happened because of you. I do not know if it is him or you that I see when I dream. I have forgotten his voice, Davidson. I cannot remember his beautiful words to me. When he talks to me it is your voice I hear. When I think of him I think of you and your strange voice."

He moved his hand timidly up her thigh, not expecting she would wriggle down so effortlessly to meet his touch. He kneaded his fingers gently into the firm roundness left uncovered by the sweater, excited as much by the feel of the fabric against her bare flesh as her sensual warmth and his desire to press his open palm urgently against her. His heart was racing, his body reacting in a way that had become unfamiliar to him.

"It is one day less, not two, so I will pretend that we have been together one day more and we will do today what we have planned." His hand stayed resting across her buttocks. "Davidson, if you cannot stay with me tonight, if we cannot be together, I do not want that you come back to me tomorrow." She raised herself onto her elbows, crumpling her notes and tossing them onto the floor. "Jean-Philippe will forgive me. Henri was strict with me this morning. He spoke to me like I am a little girl. He likes you."

"Gabrielle…"

"You do not listen to me. I do not want you to talk. We will go out and we will see Paris. When we come back we will have our dinner in my apartment. If you leave me, you must not come back and, if you stay you will also stay Friday and Thursday. I do not want to talk about it with you. There is no reason. We will know when it is time." She squirmed. "Take your hand away from me, Davidson."

He stood and stepped away, looking down as she reached for a short black skirt. She slipped her feet into it and stood beside him before tugging the zipper to her waist. She slid her feet into strapped pumps, sitting back down on the bed to cross her legs in turn and fasten the tiny buckles, ignoring him, other than to tell him where to find her wrap-around jacket. When he came back she was smoothing the comforter almost sensually and he stood behind her to absorb her every movement until she faced him. He was afraid of her, or afraid of himself. Whatever he felt he knew she would not want him either way. She wanted what he had been to her before he had walked into her life. He wanted her the way she was.

When they left La Plus Belle she took his hand and squeezed. Henri leaned over the bar and watched them leave, remembering the final moments when his young bride had died in his arms.

16

Gabrielle was one of life's anomalies. She was frustrating and she was beautiful. The day was as pleasant as the last day of summer and all he could do was think of her on the bed and the arousing warmth emanating from her.

Near the pinnacle of Eiffel's wrought-iron monument she buried her face into the cradle of his arms as he looked out over the world's premier city of love pulling her closer, warming her against the mild wind. On the Champs Élysées they were lovers, inconspicuous amongst all the others and still she did not look at him. There was so much to see and so little time to be with him. All she wanted was to go home and be alone with him. Instead they found a little café and she told him of her dreams of owning a grand hotel and fine restaurant with Marie-Claude, a dream they had once shared with Jean-Philippe. She did not want to know what he wanted from life, nor was there any need to speak of a tomorrows that would never be and he somehow knew.

Darkness came too soon and she left him at the bar to do what women do in the privacy of their apartments. She was pleased with the table setting. Henri had excelled and had a left a secret note on her bed with a promise to surpass himself each night. If whatever time was left to her that week was not perfect in every way, he was not Henri.

She did not come down and Davidson did not go up, not until Henri was satisfied he was sufficiently well-tutored in the rudiments of calling on a Frenchwoman. Davidson's skills were weak at best, made worse by years of squatting in ditches or tents while eating or scraping his food from tin plates. Henri stood back in shock, never having witnessed anyone pulling a cork from a bottle as they would a molar from a horse. He was aghast and had no intention of sacrificing more than one of his cheapest bottles of wine for the training. When all was said and done and Henri had done his best to correct years of neglect, nothing remained but to shake his friend's hand and watch Davidson climb the stairs muttering to himself.

He was to knock on the door, wait one moment, then walk in confidently with the bottle of Grand Cru cradled in his arm as one would present a box of long-stemmed roses. And then what, he had asked Henri. And then it would be too late if he did not already know. When he turned to look down from halfway up the stairs Henri had disappeared from behind the bar.

He tapped on the door and counted to ten, not certain whether he did so in seconds or heartbeats, wondering what she would be wearing and where she would be sitting. If she was in another room or busy, what would he do and where would he stand or put the wine? What would he say to her, or would she talk first? And what would he do if Henri had forgotten to put the corkscrew on the table. Suddenly the ditches and the Germans seemed very attractive to him.

The lighting was muted, Gabrielle was seated at the side of the small bistro table Henri had set for them and it seemed to Davidson as though he had climbed the stairs to heaven. Her hair was tied with a barrette and swept to one side over her shoulder, her face glowed pink and her green eyes sparkled like exquisite green jewels. Her cable sweater was creamy-white, her skirt was short and burgundy-coloured and her leotards were pale raspberry. She wore no shoes or slippers, her legs were crossed and she was turning one foot in elliptical circles with her hands clasped in her lap.

"I can't say how beautiful you are, Gabrielle. I had all my words memorized outside the door. I wasn't quite expecting to see you like this. There are no words."

"Thank you. You look very handsome, Davidson."

"No, I don't. I feel like a beggar and I know I look like one. If you're not seeing me wet and windblown, you see me at day's end looking as though I've been dragged down a stony hill behind a horse with the runs."

Her face creased. It's what she did when she didn't understand. "Is that for me?"

"Aye, it is. I made it myself. Do you think it seems real? Apart from the colour and the paper, I mean. A famous French artiste, whose name escapes me at the moment, showed me how. I hope you like it."

"I do love blue roses. They are my favourite. I will find an empty vase for it while you open the wine. The famous French artiste will not be here with the first course before a few minutes," she giggled.

The cork came out easily without the use of his knees, and Gabrielle's glass was ready for her when she returned to put the little vase in the middle of the table. She sat in a large futon by the window and patted the space beside her, knowing he would feel ridiculous sitting beside her on the settee. She curled her legs underneath her, the pale colour of her leotards becoming translucent at her knees before adjusting her skirt ever so slightly.

At the moment he wanted Henri more than he wanted her. He edited every thought to avoid repeating what he had said to her that afternoon or any other day. They were new together. There should have been much to say, however he knew that would be even more disastrous. He wanted nothing more than to sweep her up and kiss her, to slide his hands under her skirt and squeeze her soft flesh, to feel her warmth once more, knowing full-well that doing so would make it all the worse. So what was he doing there when he could simply have walked out on her to Henri's saluting finger and her fading memory of him? She had already forgotten much of Jean-Philippe. How long would she need to forget him?

"You can begin a fire, if you want. I did not know if you like them. Sometimes it can be too, hmm, how do you say, romantic?"

She made herself shiver.

"Are you cold?"

"Only a little," she lied, feeling very snug in her sweater. "It does not matter. The hot water will soon heat the pipes. They are old. It takes longer when the auberge is full."

"Do you have a sweater in the meantime?"

"I am wearing a sweater. I am fine." She straightened herself, putting one foot on the floor and crossing her legs away from him. "You have not coughed since one week, Davidson. It is a dirty habit. I am glad you have stopped for a while."

"Forever, Gabrielle. It's a pleasant change to taste my food and drink. Though I've not eaten too regularly in the mess of late."

Such was the evening's cul-de-sac. There would be no romantic flames flickering and warming them, no hand-holding, no giggles and no moments to look forward to or remember. He was a jerk and the long minutes ahead are what each had begun to count, not their heartbeats.

The first knock at the door was discreet, the second was followed immediately by Henri moving in backwards and pulling a trolley topped with ornate silver domes which he expertly swung around to face them as he pushed it to the table. He looked at Gabrielle who said nothing, then at the fireplace and to Davidson who felt he was sitting in the deepest shit-filled trench of the past four years.

The exasperated Frenchman thrust his arms upward into the air. He forgot the first courses of soup and salad and went to the fireplace where he crashed to his knees for more affect than he had intended while admonishing her with a monologue she knew better than to interrupt...until. She leaned forward, talking sharply to his back, her full lips a blur of exotic burgundy, her small hands jabbing at the air behind him. When he stood his hands were black with the newsprint he had twisted into kindling and blamed her when his hands turned his immaculately white apron charcoal grey. She stood to face him, looking down at herself as she swept her arms and small open hands down in front of her in tiny arcs, still assailing him with an endless torrent of harsh words. He wanted none of it, enough was enough and he ignored her while he went to her phonograph and put on a vinyl seventy-eight. Then he went to the table, placed the bowls and small plates in their respective places and waved a parental finger at her as he pulled out her seat with the other hand.

"And you, you big, stupid man. Why have I wasted my time with you? Look at her, this poor silly girl, look how she made herself so pretty for you, so very lovely and you cannot even light for her a fire or put music into the air for her, into her heart. You big, stupid British fellow, and you are no better," he scolded Gabrielle. "My food is wasted on both of you. You will sit down here together, you will eat and you will tell each other nice things, like what you will do tomorrow and what you will do on Friday." He exhaled a deep breath and looked at Gabrielle. "Je t'aime, ma petite fille. Tu le sais, mais que tu es frustrante parfois." He opened his arms to her. She knew he cared deeply for her and she walked into them, crying. "You see, you see you foolish young man, how easy it is to comfort them and to love them even when they are frustrating us. And you, you silly little girl, if this sad ambiance is not improved by my next course I will eat everything myself and leave you to look for a better job anywhere. Sit, both of you, and eat if you cannot think of tender words to say to one another."

He stormed out in a huff after setting the stylus onto the

spinning vinyl, filling the room with soft scratchy melodies of love, and stayed by the door. Davidson's eyes had been little more than white holes in an irregular red globe. His ears were hot, his forehead was wet and his mouth was parched because he had not wanted to chance sipping his wine, thinking she might turn on him and break the glass over his head.

"You look like a big red beet. Loosen your tie. Take it off and finish all your entrées before he comes back. He has a big kitchen knife under his apron and he will use it on you." She sipped her soup, not taking her eyes from him.

"Do you think you could blink once or twice, if only to enhance the mood, Gabrielle? It's an unnerving thing to see." The soup was delicious, and hot. "And could you tell me what that hullabaloo was all about?"

"No, I could not," she retorted. "And he will not be happy with you if you cannot talk to me. It is very easy to talk with me, monsieur. The weather is very nice today, is it not, monsieur? The soup is very hot, is it not, monsieur? Do you like the wine, monsieur? Is it too dry, or is it too sweet?" She leaned into him. "Do think you will ever learn French, monsieur, even little words? Do you know how hard it is for a woman in Paris to dress nicely for someone in 1944, monsieur, when all things are so scarce and the soldiers buy what is left to find their way under our skirts and our blouses? Do you know what it must feel like to want to dress nicely for someone in Paris, monsieur? Do you think you will remember Paris, monsieur? Do you think you will remember me?"

"Aye, Gabrielle, I do know. I know what it's like to march on a near empty stomach for days at a time, to see my new friends and old lying scattered all about me with holes in their heads and their chests and their slippery guts blown out with shrapnel. I know what it's like to want to wear something nice for I've worn the same damn uniform for over four years and I'm sick of it. The weather's better outside than in, I'll admit, although the soup is very good and the wine is perfect, not too dry or too sweet. I will learn French, since you've made me feel the fool about it and I've never had my hands anywhere but on your little bony arse or my own, not ever, if you can remotely comprehend my simple words. And, if you don't mind me saying so, it seems quite clear to me that you wanted to feel my hand there more than I did. Unless I'm deaf, I heard no complaints throughout the five minutes." He leaned in closer to her. "Besides, gypsy, I've thrown away meatier bones than the ones you're sitting on. There's no need for you to feel so proud."

She blinked once and looked down into her bowl. She reached for her spoon, forcing herself to swallow and pleased he was eating as well and not looking at her. Henri had worked so hard to make the evening perfect. She did not want to hurt him.

Is she pretty, she asked herself? Is your Emily pretty, Davidson? She kept her head down. "My bum is not bony and I do not like arse. It is vulgar, like you. You cannot squeeze bones and make them feel so good and no one will ever throw me away." She raised her spoon to her lips. Will you love her right away, Davidson, she mused? Will she lie on you in her bed when they take you from me, when they take you home? Will you remember me? She patted her lips before she spoke. "Pardon? What is it that you said?"

"I said, it felt good for me too, Gabrielle. I was going out of my mind. It's not as though your socks are very thick. Turning from you when you were talking was no easy matter. And how could I ever forget you, or any part of you. How will I ever think of Paris and not think of you, sweet thing."

"They are leotards, not socks and you did not look away. You took too long to move your hand when I told you."

He snorted. "No, I didn't turn away. It's true." He raised

his glass to hers. "Here's to a warm hand and a meaty bum. Is that better?" He pushed his chair back. "The music's done. I'll change the record and when I come back I think I'd like to see you with your toes tucked under you on the daybed, the way you were before with the warm glow of the fire on your face and flickering flames dancing in your eyes."

"Yes, that is better." She let him pull out her chair. "It is a futon, not a daybed."

"Perhaps for you, sweet thing, but I prefer the sound of daybed."

When Henri came in unannounced Davidson was lounging into the arm of the futon and Gabrielle was leaning in against him with her knees pulled to her chest as he stroked her hair and kissed the back of her head. He ignored them as he laid out their plates and filled clean glasses with wine, mumbling to himself about silly children wasting such precious time. Davidson whispered into her ear to ask the question. She shook her head mischievously and whispered something back about old, nagging mothers.

Henri stayed not a moment longer than required for deserved and appropriate apologies, which he summarily dismissed in a huff, and effusive praise which he accepted with feigned humility. There would be no dessert, he announced. They were not worth the effort. He had decided on special coffees, coffees not on the menu, coffees one would not have to sit at the table to enjoy. They danced until the coffees were brought to them and fresh linen covered the intimate table. Then she curled into him and they both stared fixated into the slowly dying flames, lost in quiet reverie.

It was eleven when Gabrielle eased herself onto her front, reaching past him to put her cup on a side table. She stayed as she was, pensively, suddenly feeling the warmth of his hand pressed into the small of her back. She pulled herself up, wrapping her arms around his unyielding neck and kissed his cheek before lowering her face against his shoulder and wondering how her breasts felt to him, pressing into chest.

He brought his other hand up, hugging her tightly around the waist before clasping her head in both hands and pressing his mouth hard against hers. She moved urgently in a slow, sensual crawl, straddling him, suffocating him, groaning with urgent suddenness from somewhere deep inside her when she suddenly felt the heat of his hands clutch the bare flesh framed between her pulled up skirt and her pushed down tights.

Time meant nothing. They both just wanted more. She could feel him. He was ready and he wanted to reach for what he knew was so close. His lips ached badly and hers were numb. He was holding her so tightly he could barely distinguish the separate pressures of her breasts and she combed her fingers through his hair. She pushed herself away, sitting on his hands and pulled her sweater over her head before she could think of what she was doing. She turned, too aroused to be shocked that the waistband of her leotards was already mid-thigh and she was naked to her waist. She freed herself of them frantically, clumsily, while he held her by her breasts. She strained to turn, pressing her face hard against his and pinning his hands between their bodies until she pushed herself away again to search for her zipper and pull her skirt up over her head. She was entirely naked and Davidson's heart was about to explode across the freshly painted room. She lowered herself, slowly, not teasingly, and put first one bare breast against his mouth. Then the other, enjoying the lingering kisses and sucking as his strong hands worked easily to knead and explore her buttocks.

She pushed their bodies apart one last time, her breathing laboured, and stretched to kiss him, her arms pressing down straight against his chest.

"I will go to the bathroom. I will not be very long."

She kissed him again, sliding from his body to the floor, and stood beside him with her legs slightly parted, letting him see. Her breasts were petite, yet full, and her nipples were small and dark and fully erect, heaving with her excited breathing. Her stomach was flat and firm, yet soft, and her skin was tight and perfection to his eyes. Her pubic hair was silky and the little she had hid nothing at all from his view. He wanted to touch her there, to feel the folds that seemed so delicate and vulnerable to him.

"Soon," she said, as though reading his mind, looking down at him for the first time with a glow on her face he knew then he would never forget.

She swung around, purring or humming to herself as she padded from the room. Her shoulders were smooth and well-defined. Her back arched perfectly toward the flawless symmetry of perfectly rounded buttocks he had made pink with his probing and squeezing and her legs ended at the smallest feet he thought he had ever seen, their toes painted to match her fingers.

She left the door open behind her and he could still hear the sweet sounds. Though when he heard the shower and the scraping of the curtain pulling across the rod he stood and walked out the door. Curfew was in less than thirty-minutes. At midnight the base would be locked down tight and no one would be allowed in or out.

17

"Hé, salut!" Henri came towards him, quickly, embracing him, which had become quite fine with Davidson. "I was wrong that day in the pouring down rain, mon ami, when I did call you a coward. You are not a coward. You are the bravest of men. There is nothing for which I would enter into that room at this very moment, not even with a white flag or a very big gun, not even behind you, you big fool."

"Henry, if I'm to stay here these three days I need a change of clothes. Yours are a good bit too small and a wee bit too fancy, if I do say so. Thanks for not locking me out and for your bicycle. It's a damn sight better than hers." He threw Henri the keys to his lock. "How about yourself, my little French friend, how will you get home? It's twenty past the hour."

"I will be fine. I know them. Anyway, a free glass of wine will wash them from my back tomorrow, if necessary. Do not worry for me. You are the one in great danger."

"Henry, if you're not too closed up for the evening, could I beg two more glasses of the cheap stuff and can you put it on my tab?"

Henri reached for a new bottle of Grand Cru, shaking his head. "The evening is too special, mon ami. I will allow only the best for her. Be gentle with her, Davidson, or I will pull out your eyes with the opener which I have left in her room by the fire. Also, I have placed more wood outside her door. Of course, she does not know this."

"Thanks, Henry. I think we might be a bit late for breakfast. I hope so."

"Possibly because she has killed you, mon ami. I put my ear to her door when you were gone. There was not one noise. Beware, mon ami. It is not for nothing that we call such beautiful women bombshells. Enough time is wasted on me. Go to her."

The hallway was lit with a single bulb and Henry had piled more than enough quartered logs for a cozy night and a day. That the door was unlocked mattered not at all. He had the spare key. He eased off his shoes, leaning against the wall. He removed his jacket before he went in and placed them quietly on the floor. His stomach was knotted, his heart was at the point of rupturing and he was certain his breathing would soon wake the dead.

Inside the small suite was dark and quiet. The doors leading to her sitting room and bedroom were open. He felt like a thief, like a voyeur. The bed was empty and had not been slept in, so was her lounging récamier. He turned, tip-toeing into the sitting room where nothing had changed in the hour he'd been gone except the barely audible sounds that had changed from her gleeful purrs to painful groans. She was on the floor, illuminated by pale moonlight and curled tightly into a ball under a blanket, rocking.

He lifted her into his arms as though sweeping an empty blanket into the air and carried her to the bed.

"Gabrielle did you think I would go that far and not come back to you. I won't leave till the very last second, sweet thing, till you push me through the doors because you're sick of me. I felt I had to run back for my clothes, and to get us another fine bottle of wine, which is on my tab by the way. I've had some help and I've got more wood for the fire. So stop your crying, sweet thing. It's our time to be happy together. Do you remember? We promised we wouldn't say anything hurtful and you didn't say anything about me not going back for my clothes. It didn't seem quite the right thing to say when you were taking all yours off. Do you think it was easy to leave a very warm and naked angel? It wasn't."

She held him tightly around the neck, nodding silently, her wet face pressed hard against the coarseness of his and trying so hard to hold back a flood of pent-up tears. He held her there with one hand as he stooped to pull back the comforter with the other and toss her new pillow shams to the floor behind them. He laid her down and pulled the covers to her chin before tugging away her blanket and rubbing warmth into her.

Her eyes sparkled with tears that trickled across her face and into her hair. She wiped them away and propped herself onto an elbow, redirecting the flow to her quivering lips as he backed away. She followed his every move, saying nothing as he uncorked the wine and filled their glasses. When he left the room and she heard the door open she sat up, crossing her legs and straining her ears as she reached for a tissue to wipe away lingering tears and blow her nose. She heard a dull thud, then several more and then silence until the door closed and still there was nothing. She leaned forward onto her elbows with her legs still crossed and her bum in the air, jerking back too late when suddenly he came through the door to her room.

"I'd much prefer you on your back till I'm done. I wasn't leaving, though if I see that little bare bum of yours once more we'll not have a fire anytime soon."

"Do not put dirt on my floors," was all she said.

He chuckled. "I won't. Besides, there's none left to fall. It's all on me. I'm afraid I'll need a shower when I'm done."

"Good. You smell like old wood."

"That is the wood." He put her glass into her hands and smoothed her hair. Then he sipped his own and did not stop talking to her as he went about the business of stoking a fire that would flicker and dance till early morning. "Should I leave my clothes where they are, or is there a place for me to hang them?"

"I will do it for you in the morning. Take your shower."

When he turned, Davidson was pulling at his tie and she was placing her glass on the night table. She slid back under the covers, following him as he walked to the door. He wanted to say something smart, something sophisticated, but he knew it was better to say nothing at all. When he stepped back out his glass was beside hers, the covers were pushed to the bottom of the bed and Gabrielle lay on her front with her green eyes penetrating his.

"You see, monsieur. I am the only French loaf on the shelf." She rested her face in her open palms. "I am not afraid, Davidson. I am happy."

"I'm glad you're not afraid, sweet thing. And I hope you're not prone to laughter in your sleep."

"I want to feel you inside me and to open my eyes in the morning with you beside me. It is what I want, what I have waited for."

"Gabrielle…"

She put her finger to her lips. "It is what I want."

"It's what I want as well, sweet thing. What I don't want is to hurt you or make you feel guilty." He sat beside her. "Are you sure? It's not too late."

She nodded, looking directly at him. "Now I will know all of you and you will know all of me. Yes, I am certain. Lean against the pillows the way you were before I went to the bathroom."

He moved more quickly than he had intended, and she giggled. He could listen to her voice for hours and never tire of the sound of her laughter that made all those around her happy. She straddled his hips, reaching for their wine as she rocked ever so gently against him and when he reached behind her to explore she slapped his hand away and took a final sip of wine before replacing her glass. He did the same and she fell against him with her arms around his neck, pulling herself up and down against him until he figured it out and yanked away his towel.

As much as he wanted to lift her and set her down to be one with her, he needed to feel every part of her, to see every part of her. He eased forward, taking her with him, laying her down in front of him. She laid with her legs apart, her thighs resting on his as he took each of her arms in his hands, gently squeezing, sensing her skin from her shoulders to her fingertips, placing each one in turn inches above the apex of her open thighs. He cupped her flushed cheeks, leaning forward to kiss her lips and her eyes and her nose, bringing his hands titillatingly down over her breasts, kissing and pinching her nipples and drawing concentric circles around her abdomen. Her virgin lips were moist to the touch of his fingertips with a texture he had never before experienced, between them her wetness was warm and exotic and as enticing as it was mysterious to him. He moaned deeply as he brought his whetted fingers to his already moist lips to taste the bitter dew.

He had heard about it and had wondered about it. He had even tried to imagine it, though it had never looked like that in his mind, nor had it ever felt like that in his mind. The little pink nodule was firm and at first he was afraid to touch it. It glistened when he parted her lips and when he put his fingertip against it she arched her back and whimpered. He pressed slightly harder, moving his finger in tiny circles and feeling incredibly aroused. He pushed her gently forward as he eased backward and brought his hands to under buttocks to bring her closer to his mouth. He kissed her there, wanting to probe with his tongue, but too afraid of the intimacy. Instead he drew the little pink gem between his lips and flicked his tongue against its sensitive tip, breathing in her pungent scent as she draped her legs over his shoulders to give him full access.

She reached out after long minutes, searching with closed eyes, locking her little hands into his thick hair and trying to pull him up over her, managing to pull herself up instead. She wriggled away from him, feeling his grasp on her wet thighs as she twisted. She let him explore for as long as she could bare the intensity of his touch, then she pushed against his side with all her strength, wanting him to turn, wanting to straddle him and do to him what he had done to her. He did turn, and she made it halfway to her objective before she felt herself being lifted helplessly into the air. She had not felt so safe in such a very long time and when she blurted out a tiny cry of pain they kissed each other's face and lips.

The bright morning light was a beautiful irritant and more than one person had giggled as they passed the remaining flecks of wood in the hallway on their way to breakfast. When Davidson opened one eye, then the other, he was alone and the bright yellow and orange flames from hours before had turned to cold dark clumps of grey charcoal. He heard a knock at the door and saw a flash of white streak across the doorway to the bedroom, then he heard the chatter of Parisian gibberish and giggles and a door closing. The platter Gabrielle carried was filled with croissants and ham, preserves and coffee. She was beautiful in the morning light and elegant, in no way demure, and what had he done?

"Bon matin. Good morning, mon amour." She stood in front of him. "I can no longer call you Davidson, unless that is what you want. It is not enough. It means my love, mon amour." She shrugged.

"And what will I call you?"

"Whatever you feel, mon amour. Before we closed our eyes you called me darling. At first I cried. I don't know why, or maybe I do. But now I know it is your name for me, only for me. "

He sat up straight. "Aye, it is for you alone, sweet thing. And what's for breakfast, darling? I've no strength left because of you. And why is it you've not yet worn your new silky things?"

"You would not understand because you are still stupid, mon amour. You are a man and men understand nothing at all, not even French men," and she fed him his first bite with a hand cupped under his chin to catch the crumbs.

Then, Friday night, another day gone, she was pouring the wine Henri had left by the table as she etched every inch of him into her memory as she watched him stoke the flames. He would soon leave her, never knowing she had earlier been with Marie-Claude and Henri, crying hysterical tears in an adjoining suite of the auberge as he bathed.

He looked so beautiful to her, so fine in the new black silk robe she had bought for him the day before, so handsome, so much a man and so alive. She wanted so badly for him to stay, knowing it was impossible. If he did he would be found and executed by his own. At least this way she would always think of him as being alive and, with him, Jean-Philippe. He would find her again, if he wanted to. If not, she would live without them.

They had not left her suite of rooms all day. They had loved and made love. He had watched her dress and undress, and shower and bathe. They sat by the fire and stood by the window, they spoke with their fingertips and lay in each other's arms stroking their skin and combing their fingers through each other's hair.

The music was Louis Armstrong's phlegmy voice made not much worse with deep scratches and a dulled stylus. There was no fine meal, yet to the young lovers what Henri had prepared for them was even more special: an exotic cheese plate with fresh fruits and crudités, a bottle of fine wine and the few remaining ounces of his own VSOP. The glow of the candles was his final touch and he left the room fighting back tears, yelling harmless invectives to anyone who crossed his path.

She had made Davidson stand in the hallway in his robe

and bare feet, not caring he might have to greet and sheepishly shake hands with a dozen couples or more and when she called to him the wait worth all the riches known to man.

She sat lounging backward on the edge of her perfectly made bed. Her pale emerald slip was pulled up high and her matching silk robe parted at her waist to drape over the down-filled comforter to show her satin-smooth legs crossed for affect. Her tiny satin slippers dangled far from the floor. His heart stopped anew. Hers beat rapidly, flushing her cheeks. She drew in her lips, tasting the sweetness of their deep mahogany colour, unblinking, barely parting them to run her moist tongue sensually along the top ridge and caress the fullness of its delicate epicentre. Her eyes seemed like sparkling green stars set in the muted blues and greens Marie-Claude had helped her with and her black lustrous hair fell straight behind her, tied at the nape of her tender neck with a barrette of blue-green polished stones she could not afford.

"There's nothing I can say, darling Gabrielle."

"Then do not. Talk to me the way you did this morning and this afternoon, mon amour, with your fingers and your soft lips."

He fell to his knees in front of her and laid his head over the creamy smoothness of her thighs, bringing his hand up under her slip to the flared lace trim of her loose-fitting silk panties and enjoying the heat of her hands stroking his face. There was so much he wanted to say, though he dared not. He was leaving her, yet he could say nothing about leaving or not wanting to that would not hurt her. There was no time left for strolling hand in hand or sipping their wine or looking out over La Falaise. He had seen her bathe and never would again, he had seen her tease him in her garters and never would again. He never would again and he found himself jealous of the future, jealous of the next man who would see her and touch her and love her.

"Mon amour, you will fix the fire and bring our wine. I am not hungry. I believe Henri will understand if we do not eat." She leaned forward, kissing his cheek. "Turn off the music, mon amour. Your voice is all that I want to hear."

When he came back she eased from the bed and pulled him close for long moments, listening to his heart. She loosened her robe, letting him guide the silk from her shoulders to the floor, and her slip, one strap, then the other as she stepped from her slippers luxuriating in the sensation of the sensuous fabric cascading over the slender curves her body to the green folds at her ankles.

She felt good suspended in his arms with her eyes closed and her body held so close to his. She purred when the fire's heat touched her skin, still in his arms as they sank onto the cushions he had scattered across the floor. He laid her gently backward, kneeling between her open legs, their eyes locked. Shadows danced on her belly and her breasts and lit one side of his face while it darkened the other. He reached out, cupping his hands and closing his eyes, seeing her with his fingertips, excited by the softness of her breasts and the contrasting firmness of her nipples. He felt each rib and the rise and fall of her concaved belly and he pressed his hands into the silken texture of her panties and under them. He raised her from the cushions, sliding his hands under her buttocks, squeezing gently before raising her legs into the air and pushing the flimsy material up past her toes. His own robe fell behind him and still their eyes were locked. She opened herself to him. She glistened and the aromas of her moisture and her perfume permeated the air around them. She reached out, searching for his arms to pull him down, inhaling deeply at the intimate touch of his fingers and their mounting urgency. When she shrieked her back arched, thrusting herself upward to meet his open arms and when he let her ease into his lap they were suddenly one and their lips pressed together.

They stayed as they were and drank their wine. His legs

ached under the strain and suddenly he gasped, falling backwards, and she fell with him closing her eyes to dream. When she woke she was in bed, spooned into his body, feeling one hand pressed lightly against both her breasts and another spread across the narrow expanse of her buttocks. He was kissing her neck and her shoulders and when she stirred he turned onto his back, taking her with him, kissing her lips and letting hot tears splash onto his face.

She had no need to reach down. She knew. She felt him and she pushed herself backwards to meet him. She squeezed her eyes tight, hot tears scarring her pretty face with streaks of green and blue and her tightly pursed lips trembled uncontrollably, though not from excitation and tiny bursts of warm spittle formed at the corners.

When their bodies shuddered in unison she dug her fingers deep into his flesh and collapsed onto his chest, convulsing. He swept her hair away from her face in gentle strokes and kissed the top of her head. He ran his hands over her body as far as he could reach, aching to say the words, banging his head into the soft pillow, grinding his teeth together and squeezing his eyes shut.

She smoothed his chest, kissing it, and reached for his hair and his face and his eyes, not looking at him. His eyes were wet and his chest was heaving rapidly beneath her. Her hips swayed, slowly at first, until she reawakened him and she ground herself onto him, pushing him deeper and deeper until they were kissing passionately and wiping each other's faces and grasping wildly at each other's slippery body. Then all they could do was savour gentle caresses and be close, forbidden from saying the words that would have made them closer.

"I know that you are Davidson, mon amour. I will never forget you, not one of our moments together. I wanted our love to happen. That you also wanted to love me makes me happy. Do not forget me. And do not die or I will always hate you. Do not die again. I could not live to know you have died twice."

"I won't d…"

She cupped a hand over his mouth. "I do not want to see you walk away from me. I want to remember your arms and your mouth and your eyes and your strange voice. I want to say so many things to you that I will not because it is too late. I have waited too long because at first you made me afraid." She pulled herself across his body to stare into his eyes, wanting to remember his fingers tracing lines across her back and buttocks. "Goodbye, mon amour, my darling."

She pressed against him, bringing his hand to her breasts and soon she fell asleep. He waited, not eager to leave her, and when her erratic breathing turned to quiet murmurs he eased himself away and onto his knees to take in her beauty one last time. He kissed her shoulders and the small of her back. He kissed her buttocks and inhaled her sweet scent. He stroked her hair and held it for a moment in his hands, wanting badly to wake her and kiss her lips as he forced himself away.

He laid his robe on the bed beside her and with nothing else to give her he pulled the heavy gold signet ring from his finger and placed it in the centre of the folded silk. He dressed slowly in the darkness, he kissed her from where he stood and he walked away making himself believe he would be back that afternoon, not expecting to see his new friend one last time.

"Goodbye, Henry. I thought you'd be gone by this wee hour and I'm very glad you stayed. Before I go, here's a wee gift for you. I was going to leave it on the bar with a note and I'd like to think you'll remember me with each drop." He pulled the unopened bottle of Rémy Martin VSOP from his duffle bag. "I hope you can forgive all the bad things and remember the good. And I hope you'll soon find someone else to love, someone who'll be as special as your first."

Henri shook his head. "I will pray for you with each

drop, mon ami, until this war is over. There is no bad between us, Davidson. We are friends, n'est pas? And for me, I am content to live my life here with my friends and be happy when it is my time to be with her once again. She waits for me and she will be angry if I do not come alone." He shrugged, twisting the cork from the bottle and filling two snifters, pushing one toward Davidson and raising the other. "Hé, les femmes, what do they know? They are always angry at us for something."

Davidson had something to say. "Henry, I..."

"It is not a time for promises, mon ami, or regrets. The future is not always as long as we wish it to be and it is never certain. She will never be alone. We will be sad together, for a while, and we will cry together, for a while." He swallowed the cognac and held out his hand, his face and his eyes showing the strain. "Adieu, Davidson, à tantôt and take care of le gros Earl. I will miss both of you very much."

"Adieu, Henri. Adieu, mon ami."

The narrow ruelle de la Falaise was dark and sunrise was still hours away. He did not look back and he did not look up, not knowing how much his life would have changed forever to see her quivering lips whispering silently behind the bevelled panes of misty glass, calling him back, telling him how much she loved him. He trudged sullenly to the top of the hill to slump against a dampened wall, dejected and depleted as he stared back at the quaint auberge and let his head sink into his chest. When the MP jeep jerked to a stop in front of him the conversation was brief before he climbed in and turned down their offer of a smoke.

There was no curfew for anyone marching into the battle of the Schelde.

18

"It'll be a hell of a thing to explain to Emily, Earl."

"I didn't hear that." Earl shook his head, exasperated. "There's nothing to explain, Little Brother. It's human nature. The girl was a looker. It's a miracle you lasted this long without it and as long as you did with her. What Emily doesn't know won't hurt her and she'll have her own secrets that you'll never ask about. It's better not to hear a secret than listen to a lie."

Davidson rolled onto his bunk and looked at the blank parchment, wanting to write but seeing Gabrielle looking back at him with her dark green eyes from between the uneven edges. His pen was unsteady in his hand and he called up to Big Earl for the date.

*

Dear Emily, the day is October 28th in the fifth year of my war. Thank you for your photo. I've just received it. You're very pretty and all the guys gathered round for a peek. I'll wear it close to my heart and hope a German's bullet doesn't ruin it for me.

We're marching tomorrow into a war that many believe will never end. It's unfortunate we can't simply be given a quota of men to kill and then go home when we're done, but the buggers keep coming and it's never done. Winter's coming and so is Christmas. I hope you get your gift on time. I'm sending it today, the first chance I've had. I hope you like it. There's nothing much to buy. If it's not been stolen, it's been ruined, whatever it might be.

I've been away a very long time, Emily, and I hate to think you're lonely on my account. It's been so long. Some of the men already know there's no reason to go home. I'd understand, Emily. I'm not the same man who left you. Big Earl took some snaps of me a few weeks back. You'll see where and you'll see how I've changed. I promise to write again soon, if you want me to.

Regards, Davidson.

*

"Earl, I want to be sick."

"That's why you're on the bottom, Little Brother." Big Earl jumped down, looking to see that no one was near. "You're a sergeant in the army, Little Brother, so stop talking like an old squaw. You did it. What's done is done." He knelt down, resting a massive forearm along the steel frame of Davidson's bunk. "Little Brother, whatever is ahead of us will not be good. We've been lucky so far in the sunny south. You know that. But winter's on our heels and it's the buggers' last chance to kill us. They're nervous and they should be. They're being squeezed and a cornered dog is dangerous, especially a rabid or hungry one. If you're lucky enough to make it home, be sure it's the home you want. Once we step onboard the ship, whenever the day comes, you will not come back to her. It will be too late. You must go where your spirit takes you, Little Brother, but your spirit is troubled and that must change. A tormented spirit feels trapped and is not free to be one with those who have departed this world before us. When we die our spirits stay close to those we love, Little Brother. They never leave us, but our own spirits must be free and yours is not. Be certain, Little Brother. Hurt one or hurt the other, there's no difference."

"How will I know?"

"I can't tell you. You came to love one without ever

having known her, and the other you have come to love as you have come to know her. You are not a man to envy, Little Brother. It is not a good reason to die and the German you don't see aiming at you because of it won't care either way, and then you will have hurt them both. Clear your mind and do it before we march."

The 29th was a sombre day of shouted goodbyes through barbwire fences, along narrow roadways and from windowsills filled with excited young women waving their scarves and hoping the men they had loved or had promised to love would see them. Davidson marched to the side of his platoon. He never looked up and he never looked into the crowds lining the narrow roads and wide avenues that led them from the city. La ruelle de la Falaise was miles away and they had said their goodbyes. His jealousy would soon fade and her memory of his voice and their time together would fade as quickly.

The city of Lille was 120 miles to the north where they would cross into Belgium and take the mouth of the Schelde at Breskens that was another fifty. For any who lived to see it the next battleground would be Walcheren Island to the north and would culminate in the opening of the German-held Atlantic ports to the City of Antwerp.

Davidson ported the Lee Enfield across his back, keeping time by smacking his bayonet against his leg and barking orders to any of his platoon who did not keep pace with his stride. The sky was dark and the days were bitter. They would be for several months to come: a dreary and desolate time of year in a colourless region of expansive low-lying polders surrounded by elevated roads atop the dykes and canals which had lost their romance years earlier. There was nowhere to hide, nowhere to run. Each man was the target of a German who had nothing to lose and each man knew there was a better than even chance he would not be going home.

The fighting was bloody and horrific. Trenches quickly

became water-filled ditches. The water was cold and the men colder. Their boots were soaked through, numbing their blistered feet and their fingers were often too cold to pull back on their triggers. Day and night the German Nebelwerfers exploded the surrounding countryside, turning polders into dust bowls on good days and into muddy bogs on the bad. At night the men tried desperately to sleep, most of them kept awake and listening intently for the blind German assaults or the engines of Allied amphibious craft attacking from the River Schelde itself.

The battle for Walcheren was vicious, fought along the unprotected 130-foot wide causeway with amphibious Buffalos fighting against a beachfront lined with heavy German artillery while other craft swept the channel for mines. The Allies advanced steadily against Germans who had nowhere to go, surrounded by the sea. It was a time to die. He would never be able to describe the noise and he wondered how long he would remember it. He once told himself he would always think of Emily in battle and, if he ever had, now he thought of no one but himself.

A slow brightening of monochromatic grey and brown tones usurped the sunrise. Both men shivered with the invasive dampness and he felt Big Earl's massive hand on his back.

"You've saved a few lives, Little Brother. You've grown to be a man since we shared our first can of beans and burnt our legs farting out Roman Candles over the campfire. Do you remember? It was much louder than it was bright and not very pretty as I recall. I am proud of you. I am proud to have known you."

"Now it's you talking like an old squaw. Keep your mud-filled skull close to the ground, Earl. These buggers are intent on seeing us dead today and I don't really have a good feeling about it below the waist."

"Calm your spirit, Little Brother. It can be a strong one if you let it, but you are still troubled and your spirit is confused. Don't let it be." He chuckled. "Here I am, crouched in a shit-hole talking to a white boy about spirits. Little Brother, belie..."

The close sound was a loud crack and Davidson recoiled, shrinking down into the narrow pit. Earl's torso had barely moved. His head snapped back once and twisted sideways, slamming back into the grassy edge of the trench. The hole was centred in his forehead, an inch below the steel rim of his helmet and his white eyes were open wide with curiosity, not fear or shock.

"Earl! No! No! Earl! You big, dumb bastard. I told you to keep your bloody head down. I'm your sergeant you big, dumb bastard. Why did you not listen? Earl!" and the name rang out over the exploding shells and the other screaming wounded.

Davidson emptied his Enfield and then Earl's, each round finding its mark. He had never killed with a vengeance, now he did, counting each one off to Earl. When he was done he reloaded both rifles and waited with every nerve-ending tingling. There was no one near him and he knew it, but when he felt the unmistakable weight of a firm hand pushing on his back he lowered his head below the edge of the trench and turned back to see Earl lying perfectly still by his side when the bullet struck his helmet and ricocheted back into the field.

The force of the impact jerked Davidson's head sideways. He winced and screamed out as much from the sudden pain that shot from his head to his spine as from the unexpected shrill resonating in his ears. He steadied himself for a moment against a muddy wall and swore aloud as he laid his Enfield flush with the ground. He waited, squeezing his eyes shut and wanting to rip off his helmet to grab at his head. When he raised himself he did so with barely enough clearance to line up the precision notches along the barrel. He breathed in slowly and with a smirk on his lips he sent a single round into the German's chest. They were coming closer.

He fixed his bayonet and sank onto his knees to cradle his friend, keeping him from the damp cold of the mud. "You've gone and left me you big, dumb bastard. Now what am I to do? Did you ever think of that?" he yelled.

It should have been so easy. How many men had he seen die? Thousands. He was twenty-six. He should have been dancing in clubs, playing tennis with Emily and having babies, not killing. Jenkins, Hillary and Gravel, all privates, were looking at him, leaning with their backs to the rear wall of the trench. So what if he was crying, who gave a shit? The .45 was ominous and lethal in his hands and, if he knew anything, he knew there was no pain in death, merely in the anticipation of it. He turned the black steel in his hands, almost mesmerized and waved the weapon at himself, struggling to conquer his will to survive. Then he laughed, and then he cried more. Not until he holstered the gun did he see the other men in the trench weeping with him. He let them be. It was enough for them to see one another.

He took off his helmet and held the big Indian's hand, interlacing his strong fingers with the already softening flesh of Big Earl's, absently turning the turquoise and silver ring. Few men could wear such a ring, a warriors ring, a chieftain's ring and Davidson eased it from Big Earl's finger and onto his own. He was now the chieftain and no one else would die, unless he died with them.

Seeing the damaged helmet he put the palm of his open hand against Earl's cheek, barely able to hear his own words for the loud ringing in his ears.

"My spirit will soon be well, Earl. Thank you, dear friend, for not leaving my side."
*

My dearest Emily, I don't mean to worry you by writing so soon after my previous correspondence to you. I wanted to tell you that you needn't bother sending any more socks and underwear to Earl. He's dead. The buggers killed him this morning and the medics are just now taking him away. I've been sitting here with him all day, in the muck, keeping him from the cold water made rancid with our blood and other foul matter and I can't even tell you where.

I believe I can feel his spirit around me, Emily. I don't know how, I just do. I know he's still with me, taking care of me, calling me Little Brother. By the time you read this it all will have been several weeks ago.

I've written a letter to his sister, Lilly, though she'll not receive it anytime soon. Might I impose upon you to visit with Lilly on my behalf as soon as possible, Emily? Her native name is Shimmering Moon and she's a very pretty thing. It's a dreadful task, I know. I also know if it weren't for having Earl by my side these past years someone like him would already have written this letter to his sister, asking that she visit with you. He was a brave man, Emily, and I loved him very much. I always will. I would have died more than once without him by my side.

Tell Lilly that each night he would stare up to the moon and sing his native verses to her. He would never have told her, he was quite stupid that way. I think now he would want her to know. Anyway, I want her to know, so there it is and it was quite the thing to hear. I called him so many bad names, Emily, in fun, and I always thought he knew so. Now all I can think is how I must have hurt him, although he never showed the slightest annoyance. He was always there for me and now he isn't.

I'm good for a while. I'm breathing and still have both my feet, but without Earl I don't know. This horrid war can't last much longer or there'll soon be only two of us left to find and kill one another. I'll write as soon as I can.

Davidson.

*

How long had it been since he wrote that he loved her? How long had it been since he had thought he loved her?

How long had it been since he had thought of her, and no one else? The River Schelde opened on November 28th and he had been gone one month.

He swore a silent and sacred oath to himself that no one else in his platoon would die. He shaved without looking into a mirror for the next several weeks. He showered in cold water that could never numb his soul and his was the smartest unit in the battalion. He was the least forgiving sergeant and he cried each night without knowing or admitting why. It was enough to believe his Big Brother knew why.

Part Two

1945 – 1947

19

Then suddenly there was nothing to do and no one to kill. Not only had they been put on reserve status once again, they felt as though they had been plucked from the war. Davidson drilled his men each day, driving them hard. They competed against other platoons for the best shots, the best hand-to-hand combat and they won most times. When they had first asked what the prize would be, he answered "staying alive."

Christmas morning he wrote the second letter in two months. He was alone in the barracks while most of the others were in Belgium homes partaking of whatever modest meal the lady of the house had managed to scrape together for their respective heroes. He opened his gift box of chocolate bars, cigarettes he would keep to barter, new socks and underwear. The lighter was gold-filled and had a stylized 'A' engraved on both sides. Big Earl's parcel from Emily contained magazines instead of cigarettes and a thick woollen cap. Lilly's box to them was on the floor beside him and he opened it mechanically. There were socks for each of them and knitted gloves. He stared at the envelope, turning it over several times, wondering what Lilly might be doing at that very moment. She would still be in bed sobbing, he thought, remembering the day the War Department had knocked on her door to tell her that her only brother had been killed in action.

He folded her letter and put the envelope away unopened. The private words were not his to read and he would return the letter in person, if he lived. He fell back onto his side and wrote another letter to thank Lilly for the gifts; anything to keep him from remembering his final night with another by the fire and their heated caresses.

By February 08th it seemed to Davidson like ages since he had left Paris. The worst of winter was over, but what about the war? When would the damn war be over? It was no longer about killing Germans. That mindset had changed with Earl's death. It was now about killing someone who might kill him. He was exhausted, so were his men. The two-month reprieve from the war had been a short-lived, a virtual stay of execution. Nothing else had changed.

The doctors and the generals called it battle exhaustion, when it was really the end result of looking down at once-living comrades and seeing one's own face on the twisted and mutilated corpses or seeing men collapse for no other reason than the pent-up fear of their own inevitable deaths. The end was near, only a matter of time, yet seemed nowhere in sight and no one wanted to die on the last day. Those deemed mentally or physically unfit to fight had been evacuated to safe zones, replaced by unskilled warriors who had little or no chance of survival against well-trained and desperate Germans.

The march to the Rhineland took four arduous and deadly weeks of trudging across German-fortified lands. They were amongst the first Allies on German soil where the enemy had an inexhaustible supply of weapons, munitions and hope. Land that should have been dry was muddy with water from German-destroyed dykes. Four-inch guns protected German outposts and a network of carefully placed anti-tank trenches made the capture of the Siegfried Line difficult and costly before falling to the Allies who ended their advance at the Hochwald Forest in the cold and pouring rain. Two weeks later the fighting was done and close to five-hundred men had been killed or wounded.

Orders came to cross the Rhine. For 1 Corps the crossing meant taking Arnhem, a city destroyed by British bombs and Allied artillery. Weary men endured twelve exhausting days accomplishing the mission and three days later Apeldoorn was taken before I Corps moved farther to the west. The Germans were desperate and that was likely to make them impulsive. Those who had not surrendered were fanatical, unwilling to surrender and 1 Corps was abruptly ordered to halt.

The Dutch were starving and a country-wide famine was imminent. If the German's were to flood the region, the innocent would be the ones to die. On May 03rd local German officials agreed and Allies began air-dropping their first supplies to the hungry Dutch as 1 Corps proceeded to destroy the defences, not looking back as they marched to Assen and Amsterdam with orders to kill any SS soldier on sight. The only enemy left to fight were frightened teenagers behind machine-guns or shooting from cellar windows and rooftops. They stood steadfast, thinking themselves heroes, possibly happy when they died for what had become a defunct cause.

The date was May 03, 1945 and Davidson Alexander had killed for the last time.

20

Monday evening, May 07th, friends gathered together in taverns or at home and families huddled around radios across North America to hear the crackling words spoken by the BBC announcer broadcasting live from a raucous and celebratory Amsterdam. Germany had surrendered and all hostile actions were to halt at one minute past midnight, May 08th. The war was over in Europe. V-E Day had finally come and Davidson, like so many others, sank to the ground or sagged against walls as Dutch men and women hugged and kissed their haggard faces.

It was strangely incongruous, so many thousands of people freed from tyranny and torture crying with happiness as they hugged and kissed men who suddenly felt emptiness and defeat rather than victory. He was finally going home. He looked up, remembering Big Earl. He was going home.
*

My dear Emily, I'm writing to you on May 08th. I'm in Assen, Holland and I've never been kissed so much by so many. I'm coming home, though I'll not be amongst the first, far from it. The family men go first, then the married ones, followed eventually by the rest of us. I suppose you already know that. Not all the war's been bad, I suppose, and I'm fairly well off as a result of it. All things figured I'm worth more than a thousand dollars and they're giving all the lads a hundred more for new suits and shoes. I'll finally look my dapper self again and not a mud-caked indigent.

On that particular matter, Emily, perhaps you might find a place for me to live, at least temporarily. I'm thinking of something modest, nothing too meagre mind you, or, if you still have half a mind to, perhaps a wee home for the two of us. Surprise me with your choice. It's been a horrible five years of chasing and killing. My fighting days are finished and I've no intention of continuing them with your tight-haired, scowling hag of a mother, in her place or ours. We'll let her clack around on her split hooves and sniff at someone else's door with her suspicious snout. I want no part of her nonsense and it's the last thing I'll ever ask of you.

I've enclosed a letter of Power of Attorney so you'll have no trouble with the bank. Though leave enough in the account for a nice meal together, a glass of wine and a ring for I've not got much in my pockets these days. I'm stationed here until we ship out, doing a bit of a cleaning up. Write when you can.

Davidson.

*

But the BBC broadcast brought no joy to the Ashton Boarding House, only hushed misgivings and uncertainty. By 0001 GMT the next day the War Office had re-issued its request for the public to stay away. The army would not have final casualty results for several more days. Emily took off her coat and sat down, watching her mother rock Noëlyn's cradle with the toe of a tightly laced foot. Her conflict had not ended. She had no idea Davidson's war had ended days earlier. She felt in her heart he was still alive, despite knowing there was always a chance she might be wrong or that he would not want to come home to her.

She had met with the couple on several occasions over the past twenty months. They were twice her age and wealthy. She was poor and Davidson had little chance of improving himself in an economy still reeling from the effects of the Great Depression. They wanted little Noëlyn as their own. They loved the little girl. They had since first seeing her and the offer still stood. They would gladly pay five hundred dollars, more than Davidson would earn in a year and enough for a down payment on a home. She would do it, but her timing was critical. She would give over her daughter to the Daniels, but not before the very last moment.

Her world stopped the day the letter came. Every woman on the street had prayed not to see uniformed officers at their door. No one wanted to think their man had died at one minute to twelve, but Emily so loved her little Noëlyn. She read Davidson's letter while standing at the open door. She was relieved he had not been killed, that he was safe and told herself she was deeply despondent for what she had done and for what she would now have to do because he would never understand, not because he was coming home.

Little Noëlyn was twenty-one-months, and well before her second birthday she would have a new mother and father with no memory of another who loved her dearly. Emily did not write a letter. It was already the end of June and the end of her happiness.

She decided she would give up the baby to the Daniels that weekend. The extra five hundred dollars would let her and Davidson begin a much better life together, in a bigger home, her own home which she would not have to share with transient strangers or a mother who cared more about utility and housekeeping bills than her own granddaughter.

Her mother had left her job at the plant as soon as the boarding house began filling with guests who, for the most part, were the first discharged soldiers arriving from the east coast. But the baby was difficult to explain and Mrs. Ashton had done so by saying the baby's father would not be coming home from the war, much to Emily's horror and the guests' quiet expression of sympathy.

Then one evening at dinner, once all the guests had been served, Emily casually explained the baby was with the family of a friend for a few days, a friend who had just proposed marriage and she passed her mother Davidson's letter before stepping away from the table to dream of her new home from the quiet of the veranda. Noëlyn would be fine. She would grow up with every advantage and Emily's new house would be ready to move into by mid-August.

Later that evening there was no further conversation between mother and daughter, just the open letter flung onto the floor of her room. Emily knew she would cry for a time and that the tears would eventually stop. She had done the best for Noëlyn, and for Davidson who was coming home to the only woman he had ever loved. He would never have to hear about Christmas Eve 1942.

21

Davidson had taken as many reintegration courses as he could while stationed in Assen and his few remaining weeks in Amsterdam. They had all been told to expect the worst: their wives and children would no longer know them, or their families would be afraid of the changes in the men they had not seen for so many years. Many of them would discover indiscretions, pending divorces and many who had once courted devoted girlfriends would possibly soon discover those girls had married. They were cautioned about being aggressive, drinking, and asking too many questions which would either have no answer or the wrong answer.

They were told how North American women had adapted to shorter fashions due to the government's restrictions on textiles that affected hemlines, how women in general were more emancipated as a result of having been in the workforce and not having to answer to anyone at home. As hardened soldiers they would now have to adapt to a new intimacy, a new vocabulary and a new bonding with children they had never seen. They would have to become their own men and learn to make their own decisions. There would be no sergeant to tell them what to do, no drills to prepare them for what lay ahead and for many of them going home had become the worst part of the war.

There would be special programmes for reinserted vets. There would be grants for those who wanted to attend university or start a business. It all sounded so good to someone who had fought in so many of the war's worst battles. By July 28th Big Earl had been dead eight months when Davidson stood amongst the hordes of unarmed soldiers crowded onto the docks of Amsterdam and looking up at the massive grey hulls that would carry them home. He was going home. He brought the big Cree's turquoise and silver ring to his lips and kissed his friend goodbye, somehow certain Big Earl's spirit would always be with him. He would never see Europe again.

He looked down at the little prayer book and fanned the delicate pages to where the frayed edges of the sepias bookmarked her three pictures. In one photo she was so beautiful with her hypnotic, deep green eyes and her long black hair blowing in the wind with La Falaise behind her. In the second, their last Thursday together, she had left him to run into the store to buy his silk robe, not telling him why and the camera had captured the smile and dark eyes he would never forget as she hurried out to be with him. The third, the one of Henri standing with Gérard, with her between them, holding her hands like a big and little brother, was his favourite. He kissed each one and closed them into the book before he put it safely away.

"I'm sorry, Earl. If only she had said the words," he murmured, looking toward the south, "if only either one of us had."

The crossing would take six days. Few onboard spoke. They were too self-absorbed with new fears and new dreams. Davidson inhaled deeply. He had made Emily a promise and would be true to his word. When his row was called out over the loud hailer he turned his back on Europe and clambered up the swaying gangway towards his journey home.

The men stayed on deck for as long as they could before the night air of the North Atlantic turned from a pleasant chill to penetrating cold. Davidson stayed as he was, alone with his thoughts, drifting amidst a billion stars and braving the fine mist carried by the artificial sea breeze.

He flipped the cap of his lighter up and down, grinding the flint to a blue flame that flickered out each time. Becoming the Chief Clerk at Morgan's Department Store was no longer good enough; not for him and not for Emily. He would be a success, unlike his worthless coward of a father. He would be a businessman, his own man with no one to tell him what to do or when. They could rent a small apartment and use his savings as start-up money together with a government loan and he would go back to school and perhaps find someone to help train his voice.

He knew Emily so well. She would take a while to find their perfect house. She was fussy about such things. He had time. They both had time to plan and to work together. She would understand and she would be there for him. They would marry and work together. They would be a family and very soon they would be a real family. She would have anything she desired, not like his poor mother. Nothing was impossible, not now, not for him.

His mother had only been forty-one when she had died in 1939. Davidson was twenty-one and had stood alone by her pauper's grave. He remembered the smell of the chapel in the hospital and the cheap wooden coffin draped in a cheap black cotton shroud, the false piety of the apathetic minister dressed in his shiny black suit and the rows of empty pews behind them.

When asked if there was something he would like to say, he had answered "yes" and told the cleric to leave him alone with his mother. He would always remember the vitality in her voice and her smile, her reddish hair and her sparkling eyes, not the tuberculosis or what had come after.

Until 1929 they had lived well, not above their means but as well as most others with his father's earnings as a travelling vender. But business had dropped steadily by the end of the second year of the depression and one day he just never came home. His mother had been abandoned at a young thirty-three and no one could say with any certainty when she was first stricken with tuberculosis. The same year Davidson was thirteen when he dropped out from school to work at the corner drugstore to supplement his mother's starvation wages. She worked two jobs as a cleaning lady in public washrooms because she wanted her boy to be someone. She knew the depression would not last forever and her son had a beautiful voice and a talent. He could also play tennis well enough to win the championship at Wimbledon in time, but it would all take money.

Then one day it was Davidson working two jobs and taking care of his mother. She was dying, dying from drudgery and he longed for the day when he would see his father once more. A beautiful young woman turned vile and sickly. The end had begun slowly with coughing, then at night he would hear her moaning and in the morning he would see her sweat-stained gown and dishevelled hair and smell her sickening breath. He would hold her frail body in his arms and sponge her with warm water, looking away as he cleaned between her legs, washed her sore breasts and changed her sodden gowns. He combed her hair and sang to her in his quietest voice to comfort her. But each day was worse than the one before, despite the food he had not eaten so that she might have more. The fevers worsened until blood began to pool at the corner of her pale lips, mixed with the stench of phlegm that filled their small living space in the worst part of town. The doctors said nothing. Finally they began to stay away, afraid of infection as her lungs rotted, and then there was no need. Bonnie Alexander laid dead, emaciated and looking too miserable to be at peace and Davidson had not cried. He had told himself she would not want his tears, finally understanding she no longer needed them. When they buried her she had no stone. She was BA-492 written in black paint on a vertical two-by-four of dried knotty pine.

There was already talk of war and a soldier's pay was supposedly good. If he stayed he would still need both his jobs to continue his voice and tennis lessons, though with his mother gone he could manage his own income, buy new clothes and be who he wanted to be. How many times had she told him that? He had always been well-dressed. She had insisted, though perhaps not in the latest fashion and that's what bothered him the most. No one would ever hire him for stage work dressed as a hobo in rags, or accept him into a tennis club as he was. He was determined to dress the part of the man he wanted to be and do so without working weekends and nights at the drugstore.

His ride home was sombre. There was no home without his mother and he was too tired to feel sadness. He loved his mother deeply. He would have cared for her forever. Instead, he would miss her forever. Or was it that he was twenty-one and felt more like forty? He had never been to high school, school dances or a prom and he had never kissed a girl. He was twenty-one and had never kissed a girl, like the prissy, stuck-up dame who had just sat down across from him.

She had climbed onto the tram a block or two after him and had stared at him even when her head was turned. She had smiled once, he thought, and had patted her skirt for no reason while he sat there reeking of death and feeling completely forsaken. For as long as he could remember he had felt inexplicably incomplete, strangely less than whole as though missing a limb, the way the legless hobo might feel phantom pain as he sat on his coaster at the corner, begging. Somehow he had always known a part of him was missing, though his mother had always been there to make him smile and forget the phantom absence he had never thought to mention, but no longer. His mother had gone.

When the young woman stood to disembark his eyes followed her, quite convinced she would not walk that way normally or tilt her hip the way she had, trying to appear sophisticated as she waited for the driver to stop and open the door. Although she never looked back, he made a mental note of the stop without meaning to and then he forgot her.

The first evening alone was long and horrible for him and he spent the night by the open window to lessen the pungency still permeating the room. The month's rent had been paid with only a few days remaining and he knew already he would leave. He would always remember the good times with his mother and work hard to become Morgan's best clerk as he continued with his singing lessons.

What was done was done. Bonnie was gone. He could grieve as much at work as he could while looking across to the bed where his mother had died and the store manager had already given him two days. The next day the girl was already on the bus and he wondered why, without caring. This time he sat in front of her, not looking across until he stood several stops later, glad all the same he had worn his second suit, a brighter tie and a shirt with a clean collar and cuffs.

Reaching for the bell and slipping his hand easily into the passenger sling for no reason other than the pretence of balancing himself, he turned his head casually to the back of the tram, then to the front, happening to cross eyes with hers. This time she was looking up, expecting him to return her smile. Instead he walked to the front footwall and stepped down. When he stepped out onto the road he was at the main entrance of Morgan's Department store.

Strangely, he had not thought of his mother at all throughout the day and, after he had tallied his receipts, he left the store feeling guilty. He stood by the tram stop with his head down, smoking, worried that Bonnie might be too cold and wanting to believe she had fond memories of him wherever she was. The steel wheels of the number 17 tram screeched to a stop against its steel rails and its overhead wires sparked blue stars at their contact point with the city's electrical cables. He stepped up, still in another world. The driver greeted him with a functional smile, like his own smile at the store. He paid his fare and went to sit in the seat he had made his own since his first day at Morgan's. He barely had time to look up.

"That was very rude of you, very rude indeed."

He looked straight at her, stretching slightly and leaning slightly at an angle to see past her parcels.

"Excuse me. Were you talking to me?"

"The tram's practically empty. Of course I'm talking to you. I would have expected a gentleman to have at least let a lady go first. You didn't even look back. I should go right back to your store and return what I've bought if that's the way all their clerks act towards their customers."

"I apologize, miss. I do. I'm very sorry. My mind was somewhere else. Normally I'm not so discourteous. Please forgive me and let me take your bags."

"I can put them down myself, thank you. And I still think you're very rude."

"I am rude," he returned, trying to smile, "but only because I'm nervous in front of lovely young women. I'm not very worldly, I'm afraid."

"I can see that. Things aren't always what we think they are." She sat ignoring him, seeming quite put off.

"Can I make it up to you, perhaps with a coffee?"

She arranged her packages more than necessary. "No, you may not and if it weren't so much trouble I would get off right now."

"Then, may I help you," he paused, this time smiling believably, "to carry your bags, I mean. We're still several blocks from your corner. I'm afraid you'll find it a wee bit of walk on your own."

"If you don't stop talking, I'll call the conductor for help."

"There isn't one. It might be his day off." Davidson

reached up and pulled down on the bell cord. "Driver, the young lady here either wants off or she's in need of your help. I don't know which, and I believe neither does she."

A wave of deep crimson flooded over Emily Ashton's face, seeing the two men exchange smiles through the driver's mirror.

"That was impertinent and it's not any of your business where my corner is."

"Then you won't mind if I sit here and watch you struggle with your bags, since I'm rude and not a gentleman. Anyway, it appears you've bought too much. If you don't already know, the store's return policy is very strict."

Emily wanted to slap him, even though he was tall and handsome and well-dressed, albeit a little too gaunt. She promised herself if he did not stand to help her onto the street she would drop all her parcels into the footwall and cause a scene. Then she ignored him for the next several blocks.

When the driver stopped she stood and began to gather her purchases, having more than a little difficulty trying to bring all the twine handles together. It was awkward and the empty aisle was barely wide enough, forcing her to walk sideways to the well and the doors. He was insolent and grinning like a ridiculous fool, she thought. She was pretty and well worth a second and third look, thought Davidson, and he waited to stand until she had stepped out and the doors had folded closed.

Somehow the driver knew to stop again moments later and the men sent a conspiratorial brotherhood grin to one another. She was still struggling with her parcels when he came up behind her.

"Miss, I beg your pardon. Can you help me? I seem to be quite lost."

"You're an idiot, and if you don't stop pestering me I'll call for a constable."

"Aye, I know I'm an idiot. And you're a little stuck-up if I do say so myself, even if you are very pretty." He went closer. "Now, will you let me help you or do you intend to fly home like a kite with your feet kicking at people's heads?"

"Thank you. This is my home. Goodnight."

Davidson looked up at the four-story boarding house. Its façade was a wall of plate-glass windows bordered by a wooden walk-around veranda.

"So you've got a room at Mrs. Ashton's. That's very nice. The place looks quite lovely."

"What I have is none of your business. Goodbye." She made her way as far as the first step, seeming very frustrated before she put down three of the bags and almost skipped to the entrance of the veranda, trying to hurry. When she turned he was behind her, setting down the three.

"That wasn't so bad, was it?" He stood straight, adjusting his cuffs. "I'll be on the same tram tomorrow, if you feel the need to avoid me. Good evening, miss."

"Thank you for the warning. I'll be sure to remember."

Davidson bounced down the steps with more vitality than he felt. The banter had actually drained him and he had little energy to spare. He checked his pocket watch. The corner grocery store had closed moments earlier and he would have nothing to eat until the morning. He spoke briefly with his landlord to advise the man that he would be leaving at month's end. Then, alone in his room, he spoke to his mother as he knelt by her bed. He wanted her to know how sorry he was for not thinking to miss her that day, despite having thought of her all the while. Then he put all his possessions into a single travel bag and left.

22

Davidson remembered every detail of those long ago days as though they had happened hours earlier, not six years before, though for the longest time he had not thought of one woman without thinking of the other. He would never see Gabrielle again, yet he continued to feel pangs of jealousy as though he had left her that very morning and his once fanciful images of Emily's body had been usurped by memories of Gabrielle's perfection. He flicked the stone wheel once more, absently. He would soon be with his Emily, Gabrielle would find her own way and they would soon forget one another. She probably already had forgotten him.

He remembered the steps of the boarding house and how steep they had looked when he arrived with his suitcase, much steeper than they had seemed that afternoon. The vacancy sign was still there, asking anyone interested to enquire at the desk and most of the lights were on.

The old lady was tall and thin; her dark hair covered with a fine mesh and knotted into a severe knob at the back of her head like a pin cushion or shock absorber.

"Good evening. I suppose you want a room."

"Aye, I do, and a quiet one. Are the meals included?"

"The room is five dollars a week. The meals are fifty cents a day more. Breakfast is at seven and the evening meal is promptly at six."

"Done." Davidson reached for his wallet. "I've not eaten

all day and I've missed the grocer by a few minutes. Could I perhaps have a sandwich from the kitchen? I'll gladly pay the fifty cents."

Mrs. Ashton looked at him as though he had commented on her mole that was also a planter for a thick, black hair.

"Just this once, in future dinner is at six sharp. There'll be no more exceptions and there'll be no guests in the rooms, no female visitors, no loud music and no disturbances. The bath is at the end of the hall. It's for the floor and is to be kept clean after each use. Gentlemen are expected to dress for breakfast and dinner and not to carry on with female guests. Do what you will outside, that's your business. This is a decent boarding home and I won't have that sort of thing going on in here."

"You'll find I'm very quiet and not much taken to cavorting, Mrs. Ashton. You'll have no trouble from me," particularly if all your female guests are as lovely and personable as you, he mused as he signed the form. "If you can tell me where the kitchen is I'll…"

"You'll take your meal in your room, Mr. Alexander. Consumption of food and drink is not allowed in the sitting room and guests are not allowed in the kitchen. The sitting room closes at ten. You may come down any time before and you may return your plate in the morning." She passed him the key. "You're on the fourth floor, the first door on the left, number 301, not 401 and now I'll see to your sandwich if there's nothing else. It won't be fancy, mind."

The room was small and austere, but smelled fresh and the linen was clean. He was already half-asleep with his suitcase not yet unpacked when he heard the quiet knock at the door. He had removed his tie, his collar and cuffs. The top button of his shirt was undone and his sleeves were rolled up. The rest he didn't know about because there was no mirror in the room.

"You!" she exclaimed.

He snorted. "So, you're working off your room and

board…or to help pay for your luxuries. There's no shame in that and there's no need to turn so red on my account. It's honest work."

"I happen to live here. This is my home."

"And that's my dinner you're holding, which is the main reason I'm here. I spent so much time trying to be kind to you that I missed the grocery store. So you can look to yourself if you need someone to blame for my being here."

She looked down at the tray. "It's a bologna sandwich with pickles and a cup of tea."

"Did you make it?"

"What if I did?"

Davidson smiled. "Because I think it's the only way it would taste good. My name's Davidson, if you care to know, Mrs. Ashton. I thought the old woman downstairs was the famous Mrs. Ashton."

"She's my mother. I'm Emily Ashton, Miss Emily Ashton," she emphasized.

He nodded, leaning into the doorway. "So, then, you're the daughter and not the granddaughter."

"That's awful." Emily laughed through her nose. "Goodnight, Mr. Alexander."

"Goodnight, Miss Emily." He held the door open as she walked away. "Miss Emily, one more thing before you go, if you don't mind. Will you be trying to catch the same tram as me in the morning?"

Her only reply was a giggle and the next morning as breakfast was being served she acted indifferently to him, even though he did his best to catch her eye. He asked for a second tea, even though the pot was within his reach and when she began to pour he asked if he might have a bit more lemon to go with it. He was about to ask for a bit more marmalade for his toast until the older man seated in front of him shook his head and waved a finger while stifling a chuckle to advise against persisting with the reckless ploy. Apparently Davidson was the one person at the table who hadn't seen that Miss Emily was about to stab him with her fork.

He dallied as long as he dared in the lobby before running down the steps to the tram that he caught with precious few seconds to spare. The seat in front of his was empty. He made a point to think of his mother and to miss her, though the day was insufferably long nonetheless. At 5:10 he had already gone from the store and mumbled to himself with his hands in his pockets and a cigarette hanging from his lips as he waited once again for the public ride home. He hated the tram. He hated the hard seats, the smell made him nauseous and the continuous swaying made reading impossible. Though all was forgotten when the young woman came from behind and stood facing away from him. He would have known her anywhere. He crushed the butt under a shoe and folded his arms.

"You know you want to talk with me, Miss Emily. You might as well turn around so I can stare at your face instead of your very beautiful…"

She swirled. "I should smack your face and report you to the store."

"To tell them I was looking at your beautiful hair? Come, I'll go with you." He uncrossed his arms, sliding his hands into his pockets. "Or you can let me walk you home. It's only a few miles and it's a wonderful day to be with a pretty girl, Emily."

"I can't. My feet hurt terribly. My shoes are new."

"Aye, I know. They were practically a giveaway at 6.95 and not even on special." He eyed her up and down, deliberately. "Did you buy that little Shiaparelli outfit to impress me as well, and that wee hat? It's all the rage, I know and too much for a poor man like me to support. So you see, you've done yourself harm. You've chased me away with a broken heart, instead of snaring me in your wanton trap."

Her mouth dropped open, watching him turn on the post

with an irksome grin and stroll away with his hands still in his pockets. The number 17 tram passed him by between blocks and minutes later she was marching more than walking directly towards him.

"You are very conceited, and completely without manners. I'm quite certain your mother would be very ashamed of you. I'm sure she did her best to raise you as a gentleman. She must be very disappointed in you."

She might as easily have slapped the smile from his face, and suddenly she realized they were no longer flirting.

"Come, I'll walk you to the next tram. Then I'll leave you to be alone with my thoughts. I've suddenly remembered I've a few things to work out."

Neither one spoke across the short distance, though at the corner Emily touched his elbow timidly, stopping him. "I've changed my mind. You may walk me home, and I think I would like a tea...if we go Dutch. Mother can wait awhile longer."

Davidson looked in both directions, as though making a difficult decision. "Will she poison my supper, do you think, for chasing after her daughter? She has that look about her."

Emily beamed. "I knew you were chasing me."

"Aye, I was, because I saw you smiling so eagerly at me on the tram yesterday and I saw no need to disappoint you. You could have simply asked me out and saved me a lot of bother." She punched his arm and his grimace was as real as their ensuing smiles. "Not that it won't have been worth it, if you'll let me treat you to the movies Saturday night."

Later, the stony-faced Mrs. Ashworth was the one to grimace when they walked in together. Neither wanted supper. Emily wanted to hear the rest of his story and Davidson felt good about telling her. It somehow validated his mother, that possibly someone else could now think of her. At ten o'clock the older woman came to the sitting room and coughed, then she stood at the bottom of the stairs until she heard Emily's door close and Davidson's footsteps continue to the fourth floor. The next morning Emily sat beside him at breakfast when she wasn't helping to serve, and suddenly the tram was a fine place to be and Saturday was too far away.

Thursday and Friday were the same and each evening the couple walked home to the corner where old poverty looked across from the east side to the new wealth of the west side and Mrs. Ashton's Boarding House. After dinner they spoke until ten, after ten he would lay awake thinking of her and when he fell asleep he dreamt of her. Saturday night Mrs. Ashton practically threw his meal at him after he declared openly that Emily was far too beautiful and dressed much too elegantly to be a serving girl as he pulled out her chair. The other guests agreed and Emily shamelessly absorbed the attention.

She was beautiful. She had spent the afternoon combing her hair ten different ways and had tried on a dozen different blouses and skirts in different combinations. Finally she had gone to one of the younger lady guests for help, knowing her mother would think her preoccupation with the coming evening scandalous. The two had worked giddily together towards the perfect result, deciding on a knit sweater belted with a ribbon to flare the waist over satin slacks, low-heeled flamenco-styled shoes and a bright-red lipstick that wasn't hers and a brooch she promised not to lose.

She was announced at the entrance to the parlour moments before dinner and her face nearly matched the colour of her lipstick when all the men stood to applaud and to tell Davidson he had done well for himself and that he must treat her properly or there would be hell to pay. Her mother simply admonished her that no good had ever come from a decent woman throwing herself at a man, particularly a man of lesser means who clearly had ill intentions.

They held hands at the movies and neither one spoke. They walked home and sat on the veranda until well past midnight, causing Mrs. Ashton to fall asleep in the parlour. Emily wanted to wake her, but Davidson put a finger to his lips and the two tiptoed to the stairs holding hands. With Emily on the second step they were eye to eye when they kissed and she balanced herself with the palms of her hands on his shoulders.

From then on the tram driver knew to stop for them only on rainy days until summer ended too quickly. They had dreams. Davidson would become a famous singer, Emily a famous artist and would one day spend her days creating in the garret of an old house overlooking the sea.

They loved to dance and they did each week. She went to his recitals and he went to her art classes, often posing for her and pretending not to like it. He taught her to play tennis and she would accompany him on the piano while he sang for Mrs. Ashton's guests on Sunday afternoons, which did nothing to ingratiate him towards the old woman. And September 03rd did nothing to change those dreams, when Britain and France declared war on Germany. However, increasingly their Sunday concerts gave way to discussions of war and listening to live reports from Europe. Neither one thought the war would ever happen. It was Europe's war, not theirs. They were young and it was becoming obvious to everyone that Emily would be Mrs. Alexander by the end of the coming year.

Christmas was austere and each guest picked the name of another so that no one would go without. Emily gave Davidson a phonograph and several big band seventy-eights, which he promised to use only in the parlour: a gift her mother thought was outrageous and frivolous for someone her daughter had only known since the spring. Davidson gave Emily a string of pearls which she commented was very nice, when she really wanted to throw them back to him. Together they bought her mother an elegant shawl, which she left in the box with a curt thank you, ignoring Davidson's remark that it would certainly keep in the cold on even the warmest day.

Emily's disappointment showed. Pearls were for old women, women like her mother in their forties, not young girls in love. When all the women went into the kitchen to help prepare the Christmas dinner, something the stolid matriarch allowed one day a year, Emily went to her room, leaving a smug-looking Davidson to enjoy more eggnog with the men and listen to Duke Ellington's big band.

The box at the foot of her door was wrapped in shiny gold and silver paper with a wide gold ribbon, a huge silver bow and weighed next to nothing. When she put the box on her bed she pulled away the card that was under the ribbon: Merry Christmas, Emily. The pearls have to be returned to the store on my first day back. They're on loan, my darling. Now open your real gift.

The satin robe was bright orange with gold lame, all the rage and very expensive. The slippers matched and then Emily peeled back the bottom layer of tissue paper and gasped. The orange satin tap pants were trimmed with paler orange lace and had clasps for her stockings. The ensemble was beautiful, worth two or three week's pay and unquestionably inappropriate. That he would even think to be so forward was wicked and she held the robe to her shoulders and danced pirouettes in front of her mirror and around her room. Then she composed herself and went back to the parlour where she slapped his face before stomping into the kitchen to join the other women with a smile on her face that left all the men leering silently at Davidson for answers.

By dinnertime she had forgiven his lewdness and by midnight they were still talking alone and dancing to Woody Herman's Woodchopper's Ball, cloaked in the green-red hues of the tall Douglas fir. It was early morning when Emily fell asleep wrapped in orange to dream of the man two floors above her, wishing so desperately that he would ask her one day soon.

Easter came early and he still had not proposed to her, though they had once again become predictable late afternoon fixtures as they strolled along the avenue after work and at the tennis club. Mrs. Ashton wanted him gone before the worst happened, not fooled by his manners or how easily her other guests were captivated by his impish charm. He paid his board on time and never asked for special privileges; neither did he offer to help with the simplest maintenance and Emily no longer did more than serve the occasional meal. She was a full-time bookkeeper at a prestigious jeweller and could well afford the five dollars each week. Davidson had no intention of seeing her do menial work for the old woman who soon had no choice but to engage a parlour maid and despise him all the more for his interference.

The ten o'clock restriction for the parlour became eleven during the week for the men who insisted on hearing news of the war and forthright conversation without the need to show consideration for the sensibilities of the women, who could join them on Fridays and Saturdays until the later hour for music and more refined conversation.

Davidson and Emily never spoke of it, not until the end of August when Davidson walked her home and told her he had given his notice to Mr. Morgan. He was going to war, as were other men from the store who had gone with him to enlist.

"I won't be gone for more than a year or so, Emily. They've promised no more than three years to quell the buggers and it's already been one year. Then I'll be back and I can take you away from your old hag of a mother. We can have our own place, and you know what that means." She was too stunned to hear what he was saying. "Did you hear me, Emily? We can marry and have our own home, away from her, maybe even by the sea where you can do your painting and raise a family."

Her face was expressionless and her eyes were glazed. She had dreamt for over a year about taking a little velvet box from his hands and how she would cry and be so happy he had finally asked. She had dreamt of her long flowing dress with a veil and her entourage, her honeymoon and making love with him. Now he was giving her a ring and telling her none of it would happen until he returned, if he did. He would not marry her before. He would have enough on his mind without thinking that one day he might make her a widow. The thought horrified her. He had ruined what should have been the second happiest day of her life and she hated him thoroughly.

"So, Emily Ashton, will you marry me?"

"When Davidson?"

He wiped the corners of her eyes. "I can't say for certain. In a year, I imagine, eighteen months at most. There's no need to cry, Emily. It's something I have to do and I'll earn much more over there than at the store. Anyway, you'll need the time to plan everything. We'll do it properly, the way it should be, at the club, and then we'll go to Old Orchard or Cape Cod for a honeymoon or wherever you want."

"I meant when did you enlist? How long have you known?"

"I went this morning with a few other lads from the store. We have until October."

"I'm supposed to be so happy, but you've made me angry with you. You'll be gone longer than I've known you."

"Aye, at the very worst, but everyone's saying it'll be over soon. The whole world's against the buggers. They've not got a snowball's chance in hell." His laugh was superficial. "Think how happy I've gone and made the righteous Mrs. Ashton, and how upset she'll be when I come back."

Emily inhaled deeply, letting out her breath in long sigh. "I'm disappointed in you."

"I love you, Emily. Does that help you? I've not said so before, but you know I do. How else could I have survived in the lioness' den with you so close, yet so far away? It's not been easy keeping my hands to myself this past year." He crossed his legs and leaned into the bench. "I think you're either supposed to put the thing on your finger or close the box and throw it at me. I'm pretty sure that's how it goes."

Emily snapped the box closed and returned it to him. "You'll have to ask me again this evening, after dinner, when my eyes are dry and I don't hate you, and in front of the others. Then we can all hate you together for doing such a despicable thing. You're quite horrible."

"Aye, I know, but does that lessen my chances any?"

She turned to look at him, smiling thinly. "I want to go home."

Emily missed dinner without explaining herself to her mother or to the other guests and took a long bath. She washed her hair to account for the redness of her eyes and changed into her prettiest party dress. When she walked into the parlour Davidson was there, looking nervous, and the other guests were either enjoying an evening tea or a sherry Davidson had thought to provide for the occasion, much to the annoyance of Mrs. Ashton who believed in strict temperance.

He knelt in front of her, trying to appear calm and suddenly everyone knew why he had gathered them together. Mrs. Ashton looked on sullenly from the doorway. She saw no reason to act other than how she felt as the others looked on expectantly and Emily seemed mesmerized by the gleaming diamond mounting as he slipped the gold band onto her finger. "Yes, Davidson," was all she could manage and she cried as the few women circled and hugged her. The men went to Davidson to shake his hand or slap his back. They understood the male need to be part of the war in a way womenfolk could not, and they surrendered the parlour to the intense emotions of a traditionally female moment. They stepped out onto the veranda for a smoke and more philosophical talk.

If Mrs. Ashton felt embittered that August evening, she was livid and fit to be tied the morning Emily left her house with a small suitcase to board a train with Davidson en route to the east coast where he would leave her to join his division. From there he would soon board a ship for transport to England. Neither one had thought ahead to their final goodbye, somehow not believing, or denying, he would be gone for as long as a year or more.

23

Suddenly, five years later, he was coming home to a woman whose voice he had forgotten. He wondered how awkward he would feel to kiss her lips, to say the words she would expect to hear and how he would say goodnight to her at the end of their first evening together. They had missed five birthdays and five Christmases together, five Easter parades and five Valentine's, countless recitals and countless tennis matches he might have let her win. She would have so much to tell him, and have so little to hear in return. He would have to discover her all over again and he wondered what he would see in her eyes when she would first see his face and his body hardened and aged.

The sea was calm and the Bedford Basin was filled with a thick, blue-white coastal fog that blanketed the sloping hills to camouflage the city of Halifax. The early morning sun accentuated the citadel like a glittering beacon as though to welcome home yet another convoy of troops. The air was damp and heavy, though to a man their coats and jackets were left behind for the ships' crews to discard. They each wanted their hundred dollars for new clothes, which was disbursed to each one in turn as the next in line touched his feet to dry land. They were home.

Most of the soldiers cared little for the sailors or the naval town still recovering from the sailors' boisterous rampage some weeks earlier. When peace had been declared many merchants had thought it wise to close their bars and liquor stores. Too late, many of them discovered they would have been wiser to remain open. Few men wanted to stay, most wanted to go and they waited long hours in line for the next bus or train out. Like many, Davidson had endured his fill of the military and one day more of sleeping in the open, each hour moving closer to the station's platform, was a small price to pay to be rid of hypocritical respect and meaningless salutes. Once onboard there was soon standing room only and rank still applied for anyone still wearing his uniform; the highest rank being anyone who happened to be a female.

Very few had any idea what they would do or what they would say when finally confronted with familiar faces, and for the most part they ignored each other to cocoon themselves into their own worlds. Davidson's trip lasted two days and he walked into Morgan's an hour after opening on August 06th. He had taken a room the night before, and when he left the store a few hours later he was employed and his arms were filled with new clothes.

He showered again until the water ran cold, and took his time to dress. He phoned the textile plant and was told she was no longer with them. He called the jewellery firm where she had worked before the war and was transferred to her local. When he heard her voice his memory of their first year together came back to him in a rush, as though he had never been gone, and he said nothing.

He went to lunch by himself and left his plate, ordering a second scotch instead and then a third. At 5:00 PM he boarded the number 17 tram, disembarking at the next stop and at 5:10 he did the same, and again at 5:20. At 5:30 he dropped his nickel into the box for the fourth time, tugged slightly at the brim of his new fedora and walked steadily towards her with his head tilted slightly downward.

Most of the seats were taken by women in knee-length skirts or dresses and with hairstyles that seemed very alluring. The few men standing seemed not to notice, though for Davidson it was hard not to look. The military reintegration teams had been right all along. The women back home had changed and at first glance he saw nothing at all wrong with it. Finally a woman stood from the seat he wanted and he tipped his hat to the women on either side of the open space before sitting. Emily was reading, paying no attention to him, which he was happy for. It gave him that much more time to absorb her and to forget his fears.

Moments before arriving at the corner they had shared for so little time, she stood facing into the back of the man who had stood first to disembark without considering that a lady might be standing behind him. When he stepped out he walked directly toward the sidewalk without thinking to turn to see whether he might be able to assist a lady. At the curb he bent forward, ostensibly to tie a shoelace as she passed, looking up to see the hem of her dress and the dark seam of her stockings centred along the vertical of her calves as she stepped onto the sidewalk.

"Thank you, sir, for your help," she said caustically as she passed. "Thank you very much."

"You're entirely welcome, young lady. Perhaps I can treat you to dinner to excuse my congenital rudeness?"

In the few seconds that followed Emily went from rigid and cold to weak and flushed, afraid she would collapse or faint.

"Aye, it's me, Emily. So you might as well turn for the greatest shock of your life. There'll not be another one greater. At least I've had ten minutes or so to decide that you still have a very beautiful..."

She dropped her book. Her face quivered and her eyes began to blink rapidly to squeeze away her tears. She turned, and her mouth opened wide. He went towards her and held her tightly in his arms. She put hers partway around him and his fears dissolved. He lifted her effortlessly. Her lips were wet and salty and her kisses were hard and passionate. He was lost in time, until he set her down and they stood holding hands, suddenly uncertain.

She had grown into a beautiful woman, and was no longer a girl. He had not known what to expect with none but the same two pictures in five years to remember her by. He stepped back to look her up and down from under the brim of his hat and walked a circle around her. He liked what he saw. She was still his Emily, though certainly not the same woman. She was rounder and fuller. He wondered what she must be thinking, feeling peculiar to see her looking at him the way she did, as if she had somehow also been hardened by war.

She stood still for him. He was Davidson, and yet he wasn't. He was not the man she had once known and somehow she knew he would never again be that man. He had changed more than she had ever imagined. She had seen the difference instantly in his eyes and in his face. The mischievousness and the cleverness were there, but the glint was gone, replaced by the invisible scars of sorrow and torment and she searched more deeply to see whether there might also be regret. In those few moments she had seen his past five years and she wrapped her arms around him, feeling sorry for him, suddenly more afraid than he had been. The war had changed them both.

He gave Emily the nickel for the phone call and while she was gone he ordered a scotch and sherry and asked the waiter to place their settings closer together. When she came to the table she was smiling.

"Mother's in an apoplectic state. She's quite unhappy about having to hire another parlour maid. I showed her your letter, Davidson." She giggled. "I think she still needs awhile longer."

"She'll have the rest of her life, Emily." He raised his glass. "So enough of the old she-beast, tell me everything I've missed about you. I had so many things ready to say, so many words I'd practiced over again in my head, but they've escaped me somehow and all I can think to say is that you're as beautiful as the first time you snared me in your trap."

"And you're..."

"Older than I should be. I know it. We all are. They told us at the very worst we would grow into our faces sooner than we want. I suppose we'll see soon enough, though I can't imagine myself looking older than I do."

She tried to laugh. "It's your hat. You're too young for a hat. I prefer you without it."

"Then it's gone." He paused to wet his throat with the scotch. "It feels very strange, Emily, everything feels strange. I still look around for my rifle when I move from one spot to another, or slap my side for the other. It's very strange, even sitting here beside you, Emily, after so long. All the same, I must say I very much like the benefits of the current fashions."

She looked down, smoothing her skirt. He did look older. "I thought you would at least phone me, or write. I thought you would be several more weeks. We heard some won't be back for another year."

"Aye, that's the truth, and many of them have no real reason to hurry. Their girls have left them, some of them even married with babies."

Suddenly she blanched. "Darling, your room...I thought I had more time."

"I've taken a wee room by the week until we get things sorted out. I was wrong to burden you with so much at once. I'll be fine."

She lowered her face, staring down at her folded hands. "I wanted you to see me in something nice."

"I am seeing you in something nice, and I can't wait to see you out of it. And I mean very soon. We have much to talk about, Emily." He waved the waiter away. "There's so much I have to know and for us to talk about. I don't see you going to work tomorrow. Anyway, it's Friday and I think they'll understand. I need you more than they do. I have so much to make up for. It's like I'm floating in a dream. I hardly know what to say or ask."

Her eyes went to one of his hands as he raised his glass, then to the other. "Why aren't you wearing your beautiful ring, darling?"

"Aye, my ring." He clenched a fist. "I removed the thing one day when I was stationed in Paris, not quite a year ago, and I left it there. This was Earl's ring. I took it from his finger the day he died. I believe he knows I have it. We were very close Emily, like brothers." He paused to sip his scotch. "I can't stay with you, not until we have our own place, unless, of course, you'll stay the night with me. You'd have to bar your door otherwise."

"Darling, I slapped your face often enough before you left me. Tonight's not the night, as much as I want to be with you. I've already spoken with the minister. The wedding will be small with a few girls from the office. Darling, many of the men at the club won't be coming home and many of the girls have moved away. As for mother, she's being very difficult and I've already told her I would rather she not come at all."

Davidson nodded mechanically, though inwardly he was feeling very pleased with himself. "I'd sooner see her stuffed and mounted on a wall to ward off evil spirits. Don't worry about her, I'll ask my manager to give you away. He won't mind at all, though I might have some trouble getting more than a few days away from the store. He and Mr. Morgan hired me back this morning with a substantial increase in salary. It was a much unexpected boon, and very generous, though I don't believe I'll be a clerk for very much longer. I've had much to think about since it's been clear to me that I'd be coming home. There were times I had my serious doubts, Emily. Not all the buggers were sloppy shots and I've got one hell of a memento that attests to it."

He was proud of what he had so far accomplished and

he knew it was only the beginning. There was much more to tell her. He had so many plans, so many dreams and very soon she would see his promise to her blossom into reality. She would have the life he wanted for her.

They ordered dinner, and by the end of the meal Davidson felt violently ill. His thousand dollars were gone and much of what Emily had saved had also gone into their new home and appliances he had given no thought to. In the five years he'd been gone prices had more than doubled and now he had a twenty-year fixed mortgage on an unfurnished home with property taxes even a Chief Clerk would find difficult to honour, rather than a small apartment, singing lessons and big plans for their future.

It was all too overwhelming, too much to contemplate or quantify. He walked her home in the dark and left her at the bottom of the stairs with a friendly kiss on her cheek without feeling the slightest need to affect any courtesy towards Mrs. Ashton. Emily had been prepared to say her mother was already in bed. There was no need. They both needed time to adjust.

He had gone when she looked for him from the top of the stairs. She closed the door behind her and fell back against it, crossing her arms and looking up at the ceiling. The evening had been pleasant. Although, as much as he had tried to conceal his glumness, his mood had changed dramatically and she understood why. What the man at the War Department had told her was true. He was not the same man, not the young vital man who had left her at the train station and whom she had dreamt about all those years. He was the man in the photos he had sent to her, the haggard man with a gun on his belt and leaning on a rifle in front of his tent, smiling with his mouth but not with his eyes.

He had expected more of her, and from her, she mused. Instead she had both denied and disappointed him. She breathed deeply, dreamily. She was right to do so, to deny him. Soon she would be his bride. She would have his children, their children, and they would have their own home. That's what he wanted most, just as she had told him in the restaurant.

When Emily pushed herself away from the door she glanced to the side where her mother had been standing framed by the squared entrance to the parlour. Her mood was dark, her expression stern and unforgiving, her eyes accusing. Not a word was spoken between them. Mrs. Ashton turned her back and returned to the parlour to bask in her bitterness. Emily climbed the stairway to her room and flung herself across her bed to plan her wardrobe for the coming day. She was suddenly on cloud nine. She was getting married. She would soon be Mrs. Davidson Alexander with her own home, privacy, and finally they would be man and wife together.

Davidson should have skipped and clicked his heels together all the way along the several blocks he had to walk, screaming for joy, when it was all he could manage not to walk past his address. For Davidson it would be one of many sleepless nights to come.

24

For Emily there had been several weeks of hectic evenings and excited days, for Davidson there were only long days at the store, singing when he could and weekends at the tennis club Emily had thought would be in keeping with their expectations. They were married on the eighteenth of October. Mrs. Ashton spent the entire day browsing through stores in her finest outfit and when she returned to the boarding house well past the dinner hour she reluctantly agreed to give her persistent lady guests all the details of her only daughter's wedding.

They were married at St. George's where Davidson had sung at so many weddings and Sunday services before the war that the venerable Anglican archdeacon gladly overlooked his Presbyterian upbringing. He had joked with Davidson privately of having explained to God with some difficulty that at such times quantity of congregation was as much sought after as quality.

The bride was stunning in her simple full-length, cream-coloured crepe gown with a laced Puritan collar, a laced fez with shoulder-length tulle veil and satin shoes which were a wedding gift from the store. The groom was outfitted with cream-coloured linen slacks, a matching linen shirt and a Mediterranean blue blazer and tie, as befitted the newest Chief Clerk of Morgan's Department Store.

Emily's girlfriends at the firm had chipped in to pay for two nights at the quaint French-styled Le Gîte and his new staff at the store had given Emily a gift certificate. Davidson had wanted a party at the tennis club when hearing of the auberge, Emily argued the club was too big and impersonal and she told him not to worry about the details. She would make all the arrangements within their budget. All he had to do was make sure she would have at least a few sunny days at the shore to show off her new imported two-piece swimsuit.

On the eve of the wedding Emily stayed at the intimate bed and breakfast where she had also decided to hold the reception. One of the girls stayed with her, to help her dress in the morning and they spent most of the evening and night chattering and giggling by the warmth of the fire. Davidson spent what was left of the night in his small rented room, massaging his temples and drinking as much water as he could to undo the effects of his bachelor party to which his best man had not been invited.

His boss had promised them earlier that he would arrive on time to escort Emily to the church the following morning, and he did, to a ceremony that was simple and with references to all things holy or divine kept to a minimum at Davidson's insistence. Mr. Morgan later agreed to drag tin cans and ribbons from his limousine as the cars trailing behind blared their horns and threw confetti at waving passers-by from the running boards. As they pulled up to the Le Gîte Davidson was too preoccupied helping his new bride from the car to notice as cameras flashed and more confetti rained down upon them.

Inside, their hostess and her staff rushed to be part of it, hugging and kissing the bride and groom and showing everyone to seats previously assigned by Emily so that no two girls would sit together. She had made certain potential couples would be as evenly matched as possible, which Davidson thought was too obvious and manipulative, particularly for Lilly who had sheepishly agreed to stand in as his best lady in lieu of the one man Davidson would have wanted by his side.

She called him Little Brother when he had asked, which made tears well up in their eyes. She accepted the honour with pride and asked if she might wear her traditional garb for the ceremony, with the permission of the bride. The bride-to-be did agree. She had come to adore Lilly who she thought would look beautiful in her beaded leather sheath, soft-soled boots and delicate headdress. And, much to the envy of every man there, Davidson found himself standing in awe between the best of both worlds.

Emily remained the centre of attraction and Davidson soon came to understand the meaning of second best. The celebration went on till well past midnight when they said their goodbyes and Davidson took Lilly aside to give her the time-honoured gift from the groom to the best man: a thin, black lacquered box with inlaid native etchings, held tightly closed with a leather thong and he told her not open it until she was home. The tiny chest had belonged to Big Earl, he told her, and inside were his personal journal and the last letter he had not mailed to the little one he had always called Shimmering Moon.

Stepping across the threshold with his bride held high in his arms and a parade of raucous well-wishers behind them, Davidson stood agape and eased her to the floor as gently as he could. His body shivered and he tried hard to ignore the sudden and violent stitch in his abdomen. He scanned the room, trying to clear his mind as she hugged him, and as she walked away he turned to lock out the pranksters and yet another urgent request for the couple to kiss.

Flushed with excitement, Emily held up two glasses as Davidson turned the bottle from the cork and filled them with champagne which persons unknown had put by the bed. Holding out an arm for her to join him by the fire, which had likely been lit by the same unknown romantics, he sighed with relief when she left him to close the bathroom door behind her. He stood mesmerized, staring down into the hot, flickering flames, keeping the glass to his lips until he had drained the wine completely to steel himself against the cruellest of innocent intentions.

When Emily stepped from the bathroom her satin peignoir was deep purple and under it she wore a matching floor-length slip. Davidson had already hurried to change into his own purple robe, choosing not to wear the matching satin pyjamas. He had no intention of standing by the bed to push down or pull off his pants on their first night as lovers, nor of unbuttoning the top or of deciding which to do first.

They stood by the fire, his arms wrapped around her, kissing the nape of her neck as he unloosed her belt and pulled her robe from her shoulders to let it fall between their feet. He cupped her breasts from behind, feeling her chest swell as he kissed her shoulders in turn. He trailed his hands along her torso and down her legs as he eased himself to the floor. When he began to inch the sensual fabric from her ankles to her thighs she stopped him and turned quickly towards the bed, throwing the cushions on the floor by the fire before diving under the covers, pulling them to her neck and patting the pillow beside hers.

He had touched her breasts only once before, through her clothes, that last evening so long ago and he had no memory of how they had felt at the time. He untied his belt and shrugged his robe to the floor. Emily closed her eyes and turned to face the ceiling as he raised the covers and slid in beside her. His hands were warm and he took his time, first caressing her shoulders and her face, kissing her lips and her eyes and her nose. Gently he put a hand to one breast, then the other, massaging more than squeezing and waiting to feel the warmth of her hands on him. He slowly pushed down the covers, kissing her breasts through her slip as his hand moved to meet her pushed up hem and search for the soft flesh of her thighs. Her body stiffened, her breathing became more laboured and when he first touched the soft fullness of her pubic curls she winced and squeezed his hand tightly in place. She wanted to giggle, instead she sounded nervous and he reassured her with a lingering kiss on her mouth that she was trying hard to control.

He waited mere moments before his hand began to knead away her tension, rubbing more urgently until she hesitantly opened herself to him and he pushed away the covers to kneel between her. He wanted her closer. He wanted to see her, to be one with her. He took her arms to ease her tenderly from the bed and onto him, to pull away her slip, but she was unsure and responded clumsily. He eased her back down, leaning forward with her. He pulled at her straps to free her shoulders and to bare her breasts, kissing each one as he lowered himself against her and reached up to stroke her hair. He could feel her stomach heaving under his chest as he worked to arouse her, turning from the waist so that she would also know his arousal.

He raised himself above her, looking down at her breasts. She closed her eyes as he pushed her wrinkled slip to her hips, raising them from under her buttocks as he pulled her towards him. He bent to kiss her belly, quickly feeling her nervous hands against his face with a pressure that told him no. He quietly obeyed with a deep sigh as he moved to kiss her face and position himself over her on steady arms, willing himself to be tender until her first innocent yelp that broke the barrier between them.

When they were done he held her until she fell asleep with her crumpled slip still gathered around her waist. He turned away only when her breathing had changed from excited to peaceful, to rest his head on his arms folded over the edge of the bed. He stared across to the scattered cushions on the floor and into the flickering bright orange flames. When he woke he had not stirred. His arms had no feeling, the flames had turned to cold ashes and for long confusing moments he was somewhere else looking toward the sound of running water. He pensively twirled the ring on his finger, not wanting to dispel his thoughts. His lips formed silent words that he repeated over and over again before finally pushing himself from the bed to pad across the room to knock on the closed bathroom door.

25

The end-of-season honeymoon was perfect and not too crowded, though the sea air reminded Davidson of the Adriatic, the Mediterranean and Ligurian Seas. He woke most nights in turmoil, one night screaming out for Big Earl to help him, and Emily could only think to hold him, though beside him she seemed so small and ineffective. During the days he refused to speak of it, saying he never would, and he never did, soon learning the longer he remained awake after their lovemaking the longer he would sleep through to morning. His sleepless nights had become lonely nights.

Emily strutted and pranced teasingly along the shoreline in her new two-piece, which was scandalous for the American coast, and Davidson both loved and hated her antics at once. He was jealous, yet not, and he took as many pictures as he could. He loved her and she loved him. She had never been away from her repressive Victorian mother save that one time when she bid him farewell and felt as though she had been reborn the day she had said "I do."

They were expected back the following Monday and the week was all too quickly behind them. Emily's first few days were spent answering dozens of the same questions and planning each new addition to her new home in order of importance. Only at Christmas did she broach the topic of her mother, to which Davidson simply replied that if God truly loved all his children He could take care of the humourless old hag. However it was suddenly important to

Emily that Mrs. Ashton be included. When she explained the reason his body jerked involuntarily and his tight grip shattered his glass.

He was doing well at the store. He was respected by management and subordinates alike, and it was not time to slow the pendulum, but she had. What was worse, she had not told him earlier. They had managed to put aside enough each week for his voice lessons. He was held in high regard by his vocal coach who was certain Davidson's future was bright and not limited to the meagre audiences of North America. Now, in the time he had taken to shatter a glass, his dreams had been shattered as well. His future had come to an abrupt end, their home was still half furnished and he would have to forego his dream piano in order to buy a crib and diapers.

By New Year's he had accepted what he could not change. What he could change was the time he spent with Mrs. Ashton. By early spring Emily had resigned her position at the jewellery firm with little more than a week's pay and by June Davidson had not sung for almost six months. He had withdrawn his membership from the tennis club and had convinced himself most things happened for a reason. If destiny had dictated that he be a father, he would be a good one, not a failure or a runaway. He would work all the harder to make a decent and ordinary life for his family.

Very early, on the last day of the month, Theodore and Katherine Alexander were born five minutes apart. That evening, after leaving his wife, Davidson went home to wake up twelve hours later, late for work and still very drunk. He called in sick, poured what was left of the scotch, and dropped onto the couch and into oblivion. By the time he arrived at the hospital his head still pounded and his eyes were streaked with fine red lines, explaining to Emily the store had been exceptionally busy the entire day and he had exhausted himself.

He waited in the corridor for all the well-wishers to leave. How could they think to raise two children when raising one would have been impossible enough? He hated them all for coming to celebrate his misery, except Lilly who understood his need and thought to give him attention as well. She listened intently as he spoke. She patted his hand that she held in her lap and when he had finished they sat together quietly holding hands, neither one noticing the scowl on the face of the old woman who was the first to leave. When all the visitors had gone, they went in together to see Emily until the twins were taken away and they were politely asked to leave. Then Lilly adamantly insisted she drop Davidson off at his home, despite his protests that it was unseemly and that he should be seeing her home safely.

By their second Christmas together their lives had changed diametrically and, Davidson thought, irrevocably. He was twenty-eight and all he had to show for his hard work was a mortgage, tax bills and a new five-year loan. To make matters worse, he had an unemployed wife who wanted nothing to change and for her two children to have the best of everything on one salary. He was already working a six-day a week and now Sunday mornings he would be singing at the city's wealthiest church, a fact that made his small wage seem particularly meagre. At least he would be singing.

They seldom had time alone. The twins were always sleeping when his day ended and when they were together they often argued about what was wanted or needed and how they would pay for it. Sunday afternoons, after rehearsing the next week's hymns with the organist, he would sleep on the couch until dinner, drink a scotch alone while she did the dishes and in the evening he would sign the smallest cheques he could get away with.

He hated that Emily's mother was increasingly at the house more than him and that he could not afford even the least expensive suit at the store. He hated they had not made love more than a few times over the past year and what the passage of two children had done to her belly and her breasts. When she did come to him, the intimacy was a prelude to sleeping and functional at best. He hated that she had begun calling him father and he found himself thinking more often about his own father. He hated that he began thinking differently towards Lilly. She was like a sister to him, but she was also a beautiful young woman. She was exotic, alluring and untouched, while Emily had begun dressing in comfortable frocks for her artwork, or housedresses she would still be wearing at dinnertime. His wife never went to church to hear him sing, though Lilly often would, and on those days they would ride partway home together on the tram and stop at the station for coffee.

He had taken his wife dancing on their first anniversary, but Emily had needed a new dress and new shoes to complete the outfit. By the twins first birthday Davidson wondered if Emily had ever thought back to their first encounter on the number 17 tram, or if she remembered the first time she had slapped his face. The following Saturday he chose not to come home, turning instead to his only real friend.

26

Lilly had known he was coming, and why. She had not been expecting it, though neither was she surprised when he phoned her one morning from the store to ask if he could invite himself for dinner. For Lilly it was a simple matter. He was her brother and he was in need. She would have done as much for Emily, though Davidson was the one to whom she felt the most connected. She loved him deeply and she wanted to tell him so. There was nothing she would not do for her Little Brother.

He laughed. "Thank you, Shimmering Moon. I needed to hear that, though I must say the endearment sounds comical coming from such a wee thing as you."

"Sit, Little Brother. I will give you one small scotch, maybe two, no more. Then we will eat and after you will drink my special tea. It's not the tasteless white man's tea. It will make you feel much better than you have for a while." She giggled at his reaction and shook her head. "No, it's not what you think, you silly man. It's tea. I'm much too young and much too beautiful to be a shaman and if you even think to call me a witch doctor…"

"There's no calling you a witch of any sort, Lilly, and I'll clout the ear of anyone who does. Though I have to suppose that if you didn't spend your days with all those ancestral bones you like to pick at that you'd already have yourself a living man, and one who would have passed by me for approval. I'll not see you with just anyone. You know that for a fact."

Lilly hugged him and told him where to sit. Her home was a hodgepodge of books and papers, many of which she had authored as one of the youngest and most talented and successful anthropologists in the country specializing in Native Studies. She poured the first scotch, and the second, sitting by his side as he spoke about Big Earl and their good and bad times together, waiting patiently for Davidson to decide when to tell her what she already knew to be true.

"Lilly, I should never have come home from the war. I should never have married her. I came back as half a man. There's a part of me that's still over there."

Lilly closed her eyes slowly, lowering her head, which was in no way submissive or timid.

"Davidson, you left Gabrielle for the first time three years ago, and again two years ago when you chose to leave Europe." His look of absolute disbelief begged the question. "Yes, I know of your young Gabrielle, Little Brother, and of your deep love for her. My brother wrote to me of her with words he never spoke to you. He should have, however men are men and, red or white, they are really very stupid when it comes to women. It could be that you hurt Gabrielle and that you made a terrible mistake by leaving her, perhaps not. But now you have a family and your mistake must either be accepted or forgotten unless you are prepared to live with a terrible guilt." She took his hand. "I will always love you, Davidson. I will never judge you, but your path is yours to decide, Little Brother. I cannot help you. I can only be here to listen and to comfort you when you fall."

"I can't forget her, Lilly. I still dream of her each night. I still think of her and she seems so real to me."

"Because you punish yourself and your spirit is agitated. It's your decision you must forget Davidson, the choice you made, not Gabrielle. It's better to remember those few days of love with her, than five years of war. Your memories of her may fade with time, and if they don't you will know the reason."

"Aye, but I don't have to wait. I know the reason now."

"What's done is done, Little Brother. You came back. For whatever reason, you chose one and not the other. Your time has come to be at peace with yourself, to let your spirit find peace."

"What is it they say, Lilly? Time cures all."

"No, it does not. It's not true."

Davidson put down his glass, nodding. "Aye, there's not a day goes by I don't think of the big oaf."

"He knows that, Little Brother. He's told me many times. He knows your spirit is still troubled."

"I felt his presence, Lilly. I felt his hand on my back. I know I did. He saved me that day, and for what?"

"Perhaps my brother's spirit knows what you do not. Those who go before us are always with us. They can see what we cannot."

The colour drained from his face. "Earl told me almost those very words moments before he died. I wish I felt more of this spirit stuff, Lilly. That day in the ditch, when I held him, I knew he was there with me and nothing's changed for me. I don't feel whole, Lilly. I never have, except for those few days with Gabrielle. Being with her made me feel like such a different person, but that person's gone and he'll never come back. Perhaps that other person was my spirit. My spirit's not troubled Lilly; it's been taken from me."

He enjoyed his time with Lilly and had wanted to speak for hours with her, but her dinner and tea quickly culminated all his sleepless nights and he soon fell asleep on her couch. She called Emily to explain in a way that precluded suspicion and unnecessary questions. She asked about the children and promised Davidson would be home Sunday afternoon as usual.

Emily would not be going to the church to hear him sing, not with the children and not when Lilly offered to take them for the day. When she hung up the phone Lilly felt overcome with sadness and after looking in on Davidson she went to her bedroom to worry about her friend she knew was trapped between two inescapable truths. She went with him Sunday morning, they stopped at the station, and when he arrived home alone Emily met Davidson at the door.

They spent what remained of the day talking about their futures that to Davidson suddenly seemed divergent. In the evening they made love that seemed real to her, not to him, and when she fell asleep he eased from the bed and poured a scotch. Nothing would change anytime soon, not unless he took the first step. He loved her, but they had forgotten how to love. They no longer spoke of their dreams, only of their disappointments. They no longer shared time together and had forgotten how to laugh. Their life had stopped them from living and it would never be better. At thirty-five he would still be in debt and the bank would own his home, so what could he expect at forty-five or fifty-five? And what if he was ever to lose his job, or his health? It was not what he wanted, and he blamed himself for ever thinking a thousand dollars had made him rich. He wanted millions, not mere thousands. He wanted more than being Chief Clerk and he wanted a woman on his arm he could be proud of, not a housewife in a frock stained with oil paints and baby spit. He wanted an education and a career, not just a job, though if he stayed with her that would never be and she would never have her home or her studio by the ocean. He poured another scotch and hated that new dimension of himself as well. It didn't help much, though for a time he felt as though it did.

He spent the day deep in thought, deciding against telling Lilly. She would not approve, and he thought more about not telling his friend than confronting his wife. Emily had not called him darling in a year, and he was no better, so what was there to lose? Monday afternoon he left the store early and came home late.

Emily alone would be the one to define what he had done as a decision or an ultimatum. One would mean a new life together, a new beginning. The other would mean following his heart. They argued heatedly throughout the evening and into the night and he saw Emily rant and rave for the first time since he had known her, but he was adamant and unflinching. He wanted more than grade seven for himself, he wanted an education and to become somebody. He wanted more than overdue bills and sleepless nights.

The realtor would arrive the next morning to post the sign and the bank would be paid off as soon as the house was sold. She would go back to work, he would study at night and the twins would be given to a family who could care for them until the time he and Emily could afford to do the job properly themselves. It would mean two years at most in a foster home, he promised her, and in the meantime they would live in an apartment and not above their means. They would have friends once again and be able to work towards a life that would mean something. She could have her home by the sea and they could dance at the club to Billie Holiday and Ella Fitzgerald and be young. The twins were only a year old and would never know differently. However, in fifteen or twenty years, he argued, they would know the difference and would hate their parents for not having done everything possible to improve their destinies.

Emily cried through the night, struggling to believe and comprehend what was happening to her. How would Davidson ever understand her grief, and how would she ever explain away the pain of doing to Katie and Theo what she had callously done to Noëlyn.

Tuesday morning she stood by the front window feeling nothing as she watched the man hammer the For Sale sign into the ground, the moment when the gravity and the finality struck her. Davidson had been serious. She was losing her home and her husband was fully prepared to leave her. He had taken the day off from the store and sat quietly in the corner. She looked into his eyes, eyes that had never regained their glint and she wondered if the war alone had robbed him of the once mischievous sparkle. She had always secretly suspected, or at least she had always wondered. He had never really been the same following his discharge. His nightmares were less frequent, but mostly she noticed the little things and at that very moment she hated him.

He suddenly seemed empty to her, defeated, yet determined in a way she had never before seen. He had said the children would be back in less than two years, but he had promised even less than that once before, and what of her mother. She loved him, yet she had not been in love with him for at least a year and she needed to know and understand why. She had given up her daughter for him, and now he was asking the impossible of her after he had promised to never ask anything of her. What had he given up for her? What had he ever lost? He had wanted the house and the family. He had told her so. Now he was turning his back on both and she wanted nothing more than to hurt him for what he was doing.

He had won, and she sensed he had known all along. He knew no man would want a woman with two children, and alone she would have no hope of ever having a home or a good life. She despised him for having manipulated her. He had won, and had not said a single word since breakfast: "Emily, I promise you, one day soon we'll have our children back, if it's the last thing I ever do. And one day, Emily, we'll have all the money in the world. You'll see. I've no intention or desire to live through a life of poverty. It was enough I had to see my dear mother die in a filthy bed that was no better than an infested mat on the floor, with nothing to do for her but clean her and hold her frail body as I sat there feeling useless. It's done, Emily."

When the agent had driven away she went to Davidson and slapped his face with such rage that his head snapped violently sideways into the couch.

Part Three

1972 – 1973

27

James Parker spent his first night at the Muir Hotel because the flashing purple sign was the first he had seen on his way into town and he had stayed in worse. It was already 2:00 AM and he was exhausted. His eyes burned from the strain of peering through the greasy windshield of the rental into a violent whirlwind of icy snow which the headlights had turned into a merciless onslaught of hypnotic, white shards. He didn't think much about the flashing neon, what he cared about was closing his eyes and sleeping for only five dollars.

The room had two beds and the lights were too dim to distinguish any known colour. The bed sagged, the furniture was splintered to the point of disintegration, the single closet had no hangers and the shag carpet was sticky in some parts and crusty in others. The room reeked of gastric acids and the heavy smell of booze-tainted urine emanated not only from the bathroom. He laid worn towels over the tiled floor and sprinkled generous amounts of his own cheap cologne randomly into the air. Then he emptied the bottle onto the bed and pillows to mask any previous disease that might not have been washed out, or was too deeply embedded into the mattress to be expunged. Each smeared pane of the window that faced a brick wall was cracked and the black and white television produced only one station. When he turned the on/off dial he wore his winter gloves and when he fell onto the bed he was fully dressed and had covered the pillow with his leather coat, but the uneven door was no barrier to the laughing, the shouting and the loud music from down the hall.

He had left his luggage in the car, where it would stay safe from infection. What he did bring with him was a bottle of cheap scotch, and he thought of sitting on the bed with his back to the wall until the noise didn't matter and he could fall asleep after a few shots. His second thought was that the walls were covered with historical yellow stains of previous lonely residents and crusty edges of once-green and stringy flicks that had not been entirely brushed away, not to mention he had begun to hate drinking alone. He swung his legs from the bed and stood to put on his coat. He swallowed what was left of his three-finger shot and went to the bar.

The ambiance was a large room with a juke box, purple and green neon lighting, a collection of mismatched furnishings, a dozen whores and an unequal number of pathetic johns who had watched him walk in. James Parker liked whores. They were inexpensive and never asked him for love. They were also great language teachers and some of his favourites along the Mekong River had made him fluent in Vietnamese during his back-to-back tours.

The men at the bar who apparently had not wanted to invest an extra five dollars for the privacy of a room were openly enjoying the women on round wobbly vinyl stools with what James imagined would be less hassle with the same end result. The whores all looked the same, no different than the cheap dollar-dips in Vietnam. Their fake red or blonde hair was greased and pulled back into cones or tails. Their faces were thick with cream that had begun to dry, their lips were painted blood red and their eyes were dusted in blacks and greens that were smudged and seemed exaggerated and garish in the dim light. Some had their skirts hiked to their waists with potted and bruised flesh swelling from the tightness of dark nylons and the straps that held them in place and their blue-streaked breasts were covered only by groping hands.

James pointed to the bartender, then to the scotch bottle and held out three fingers. If Vietnam had taught him nothing else, his time there had taught him how to drink. He had come to think of the killing as secondary, of primary importance was the drinking to forget and he had forgotten when he had stopped thinking how easy both had become. Some of the women looked his way, some smiled invitingly and others winked and blew him kisses. One that he took to be in her late fifties sauntered over to his table and stopped at the very moment a large droplet fell from somewhere under her skirt, splattering onto the floor between her salt-stained knee-high boots with a loud smacking sound. He stared down at the tiny puddle that looked like white snot and he decided she smelled the way she did because she had splashed her body with her cheap perfume when she should have bathed in it.

He waved her away with words common to her trade and stayed as he was, lost in his own world, sitting in his coat and nursing his scotch until he left to go back to his room about an hour later with his second three-finger glass. No one bothered him. They had no reason to confront a man whose chilling look left little doubt how little he cared about himself or others, and certainly not over a whore. No one dared, and he thought nothing about it. But that was not the real James Parker, rather what two tours of duty in Southeast Asia had made him. He liked whores, just not female trash in short skirts and tight blouses that hadn't been washed in weeks. Before he slept on the only chair in his room he positioned himself against the door and fell asleep in his coat to remember the face of the last man he had killed in a war he had joined for no other reason than to find himself.

He left the hotel early the next morning without showering and without noting the time. His breakfast was another mouthful of gut-rot scotch and he had no idea where he would be by noon. After returning the rental he had no timetable. He had no job and he had stopped wearing a watch, content to be alive for however long that would last. Everything else would fall into place, and if not, how would he know the difference? For James Parker, fate meant looking into the past to remember the fate of others and nothing at all to do with his own destiny.

The brownstone boarding house was near the corner of Keel & Bloor in the High Park area of Toronto, a town he passionately despised. The only parents he had ever known had moved so often he had no memory of his last known address as a child. He vaguely remembered Montreal, but he knew his lack of French would make him undesirable in an increasingly Anglophobic Quebec and the many American companies he had gone to seeking work had turned him down.

Each time he could see in their eyes the reason why. He would stay for two weeks. He knew he was fooling himself, putting off the inevitable, what he could do right away. In two weeks he would leave to find a seafarers union on either side of the border and return to the life he had abandoned to fight a miserable war along the Mekong. The sea and soldiering were all he knew. They were his life. The rent was twenty dollars a week with no food or cooking privileges, which was fine because he had allotted very little of his money for food.

He got into the habit of going into restaurants between peak hours where he would order water with the cheapest sandwich on the menu for lunch and read through want ads before leaving with his pockets filled with soda crackers. He bought his newspaper each morning from the dispenser outside the subway station that he paid for with coins moulded the previous night from chewing gum, letting each one freeze on the windowsill. Coins were not required to open the door of the dispenser, though there was always a cop standing nearby and hearing a faint clink was better than no clink.

The house had three floors. The main floor was private with a kitchen and parlour that were off limits. James was on the second floor that had three bedrooms, a bathroom and a common room shared by the other floors. Late at night he would penetrate the sanctity of the DMZ kitchen for the ketchup he needed to mix with his crackers and hot water for a simple meal, until the end of the first week when he arrived after a day of futile job hunting to find one full bottle of the condiment and a homemade meat pie by his door.

Early Friday night, January 21, after he had devoured the exquisite dinner, he poured a deep scotch and went down the hall to what he thought would be his first bath since his childhood. He had no idea why. He just wanted a bath. The old Victorian home was all but devoid of the other guests he had ignored over the week, most of them having left for reasons he cared nothing about.

They were flower children, spoiled brats with a lot of their parents' money who preached peace and love. When all they really wanted was a piece of ass with whoever was closest to them with decent tits to feel and a weed to choke on and burn their eyes. Bullshit. Life was shit. The fat white guy down the hall was one of the worst. He had given James the sign and called him "bro." His bright red hair had been tied in pigtails and he wore no shirt under his U.S. Army jacket. His pants were striped with wide red, white, and blue lines and his bare feet were strapped into heavy leather sandals in the dead of winter. His beard looked like a clusters of raspberry dust balls, his shoulders were rounded, he had no hair on his chest and his nipples were small and girly pink. James simply said "fuck off" and looked down at the guy's crotch for a watermark before walking away.

The other guy, across the hall from him, was tall, skinny and black with a purple comb protruding from his exploded Afro and white cue ball eyes rolling in his head. He wore black sandals, black jeans, a black leather vest without a shirt and a plastic brass-coloured medallion around his neck. He looked like a burnt cotton swab, or a chimney sweep's favourite wire brush. He gave James the sign and said "down with war, man", sounding high. James gave him the finger and told him to fuck off, though this time he didn't walk away. The other guy did.

They had both gone very soon after, and James had the place to himself. The water was steaming, punitively hot enough to sting his skin and expunge his week. He was alone in another world, alone in a deep porcelain bath he had filled to the rim and nothing had changed. He had always been alone, and always would be. The quiet and the steam wafting around him were all-encompassing. He stared absently at the oxidized green-blue brass faucet that was dripping incessantly, trying to staunch the drops with his big toe. He thought about everything and thought about nothing, letting his mind wander.

Sometimes he wondered why he had never cried, or why he had never felt remorse for having killed hundreds of men. Other times he wondered if he would ever kill again, and for what reason. Mostly he wondered why he had ever been born. He sipped his scotch, thinking his whole life had been reduced to killing men he had no reason to kill, and fornicating with women who might have been their sisters or wives.

The door seemed to open suddenly, only because he was lost in thought. She didn't see him at first, taking the time to close and lock the door with her back to him as she made a swishing sound and fanned the air around her. When she did see him, sprawled with his ankles and feet hanging over the top edges of the bath, she brought a hand to her gaping mouth and stared down at him with very wide eyes. James Parker simply looked at her and tilted his half-empty glass.

She was far from drop-dead gorgeous, he thought, though definitely on the chart in faded blue jeans, a zip-front hooded sweatshirt he could never afford and blue suede mukluks trimmed in real fur that had never seen snow. Her cherry-blond ponytail was too 'bobby-socks fifties' and her face needed some makeup. Despite the flaws she was definitely doable. She was spoiled, he determined, and very doable.

It should have been one of those opened-mouthed monologues replete with nervous exclamations and she should have run out, yet she stayed. After the initial shock she leaned against the pedestal sink, slipped her hands into her pockets and suddenly James did not want her to leave. Inexplicably, he wanted Helen North in his bed or in his bath. He didn't care which, he just wanted her.

She looked down and said hello, very nonchalantly glancing around the bathroom and told him her name. She asked about the house and he told her what he knew, introducing himself when he had finished. Then he asked about her and she answered after a close-mouthed smile and a non-committal shrug.

She had arrived Friday and was on the same floor. She sounded educated in a non-erudite way. She seemed cultured, but not prissy, though she was definitely her daddy's little girl and her mommy's pride and joy. She was obviously privileged, everything he was not. She should have been staying at the Hilton and luxuriating in a spa, not in a low-rent boarding house bathroom looking down at him and talking as though living the natural order of things. She'd be gone by the end of the week, back home with mom and dad where she belonged.

The water he was sitting in was turning cold. When he reached for his towel, he hesitated, asking if she was just going to stand there. She said "yes, of course", adding matter-of-factly that she was an artist and saw nothing wrong with being able to appreciate the human form. In fact, she had often posed in the nude for her fellow students at university, she boasted.

He leaned forward, threatening to pull the plug, garnering no reaction, so he stood. When he stepped out to towel himself she took his empty glass and stepped back to observe him as though she were taking notes, putting her nose into the glass and making a face. His clothes were neatly folded on a small bench, and clean, which he was thankful for, but he wasn't accustomed to being watched and certainly not studied. Although he had no reason to be shy. He'd been naked in front of dozens of whores and, he thought, it was more than a little ironic that she might be trying to shock him. He reached for his clothes, leaned in to kiss her mouth as he took back his glass and walked out holding the towel in front of him. The bolt action locked the door behind him.

An hour later he was already lounging across the sofa in the common room when she walked through the double doors. Her ponytail had been brushed out and her straight cherry-blond hair hung down past her shoulders. The mukluks were gone and her short wool skirt made him want to see the little of her that was covered. Her legs were long and bare and she had left the matching cardigan unbuttoned enough to accentuate the swell of her breasts. James stood, showing his appreciation with a gleam in his eye and wide smile. He went to the door, kissed her again and went back to the sofa without saying a word. She trailed behind him, curled herself onto the sofa beside him and reclined, not bothering to adjust her skirt that had commanded his fullest attention. At first they both stared into the hypnotic flames.

The evening seemed to go on forever. They spoke for hours, listening intently to one another until she quietly leaned back onto some old cushions to put her feet up so that her legs lay over his and she wiggled into a comfort zone as her skirt was pulled higher by the unforgiving cloth of the worn sofa.

Her pale legs were warmed by the fire and tinted by its glow. They were smooth to his touch as he first raised one knee to kiss, then the other. She was serene, her eyes were closed and she moaned dreamily, enjoying his gentle squeezes and not minding the increasingly bold probing that pushed her skirt higher. When he sensed she was ready, his hand covered her wine-coloured silk panties. His fingers curled and locked into the softness hidden beneath and his thumb caressed the tiny firmness between her supple and moistening folds. Her breaths were deep and long, more of a purr, and soon she lowered her outer leg to the carpet as much to stretch as to help him, widening the apex of her panties and letting him see the lower and shadowed curvature of her buttocks.

He needed to touch her breasts, to feel their contours and their rhythm. His free hand worked slowly at the few remaining buttons, pushing apart the two edges of her sweater across one breast, then the other. She opened her eyes and looked at him without words, one breast covered by the warmth of his hand, the other by hers as she reacted to the pressures of his other hand until she quivered and arched her back. She rolled languorously into him, feeling his hands slide under her to lift her as he stood.

His room was not impressive, neither was hers. The winter wind whistled between the warped sill and loose-fitting wooden storm window and an ancient radiator worked hard to compensate as it dripped and hissed. The window ledge was where he kept his soup bowl with its dried clots which had earlier been the stolen crackers for his potage du jour, the glass for his cheap scotch and the half-empty bottle. There was a mirror, a bureau, a wooden chair that once had cushions and the walls were painted robin-egg blue to match a mostly threadbare carpet. His duffle bag was open on the bureau, filled with dirty on the left, clean on the right. He was in transit and he needed to not forget that fact. The bed was a single and belonged in a cell. It was in a cell and the blankets were beige with institutional blue stripes along the top edge.

James lay on the bed with a thumb hooked into his belt, propped on one elbow to watch her. He had kicked his boots into a corner and his sweater was draped over the chair. Helen stood, scanning what there was to see in the room as though memorizing each detail or comparing the imperfections with those in her room.

Her face glowed. She shook her head slowly from side to side, uncertain what to say, yet very certain she wanted to be with him even though she had no idea why. Her sweater was still unbuttoned and came away with seductive shyness as she gazed into the window that was frosted and white. He wanted to ask her thoughts, already certain she was thinking of him. In the darkness she was a delicate silhouette, a perfect figurine. She slid her open hands down between her skirt and her hips and pushed it to the floor. She was marvellous. She went to the bed and stood in front of him, putting her fingers into the elastic of her panties to slowly push them down until she could kick them free of her ankles.

Her body was still warm from the fire's glow and the heat she was feeling inside as she lowered her body over his and pressed her mouth onto his, letting her hair cascade around them. Soon they twisted impatiently and he pulled her onto his chest to free his hips and push away his jeans. She leaned over him, enjoying the sensations of his hot breath and the pressure of his lips on her breasts and her nipples as his fingers probed and dug into the soft flesh of her buttocks and caressed the length of her dampened back.

She reached behind her and moaned before sliding backwards to meet him. She needed to feel him, to engulf him as much as she knew he needed more of her.

She was unlike any woman he could remember. The others since coming home had all been one-night stands or paid for by the hour, and during his two years of service most had been diminutive and shapeless with no breasts and meatless buttocks. Young or old, they were all old and often he would make them turn away rather than look into their expressionless faces and dull black eyes. Many of them had smelled of recent use or neglect or had taken him into rooms that did, and most of them were blotched with bruises or corrugated with welts and the scars of badly healed cuts. He had never kissed them and had always washed himself thoroughly after paying them. He had never sucked their nipples because they were often coated with poison to incapacitate a customer who would wake up sometime later feeling like shit and without his money or his papers.

Helen's skin and her mouth tasted sweet and the smell drifting up from between her legs was sensual. He tried to block it from his senses, promising himself he would not love her or wake up with her. She was a one-night stand, nothing more, something they both needed and wanted. It was the seventies and guilt meant nothing at all when wet bodies melded and squirmed to be closer, but she never took her eyes from his. He was no better. He noted even the slightest change in her expression, from ecstasy as she first eased him into her, throughout an increasingly urgent crescendo of passion that ended with her violent release. She lay completely exhausted with him still inside her, looking into his eyes with her arms folded across his chest.

"You want me to go. You do, don't you?"

James breathed deeply, shifting Helen slightly. "I want you again. You never stopped looking at me. Your eyes are green-brown."

"They're hazel, so are yours." She giggled. "So you were looking at more than my breasts and my panties on the sofa. Nice touch, so to speak."

He nodded his head into the pillow. "Yeah, I was, but not for long. Your body's fantastic."

"Does this mean we're doing this again tomorrow night, or do we get past it?"

"I don't know. I'd be stupid to say I don't want you lying on me like this, but I don't know."

"Don't know what?"

"What I'm doing here for one thing, lying under a beautiful naked woman and feeling myself growing inside her again. We may not have to wait until tomorrow."

"You're right." She began rocking on him, pressing her hips into his. "What else don't you know?"

"Lots of things, like why I came to a city I can't stand to find a job I don't want because I'll probably be gone by the end of the week. Why you came here when you did? Why you walked in on me and why this? It's not like I'm the best looking guy in town. I should have scared the hell out of you, I do everyone else. Instead, I'm in this hole of a room fucking you."

She kissed the thin scar on his face. "I knew as soon as I saw you. I wasn't even blown away, the way I should have been. I knew you wouldn't hurt me, like I knew I wanted to talk with you and that I wanted this. I just never thought it could be this good." She put her hands on his shoulders and pushed herself into a sitting position with her knees close against his hips, still rocking. "Let's see what happens tomorrow. Maybe we'll just laugh about it, or maybe we won't see each other at all. It's a pretty big house."

James felt himself on the verge. He held up his open palms lightly against her breasts, feeling her nipples harden before wrapping his arms around her to pull her down. "A week can be a long time or a short time. I think this one's going to be short."

"But you still want me to go back to my room when we're finished. I saw it in your eyes. You see something in mine that scares you. What was it?"

"Do you always have serious conversations when you're fucking strange men?"

Helen raised her arms over her head, letting him bear the full weight of her body. "You're not strange to me. There's something drawing me to you and I've never given myself to strange men. You're..." she gasped, and her body shuddered. "Sorry, I was about to say the first strange one. So what was it? Tell me, or I'll jump off and can finish this on your own."

"What was what?"

"What you saw in my eyes."

"I saw myself looking back from them, and I didn't like what I saw. That's what you saw: me, looking at me. You kind of walked in on me at a low point in my life. So jumping off right now might not be such a bad idea, before you drown us."

"Sorry," she pressed into him, "I'm not ready, and I have no idea why I came here. I just did. I was driving by, I saw the sign and I stopped. I love old houses. I love to paint them, and I walked in on you because you didn't lock the door. Okay? But at the moment all I want is for you to get me off. So can you put your little issues aside and help me do that?"

They brought each other in as closely as they could. After their bodies shuddered once more in unison, then again, she laid on top of him, shivering as her skin began to dry. She watched him drift away from her, into a deep slumber, enjoying how she rose and fell in concert with each of his breaths. She felt weightless on top of him, curious about the enigma lying so peacefully beneath her and the coming evenings. She was happy he had fallen asleep. It made leaving him easier.

She eased herself gently away, with slow precise

movements. She didn't bother to dress. At 3:00 AM the hallway was dark. She leaned against the closed door with her clothes gathered in her arms. She had a million questions flashing through her mind. Uppermost was why she had acted like a slut for a man she didn't know, and why she hated to leave him.

Helen North was a graduate of Simon Fraser University on the west coast, struggling between wanting to be a free thinker and wanting the approval of her parents who had raised her to be a good catholic and a decent young woman with solid social values. She had left their suburban home on the outskirts of Vancouver at the end of August, ostensibly to work her way across the country. In fact, she wanted and needed to find her way, to find herself. She had upset her mother and had frustrated her father, both of whom had been vehemently opposed to the scatterbrain plan. She still had no idea where she was headed, or when she would get there, disappointing her parents not for the first time. Her father had wanted her to one day join his law firm, and her mother had always wanted her to become a general physician and perhaps one day join her in private practice.

In her preteens she had not thought much about the family debate, though the issue became increasingly important to her parents the closer she came to finishing high school. When she had finally told them of her decision to pursue the arts, they were speechless. She had always been the perfect daughter, her daddy's favourite girl who had decided to abandon them and devastate all their dreams they had once hoped she would embrace and achieve. They had always given her free rein to learn and to live. Now they believed they should have been more parental and less loving.

She was twenty-five and still living at home to placate her socialite parents, feeling as though her life was going nowhere. During the week she was an emerging artist, working at perfecting her natural inclination toward abstract nudes, and a popular local folksinger selling her increasingly popular canvases at various bars and coffee houses where she performed most weekends. She needed out. How could she sing and paint about freedom when she wasn't free herself?

She wasn't a virgin and chortled at the thought. Who was in the seventies, no one she knew, but she had never done anything like that before, not that she was going to cry over it. During high school she had been with several boys who had always moved on as soon as the novelty of another naked girl had worn off. At university she had gone through a series of semester-long affairs, and she had no idea what she had just done.

In the morning she would begin looking for a club to sing in or a portrait to paint in a hotel lobby or train station for ten or twenty dollars per sitting. Saturday night is what she was thinking about, and whether she would be with the man who was sleeping soundly on the other side of the door.

She couldn't sleep. She couldn't stop thinking about his clear and penetrating eyes, the thin scar on his face and the thin welts she had felt on his chest and his back. They had spoken for hours before he had taken her to his room, lifting her in his arms with no effort, yet she had learned virtually nothing about him. She wanted to, she wanted to go back to him, she wanted to love him again and learn more about him. She also knew if she did go back to him, to wake up with him, he'd be gone by day's end.

The unseen sun rose behind thick clouds and heavy snow a few hours later as Helen sat on the edge of her bed. It was 7:00 AM. She would have to leave soon to find a hotel where she could set up her easel in the lobby. Then she would have to finish her painting early enough to barhop to any gig that would pay her way to the next bigger one. The temperature was hovering at 22° F, but to her the weather was frigid.

Cold winters were one factor she had not considered when she had left the moderate climate of the west coast weeks earlier and now all people could speak about was lake effect snow. She still needed to warm her car, to avoid damaging her art supplies and before carrying down her guitar. James would either look for her that night or avoid her. She might have been too easy, or too aggressive. Either way, he hadn't seemed to mind. She pushed herself from the bed, trying to push him from her mind as she walked out.

James was laying spread across the floor between their doors in blue jeans, polished cowboy boots, a crisp white shirt and a full-length leather coat he had not closed. He was sleeping. Helen looked down at him, studying him. He had no gloves, no hat, his dark hair was cropped short and his dark aviator glasses were halfway down his nose. He was as tall as her, about 5'10", slim and he filled the hallway with his attitude as much as he did with his body. She doubted anyone would dare to walk over him, and suddenly she needed to hurt him the way she felt hurt. When she kicked his boots he woke without showing surprise, as though he had just closed his eyes moments before.

There was no surprise left in him, merely pent-up tension. He had long ago made a habit of understanding where he was and what the consequences might be. He knew where he was safe, and where he was not. James Parker had run away from an abusive home at fifteen. He had not finished high school, he had been in trouble with the police and had spent the next eight years of his life working for slave wages on some of the worst ships sailing the seven seas. He had always known he wasn't good enough to work on the best, but he had seen the world and that had been enough for him until he had thought of Vietnam as an opportunity to make some real money. Not very long after he realized he would die young, either quickly from a bullet or over time from a cheap whore and hard drinking. At the time he had hoped it would be from a cheap whore or cheap scotch. It would take longer. So what? The pain would dull with time. Anyway, he didn't care. He was used to it. Pain was all he had ever felt, all he had to remember

At one time he had wanted to kill his father for beating his mother, but then he had realized she wasn't worth saving. She was a drunk and she had friends, close friends who would come to the house when his father was gone and he was supposed to be at school.

He left them one day in '61, when his parents were too busy arguing to notice and he never looked back. He was half certain they were still alive, somewhere. He didn't care. He cared about himself and, even then, not very much.

"Good morning." She kicked his boots again, but not very hard. "Hello. Get out of my way."

James uncrossed his legs, looking up at her.

"Sit with me…" He snapped his fingers twice, as though searching for her name. The first time she kicked her foot into his thigh. The second time he caught her ankle and raised a hand to meet hers arcing towards his face, pulling her onto him. "You left me."

"You wanted me to, you bastard."

"Yes, I did, but I didn't. I'm sorry. It was special."

"Oh, screw off, it was special." She pushed herself away and stood, kicking him in the stomach. "Screw you, asshole."

James grabbed her foot that was coming back in a wider arc.

"Hey, listen. It was special for me;" the smirk on his face made the confrontation worse, "the way you smelled, the way you moved…everything. It was special, really. I just couldn't ask you to stay."

"Prick!" she hissed.

"See? That's the reason, right there. It's not like we're going together. We happened. So what's the difference whether you left last night or this morning?" She struggled to get her foot back. "Besides, you left me, so why the attitude? And prick? I'm not a prick, an asshole maybe. I can live with asshole."

"I can live with asshole," she mimicked, twisting her face into a snarl and pushing herself away.

She brought her foot back one more time to kick him and he dropped his hands to his side to allow it.

"Go ahead. Get it out of your system." It was as though he had said "you've hurt me enough" and she collapsed onto his lap. She stared deep into his eyes and let him kiss her. "Spend the day with me," he said, evenly. "You know, you could have stayed. I wasn't sleeping when you left, Hellcat, and letting you go was wasn't easy. I wanted you, but I knew you'd be better off not staying." He waited for her to say something. "Believe me."

As much as she wanted to believe him, she didn't.

"I have to go. I have to carry all this stuff to my car and do my thing. I came here to work, remember?"

"I'll go with you. Besides, I'm already dressed to go out and I have nowhere else to go till Monday."

She wanted him to, badly. "No. You look like Paladin, except without his guns. You'll scare people away." She paused, looking into his eyes. "You like that, don't you, James? You like scaring people away, like me?"

"Guns aren't cool, Hellcat. But you wouldn't know that." His lips took on a curious smile and his eyes seemed cold and even more distant. "Kill a man with your hands, that's cool … until the thousandth time you see his face in your   sleep,   asking   you   why."

She blanched as her mind reluctantly absorbed the words, processed them and jerked her body upward as though she had been wrenched away by invisible hands.

She slammed back against the wall, horrified.

"Shit. I was only joking."

He stayed as he was, dividing the hallway. "Three hundred, maybe four, after so many there's no difference. It's just a number."

Helen's face grimaced. "What?"

"I was in Nam, two years' worth. Most of them were done from the boat I was on. They were easy...silent.¬ Sometimes we did shore patrol, more like shit patrol. That wasn't so good. It was always hotter than hell and worse when the rains came. That's when we did them by hand, when it rained. I did about thirty that way; those I remember." He sighed. "Two sounds you never forget, Hellcat: a snapped neck and blood pissing through a man's throat." James stood and looked straight into her eyes. "That's why I didn't want you to stay. I wake up with the sweats most nights, sometimes I scream and there's never enough shit in the bottle by the window to make it all go away. That's why." Helen stared at him in disbelief. "I'll take your stuff to the car and don't worry about tonight. I won't be here." He gathered the instrument and her art supplies easily. "I wish I could say something nice you could remember, like I'm a doctor or a lawyer, or a nice guy who'd like to go dancing with you. But I'm none of those things, never will be." He stepped aside, wanting her to precede him. "Last night was special for me, Hellcat, but what you see is what you got. Next time you'll have to remember to knock first. Sorry."

"So now you think I can just go out to paint some guy's wife or fat kid after what you've told me? Are you completely insane? And let me tell you something. What do you know about being a doctor or a lawyer? That's my parents' thing. It's not who I am. And who are you to tell me what I like and don't like, asshole?"

"You're upset."

Her eyes flared. "Oh, excuse me, miss, whoever you are.

I really enjoyed screwing you last night, but, by the way, I've killed hundreds of people and that's really cool."

"Yeah, you're angry alright. I can tell. But what I said was: until you see his face in your sleep, asking you why. Your name is Helen North, not whoever, but I'll remember you as Hellcat because you are one and your eyes are hazel. So are mine. I don't think I ever knew that because I never look at myself in the mirror that way. You're also fantastically gorgeous, even if I didn't think so at first. You smell like a bouquet of spring flowers and your skin is satiny smooth. Okay? Now, move that tight little ass of yours."

"I am not angry. I'm shocked, and I would have been better to hold than a bottle of cheap scotch. You're fantastic too, maybe a little scratched and bruised, and your body certainly didn't think I was ugly when you climbed out from the bath last night. You smell clean, but not like flowers and your body is good enough for me to paint. I think you know that. You're conceited, in your own charming way and my tight little ass is the best you'll ever see. So put that stuff down." James hesitated. "I said put it down. Anyway, I was really looking for a reason not to go out today, except maybe for lunch. My painting can wait one more day, unless you're going to volunteer and after I take you for a real lunch, without booze, you can help me find a club to sing in. Only successful recording artists have mean-looking bodyguards and it might make them think I'm better than I really am."

He pulled at the edges of his coat. "Sorry. I'm already dressed to go out and I've got plans for tonight."

"No, you don't, except to be with me, and you don't have to steal anymore soda crackers for supper. If we're still hungry after the gig we'll call out for Chinese or a pizza when we get back. So you have no reason to go out either, not even to waste your money on chewing gum, unless you think chewing gum makes you look like a tough guy behind those stupid glasses."

He grinned. "It sounds as though you want to forgive me for being a jerk."

"I certainly don't for thinking I was ugly."

"I never said ugly. I must have had soap in my eyes."

She ignored him, opening her door before grabbing her guitar from his hand. When she turned back he was grinning, holding out her satchel in one hand and the easel in the other.

"You can put all that in my room by the door for me, and then you can leave. I'm going to make myself coffees and soak in the bath, which, by the way, you didn't clean last night. So not only am I very ugly, I'm going to smell like cleanser. Thank you for that, and I'll be ready for lunch by eleven."

He did what he was told. "You said coffees, in the plural."

"I also said I would have been better to hold than a bottle of cheap booze."

When she closed the door behind her, James went back to his room. He opened the window and threw the bottle as far as he could into the backyard where he didn't see it sink into the snow. Then he lay close to the door with his face pressed to the narrow opening and waited to see her feet. What he saw were her feet and two cups between them as she reached in to close the door to her room. When the bathroom door opened and closed he tiptoed down the hallway and the stairs to beg his landlady who was in the kitchen to let him buy Danishes or anything else that was sweet and sticky. When he knocked on the bathroom door there was no answer, when he called her name there was no answer, and when he tried the doorknob it was unlocked.

He had been right about their week going quickly. Thursday night had already come and he was leaving the next morning for Montreal to sign up for work on any steamship line that would hire him for the coming season. The sea was all he knew, and Helen had found a coffee bar in Toronto who wanted her four nights a week. He had already bought his ticket the day before when she thought he had gone for a job interview and he waited until they were back at the house to tell her the truth. It was to be their last night together.

They stayed in her room, savouring their final hours and minutes until Friday morning inevitably encroached on their lovemaking. The room was warm and quiet and they were naked on the bed. Their closed eyes enhanced tender caresses and her gentle whispers lightly touched his ears mixed with the sounds and tears of changing emotions. James was wedged into the corners of the wall with cushions against his back and Helen was spooned against him, enjoying the feel of his warm hands cupping her breasts and his fingers tenderly pinching their responsive caramel crowns. The dark hews of evening changing to morning's cold light went unnoticed until she squirmed to face him. Her face and her lips were quivering, a mirror of his own sadness. Her glistening eyes searched his for even the faintest hint, but his were suddenly cold and dry when he eased her away.

She sat quietly despondent, oblivious to the howling winds shaking the frosted panes of her window, watching him dress, absently reaching for her own silk chemise and flared panties she had worn just for him to remove the night before. She looked so peaceful to him, so angelic and so vulnerable. He wanted to remember her flushed and content, not framed behind the cold starkness of a distant window and mouthing words he would not hear. He would not turn back to see her standing at the window, he promised himself. His time with her was done. His time had come to go. He would be a seafarer again and she could be whatever she wanted to be.

She was quiet, pressing her hands into the top of her

inner thighs. Then she stood and pushed her panties to the floor, raising one knee slightly to free the fragile fabric from one leg and raising the other to pull them away. She went to stand against him, pulling him close in an embrace that seemed eternal to him. He steeled himself against the final touch of the soft rounded flesh of her buttocks, her slim waist and the satin smoothness of her neck. She turned, pushing her back into him to feel his hands on her breasts one last time and against the soft moistness centred below the firm contours of her belly.

She hated feeling the pressure of his hands at her shoulders, wanting to turn her. She surrendered. She rested her forehead against his chest. Her embrace was hard and unyielding, her hair and skin were still an intoxicating bouquet to him, but he had already stayed too long. He pushed her away, following her hands as she pulled at the lapels of his coat to tuck her silk panties into the inner pocket.

There were no words, there was nothing to say. Her panties were infused with a scent he hoped he would never forget, but a white picket fence in the suburbs had never been intended for him. By March he'd be whoring again in some foreign port, forgetting he had ever stopped drinking and one day soon she would also be forgotten amongst a string of convenient one-night stands. He was a loner, he always would be.

Engraving images into his mind he knew would fade with time he walked away from her, into the hallway and out into the bitterly cold artic air that bit at his skin as he left long footprints in the snow that was white, blinding and crisp. He kept his back to the window he knew would be opaque from the heat of her breath against the frosted pane. Not looking back was the first leg of another unknown journey for him. He had learned to never look back. It helped him not to see their faces in his sleep.

28

Helen felt completely empty, cuddling into her pillow and blankets for comfort that wasn't there. A week earlier she had wanted to believe they had come together to fill each other's void, now a part of her had gone through the door with him, a part of her she would never regain, never understand and always lament.

One week before he had walked in on her bath with cupcakes and had sat on the edge of the tub watching her bathe, letting her lick off the icing. Later in the evening they had been too exhausted to order in pizza and had fallen asleep in her bed. He hadn't screamed out once and had stopped drinking. Now she was certain he would start again, driven by the part of him that had remained behind to haunt her for the rest of her life.

She stayed in bed until noon, trying not to think, wanting not to sob and suddenly she was unable to stop. But now she had a gig, one that paid real money and she had to be good. The landlady agreed she could practice in the common room, as long as she was alone or with guests who wouldn't mind. She made a coffee to take with her and took her guitar from its case. The envelope held in place by the strings was pink and addressed to Hellcat. But the coming days and weeks were going to be tough enough without some teary-eyed Dear Jane letter from some guy who couldn't deal with being an asshole.

Helen thought of every reason not to open it. She had nothing to remember him by, nothing at all and suddenly she hated him, knowing she had given him what was more than a pair of panties. She had given him a physical part of herself, something they had shared and thinking of it made her want to be ill. She threw the letter in the wastebasket and left her room.

The music coming from the common room was beautiful and melancholy; her lyrics were being sung above a whisper. Listening to her made James Parker lower his head, wanting to bury his face in his hands, quietly snickering at how silly he would look to anyone who might see him. He was far from being self-absorbed and light years from feeling self-pity. It wasn't him. It wasn't his style. What the hell did he think he was doing? He stood straight and tensed every one of his muscles at once. He walked down the stairs to the entrance with a purpose, wanting to avoid any conversation. He waved goodbye to the older couple and thanked them as he stepped into the blizzard for the second time.

By the time Helen had narrowed her selection for the evening performance the snow had abated and the air had warmed to a moderate cold. In her room she still felt too empty to eat and wanted nothing more than to sleep. She looked at the envelope resting on an angle at the top of the pail filled to overflowing with sheets of music paper. He had wanted to see her write music and to sing the notes. He must have told her a hundred times how he loved her voice and now he was gone and she would never see or feel him again. She stared at the envelope, almost in a trance before she took it from the pail. She knew what he had written: that he was sorry for doing what he had done to her, for leading her on and for leaving her, that he would never forget her. She steeled herself thinking bullshit, bastard, asshole, how much better off she would be without him and how much she loved him and wanted him.

She pulled out the flap, not wanting to open the letter when she already knew. She hated him, before she was stunned into more disbelief. Her stomach constricted into a tight knot and she felt physically sick. She read the words over and over again until they blurred: Marry me, Hellcat. I wasn't strong enough to hear you say no. I'm sorry. My bus leaves at noon and I expect to sign on Sunday PM. Then I'll be married to the sea. I'll understand and will always miss you and think of you, yours, James Parker.

She brought sheet of paper closer to her eyes, not believing the incredible words. It was after 6:00. He would already have arrived in Montreal. She turned the letter over, hoping for more. There was nothing more and she cursed him. The man was an absolute fool. There was no address, no phone number and what did he think she would know about seafarers' unions? She ran downstairs and into the sacrosanct parlour with the note. She had nowhere else to turn.

"No, dear, Mr. Parker left after lunch. Well, "Mrs. Baker paused, "he did leave earlier on, then he came back unexpectedly, saying he had forgotten something important and he asked if he could have his room key for a few hours longer. Of course, I said yes. He's such a nice young man." The landlady patted the cushion beside her on the couch. "When he left the second time he looked terribly sad, Miss North, and I wondered why because I know he heard your lovely music. I saw him in hall, standing by the door of the common room listening to you. When he left he was in such a hurry and he ran out the door. I suppose he forgot his timing and was afraid he would miss his bus."

"He was upstairs, listening to me?"

"Yes dear. It seemed to make him very sad and I thought that strange because your music was so lovely. My husband offered to drive him, but Mr. Parker thought the weather was too bad for him to be driving and he turned us down. He said the subway would be faster and safer. I do wish he had stayed the night. They closed the highway shortly after he left us. The storm's still moving to the east, dear. I can't think where he might be right now. I do hope he's alright. He was such a fine young man, much kinder than he wants people to think. He didn't fool us for a moment." Mrs. Baker smiled, patting Helen's knee. "Did you know he took all our ketchup during his first week with us, thinking we didn't know? It was so sweet. There was no way we could be upset with him. We knew all the while. I made him a special meat pie and gave him his own bottle of ketchup." Mrs. Baker nodded. "I never expected he would come down and hug me in front of my husband. I was quite flustered. He's very handsome, isn't he, in a rugged kind of way?" The old woman blushed. "Then he left us and went back to his room."

It was all too much. Helen ran up the stairs, grabbed her coat and came back down in tears. She had no idea where the bus station was or how to get there by subway. She didn't care. His bus had been cancelled. That was all she had to know.

She exchanged a few words with Mrs. Baker before running out the door. She ran as fast as she could along the unplowed street to the subway station at the corner and down the moving escalator, ignoring curious looks and occasional remarks from those she bumped into, not thinking what she would say to him. She knew what she would say, after she smacked his beautiful face for being so stupid.

She asked the crowd where to go, and once onboard the ride seemed interminable. She asked where to get off, and where to go next and annoyed many more people as she ran to the next train, missing it by seconds. She stamped her foot, groaning loudly from the deepest part of her, furious with herself. When the next train did come she was the first through the doors and cursed them for not closing faster. At the inter-provincial terminal she ran up the granite stairs, two at a time and asked everyone around her for the Montreal counter. When they all pointed she ran, leaving some smiling and others frowning behind her.

She described him to the clerk behind the wicket who remembered the man with the scar and dark glasses right away, pointing to the bar and looking at his watch. James Parker had been in there for at least five hours and all hotels were fully booked. Her shoulders sagged.

She had never been in bus station, let alone a transient bar, which left her without a proper barometer to know whether what she was seeing was actually better than it looked and smelled. Smoke permeated the air and she could see the blue-grey air wafting in small whirlwinds around the waitress as the girl strutted between the tables. No one seemed to want to be there. No one smiled and no one spoke. They all sat quietly at the bar or at tables, looking down at their drinks. Some were squeezed into corners and others were lined up against the walls and she wasn't any better.

Her hair was windblown from running and hanging down in damp tangled strips. Her face was red with cold and exertion, her jeans were wet from the knees down and her feet were cold and wet from where her mukluks had leaked in melting ice and snow. Helen stood motionless, staring at his back, feeling sick and disheartened and wanting to cry as she watched him order yet another. She waited until he was served, wondering why she should even care and what the point would be.

"If you take one more sip I will never, never marry you, Jamie. Please, don't do it, for me."

James Parker sat straight and swivelled on his stool, looking at her through the dark aviators as though seeing a vision. There was no smirk for her to slap and no smart retort for her to despise.

"It's club soda, straight, no lemon, just the way I like it." He held out the glass to her. "I've gone to the john a dozen times already. By the way, I do love you, Hellcat. I just couldn't say it when we were naked ...and we were always naked. I didn't think you'd believe me."

"You came back for me. Mrs. Baker told me you came back."

He nodded. "Yeah, I did. I thought at first you'd find me, if you wanted to. Then I thought I should grow balls and go back for you, to be a man for you. But when you came out with your guitar, and didn't seem to care, I knew you'd seen my note. So I just assumed. I listened to you sing for as long as I could. Then I left. That's all she wrote, Hellcat. That's the story."

"That's it."

"Yeah, that's it. I'm broke, I'm unemployed and a lot of people don't seem to like me. All I can promise is to love you, get myself educated and become somebody you can love. I already love you and I can get into some university on a maturity programme. Being somebody you can love is up to you. It won't be easy, but I think I can help pull it off." He put the back of his hand to her cheek. "You look horrible and you're not saying very much."

"You bastard."

He chuckled weakly, lowering his hand. "A bastard you'll marry or a bastard who gets on the bus in another twelve hours, if he hasn't already drowned in this stuff?"

She eased herself onto his lap, facing him with her arms wrapped around his neck. "A bastard I'll marry, and who owes me another pair of really expensive mukluks, if he doesn't run away again."

She leaned in to kiss him, opening both her eyes with surprise at the sound of the cheering applause. James went to pay the bartender who grimaced and waved him away with a flick of his wet towel, telling him in a hoarse voice that anyone who could drink that much water in any bar deserved not to pay for it.

29

They stayed at the Baker's boarding house for another two months. Helen sang at the bar Thursday through Sunday, with James always in the front row and during the day she rehearsed while he worked at whatever part-time job he could find. February 14th was a Monday and she had the night off. He took her for pizza and gave her a brand new pair of fur-lined boots in the restaurant. She only felt the ring when she slipped her foot into the soft suede, completely ignoring what he was saying about her still having time to change her mind. By the end of March he had been clean for two months and had been accepted into the adult programme of Loyola University. By the end of April they were living in Montreal, at the foot of the mountain, very much in love and inseparable.

He worked days in construction while Helen created canvases to sell at weekend flea markets. In the evenings he attended classes while she sang at the campus bar. She helped him with his studies and at the end of the first semester, the end of August, he felt like a little boy running home to show his mother his report card. He was at the top of all four classes and on top of the world.

It was a celebration and he also knew there was something she had wanted to tell him for some time, but she hadn't wanted to affect his studies and he had long ago learned patience. She wore his favourite dress for the occasion: short and in fashion, the way he liked to see her and styled like a shirt with buttons from top to bottom.

She was lean and tanned and had changed her hair colour back to auburn for the summer. She was superlative, flawless, and after all their months together he still could not take his eyes from her. James had let his hair grow long and wore it slicked back into a sleek ponytail, which suited his look when most men would have seemed more like effeminate sissies. He wore black leather with dress boots when he wasn't working, and by August his tan was deep and dark. He no longer looked sinister or threatening, except to other men. Helen had promised to soften his look and she had, teasing that he was only years away from being a real gentleman. He spread out the blanket and lay flat, looking up.

"You're a pig."

"What's your point?"

She knelt beside him, enjoying how he was looking at her. "I'm proud of you, Jamie."

"You should be proud of yourself, Hellcat, for turning me around. I could've been sweating in the filthy boiler room of some Taiwanese rust bucket instead of seeing a gorgeous girl in the moonlight. You did this to me."

She lay beside him, looking at the stars, slapping his hand away each time he plucked at another button. "I'm so glad I read your note, Jamie. Thinking how close I came to not reading what you wrote scares me so much."

"I always tell myself I would have gone back again, to make you read it."

She stroked his hair. "Jamie, I want a January wedding, this coming January."

He kissed her chin, her mouth and her nose. "You just tell me when to be there, Hellcat."

"The twenty-first; it's a Sunday. And I want a civil wedding with a justice of the peace, my parents and maybe a few friends by then. Besides, finding a church would be a hassle. It's taken my parents this long to adjust to you not being catholic. Can you imagine a priest trying to deal with someone like you?"

"A judge is fine, pretty girl. I've met a few in my life. They're not so bad."

She jabbed him. "I want it to be in the country, Jamie, with lots of snow falling and a big fireplace."

"And if it's not snowing?"

"It will. I know it, like the day I met you."

"I'll be there, Hellcat."

She rolled onto her side, punching him when she realized he had unbuttoned most of her buttons. Then she undid the last two and held herself against him. "Jamie, about my parents, they'll be here next week. Mom phoned this morning. I'm sorry I didn't tell you earlier. She sounded funny. I suppose they're a bit anxious about meeting you, now that they're almost certain you love me and that I won't be condemned to hell because you're a heathen Presbyterian."

James snickered, kissing her neck again and rubbing his hands over her arms. "That would be ironic, since you're the one who saved me. Don't worry, Hellcat. I'm anxious to meet them, to hear all those little secrets you haven't told me and see all those little bare-bum baby pictures. And I more than love you. I adore you. They'll see that right away and too bad if they don't. Now," he propped himself up and scanned the dark hillside, "if you haven't noticed, we're pretty much alone."

James eased his hand under her open dress to her bare hip. She let him gently ease her onto her back and caress her bare belly, breathing deeply as he gently pressed his fingertips under the thin band of her panties.

30

The Norths arrived the following Saturday. James had seen nothing wrong with inviting them to the apartment for the evening and was openly put off when Helen explained why the invitation had been refused. Mr. North preferred not to see the home his daughter shared with a man who was not yet her husband. Mrs. North had concurred and James could only shrug when Helen told him that her father was to pay for the evening at the Ritz. He had never been to the Ritz and had never eaten a meal of more than three courses. Preparatory to the visit, he had taken Helen's lessons in stride and had promised her not to dip his hot roll into the butter dish or tuck his serviette into his collar or pick food from his front teeth with a fork. When Saturday night arrived she was dressed to kill and he was James.

Helen had recently sent her parents the best of the photos she had taken of James. Most of the others had been of her sitting on him, or of James standing behind her, hugging her, or him alone behind a desk or sitting in a chair. In most shots he had been wearing his signature aviators. These were more like studio shots of a man in black leather who did not like to smile for the camera.

James had always refused to speak with them on the phone, not wanting to endure a banal conversation about himself with someone he had not met face to face. Not one of the photos had prepared them for the man who strode into the restaurant with their daughter on his arm.

Mrs. North brought her hand to her mouth to muffle an "Oh my God, Herbert", as her husband stood to meet the man everyone else in the restaurant had also turned to see. The men shook hands, and James tilted his head towards Mrs. North after she had finished hugging the daughter she had not seen in close to a year. James had made it very clear to Helen that there would be no false or effusive emotion by him towards her parents. Not only did he not know them, until proven wrong, he would consider their mission as an opportunity to evaluate and undermine him. Though he did concede her father had been smart to meet with them on neutral ground.

Through the salad and soup the conversation had all been about Helen. James had remained silent, knowing full well Mr. North was using the time to sum up his body and facial language, both of which were intentionally and casually inert. When the sommelier began to fill his wineglass, James stopped him with a casual stroke of a forefinger, asking for club soda without ice and offering no explanation.

"Helen tells us you're ex-combat, James, that you spent two years in Nam. Two tours must have been very hard on you."

"That would be Vietnam, and yes it was hard." James paused to spear the lemon slice and remove it, visibly irritated that yet another non-combatant who had never seen action thought it was alright to say Nam. It was not alright. "It's what kept me alive. Now I have your daughter to live for."

"Wasn't that a rather peculiar decision to make on your part, signing up to fight another country's war?"

"No. I signed up to test fate, not to fight a war. Call it a death wish, or a hair shirt. Call it whatever you want."

"It sounds as though you had something to forget or leave behind. Did you achieve your objective?"

"It was a long time ago. What I achieved was staying

alive. Nothing else matters in a war. When I was a kid I ran away to sea to get away from the people who raised me. I haven't seen them for eleven years. That was also staying alive. I went to sea instead of going to prison for killing them." He smiled, placing his hand over Helen's "Actually, I went to sea instead of killing them. What goes around always comes around." He grinned. "Hellcat knows the story and she's okay with it."

"About your parents?" her father asked.

"No, about the ones who raised me, after they bought me."

Mr. North showed no surprise; his wife stopped eating. "You know you were adopted? Your adoptive parents told you?"

"Your choice of words, not mine, but in a word, yeah. It's as good as any. I was told my real parents were having a rough time making ends meet, so they gave me away through some social aid centre. It was a big mistake. I would have been better off growing up poor; enough said. They screwed up, big time."

"You were treated badly?"

James chortled through his nose, looking at Helen. "Is there any other reason for a kid to spend half his life at sea?"

"I can imagine how difficult your life must have been."

"If you say so. I lived it, and I can't imagine. So I think you might come up a little short. No offence."

"So, you're twenty-six."

"You already know that, with all due respect. I was adopted on July 15, '47, on my birthday. I was never told where and I never asked. I just wanted out and I've never cared enough to find out. All I remember is moving around a lot, the man leaving each town to work on the road and his wife entertaining at home while he was gone."

"Your mother did housewares parties, James?" Mrs. North asked, tapping the corners of her mouth.

He snickered. "No, ma'am, she didn't. She slept with men for less money than she could have made doing them on the street. It wasn't quite like having a lawyer and a doctor for parents, I suppose."

Mrs. North coughed her wine through her nose. Helen lowered her head and tried not to giggle. He was her man and not entirely defenceless on his own, not that he hadn't warned her.

"Helen says you're Presbyterian."

James sliced into his filet mignon. "That's what it says on my papers. All the same, the point is moot. I don't believe in a God, not that I might not if there was one. That's why we're having a…"

"Mom, the wedding's going to be in January, like I always wanted, and very intimate. Did you hear me, dad? I said very intimate, that means you guys and maybe a few friends."

"I'm not deaf, young lady, and I happen to be talking with James." He signalled the sommelier away and poured his own wine, ignoring the women. "So your adopted name is Parker. Is that so?"

"Yes. What went before means nothing to me. I spent twenty-six years being born. I only began to live eight months ago and I don't mean this born again crap. So where are we going with this? I will never let anything happen to her and I believe that's where this particular conversation ends. I'm not very good with questions, and less good with bullshit, particularly when I don't have all the answers. All you have to know, Mrs. North, Mr. North, is that I love her more than my own life and, if Helen loves me half as much, I'm very lucky. You also have to know that I'll call you Herbert and Doris when I feel right about it. Until then I'll look at each of you when I'm talking." He sipped his water and enjoyed the quiet with his last morsel of succulent beef.

"There's one more thing." Mr. North gave James his full attention. "I'm paying for the wedding. She's mine now, and I'm hers."

He sipped his water.

"I'm afraid not, Mr. Parker."

"It's not open for discussion. I'm paying."

"You misunderstand me. I'm afraid there won't be a wedding, Mr. Parker. She is not yours now, and she never will be." Mr. North dabbed the edges of his mouth and folded the napkin authoritatively. "I've taken the liberty to arrange for dessert to be served in our suite. There's something very disturbing you both have to hear, something best said in private."

Helen went cold. "That's not funny, dad. Why would you say anything so cruel?"

Mr. North was already standing, pulling out his wife's chair. "Helen, we'll give you and Mr. Parker a few moments alone. We are in suite 1518. Shall we say...ten minutes?"

"Pardon me for not standing, Mrs. North. Mr. North, go fuck yourself. January 21st is the day and you've got shit all to say about it. Whether you and wife attend means absolutely squat to me. It's Helen's day. You hurt her, I'll hurt you."

"Very fine bravado, young man, if not a little melodramatic. I expected nothing less from a man with your turbulent history. Please be in our suite in ten minutes, both of you."

James and Helen remained silent, watching her parents sign for the meal and leave without turning back. Helen grabbed for his hand. "I've never seen him this way, Jamie. They've known about us for months, and I've never seen my mother so passive, or him so aggressive. I don't understand. This goes way beyond the catholic thing. There's something very wrong. I thought they'd be a little anxious about you taking me away from them, but I never imagined this."

"I'm not surprised, Hellcat. I guess the scar doesn't help

much. Don't get hyper over it. You're mine and that'll never change. January is all you have to worry about, in the country with lots of snow, as requested."

She squeezed his hand. "Tonight was supposed to be such a special night for us. I was going to tell you at the mountain, Jamie, but then you started acting like you always do and I decided to surprise everyone tonight. I was so excited."

"Keep those eyes dry, Hellcat. They're not worth it. You can surprise me. Nothing else matters. What's got you so excited?"

Helen brought his hand to her lips. "Our baby."

*

James left a message for 1518 at the front desk. He had no intention of using a courtesy phone. They would be late, on their schedule. When they did arrive an hour later the door to the suite was open. Mrs. North was seated in the sitting room and her husband stood stoically beside her.

"Please sit down, both of you."

Helen sat. James remained standing.

Mr. North dropped an enlarged photograph of their daughter and one of James side by side on the table. He looked at his daughter first, then James. "How did the two of you not see it?"

"See what?" James asked. "Talk anymore bullshit and we're gone. So start making some sense because I'm starting to get royally pissed."

"Mr. Parker. It is quite true that you we're adopted on July 15, 1947, which happens not to be your birthday. You were born June 30, 1946. You were given up for adoption a week after your first birthday and spent a week at the adoption centre before being selected by the Parkers. Hence what you thought was your birthday. Apparently your biological parents had intended to take you back when their economic conditions improved, from what I've been able to ascertain. However, as you said earlier, your adoptive parents moved around quite a bit and we are talking about the forties. Things were a bit primitive back then, to say the least, what with all the war babies. Your real name is Theodore Alexander. You were born here in Montreal, where your biological parents still reside."

James stared at him. "My name is James Parker. It's who I am and I don't give a good shit who lives where. I also don't see that it's any of your business, or what it has to do with us getting married." He looked down to Helen, holding out his hand. "Let's go, Hellcat."

"Both of you stay as you are. I'm not finished, Mr. Parker." Mr. North looked at his wife who was sitting with her back straight and her hands folded in her lap. He squeezed her shoulder to comfort her as he looked down at the photographs, shaking his head.

"We know all this, Mr. Parker, because we wanted and needed to know about the man who would be marrying our daughter. More importantly, we wanted to know about the man in the photograph. We wish we had seen the truth earlier, we sincerely do, but it's the only real close-up and, as you can see, you're not wearing your usual dark glasses. Understand there is no one we love more than our daughter, ever since the day we first held her. We had once thought of telling you, Helen, but for some reason we never did. The timing never quite seemed appropriate. Admittedly, in retrospect, we have done you a terrible disservice. To us it was just a paper, a formality and we never meant to hurt you or to see you suffer. You're our daughter in every way, our little girl. We need you to believe that." His shoulders slumped. "You were also born on June 30, '46, Helen, you know that, but not to us. You were born to Emily and Davidson Alexander. You were baptized Katherine Alexander at St. George's Church with your twin brother Theodore. You and Mr. Parker are brother and sister."

James moved quickly to grab Helen by the shoulders as she fell forward clutching her stomach and screaming in a strained groan. She rocked back and forth, calling his name repeatedly. Mr. North did his best to remain stoic, feeling his emotions rise as his wife began to cry, wanting to go to her daughter, but James Parker suddenly seemed threatening to her.

"No one could ever have imagined this would happen, child. The Alexanders did try to get you back, at least once that we are aware of, but we had moved to the west coast and, as I said, many things were primitive back then. I suppose we didn't make it very easy for them. He's in real-estate, a developer of considerable reputation and she devotes most of her time to being a patron of the arts. So, you see, there's absolutely no way you can be married." He paused. "Helen, there's still a place for you at home. You know that. We want to take you back with us. No one need ever know about your relationship with Mr. Parker."

"She's going home with me."

"I understand, Mr. Parker..."

"His name is James!" Helen screamed. "James!"

Helen's crying became the only sound.

"We understand how you must feel, Helen. However the reality is that no priest will marry you, not once they know, not even a minister of another faith. You are fraternal twins. How did you never see it? My God, the photo, and when we saw you come in together we were horrified. How did you never see the resemblance?"

"This is bullshit."

"No, Mr. Parker, it is not. Our investigation was very complete. We welcome you to review the findings, though it won't change a thing. You were both taken to the centre at the same time. We adopted Helen two days later and gave her a new name, but kept her birthday. Helen, we're sorry. We've reserved a room for you. We would like to leave as soon as possible. We can make arrangements for your personal belongings to be shipped back at a later time."

James stood. "We're leaving, together, and right now."

"I'm afraid that's quite impossible. To do so would be an affront to everything Helen has ever been taught, to her religion and to a decent upbringing. How can either of you possibly think of living together as husband and wife with the knowledge that you are brother and sister? It's unthinkable, and a despicable sin, a crime against God."

"So is buying a child and never telling her. What would any God think about that? So be careful what you say from this point, Mr. North. Helen hasn't changed me that much and at the moment I'm a little on edge."

Helen eased herself forward, ready to stand. "How long have you known?"

"We received definitive information the evening before we called, a week."

"James and I have been together for almost eight months, and all this week. What makes tonight or tomorrow any different than yesterday, or the night you called?"

"Helen, you can't do this. You can't possibly think to leave here with this man."

"Yes, dad, I can. And I will." She looked up. "Jamie."

"Think of what you're saying." Mr. North grabbed the back of his wife's chair to steady himself. "It's a terrible shock, we realize, but we can't let you do this. Think of the future, think of the ramifications. What happens if there are children? What then. It will be an abomination, a sin. It's horrific enough that you've practiced incest with him, but now that you know. Helen, this could mean prison for you and excommunication. And think for a moment of what you'll bring into the world: a sick child, or one that's lame or demented. Think of your mother," he pleaded.

Helen squeezed James' hand. "There won't be children. We'll make sure of that." She stood, slipping her arm around James, her face streaked. She looked directly at her mother, then to her father. "I was meant to be with James, and I will be. If that means not getting married, we won't. It's a piece of paper, no different from the paper that made me a daughter. James is right. You lied to me. We might have known if you had told me, but you didn't. Just knowing our birthdays were the same, or that we were given away, but we didn't know. So thank you. Thanks, dad. Really, thanks. By not telling me you helped to bring us together. Thanks, mom." She crossed in front of James. "There will be no invitation, and no wedding. Thanks, both of you."

"You can't leave, Helen," Mr. North implored.

"Thanks for sitting there like the perfect wife, mom. You were very comforting," she answered, slipping her arm into James' "I know what I want, and I'm going home to be with him. Don't do anything to make me despise both of you more than I do right now." She looked at her watch. "Take note. Helen North's time of death was 8:16 PM, September 02nd."
*

Undeterred, the Norths delayed their return flight. They attempted several times to speak with Helen throughout the days and nights following the disastrous evening, finally enlisting the help of a zealous priest who heatedly confronted the young lovers with ecclesiastical threats of eternal damnation and exclusion from heaven on high. The cleric quickly learned the hard way that the angry atheistic fist is mightier than the invisible shield of pious self-righteousness.

The Norths persisted despite the setback. They stood for endless hours outside the ardent couple's apartment in the hopes of confronting them one last time to convince them of their shared sin. The following Friday when their vigil came to an abrupt end with the news of the couple's departure, inadvertently delivered to them by the superintendent, Mrs. North understood she would never again see the young and vibrant woman who had once been her daughter..

The bands were posted at the Halifax City Hall at the end of December and on the twenty-first Helen North became Helen Parker in a very private seaside ceremony in the middle of Nova Scotia's first snowfall of the New Year. Their honeymoon would come later. James had already begun his second semester of studies at Dalhousie while working with a small construction firm. Helen continued her painting while counting down the days to April 10, and trying her hardest not to think about it.

Jackson Parker was born at 5:10 AM. Four days later, on April 14th. His name was legally changed and he would never know the heartbreak of his real parents who gave him up to a couple whom they had never met and would never know.

Helen cried copious tears and no one cared but James. No one had ever cared about her as much as James. Two months later, after his exhaustive exams, he gave her the travel portfolio for her birthday. The next day they left for a three-week honeymoon on the Spanish Mediterranean, not to forget or escape, just to be alone and to love one another as much as ever.

PART FOUR

1972 – 1983

31

Davidson had never forgotten that vicious slap and he had never forgiven it. What he had forgotten were her gentle and coquettish slaps during their innocent courtship. Emily never had her house by the sea and she never forgave him for sending her children away. In the years that followed, as much as she had thought she should have loved him, those magical days of youthful flirtation had gone forever.

A week after they had given up the twins their home was sold at a profit, though Emily would always think of it as having been taken from her. She had never forgotten the deep humiliation she felt the day she moved from her perfect home to a small one-bedroom downtown apartment. Nor had she ever conceded that it had been the beginning of a new and privileged life. It was what Davidson had needed to do, the catalyst that had been eluding him, what he could not have done had he not made that one crucial decision which he still regretted so deeply.

Davidson said goodbye to Mr. Morgan. He studied real-estate during the day and attended night courses to obtain his high school leaving certificate two years later. He was accepted into McGill's Business Programme, attending daytime classes while he bought and sold a dozen or more houses and Emily studied art and design, constantly searching for new real-estate opportunities. By the time he had graduated with honours they weren't buying houses, they were building them and by the time he obtained his MBA they were selling land to developers and planning whole communities.

In 1956 Katie and Theo were ten years old and seemed to be all but forgotten. For Davidson it was enough that he had kept his promise to Emily to one day become successful. When the twins were three he had tried in vain to locate them, and for Emily that one failure would forever be Davidson's greatest. They had never spoken about the children, though Emily would never forget them. Each year she would quietly celebrate their shared birthday and imagine how they would look, how they had grown.

The Alexanders were part of a new affluence and well on their way to becoming wealthy. Emily no longer pursued her painting. She preferred to appreciate the work of others. Davidson had not sung in years and each day what had once been important to them became less discernible to where they no longer thought of the past. They had become the Alexander Corporation. Emily and Davidson no longer existed. They no longer shared their dreams or memories. Neither one existed, each having been subliminally bartered for expectations, ambitions and deeply rooted regrets.

Emily never really thought of her mother and rarely visited the grave site when she did. Those occasions were perfunctory and she went alone without flowers or melancholy. She was the sole beneficiary of the Ashton estate, which was the boarding house, and Davidson had steadfastly refused to benefit from any subsequent monies derived from its sale. He had insisted his success would be his own, that what he accomplished in life would never be mistaken as a fortunate consequence of a windfall they had both known would come their way one day and he never enquired as to what Emily had done with the inheritance.

They were becoming prominent members of the business world, envied and much sought-after members of the new social elite. By 1972 they were living an opulent existence that made no distinction between work and play. Not only were they members of the city's most prestigious club for the who's who of business, they owned it.

Davidson worked most evenings, spending increasingly less time with Emily. The only occasion they danced together was to open the annual ball and they no longer accepted wedding invitations from friends or associates whose children they had seen grow up, instinctively avoiding any occasion that might inspire painful reminders of what might have been. They almost never entertained away from the club, their first rare nights of sleeping apart had become routine and Emily often vacationed alone or pampered herself with selected friends during extended stays at luxury spas.

It had been years since Davidson had planned a vacation: for him, occasional long boating weekends at their lakefront property in the Thousand Islands with friends from the club or business associates were time enough away from the office. His private secretary had been with him since the day she graduated from secretarial college at seventeen, when she had agreed to work with the Alexanders for practically nothing. At the time she had believed him that one day she would not regret her decision and she never did. She was his right arm and confidante, not Emily's, who knew enough to understand the close bond more than respect it. Both women clearly understood the underlying complexities of their own relationship that Davidson did not. No one got passed Bernadette Dubuc, not even Emily.

The BOAC flight from London's Heathrow Airport touched down one muggy July afternoon. As passengers scrambled to disembark, one man remained seated at the window of his First Class row, finishing his drink as he perused the final few pages of the extensive report he had both commissioned and contributed to personally. When the stewardess cleared her throat with a meaningful intonation he answered her with a smile. He unbuckled his belt and side-stepped into the aisle exuding a natural confidence and charm.

The following morning he arrived at the head office of the Alexander Corporation by the time Madame Dubuc walked in. The young girl working at copy typing a lengthy telex message from behind the reception desk looked up to stop her, to explain that the gentleman standing off to the side of the expansive and modern lobby was waiting to see Monsieur Alexander. He had no appointment, though he did seem very nice.

Madame Dubuc would normally not have bothered, however the young man had come from Europe and deserved at least a polite refusal.

"Good morning, sir."

He tilted his head. "Bonjour, Madame Dubuc."

She smiled, pleasantly. "Bonjour, monsieur. I regret that Monsieur Alexander's appointments will make him unavailable throughout the day. His appointments are usually made quite a few weeks in advance."

"As the young lady has already explained to me, and I understand entirely, madame. Regrettably, I was unable to call in advance of my visit. However, I am quite certain that Monsieur Alexander will want to see me, and that he would prefer to see me here, rather than at his home this evening on Fleetwood Drive." The man's expression was good-natured and inherent, neither smiling nor determined. There was something about him that made her like him. "He will see me, madame. I assure you. Please, give him my card, with my sincerest apologies for having disrupted his schedule. I have travelled a very long way to meet with him and cannot return home without having done so. My flight departs tomorrow, madame, and it would be impossible for me to stay longer."

Madame Dubuc took the card, not recognizing his name or the name of the law firm. She looked at him, creasing her forehead just enough to show mild frustration with the young man and the very unorthodox request.

"Monsieur…"

"Madame, my leaving will change nothing. Monsieur Alexander will see me whether we meet here, or elsewhere."

"May I…?"

"It is a matter of some discretion, madame, between Monsieur Alexander and me. Although, if it will help to alleviate your anxiety, I can tell you that my business with him concerns the evening of October 28, 1944. He will understand the significance of that date, madame. I assure you, there is no doubt."

The date meant nothing to Bernadette Dubuc. Davidson had never spoken with her of the war years, or of what hung on the wall by his desk. She left the young man to wait without promising an immediate appointment. He nodded appreciatively and stood with his hands by his side.

She walked into Davidson's office without knocking. He never expected that she would so early in the morning. "Davidson, a gentleman has arrived who wishes to see you. He won't say why."

"Bernie, are you going soft on me? Need I remind you, you're the one who started the appointment rule? Please attend to the gentleman. See if one of the others might not be able to accommodate him. I'm really in it up to my shorts today."

"I know, and your agenda will be busy enough without unexpected interruptions. However I believe you will want to see this young man."

"And why is that? Is he a potential candidate for your lovely daughter?"

"My daughter has enough men to sort through, though I have to believe she would want to walk slowly enough for this one to catch her."

"He must be quite a talker if he's warmed your heart, Bernie."

"Eloquence apart, he's very adamant that he meet with you, whether here or at your home, Davidson. He mentioned the address."

"At my home?" Davidson raised his eyebrows. "Is that a fact, and he won't say why he's here?"

"No, he won't. He claims what he has to say would be indiscreet for anyone other than you to hear."

"Then, do you at least have his name. Or is that also a deep and dark mystery?"

She passed him the card and watched as the smile and colour vanished from his face.

"He says it's regarding the evening of October 28, 1944, that you would understand what that date means." Bernadette stepped forward quickly and reached out over his desk. "Davidson, what is it?"

32

The young man came through the door, acknowledging Madame Dubuc as she closed it behind her. She had been instructed not to disturb them for any reason and to reschedule the entire day's appointments. In those first seconds Davidson felt his entire body moisten with cold sweat, wanting inexplicably to scream out that he had wasted his entire life.

"Good morning, sir. Thank you for not refusing to see me. Allow me to introduce myself. My name is Jean-Alexandre de-Saint-Valéry. I am the son of Gabrielle de-Saint-Valéry."

"And mine."

The young man nodded, nonchalantly. "Yes sir, and yours."

"Aye, there's no mistaking those green eyes." Davidson stood, coming around his desk as he gestured toward twin leather armchairs. "Je vous en prie, Jean-Alexandre."

"There is no need for us to speak French, sir. My English is perfect, as I know your French is impeccable. Much of my education was completed in Glasgow, your birthplace. My mother insisted."

Neither man thought to extend his hand.

"How is she, lad?" He leaned, pressing his elbows into his knees. "Tell me you've not come all this way to say something horrible has happened to the sweet thing."

"My mother is well, sir, and a very successful hotelière and restaurantrice in Paris. Neither have I come here to embarrass you or to ask anything of you. My mother is completely unaware of this meeting. She believes I am in England. I thought it best to fabricate a story that would not alarm her or cause us to argue, as much as it has troubled me to do so."

"Why did she never tell me I had a son?"

"She has never said, and now it is too late to know why, or to care. Perhaps, in her heart, she believed you to be dead, or needed to believe that you were. It would, after all, be easier for her to eventually accept your death than to always believe how you loved another more than her, a woman you had not seen in five years." The smirk was genuine. "She never speaks of you to me. I suppose she's afraid I would, at some point, try to find you. Gérard and Henri, who still remember you with great fondness, continue to talk of you when she is not there to listen. Gérard is my brother. My mother adopted him the day I was born, July 28th, which has since been his birthday."

"July 28."

"Yes sir. The day after tomorrow, the day you left Europe from Amsterdam." The young de-Saint-Valéry relaxed. "I know a great deal about you, sir, as you will soon discover. The truth is I probably know more of your life than you do yourself. However, I am not here to impose myself, nor have I come here to threaten you or cause you distress. Though I do regret that may inadvertently happen and I apologize in advance for any grief I may have brought to you. I have come simply to tell you a story. I warn you, however, that I will tell you the whole story or nothing at all. I also warn you to be prepared." He paused, looking at Davidson unflinchingly. "If you would prefer that I leave, I believe this would be the appropriate moment to say so. She will never know of this meeting. I give you my word. And you will know nothing of her."

"No." Davidson's voice was commanding. "You'll stay right here and tell me all that you know." Davidson sank back into the chair, his face devoid of any colour. "Not a single day has passed that I've not thought of your mother, lad, not a single day. I struggled with myself each day from V-E Day to the moment I stood on the dock, knowing deep down I didn't want to leave. I loved her so much, but I had nothing to offer her and I knew she wouldn't be alone for long, if someone else hadn't already captured her heart. Who would I have been to ruin that? I'd been gone from her the better part of a year. I'd killed hundreds of men, lad, yet your mother turned me into a nervous schoolboy each time I looked at her." Davidson was looking past his son. "I told myself for years it was for the best, that I would never have been good enough for her. I've always known I was not the one she really wanted. She wanted the thought of me. I would never have been more to her than her memory of another."

"You're speaking of Jean-Philippe de-Montparnasse."

"You know that much."

Jean-Alexandre nodded. "He is a small part of what I know, of what you are about to hear. She still wears the locket. I have spent the past few years piecing together the information, a matter of more than a little regret to me. I began as soon as I was able to act on my own, without my mother's knowledge or intervention. My information is very complete."

"Tell me your story, lad. We'll not be disturbed."

"First, sir, you must know that you left behind the most beautiful woman in all of Europe, an opinion shared by many." Jean-Alexandre reached into his attaché for the manila envelope that he passed to Davidson. "I have copies, sir. You may keep these to review at your leisure.

Davidson shivered visibly as he slowly removed the coloured enlargements. He studied all three, sombrely, lost in time. When he spoke, his voice was barely above a whisper and tears welled in his eyes.

"When were they taken?"

"One week ago."

Davidson cleared his throat. "You've got a terrible mean streak in you, lad, or a natural inclination toward the dramatic."

One of the photographs was taken as Gabrielle sat alone at La Falaise, another showed her standing between two men whose faces he still remembered and a third showed Gabrielle walking along the Champs Élysées. Davidson placed them on the table as though they were fine sheets of gold and went to the side of his desk for his own briefcase. He took out a small leather bound book. Taking his seat, he passed it to Jean-Alexandre.

"I've never forgotten her, not for one day. That book was given to me by a navy pastor in the hope it would bring me peace and comfort. Unfortunately, it brought neither. I've not read a single verse from its pages since a very dear friend of mine passed away from a German bullet in his head."

The young man looked up. His dark green eyes expressed what his face did not.

"Big Earl was killed?"

Davidson's surprise was real. "Aye, he died at the Schelde. So, you've heard of him."

"I have, and I've seen his picture: a man bigger than life."

Davidson stifled a weak laugh. "You've no idea what you've just said." He turned and pointed to the shadow box mounted on the wall; encased inside were his helmet and .45.

"I presume they're souvenirs of a five-year hell, monsieur."

"They are indeed, lad. Though what they really are, are constant reminders of desperation. The hat reminds me that in difficult times I'm never alone, even when it appears that

I might be. The gun reminds me of a brief moment in my life when I thought of it as a remedy more than a weapon."

"It was that bad, the day he died?"

"There's not a word to describe it, and much worse for Earl and many others."

"Henri still talks about him constantly, about the night the huge Indian made him drunk. Earl's memory is still very alive with Henri, and those who have heard his stories. Henri continues to believe each new headache is a lingering result of that night, a persisting phantom as it were."

"Aye, I remember the day and the morning after, which is a miracle in itself. I still believe your mother tried to kill me for my stupidity with her vile gypsy concoctions." Davidson's weak smile disappeared. "It happened just days after we freed the River Schelde. It was quick, lad. He felt nothing. I still remember the quizzical look on his face." Davidson pointed to the prayer book. "The one purpose it's ever served since then is to preserve the three precious photos I possess of Gabrielle. It's been with me each day."

"After all these years you carry her pictures with you each day."

"I made a very terrible mistake. I was young, and as stupid as Gabrielle always said I was. I should have listened to Earl. He knew the truth."

"What truth was that?"

"That I loved Gabrielle so much, and that I should never have boarded the bloody ship that took me home, or to where I thought my home should be. I should have stayed. I've always known the truth."

The young man opened the prayer book to the sepias of Gabrielle. He recoiled, wincing as though prodded with a hot iron and he was suddenly sad.

"Sir, I had no idea how closely my photographs would resemble these three. I'm truly sorry. I had no ill intent. My purpose was not to cause you grief, rather to show you old friends in Henri and Gérard. Often, in the autumn, my mother will sit for hours at La Falaise. I believe I have discovered the reason why. I have never seen these pictures before, sir. My intention was not to replicate them. I am truly sorry and I apologize." He handed the book back to Davidson. "She does not talk of you because she does not want to dilute her memory of you. This I know because my aunt Marie-Claude, who is not my real aunt as you know, has told me. She has also told me of Jean-Philippe and how my mother once confessed to her that she had stood crying at her window the night you left her, begging you in silent whispers not to die and to come back to her. She cried for more than a week, monsieur. To my mother she was losing Jean-Philippe all over again. The only two men she has ever loved, but you are the one she called out to from behind her window, not Jean-Philippe." He sighed deeply. "May I stand?"

Davidson nodded mechanically. "Yes, of course."

"My heart will always ache to know how much pain her loneliness has brought to her because she once met you, and because she has never forgotten you. Can you imagine what it must be like to live so many years of lonely days and much lonelier nights not knowing whether the only one you have ever loved, or will ever love, is alive? I cannot. To think of living such a life is beyond me. That man whose pictures I have seen is not you, monsieur, nor is the man Henri keeps alive in his exaggerated stories. That man would have run to her, to love her. He would not have abandoned her to spend his life living a horrible lie." Jean-Alexandre pointed to the photos in Davidson's hands. "She never married, monsieur. You were her first, and her last. See how young and beautiful she looks, easily young enough to be my sister more than my mother. She has many close friends, of course, and her hotels are well known in Paris, as is her restaurant, which is one of the finest." He shrugged. "I believe, even now, she would walk away from all she has achieved to know you still think of her as you say you do. She loves you still."

The young man walked to the window and looked out over the city's panorama, surprised by the sudden exhaustion overtaking him.

"Despite the early hour, lad, I believe a stiff one is called for. Will you join me?"

"Yes, I will. Thank you." He turned to look at Davidson and saw the photograph of Big Earl on his desk. "I would suggest doubles, sir. It will help both of us."

"Will scotch do?"

"Straight, thank you. No ice."

"Spoken like a true Scot." Davidson handed his son a crystal glass.

"With your permission I will begin what I have come here to tell you, something even my mother does not yet know." He paused. "Perhaps she never will. I believe, as you soon will, my story will be too impossible for her to believe, or to accept. I have questioned myself a thousand times as to how I would begin my story which goes back many years and has many characters. Some of whom you know, and others you would never have suspected. My information has been well-researched and each event has been confirmed. When I am finished, I will leave you a copy of the full report." He swirled the scotch in his glass, taking a moment to look again at the photo on the desk. "I am sorry for the death of Big Earl, even more so that I can never speak of his passing to those who continue to think fondly of him. You may want to know that Jean-Philippe's body was never recovered from North Africa. My mother buried him one year after the war ended, beside his parents, in a grave that remains empty to this day."

Davidson raised his glass. "To Gabrielle, lad, and two very brave men."

"Yes, indeed, to three very brave people."

Father and son took their first sip.

"When she was eighteen my mother fell in love with the

only son of Jean-Pierre de-Montparnasse, a French Reformist, and his wife Suzanne-Amalie. You already know both Jean-Pierre and Suzanne-Amalie were executed by the Germans mere days after the invasion of France in 1940, alongside my maternal grandparents, and shortly after Jean-Philippe had left France to fight with De Gaulle's Free French with promises to return. Of course, he never did. His death was the end of a family and her dreams. You can imagine."

"I don't have to imagine. I remember vividly."

"She never gave up hope that the reports of his death were wrong, that one day he would walk through her door to be with her. However, the story does not end the day you walked through those doors, monsieur, if that is what you infer, rather the point at which the story begins in the year 1917, to be precise. A British Captain whose name was Perceval Howell III, by all accounts someone who considered the war as an interruption to other more entertaining pursuits, such as naïve young women, became a causality of the campaign during which the village of Messines, France was taken back from the Germans. His injuries were minor, still he was an officer and that status allowed him certain privileges such as choosing not to die with his men. He is the most repugnant of the characters in my story: a man of unenviable character and certainly known by many as a man who lacked even the smallest trace of courage. In any event, he spent several weeks convalescing, during which time he came to know a young and pretty French nurse, Antoinette de-Clèrcy, and it did not take the coxcomb and charming captain very long to cast his practiced spell over her. I know this in great detail by virtue of the fact that Madame de-Clércy is alive and well. I have met with her on more than one very enjoyable occasion. This so-called captain, whom I refer to out of strict necessity, is believed by Antoinette to have been killed in battle very near the end of the year. I have not seen the need to destroy her memories of him. The loathsome swine died a few years ago in England."

Davidson leaned forward. "I trust there is no insinuation there, lad."

"No, sir, there is not. In the spring of 1918 Antoinette gave birth. Imagine the shame she must have felt, the hardships she must have endured. It was 1918, without the openness or free-thinking we enjoy in the seventies. She was, in the eyes of many, no better than a street tramp, a whore, if I may say so. She is now seventy-five and in very good health. However back then she lived in disgrace and shame. Her life would have been ruined, and not hers alone, if she had not acted to do what she thought was right. Her first few months alone in Paris were very difficult, strained to say the least, with no work and no one to provide for her. She was reduced to begging in the streets and demeaning herself to earn meagre scraps of food or a few centimes, until the day she met a couple, a young couple who gave her food and treated her with kindness and dignity. That couple's name, monsieur, was de-Montparnasse and that day she courageously gave up part of her life and her soul. She regrets what she did to this very day, even though she had no choice."

Davidson sat on the edge of the window with his back to the city. "Does she know of his death, and the death of the de-Montparnasse couple?"

"She wept openly when I told her. Yes, she knows of both events."

"Does she know how much Gabrielle loved her son?"

"I told her I am certain he died very bravely, and knowing how deeply my mother loved him. She would not love anyone who was not." Jean-Alexandre moistened his mouth. "Still, Antoinette could not find work and soon she travelled to England. Her journey was difficult, mostly on foot, and took her several weeks because she had no money and relied on the scarce generosity of strangers. Eventually she found factory work, which never lasted more than a day or two. To them she was a foreigner, a Frog and a Frenchie. Men wanted her in their beds and women wanted her to leave. Her life had not changed at all, merely her venue. She had little to eat between menial jobs and what little she had she gave to another whose life, she knew, would otherwise soon come to a tragic end."

"Who was the poor thing caring for when she had so little for herself?"

"Only weeks after meeting Jean-Philippe and Suzanne-Amalie, her life was still so desperate. It's then that fate introduced her to another young couple who had gone to London to find work. Antoinette knew she was doing what was best for the baby, for Jean-Philippe's twin brother. In her heart she knew, despite her tears. The couple's name was Alexander, Jonathon and Bonnie Alexander. They later immigrated to Canada, when you were four years old." The young de–Saint-Valéry raised his glass. "May I suggest a toast to your mother's continued good health, monsieur, and to my grandmother? I have told her what I know of you and it is with the deepest regret that I am unable to tell my mother."

Davidson dropped his glass and stumbled forward, his eyes glazed and his face contorted with disbelief. He couldn't think, one thought erased another and he felt sick. He shook his head in denial, mumbling words he didn't hear.

"Good Lord…"

"Jean-Philippe was your twin brother, monsieur. There is no doubt whatsoever. Now you know why my mother's tray fell from her hands that night so many years ago. You were Jean-Philippe in every possible way, save your name." He paused. "Your name was to have been François de-Clércy, if you care to know. That is how Antoinette still remembers you. She cried as much to know you are well, as she did to know your brother is dead."

"None of this can be true. It must be complete fabrication," Davidson muttered in a daze.

"All that you have heard is true, and all of it has been documented for your later perusal. Though not all the story has been told." He looked into his empty glass. "Somehow coffee seems inappropriate, sir. May I bring you a fresh glass?"

Davidson nodded distractedly. His mind was working feverishly to understand. He pushed the palm of his hand flat against the intercom, telling Madame Dubuc to clear his agenda for the week and to refuse or redirect all calls without exception. He loosened his tie and faced into the soothing heat of the sun coming through the window. He took up the drink his son had put in front of him without looking at it and swallowed half the generous portion.

"My life has been wasted, completely and utterly wasted." He drained the glass. "When I went to war I loved no one more than my wife. She was all I ever dreamed about, all I ever spoke about. I'd felt alone all my life, feeling incomplete, feeling as though something had been taken from me that I'd never get back. Then my mother died. It was the greatest loss. I loved her dearly. It was then I met my wife and I thought I'd never be sad another day in my life. Then I went to war. I'd been fighting to stay alive for four years and killing many a man in the process. This one night, in October, Earl and I went into town to get drunk. I can't remember how long it had been since I'd slept in a warm barrack and not in a damp tent or thick mud. Anyway, it was the night I met Gabrielle. I scared the bloody daylights out of the poor girl and couldn't make any sense of it. I went back the next morning to succeed in making things much worse between us. As much as I tried, I couldn't stay away, knowing all the while it wasn't supposed to be, that she didn't want me there."

"She wears your ring faithfully on her finger, she has never removed it. Marie-Claude has also told me of a black silk robe. I should hate you, monsieur; instead I feel a deep sense of pity for you. What I have told you thus far has been the good news. There is more, and you have agreed to hear it all. May I continue?"

"What could possibly be worse than knowing you've wasted your entire life, to know you should have been with someone else? What?"

"Perhaps having someone, a stranger, confirm it to you. I suspect you have never spoken of my mother to your wife, Emily."

"You know her name?" Jean-Alexandre answered with a tilt of his head. "No, I never have. We made a promise to one another on our final day together before the war. I broke that promise with Gabrielle."

"We all break promises we cannot keep, monsieur, and you were not the first you break yours in this story. And we all have secrets. I now have a secret I must keep from my mother. You and your wife share a secret you have kept from your friends, that, like Antoinette de-Clércy, you gave away your two children, although you were not starving of hunger and living on the street. Your son, Theodore, had an unfortunate life as a child. His parents were abusive towards him. He was in trouble with the law, he ran away to sea in his teens and at twenty-three he went to Vietnam. I have lost track of him since his discharge and have no particular interest in knowing more of him than I do. It's all in the file. His current name is James Parker. Your daughter did better for herself. She's educated and lives well with her parents on the west coast, though she has not yet achieved much on her own in life. In short, I would say she's been spoiled. Her name is Helen North, if you're interested."

"You've done your homework, Jean-Alexandre. I can't deny that." Davidson looked stunned and beleaguered. "Where would I even begin to tell my wife? They were supposed to be sent to foster homes, not to be adopted. She's never forgiven me. It's the moment she began to hate me. To tell her after all these years and to explain a son from the war would devastate her."

"You stand corrected, sir: not a son from the war, a son from Gabrielle, my mother."

"I'm sorry. You know what I meant."

"Perhaps your wife, Emily, would welcome the revelation."

"Say what you mean, lad. This is no time for riddles."

Jean-Alexandre continued unperturbed. "Perhaps your wife would feel sufficient compassion towards you to confess her own burden, which she has carried for so many years, to tell you of her daughter Noëlyn. Perhaps the time has come for her to assuage her own conscience."

Davidson could only look at Jean-Alexandre with his mouth agape as a penetrating chill expelled the warmth of the sun from his body. He put his empty glass on the ledge and rubbed his haggard face. Jean-Alexandre continued matter-of-factly.

"Your wife gave birth to a baby girl in September of '43. The father was listed as unknown, though simple arithmetic would indicate the event was initiated at Christmas, while she was working at a munitions plant. She was released from her position soon after. I will let you decipher the child's name for yourself. For my part, I find the choice distasteful. Your wife kept the girl for two years, before selling her to an affluent family for 500 dollars, though it would appear not until she was quite certain you had survived the war. If you had not come back to her, monsieur, I have no doubt the girl's name would still be Noëlyn Ashton, not Noëlyn Daniels. She currently lives in New York. She's married to an investment banker several years her senior who has nurtured a rather expensive lifestyle, she has one child whom he did not father and she kept her maiden name when she married. Her father died recently of a heart attack. Her mother still lives somewhere out there, in this city."

He waved a hand across the cityscape.

Davidson looked at his watch. His head was pounding. Big Earl invaded his thinking and what his friend had said moments before his death. He had chosen the wrong home and had hurt the wrong woman. He had abandoned one son he had never known and had ruined the life of another. Then he thought of Emily, that day on the tram, the first day he had seen her in five years and his crystal glass exploded against the wall. A second later the intercom buzzed.

"I'm fine, Bernie. Thank you for checking in on me. I was just being a little clumsy. Delegate all my appointments to the appropriate department head until further notice and tell McAllister I want to see him this afternoon. I'll advise him when, but he's to clear his agenda and remain available to me."

His son walked back to the leather armchairs. He remained standing.

"I am at your disposal for the rest of the day and evening, sir, unless you have other commitments. I doubt whether you care very much about your adoptive father. He wasn't much of man to do what he did to his wife, and no better than Howell. The fact is, there is no information at all as to whether he's alive or dead. He simply disappeared the day he walked out."

"Then he's dead, and good riddance to the filthy bugger."

"There is more I would like to tell you about my mother, Henri and Gérard. Perhaps I might do so over lunch, if you would care to be my guest, or perhaps at dinner if your afternoon is booked."

Jean-Alexandre saw a man whose life he had shattered in the short time they had been together. When there was no response he reached for a thick file folder in his attaché.

"This is the complete file, as I have promised, complete with names, addresses and much more than I have told you. I have said enough, and have accomplished what I have come here to do. It was interesting meeting you. Thank you." He closed his case and walked to the doors before turning. "One last question, if I may." Davidson nodded. "Would you have gone back to her? Would you have stayed with my mother had you heard her voice calling after you from her window that night?"

"Yes, lad. There's no doubt. And if the MPs hadn't come to me on the corner there's no doubt I would have run back to her."

The young man closed his eyes and pursed his lips. "Then I leave you with your memories of what might have been, monsieur. Good day."

"Jean-Alexandre," Davidson called out "one moment."

"Sir?"

"Tell Bernie where you're staying. My car will arrive for you at six."

The young man's smile was thin, his nod discreet. "I will. Thank you once again."

The door closed quietly and Davidson collapsed into the leather chair across from the one where his son had dropped the file. Moments later Bernadette Dubuc walked in.

"Arrangements have been made for a private dinner at the club, Davidson. Would you like some lunch?"

"No, Bernie. Pour me a scotch, a bloody big one and tell McAllister to be here within the hour." He opened the file. "Also, phone Emily. Tell her I'll not be home tonight and then book me a room downtown at a different hotel from the lad's. When you're done doing all that I need a favour of you, a mother's touch if you don't mind."

33

By 4:00 PM his meeting with McAllister had concluded, he had changed for the evening and by six o'clock Jean-Alexandre was stepping into his limo. The men seemed like casual business associates more than father and son and Jean-Alexandre did most of the talking as Davidson hung on his every word.

Gabrielle still owned L'Auberge-de-la-Plus-Belle-Gitane and two five-star hotels she which co-owned with Marie-Claude. Her restaurant was L'Assiette Élégante, which was as elegant as the name implied and counted amongst the most talked about in Paris. There were photos for him to see from each missed year and copies for him to keep. He saw his son and Gérard grow to be young men and Henri grow old. There were pictures of Gabrielle, Marie-Claude, La Plus Belle that had not changed and several of Davidson's mother, Antoinette de-Clércy, sitting with his son. The last page of the last album was a candid photograph of Gabrielle placing flowers over his twin brother's final resting place.

Jean-Alexandre accepted his father's offer to drive him to the airport the next morning, though he insisted he would walk back alone to his hotel after dinner. He needed the air, they both did. Davidson spent the night studying the details of each photo, remembering and crying until his eyes stung. Gabrielle at fifty-one looked no older than her mid-thirties and was as beautiful as he remembered. There were a thousand expressions in her photos, in her eyes, and he had forgotten none of them. It was as though he could talk to her and more than once he looked over to the phone.

He had not gone to bed and hadn't slept. When he left the hotel the following morning he had not eaten and wouldn't until having dinner alone that evening before going to the house on Fleetwood Drive. Late morning, when Jean-Alexandre joined him, the mood in the limo was solemn, neither man really knowing what to say. What could be said without frail promises? He told his son how much he loved Gabrielle, when he wanted to tell her himself. What he felt for his son was pride, not love. What was happening was all too new for false emotion and they both knew it was also too late. He wanted Henri and Gérard to know they had never been forgotten, as he had not been forgotten by them, knowing full-well they would never be told. All he could do was to hold out the box wrapped in silver paper as they slowed into the Departures lane of the airport and hope the young man would not refuse his gift.

"Happy birthday to you, Jean-Alexandre. I hope one day you'll think well of me. I'm proud of you, albeit much too late to say so. You'll grow to be a fine criminal lawyer one day, one of the finest in France. I've no doubt of that." His son took the box with some hesitation. "I'll leave it to you to explain the gift, if you don't toss it away once I leave you, though I wouldn't blame you at all if you did."

"This was not necessary, sir."

"Yes, it was."

"May I open it?"

"Aye, it would please me very much if you did. Take your time. The police never question limousines. They seem to always believe the passengers inside might damage their advancement up the ranks."

Jean-Alexandre opened the box, his eyes once more showing more expression than his face. "Sir, your gift is not appropriate. It is far too extravagant."

"Divided by twenty-seven and a law degree it's far too inadequate, and don't think I don't know it. Take care of her, lad. I won't ask you to have faith in me. I don't deserve your good opinion. All I can ask of you at the moment is to believe me when I say there's no person on earth who'll ever love her more."

His son slipped the gold Rolex onto his wrist. The blue face glittered under the crystal.

"Thank you. It will always give me a time to remember, so to speak." He paused for a long moment, holding up a hand when Davidson went to talk. "Sir, yesterday I mentioned how we all break promises and none are free from the guilt of telling lies. Do you remember?"

"I do very clearly."

"I lied to my mother, by making her believe my true destination was England and I have since lied to you in order not to betray her trust. I wish to correct that lie before I leave you, and by doing so I shall be breaking a recent promise made to my mother, though I do so with a clear conscience."

He turned his head, looking deep into his father's stern, unblinking eyes.

"What was that, lad?"

"Not to tell anyone she's dying."

34

The conversation went on for thirty more minutes before both men shook hands and Davidson returned to his office. He had not thought of Emily once since McAllister had left him the day before, when he couldn't take his eyes from the pages of the extensive report or stop thinking of the time he had walked through the bathroom door after knocking and she had thrown a towel at him, screaming. Lovemaking had never been erotic with Emily, never exciting with her and he remembered how, after their first time together, he had thought back to the last evening he had spent with Gabrielle on the cushions by the fireplace, the burning logs and their heated passion.

He was furious with Emily and felt deeply betrayed by her, but the reasons for those emotions were unimportant to him. All he could think about was Gabrielle and what he had done to her. He ordered dinner without looking at the menu and when he finished the meal his car was waiting for him outside the lobby of the club.

The mansion sitting atop Fleetwood Drive overlooked the city, though he hadn't really taken time to appreciate the view in years. Emily was there to meet him at the door, not surprised that he didn't kiss her. She stepped back into the entrance as he walked past her and put down his briefcase, leaving the chauffeur to drop off his valise and close the door behind him as he left.

"Was your trip a success, Davidson?"

"There was no trip, Emily. I had dinner with an unexpected guest from out of town and I chose to stay at a hotel." He turned his back to her. "I would appreciate a drink in the front room. I'll join you momentarily. It's been quite an interesting two days and I would like very much to share them with you." He took up his valise and started up the stairs. "I'll be a very few moments, and would like that drink."

"Yes, of course. I'll see to it right away."

Davidson did nothing more than throw the suitcase on his bed, open his briefcase to retrieve the file, and spend a few moments to calm himself before joining Emily who had just finished pouring a glass of wine for herself.

"Please sit down Emily. What I have to say will be paradoxically easy and difficult for me. What I need from you is not to interrupt me until I'm done. Do you understand me?" She nodded her head in agreement, blushing involuntarily and surprised by his tone. "When I was stationed in France, in '44, I met a woman, a very young and very beautiful woman. Her name was Gabrielle. I should have walked away from her the very first moment I saw her because I had frightened her badly. The next day she told me why, before begging me again to stay away and she meant it. Suffice it to say, I didn't. She sincerely wanted me to stay away because she had recently lost the man she was to marry. He'd been killed and I bore more than a slight resemblance to him. Anyway, we became lovers. The affair didn't last long because it couldn't. We were marching to Belgium. I'll make no excuses for what I did. Suffice it to say I've just discovered I have a son. He came to see me yesterday. He's twenty-seven."

Emily sat poised on the couch. Her dry eyes were filled with animosity and disgust.

"Was she the only one you had in all those years?"

"Yes."

"Really, and you expect me to believe you?" she retorted with a curt laugh.

"I don't bloody care if you do, Emily, and I didn't have her. I was with her."

"Were you in love with her?"

"I never said those words to her and she never once spoke them to me. We each believed the other had their own reasons to be with the other. But, yes, I was in love with her."

"And now you're telling me you regret it because someone telling you he's your son has come looking for something?"

"No, that's not what I'm saying. And I don't regret it."

"So you regret me," she accused tersely.

"It's not been easy between us for some time, Emily. We're not even like brother and sister. We've become more like distant cousins. When I came back I did so to marry the woman I loved, you. But it was someone else I married. I made a choice as I stood on the docks before boarding the ship, a difficult choice, to come home to you, Emily." He swirled his drink. "You know as well as I do, you've always known how much better things would have been if I hadn't come back, if I'd stayed there."

"That's cruel, and unwarranted. I counted each of those long days and spent my nights writing letters."

"Perhaps so, though it's neither cruel nor unwarranted. And you know it. The day Earl was shot I might just as well have been the target, we were that close. If the German bugger had even taken a breath or blinked, I might have been the dead one."

"My mother said you'd do something like that. She told me every day and I never believed her. I believed in you."

"Your mother's best off where she is. So I'd be grateful if you were to leave her out of it."

"Perhaps you should have stayed, and not come home."

"I had dreams, ambitions, things I wanted to

accomplish, then so many things went wrong in so short a time and I saw it all being thrown away. That's why I asked you to give up the children. What happened to them was a dreadful mistake, and you know that as well. I never intended for events to turn out the way they did, and I'll bear the guilt alone if you won't share it with me. You'd not have had this fine life of yours if we had kept them. You'd be wearing housedresses, washing your own dishes and doing your own cleaning. I told you two years, and I did what I thought was my best to bring them home. I'll always regret that my best efforts were not good enough."

"We both will."

"Aye, we both will. Still, what's done is done."

"You should have kept this to yourself, Davidson. I can't see why you would have thought to tell me this after all these years. What does he want, money?"

"He wants nothing, it's quite the opposite. The young man's invested a good deal of time and money to find out about me. When I offered to reimburse him, he refused outright. There is no hidden agenda, nor malice. He came to tell me a story, nothing more, a very fascinating story indeed, which is contained in this folder and begins with the reason Gabrielle was so terrified the first time I saw her. The man who Gabrielle had intended to have as her husband was my twin brother. To her, Emily, I was a man come back from the grave. It seems I was also adopted, given away. My real mother is still alive in France."

"And you believed him?"

"Aye, I did."

"It's preposterous. You know who your parents were."

He sipped his scotch. "Emily, during his investigations he also discovered the twins. His file is very complete, shockingly so."

Emily leaned forward. "Has he spoken with them?"

"No, he hasn't."

"What did he tell you about them? Have they done

well?"

Davidson nodded. "Katie, yes, she's on the west coast. Theo wasn't as fortunate, though he's found his own way. It's in the file. I'm sure he'll do well for himself. He's strong and he's a fighter."

Davidson brought the snifter to his mouth, watching Emily's eyes still burning with hate as he swallowed, pausing as long as he could for affect. "He's found all the children, Emily, including yours. Your daughter Noëlyn lives in New York. She's done quite well for herself and, clearly, I must admit to a certain, morbid curiosity. What did your dear mother have to say about that during the two years you kept the girl under her puritan's roof?"

Emily stiffened, inhaling a sharp breath through her nose. She suddenly felt cold, yet her face reddened and her heart all but stopped. When she spoke she did so slowly, not wanting to stumble or use the wrong word.

"She wanted me to have an abortion. She said losing the baby would be a small price to pay. I didn't, because I didn't want to risk ruining my health and our future together. Then, when she was born, my mother wanted me to give her up."

Davidson sipped his scotch patiently, watching her eyes glaze over and her throat worked to lessen the sudden dryness.

"And you didn't, at least not until you knew whether or not some German had done his job. You didn't want me back, did you? I should have stayed away and you would have been all the happier for it."

"Don't stand there being so superior. We're both guilty of the same thing, as well as lying about it."

"Do you think so, Emily? Do you really? Do you really think opening your virgin legs as a party favour is the same as having fucking bullets flying around your head while you're kneeling waist-deep in shit and pissed-filled water? I don't think it's at all the same as fucking at a party."

Emily clasped her hands together, not trusting herself to reach for her glass. "It was only one night, Davidson. I made a mistake because I was lonely. I can't even remember how or when. It all happened so fast and was so long ago."

"I don't give a bugger's damn, Emily. It happened, and I have no interest in hearing your mournful laments."

She hesitated. "Do you know how she is?"

"I don't care a bloody hell how she is. There's no need for me to know. Two years Emily, two years of sweet words and sharing our dreams and all the while you were nursing another's brat and waiting for me to take a bullet. You should have told me, Emily."

"You're not without guilt."

"Aye, I agree. I broke my promise to you. Still, I didn't know of a son, which is not the same as keeping another man's child for so long in the hope I'd not come back, knowing full-well there was only one reason I wouldn't. It makes me sick to think what we did to Katie and Theo for no other reason than our own success. It was a very fine act you put on as a virgin bride our first night together, Emily. Do you ever think back to it?"

"It doesn't matter. It's been too long." She reached for her glass. "That doesn't mean we still can't help the children."

"No, we won't, neither one of us. The twins have their own lives, which we have no right to upset and the other two have no need of us, not now. They'll make their own way in the world, as we did, for better or worse. Do you remember those words, Emily?" His expression changed to a sardonic smirk. "By the way, you're a grandmother. Her name's Jodie. She's two years old. Congratulations."

"Noëlyn's?"

"Yes, though you needn't worry unduly. Both her other grannies are still alive. I doubt she's lacking any attention."

Emily's tears began slowly. "You're enjoying this."

"No, I'm not. I want done with it, Emily." Davidson stood to fill his glass. "I'm taking a vacation, Emily, a very long one."

"Do I have to ask where?"

"No, you don't."

"How long will you be gone?"

"I don't know."

"Do you intend to come back?"

"Gabrielle's dying Emily. She'll not die thinking the worst of me. When the time comes, I'll be with her. I was wrong to leave you to fight a hideous war that you'll never know the real tragedy of, and I was wrong to do what I did to her and leave her alone. You and I have lied to each other, Emily, and together we've done a terrible thing to our own children. Gabrielle's done nothing but love one man and try to forget another. I don't know whether I'll come back, I really don't. And what does it matter? We can't ever go back. There's no point. What memories we thought we might have are all gone. They've changed to regret for what each of us has done and disappointment in each other. The events took place a long time ago, Emily, yet the wounds are recent and very deep."

"Should I expect a divorce?"

"McAllister's drawing up the papers for you to sign. He'll come by tomorrow morning if that's convenient to you. You'll get fifty percent of everything, excluding personal investments, which I believe you will agree is very generous given what we know."

"I suppose you'll buy out my shares?"

"No, I won't. We'll each keep our own. I've already initiated the sale of the company and the club. When the transaction is completed I'll step down. I want nothing more to do with it. You'll be given half of that as well, if you don't contest."

"I won't." Emily chortled, after a long pause. "So, Davidson, I finally get to have my cottage by the sea."

"You'll have whatever you want by the sea, Emily. You've just become an extremely wealthy woman."

35

Jean-Alexandre grinned expectantly when his secretary walked into his office to say with almost girlish excitement that a birthday gift had been delivered to him. She asked eagerly if she could bring it in for him as though she was the one who would read the card and tear at the ribbons and paper. He said yes, thinking Gérard had put her up to something mischievous as usual. She ran from the room like a giddy schoolgirl and when she came back through the door Jean-Alexandre could not have been more taken aback.

The man on her arm bowed to her and kissed her hand, before she left them to run to tell someone, anyone about the visitor.

"I trust I'm not here at an inappropriate time, Maître de-Saint-Valéry?" he asked.

"No, sir, though I must admit your arrival is more than somewhat unexpected."

"I imagine so, Jean-Alexandre."

"I left you just yesterday, monsieur. I don't know what to say."

"Then imagine how I feel." Davidson looked around the office that appeared more like a library. "Tell me, do officers of the French court store their fine liquor anywhere close at hand?"

"Yes, they do, sir. Will scotch do? Straight, no ice?"

"Aye, that will do very nicely, but I don't have much time to sit and talk with you about it."

Jean-Alexander nodded, thinking he knew. "A brief vacation to ease a troubled mind."

"No, lad, I'm here to stay and what I need most from you at the moment is to know where she is and how to get there." He put up a warning finger. "And she's not to know about my being here."

"To stay," Jean-Alexandre's brow arched inquisitively, "you mean an extended vacation?"

"I mean to stay with her, if she'll have me, for as long as we can be together." Jean-Alexandre poured their drinks, doing his best to maintain his composure. "Would you mind terribly, lad, if your mother were not to attend your birthday party and Gérard's. I'm thinking she might have other plans, though I can't say with any certainty at the moment."

"I would have reason to reprimand her severely if she dared to show herself, very severely." His voice was gleeful and his eyes beamed.

Davidson studied the office walls. "To much success in your career, Jean-Alexandre, and to your mother. May she not have a weapon too readily at hand when we meet. It wouldn't be the first time and she's not one to hide her emotions. Are you quite certain she'll not want to kill me?"

"Those closest to me call me Alex, sir. And her eyes are what I remember fearing the most as a child, and often enough in the present."

"Aye, those damned unblinking green jewels. Get me to her, Alex."

"She's always at her restaurant at this hour. I'll call." He took up the receiver. "Where are you staying? I'll arrange for a suite at Les Fontaines and the transference of your luggage."

"I'm there already, lad, though I left my bags with the concierge. I was a bit eager to be on my way."

"The restaurant is less than a block from there."

He chuckled and spoke for a moment into the phone before being transferred to the restaurant to tell his mother the plans for the evening had changed. He would meet her at her office at Les Fontaines, and from there they would drive to his party at La Plus Belle.

"You have stolen my day, monsieur, and I thank you." He raised his cuff. "It keeps perfect time, though I must confess it is not my best birthday gift."

"I'd prefer Davidson. I won't leave her twice lad, not if she still wants me."

"So, Davidson, how will we do this? First I must sneak you into the hotel. Her green eyes are everywhere. She's like a hawk. She misses nothing. As you have heard, your bags will be in your suite and the concierge will ensure your clothes are presentable before we arrive." He chortled. "Gérard and Henri will understand, once I tell them, but I will wait until they have had too much to drink and are angry with her for not sharing you with them. Come."

The drive through snarled Paris traffic was long and came to an end too soon for both men who worked at perfecting their conspiracy. The valet had the car gone within seconds and the concierge was waiting for them alongside the doorman. Everything had been laid out perfectly in his room by the concierge, and by the time Davidson turned on the shower Jean-Alexandre was already walking through the door of his mother's office.

"Mama, you look more divine than an angel," was all he could say without giving himself away.

"Thank you, darling. I wore it for you because I know it's your favourite on me."

"You're enchanting."

"And you're incorrigible."

"Come, mama. I have a surprise. It has been too long since I have treated you to something special. My birthday has much to do with you, after all." He took her hands and guided her from behind her desk. "Tonight is also your night, as much as mine, and you will not argue with me. Come. You will enjoy an hour of relaxed luxury in the spa and the hair salon has made place for you. Then we shall go to the boutique and you shall have the most beautiful dress."

"You are not a rich lawyer yet, darling. Thank you. I'm fine as I am."

"No one is more beautiful than you, mama, though I must confess that I am doing this for myself with complete selfishness. It will make me happy on my birthday to know I have done such a little thing for you. You cannot refuse me on my birthday."

"I have work to do, you silly boy. Go now, and leave me to it."

"Your work is finished for the day, mama," he insisted. "Come."
*

Davidson was dressed and pacing his room like a nervous schoolboy, not wanting to sit down for fear he would crease his pants and not drinking because he wanted to be perfect for her. He looked good, though he didn't think so. He was in better shape than men half his age, his stomach was flat, his body toned and his hair was as black and as full as the day he had walked away from her. He thought the phone would never ring. When it did, he jumped back.

Eighteen floors below Jean-Alexandre excused himself, telling his mother he would be back soon to escort her to the car. Moments later a discreet knock came to her door.

"Madame, I am sorry to intrude."

"What is it, Claude?"

The maître d' walked in holding a dome-covered silver tray. "Madame, may I say how heavenly you look? You are a divine image this evening, as you are every evening."

"It seems the men around me are very gallant today, Claude. Thank you for noticing. It is a gift from my very extravagant son. He is being very silly today."

"And you are our gift from heaven, madame."

She giggled. "Thank you, Claude. Now, what is it you

need?"

"There is a man, madame, in the dining room. He wishes to speak with you about the meal."

"Claude, you are the maître d'. Our dinner guests are your responsibility."

"Indeed, madame, however he insists that he speak with you alone. At this very moment he is enjoying our best wine with your compliments. Still, he insists."

"What was wrong with his meal?"

"There was nothing wrong with his meal, madame. He has not yet ordered. He simply waits for you to join him" Claude held out the silver tray, lifting the dome. "It is from the gentleman, madame, with his compliments."

Gabrielle stared at the little box before taking it in her hands as Claude moved the tray closer. When she finally opened it, she gasped. "Claude, what kind of joke is this? Who put you up to this?"

"Madame, the gentleman wishes to know whether he might have his own ring back, the one on your finger, and whether there is any hope that you might be his bride." Claude paused, trying to contain his own mounting excitement. "What do you wish me to tell him, madame?"

Gabrielle blanched, grasping the little box in trembling hands. "Claude, this man, what does he look like?"

"Madame, I believe him to be the gentleman in the photo on your desk. He seems to be very charming for a foreigner."

Seeing his mother running so quickly down the corridor from her office towards the restaurant Jean-Alexandre knew he had done the right thing. He leaned back against a marble pillar, an irrepressible air of self-satisfaction conquering any effort to appear innocent.

"Alex, what have you done?" She pleaded, completely beside herself with panic and joy, grabbing his arm. "What ridiculous and crazy thing have you done, you silly man?"

Jean-Alexandre brought his mother in close. Not once in

his life had he seen such an expression on her face: a look of fear mixed with excitement and confusion.

"I have done nothing, mama," he whispered, stroking her hair reassuringly, "and all he knows is that you have never stopped loving him. Tell me if it is not true, and I will undo what I know you truly want, what your heart truly desires. He knows nothing, mama. Do not be afraid. He is here because he wants to be. I like him, mama. I like him very much." He cupped her face in his hands. "Mama, this time you must say what you mean. Go to him. You have been apart long enough, too long. Go. You will not be disappointed in what you see and do not make me regret my lavish gifts." He took Gabrielle by her shoulders easing her tenderly away. "You are ravishing. Now go to him, run to him."

Gabrielle slowed to a stop at the hostess' lighted lectern. Her heart was pounding and her legs were barely able to support her, her mind refusing to believe what she saw standing before her. She shrank back, smothering a shriek with both hands. He looked so elegant and sophisticated. He was beautiful and younger than she had ever imagined in any of her nightly dreams. She stood there, frozen, watching him until the young hostess whispered: "Allez vite, madame. He has not stopped fidgeting for a moment. Go to him."

She knew. They all knew.

Davidson lowered his arms and hands from the plaintive stance he had taken, not knowing how else so stand. He stood by his table as she came at him in a whirlwind of hair and silk, the hem of her cocktail slip rising and falling around her thighs, bracing himself against the impact well before her feet left the ground and her arms clung to his neck. She was still the most spectacular woman in all of France and, as fluent as he was in French, he understood not a word she was saying.

Jean-Alexandre had trailed nonchalantly behind his

mother. The soft collision was all he had to see before he turned to leave them alone. He gave a contented thumbs up to the maître d' and concierge and was completely oblivious to the admiring eyes of the pretty young hostess who thought she had never seen such a handsome and chivalrous young man.

Chantal DeNeuve was oblivious herself, to the two older men who had noticed her captivated gaze and had followed it to the back of the young man disappearing around the corner. It was her first day of work at the hotel and did not realize the two men standing at her lectern had, at that very moment, decided her destiny with yet another conspiratorial handshake before turning their attention back to Gabrielle and Davidson.

"Might I interpret whatever it is you're saying as a yes, darling Gabrielle?"

She plastered his face with images of her muted red lips, her own face streaking with dark rivulets of tears. "I love you, Davidson. I love you, mon amour, my darling. I have never stopped loving you."

"That certainly sounds like a yes. I love you, Gabrielle, as deeply as ever, though would you mind not strangling me before the wedding. And might I now have my ring back? You've had it a good while."

She couldn't speak. She shook her head in a definite no, loosening her grip on his neck and when he set her down she wrapped her arms around his waist and buried her face into his chest to hide her tears and stain his shirt.

There was no meal, only a bottle of the hotel's finest wine and a platter of their finest cheeses delivered to his suite, compliments of their son. They spoke for hours as though they had never been apart, and he kissed her a hundred times. They made love with the passion of their youth, satisfying unwanted interludes with tender caresses until their passion reignited over and over again. At nine o'clock the next morning Gabrielle called down to the front desk to ask why their breakfast had not yet been delivered. The excited clerk transferred the call. There would be no room service, she was told by Henri. Their table had been set in the dining room and they were expected.

Davidson tried to persuade her to change her mind. The last thing he wanted to do was share her with a restaurant full of strangers, he insisted. Then suddenly Gabrielle's brow knit into frustrated lines, when she realized her predicament which was causing Davidson to double over on the bed with laughter. She had nothing to wear and had to call the Housekeeping Manager to bring her a change of clothes from her private suite. She begged Davidson to answer the door.

He didn't. He refused steadfastly with a long-lost glint in his eyes. She called him a stupid man, and when she opened the door, wrapped in a bath towel, he called out to ask where she had put his pants. Her pink glow deepened to beet-red when the woman at the door winked and told her how all the other women in the hotel were envious of her for having such a debonair and handsome lover, adding that she would be pleased to help them look for his pants. She walked away giggling and by the time Gabrielle had closed the door Davidson had already dressed and was sitting in a chair to watch her dress. When she had finished, he stood. She could see how his expression had changed.

"Sweet thing, I've something to tell you before we go down. Can we talk?"

"Yes, of course. What is it, mon amour?"

"Our son came to see me in Montreal, you know that."

"It is not the first time he has misled me, but it does no good to scold him. He is too much like you. He never listens. Once he has something in his head he listens to no one, not even me. He has always been very protective of me."

"Aye, and I'm glad for it, when I should have been here to protect you. I have much to be sorry for, Gabrielle, a great deal. Though what I have to say now is much more important. Come, sit here beside me and take my hand."

"You already have my answer, my darling. It's yes."

"And there's not a happier man anywhere. But Gabrielle, before we go down there's something you have to know. Jean-Alexandre and I have agreed I should be the one to tell you."

Gabrielle sat on the edge of the bed, thinking the worst, thinking her son had been foolish enough to betray a trust and suddenly felt her joy escape her. Her sick heart was racing, thinking of what he was about to say.

"What is it, Davidson? You know that you can tell me anything."

"That first night, darling," he began, "you dropped your dishes and you screamed, and the morning after when you showed me your locket and told me never to come back to you because seeing me was too painful a reminder of Jean-Philippe. Do you remember?"

"How could I not? I hated you so much, mon amour, without knowing how much I would soon love you. As I have said, our son inherits it from you."

"Gabrielle, the resemblance I shared with Jean-Philippe was no coincidence. Your Jean-Philippe, the man you loved so dearly, was my brother … my twin brother. Our mother still lives on the outskirts of Paris. It seems we were each given up at the end of the first war to different families. That's why I scared you so, sweet thing" Davidson gently squeezed her hands. "Our son's research was shockingly complete. If he had not come to see me, I would never have known. Be proud of the lad, sweet thing. Don't be angry with him."

She shook her head. "No, Davidson. What you are saying cannot be possible."

"Yes, darling. It's the truth. There is no mistake. I'm sure of it. We're both sure of it." He pulled her closer, feeling her body shudder.

"I loved your brother, Davidson?"

"Yes, you did, and now you love his. I'm certain our son would have told you, had I not come back to you." Davidson stood. "I still don't believe it myself, so don't hurry to comprehend the unfathomable."

Nothing was said between them until eventually Gabrielle pushed herself from the bed and wrapped her arms around him.

"I have visited with him many times, and many times I have been to La Falaise to remember both of you. It is Jean-Philippe who has brought you back to me, Davidson, not our son. He was only the messenger. That is what I know...what I will always believe." He squeezed her, saying nothing. "Darling," she whispered, "we must go now. They are waiting for us."

"And who would that be, sweet thing?"

"Who do you think, you stupid man?" She kissed him. "All of them."

36

Walking into the restaurant, Davidson's eyes blurred with heartfelt tears. Henri had commandeered the kitchen to make the couple his finest breakfast, Gérard rushed to shake his hand and Marie-Claude squeezed between them to hug him as though he had been her brother all along. Jean-Alexandre had told her how Jean-Philippe had been adopted. She didn't care. Jean-Philippe would always be her brother, as would Davidson. When they all heard about Big Earl, and how he had died so soon after knowing them, they wept for him.

Henri wiped the back of his hand across his reddened eyes and left the table. When he came back he was at the head of a procession of waiters, with two of Gabrielle's most expensive bottles of champagne. She rolled her eyes and expelled an exasperated sigh, telling Davidson loudly enough for everyone to hear that Henri had never changed, that she should have fired him one morning when he was so pathetic, or smacked his head between her pots instead of making him head chef of her premier restaurant.

The first toast was to Davidson and the couple, the second was to Big Earl and Gabrielle admonished Henri not to have a headache later in the day. The third was to Jean-Alexandre, made by his father. In the afternoon their son drove them to see a flustered Antoinette de Clèrcy who had endless questions and so many regrets. She lived in a small but comfortable cottage on a pension from the hospital where she had worked until ten years before. She served tea in the garden and made very clear to her son that she would never think of moving from her home. Nevertheless, on their way back to Paris, Davidson instructed his Jean-Alexandre to make enquiries at her bank and to tell them to expect a sizeable deposit from a corporation in Montreal. Antoinette de Clèrcy would live out her life free of mundane worries.

Arriving before dusk, they drove to Gabrielle's home where she changed for dinner as the two men exchanged more questions and answers. When she joined them she was striking and still every bit the gypsy who had once walked down the steps of La Plus Belle, when she had ignored him as she walked passed him on her way to the door. As youthful as she had looked in Jean-Alexandre's photos, she now looked even younger with an aura her son had never seen. She wanted to stay there with Davidson, in her home, to love him, but they could not and she blushed like a teenager at her son's snicker when Davidson reminded her he had not slept since leaving Montreal. She scolded both men for their foolishness. She felt strange speaking with Davidson in French and it was one of those times she slipped into English.

Jean-Alexandre tapped his new watch for Gabrielle to see, reminding them Henri had insisted they dine at her l'Assiette Élégante where he would personally prepare their meal, and Davidson had yet to change. Even the busiest employee at the hotel stopped what they were doing to watch the couple stroll through the lobby hand in hand. They had never seen their boss in the company of a man and Gabrielle felt her cheeks explode with colour at seeing their smiles as he tugged her into the elevator. She wanted to wait for him in her office, but he had other ideas and she knew everyone in the lobby knew what those ideas were. Once inside, she punched him and when he picked her up like a doll she punched him again, telling him about the tiny lens in the ceiling. He didn't care. He wanted to kiss her, and he did for eighteen floors.

Her staff at l'Assiette Élégante was no less indiscreet, waiting anxiously to see the man who had come back to her after so many years, and she scolded Henri once again for being such an old gossip. He ignored her with a patronizing tap on her shoulder and threw his arms around his old friend. Until then Gabrielle had eaten only the occasional meal in the restaurant's kitchen. Her staff had never served her and she didn't like the effusive attention or Davidson's teasing grin each time a waiter or the maître d' went out of their way to make her feel special.

Later they fell asleep as they murmured tender words against each other's lips. The next morning they woke with the sun, each one startled to see the other naked and still locked into each other's arms as though the previous day had been a dream too wonderful to be true. Gabrielle gasped, waking him, and Davidson jerked involuntarily, bumping their heads before smothering her with more kisses.

He asked to have the morning alone. There were details he had to attend to, not the least of which was arranging for a transfer of funds to his mother's French bank. When he saw the look in her eyes he kissed her cheek and propped himself on one elbow to tell her all about the beautiful woman he was going to call, teasing her at first, before telling her of Big Earl's Shimmering Moon, the old Indian woman, and why he had to call her.

Lilly listened intently to her friend ramble on like a love struck adolescent, happy for him. Emily had not called her and Lilly doubted she ever would. She had always been Davidson's friend and confidante more than Emily's. They spoke for an hour or more and Davidson promised to call her soon after with the date, understanding yet disappointed when Lilly gracefully declined the honour of being his best man. When they were finished he called McAllister who told him Emily had signed the papers. There would be no contest and McAllister would work as quickly as possible to finalize the divorce proceedings. With well-placed contacts at court Davidson could expect full closure by mid-September at the very latest.

McAllister transferred his call to Bernadette Dubuc and they spoke for another hour as he scribbled notes into his agenda and verified dates. When he ended the call he was ecstatic and anxious to tell Gabrielle the wedding could be as early as the end of September, subsequent to their trip to Montreal.

When they arrived in Montreal at the end of August, Lilly was at the airport to greet them and both women shunned him immediately for his childish sense of humour. Gabrielle had been expecting to see an old woman wearing moccasins and wrapped in a thick woven blanket with braided hair, feathers and henna facial markings on roughened skin. What she saw was a beautiful woman with long, silky black hair and flawless amber skin. She was wearing desert boots, khaki shorts with ankle socks and a denim shirt with the sleeves rolled up and holding a dozen red carnations that she knew were Gabrielle's favourite flower. By the end of the day the women were more like sisters than strangers and Davidson was still in the dog house.

When Gabrielle had begun to argue that a taxi would do just as well as a limo to get them to the hotel, and that she didn't need a limo to make her feel any more special, they chuckled at her reaction when the chauffeur stepped forward to call Davidson by name and metaphorically welcome him home.

McAllister had already negotiated the sale of the hillside mansion and Madame Dubuc had leased an exclusive pied à terre to meet his needs for the next several months, as well as seeing to the transfer of his personal possessions to the newly furnished apartment and Paris.

He had told Gabrielle about his business, characteristically understating his success, though not until she saw his corporate offices and the extent of his existing and future projects did she realize what he was sacrificing to be with her. Davidson put an end to her doubts abruptly with a firm finger pressed to her lips. He could live the rest of his life without limousines and private clubs, not without her. Inwardly she knew differently. She knew he could never leave it all behind.

They stayed for three weeks and went to the High North with Lilly to see her work. Gabrielle ate caribou and white-tailed deer and listened without understanding a word as Shimmering Moon noted ancient recipes described by tribal elders which Gabrielle would be the first to serve to the ever-pretentious elite of Paris. She saw the oldest walled city in North America riding in a calèche through the streets of Le Vieux-Québec. She was in love and she cried happy tears each day. She had girls' days with Lilly when Davidson had business to attend to and what she learned about the man she was about to marry fascinated her. She learned how he fussed over Lilly and had become a brother to her, doting over her to where Lilly would often have to put him in his place, despite loving every moment with him.

Gabrielle told Lilly about the times she remembered with Big Earl, the day they had brought her the mattress and filled her bistro with carbon monoxide, how she had yelled at them both and how Henri had run out into the pouring rain to scream at them. They laughed and cried together like sisters and late one afternoon Lilly put a hand to Gabrielle's cheek and asked her what was wrong.

Lilly replied: "There is nothing he has to know, Gabrielle. He knows everything. He has also confided in me. All you need to know is that you are all he wants in life, for as long as he can be with you. There is no reason to be afraid"

"Jean-Alexandre has told him."

Lilly nodded. "Yes, of course. Would you expect otherwise? You are his mother and Davidson his father. He did what was right, a secret you must keep from him. He would be deeply hurt to know you have discovered the truth."

"That is why Davidson came back to me."

"No, it is not, and do not even think such foolishness. Jean-Alexandre waited judiciously to reveal the truth until moments before boarding his plane, until he was certain of his father, the day after Davidson had already made his decision to find you."

"He should not have come back."

Lilly shook her head. "He should never have left you. It has haunted him for years. It's the first time I have seen him not pretend to be at peace. He will take care of you, if you let him. You need not question how much he loves you."

When the day came to leave, the women hugged each other tightly and Lilly punched Davidson in the stomach when he gave her the return airline ticket and the confirmation for her stay at Gabrielle's Les Fontaines. The women cried as though they would not be seeing each other for years and not weeks, and hugged again. Davidson rolled his eyes and walked away from them after his mandatory squeeze and kiss from Shimmering Moon.

En route to France he ordered champagne to celebrate: the day before he had signed the divorce papers. McAllister had done his job diligently and he had been well rewarded. Davidson was Gabrielle's entirely and they danced in the aisle over the Atlantic. All that remained for Davidson to do was to put his signature to the final documents that would complete the sale of the corporation and club upon his return to Montreal after the honeymoon. Hearing that, all Gabrielle could think about was returning to spend more time with Lilly.

Davidson would never have thought to exclude Bernadette Dubuc. Her future position with the incoming directors of the company had been secured and the personal cheque he issued in her name would more than ensure her a comfortable life. Then, when she opened her invitation to the wedding, she could barely contain herself.

The 29th had been an evening none of the women would ever forget and one the men would never hear about. Not to be outdone, the men had planned their own evening requiring a limousine service and various forms of self-medicated remedies by sunrise. Saturday, September 30th, was a beautiful cloudless day with a warm gentle breeze and the bride could not have been more beautiful or flustered.

Jean-Alexandre walked proudly down the carpeted aisle with his mother on his arm as Henri whispered to a nervous Davidson. The threat was good-natured: he had always known the day would happen, that they were meant to be and that if Davidson ever hurt his little Gabrielle, or ever disappointed her, Davidson would see another side of him. No one noticed as both men smiled and shook hands. All eyes were on the bride.

Marie-Claude and Lilly went before the bride who wore a midnight blue silk dress to above her knees with an Asian high-neck collar and matching low-heeled pumps that sparkled in the sun. Henri gripped Davidson's arm to steady him as Antoinette looked on. Gérard interrupted his flirtation with Bernadette as his mother stopped by Davidson's side at the alter overlooking the City of Lights from the grassy plateau of La Falaise. The weather was as perfect as the bride.

The intimate reception was at l'Assiette Élégante where they danced until the early hours, the bride and groom scarcely managing a few hours' sleep in Gabrielle's private suite before catching a flight to the French Antilles for a month-long Caribbean cruise. Gabrielle already looked forward to wearing the bearskin parkas Lilly had given them as gifts with matching fur-lined mukluks and mittens when Davidson would take her to the High North once again in December.

She had never before gone so long without working and took several days to slow her pace. She had never been so tanned, and had never worn such a small bikini. She had never made love in waist-deep water and had never been so pampered or so happy in a month-long dream she knew would not end for years. She had been told at least four or five years for a woman her age, possibly more if she cared for herself, although no one told her how.

There were no experts in the field of congenital heart disease, what they described as an atrial septal defect, a hole in her heart between the atria. She was merely supposed to believe advances were being made every day. That had been four months earlier, the time she decided to confide in her more pragmatic son, the time he had decided to betray her trust and once again contact the private detective in Montreal for the most recent information on one Davidson Alexander.

She had never taken so many pictures, or had them taken of her with Davidson. It would be all she could one day leave a man who already had everything.

When the couple returned to France everyone stood in amazement at how different she looked, at how different she was. She worked half days and converted a hotel suite into an office for Davidson whose time was mostly spent on the phone with McAllister and Bernadette. The Thousand Island home and forty-foot motor yacht had been sold with Emily's consent and a final price had been successfully negotiated for the entire Alexander Corporation which now boasted a private club.

She had never seen city snow as deep, quickly deciding she didn't like the sting of winter's sub-zero bite upon her skin until her first horse-drawn sleigh ride through the barren woods and rolling hills and occasional sips of Rémy Martin. Throughout the entire week at the retreat she hadn't believed him, convinced he was being silly and when she spoke with Lilly she saw no reason to believe what either one. They were both as incorrigible as her mischievous son.

She sat by the pilot during most of the 1300-mile flight northward to Rankin Inlet in Nunavut, listening intently to the stories of the man's life as a bush pilot, thinking she had lost all track of time as they flew into the encroaching daytime darkness of the winter solstice. She looked back to Davidson who sat alone, looking smug and pointing to his watch that showed two o'clock in the afternoon. She blew him a kiss and ignored him as though she had been right not to believe him.

As they disembarked she saw the doors of the huge research vehicle open. Shapeless forms were running at them, narrow beams of light zigzagged erratically and she heard the sound of blowing snow as she had never heard it before. Her nose and mouth were protected under a thick woollen scarf from the minus 52° that blurred her eyes instantly with cold tears and she felt her lungs burn. She tried to turn, to search for Davidson as the forms scurried her along to the tractor. Two of the bigger bodies lifted her into the air and slid her through the narrow door. Davidson followed with somewhat more decorum and chuckled to see his wife sprawled on the floor when he scrambled through after her. The luggage followed, then the pilot with Lilly and her crew close behind and Gabrielle understood why Davidson had bought her so many new clothes.

They would stay for ten days and Lilly had each one planned. When Davidson joined the pilot and the other men for the evening, the women gathered with hot drinks to see Gabrielle's wedding and honeymoon photos. Lilly explained quickly that the women weren't laughing at her. They had only ever seen pictures of bikinis in magazines and had never known anyone who had been so naked except under blankets or furs. They all had something to tell her, and something to show her. They had all made her little gifts and Gabrielle looked to Lilly for the proper timing. She had told Gabrielle to expect openly warm hospitality and had suggested a small token of her appreciation might be appropriate, stressing the importance of small, and Gabrielle had brought them all Belgium and Swiss chocolates. Davidson had taken care of his own obligation with a case of single malt scotch and ten-inch Montecristos.

She awoke in the dark and by noon no more than a faint golden glow highlighted the horizon. She could never have imagined the barrenness or vastness of the sub Arctic's flatlands darkened snowscape, or the ferocity of the wind. She ate traditional stews and slept under thick furs with Davidson in an igloo she had helped to construct, a special treat arranged by Lilly, the only light coming from oil lamps filled with oil from thick slabs of whale and seal blubber. During her days she ran with teams of huskies that stopped when she slipped from her sled. She stroked the pelt of a sedated polar bear being tagged. She went on hunting expeditions for seal, learned the bow and arrow and how to throw a spear with an atlatl. She ice fished and from whalebone she carved her own eye protection against an Artic sun and blinding snow.

She wanted Lilly to spend Christmas with them in Paris, disappointed when her friend refused, insisting her workload would not allow for that kind of travel and Davidson refused with a shrug and sheepish smile to get involved. They agreed on the spring, to celebrate Gabrielle's birthday, and they hugged and kissed each other before running like children to the research vehicle that would take them to the plane that had been warming up for the past hour.

The couple would be at the Montreal pied à terre by late afternoon and Davidson would meet the following day with a team of corporate lawyers and accountants to bring an end to the Alexander Corporation. Emily's presence had neither been required nor desired, though by the end of the day her bank manager in South Carolina had called her seaside home to confirm the deposit of fifty-five million dollars. She would never again see Davidson Alexander.

37

August to December had been a whirlwind of travel and excitement and Gabrielle often wondered when her dream would end, hoping it never would. She had always insisted Christmas be celebrated at her home, a traditional time for family and friends without lavish gifts. Her first Christmas with Davidson and Antoinette would be no exception.

Gabrielle confiscated everyone's shoes before the midnight réveillon meal and lined them up in front of her fireplace. Not until all were filled with food and wine, and more boisterous than before the meal, did they find their way into the salon where their shoes had been filled with gifts from Père Noël. Davidson was the only one with a stocking hanging from the mantel and Gabrielle had so many gifts that her shoes lay atop the pile, for which she scolded them all.

Each gift from Gabrielle was wrapped in the same royal blue velveteen cloth. Marie-Claude's was Gabrielle's share in the two hotels. Henri's was full ownership of l'Assiette Élégante, its mortgage paid in full. Gérard's was the deed to La Plus Belle and Jean-Alexandre read a note attached to the cheque, of which he was never to reveal the amount. She gave Davidson a ruby and sapphire ring that held together the deed to her home, though not until she put a stop to all the murmuring.

She had done what had made her happy and Davidson had agreed with her. Her time had come to step down, her time had come to enjoy. It's what they both deserved and what they both wanted. Marie-Claude was the most upset. She was losing a closeness she deeply cherished.

Gérard and Henri glanced over to Jean-Alexandre waiting for him to say something, and were all the more confused when he simply said "Thank you, mama," adding with a mischievous smile, "but we see no gift from Davidson? We see nothing to you from him." He looked to his brother and Henri. "We shall deal privately with the cad," he joked.

His father raised his hands in surrender and pointed to the brass scrolls by the fire. He chuckled at the pursed lips and piercing green eyes, seeing Gabrielle uncurl first with meticulous care, following the plotted course with her finger that would take years to complete. She concealed her confusion badly, urged on by all in the room as Davidson stood stoically by. When she uncurled the second scroll she clutched her chest and gasped as both Davidson and Jean-Alexandre ran to her. She stared at her gift in disbelief: a full-colour blow-up of a sixty-five foot, double-masted schooner with an emerald green hull and pure white topside that was resting in its cradle and very near completion. The name on the transom was Gypsy Bride and the seemingly small man standing under it, between its twin brass propellers, was Davidson.

The maiden voyage would be in the Mediterranean and would last throughout the spring and summer, he explained. The rest of the world would simply have to wait until then to see her. First, however, they would enjoy week-long trips to Switzerland, Germany, Cape Town and Chicago. That's all anyone had to know.

The first night of her honeymoon she had cried in his arms for hours when she had told him of her talk with Lilly. He stroked her hair, defending their son's well-intended indiscretion and told her he would never let her go. If the doctors knew so little about her disease, how could they know how little time was left to her?

By the end of February the Europeans and American cardiologists had conferred and had agreed. Surgery would serve no purpose, and might worsen the condition of her heart. A reasonable prognosis, they agreed, was between five to seven years, possibly more, though none was willing to comment on the possible consequence of a life at sea in search of the perfect island.

38

By the time the masts were stepped and the Gypsy Bride had been tested for sea worthiness in late April, Lilly had arrived in Paris. Two days later they were nestled onboard the schooner at dock in Saint-Malo. Henri brought his finest champagne to pour onto the bowsprit, he doted over Lilly and Jean-Alexandre stood back in awe with Gérard at what their mother was about to undertake: sailing eleven hundred nautical miles to the Mediterranean, then thirty-five hundred more from Seville to Damascus and back, with dozens of ports of call along the northern coast of Africa and the jagged European coastline.

Antoinette thought it was all very nice, that the boat was very pretty, though only the men were impressed when Davidson asked for help to board the two steel cases of scoped rifles and laser-guided handguns. The weapons were the single part of her new life Gabrielle did not like, yielding to Davidson's insistence on proper training. They set sail May 05 and Lilly disembarked a month later in Barcelona, delighted that Gabrielle had never looked or felt so good. She had a special treat for them, a surprise she had kept to herself for a month resisting the temptation to tell them: Henri would her in Barcelona to drive her back to Paris, which they already knew. What they didn't know was that the trip would take the new couple three weeks.

Davidson threatened to shoot Henri on sight and made Lilly promise to note each and every impropriety. The women ignored him, of course. It was more important for Gabrielle to know if, if, and if. When Henri arrived at the gangway Davidson refused him boarding privileges, wanting to know his intentions, until Gabrielle pushed him aside. She took Henri by the arm to hear the other side of the story, leaving Shimmering Moon and Davidson standing looking at each other until the moment came to hold each other in the tight embrace of brother and sister.

Each man charged the other with protecting their women, bidding one another farewell with firm handshakes and repeated slaps to their backs. Then they slouched against the high gunwale to wait it out as the women hugged and cried some more. Moments after their departure Gabrielle smiled up at Davidson, telling him how certain she was that one day soon a beautiful Cree woman would soon be living in France and how happy she was that Marie-Claude would soon have a new friend. It was the first time Davidson had walked away from her without saying a word, the first time Gabrielle had heard him crying in the privacy of their stateroom.

She went topless on the Isle of Crete and rode camels in Damascus and Algiers. She saw the birthplace of Christ, the Sistine Chapel and listened to the Pope. She saw the Red Sea, the pyramids and threw up off the coast of Sicily in agitated seas. She saw Ortona and places Davidson had never forgotten. And she saw a man who could not be real, a man she would love until her last breath.

Late in September, after twenty-four weeks at sea, a peculiar message had suddenly been relayed to them off the shores of Portugal, a message translated from French to Spanish to Portuguese and then into broken English: Urgent you return to home very ASAP. Henry will marry with John Alexander. Please to confirm earliest arrival. Very much love from all of them. And there was nothing for them to do but wait until the next port of call, which was twelve hours away in Lisbon and still nine hundred miles from their home port. For Davidson the twelve hours proved to be an eternity and when they touched the dock he sank to his knees to give thanks as Gabrielle left him and hurried off to the nearest phone.

Yes, Gabrielle insisted to Jean-Alexandre, she was fine. She had not had one moment of fatigue since leaving Saint-Malo and not once had she lost her breath. Now what was going on, she wanted to know, exasperated with Davidson who stood beside her as though he knew everything already, when he knew nothing at all. Jean-Alexandre had finally proposed, she repeated to Davidson, and Chantal had said yes, she repeated, and they were already engaged! She tugged at Davidson's arm excitedly as Henri came on the line. After so many years he had found himself a wife, Gabrielle repeated, one who often spoke Cree to annoy him. Lilly was already living with him in Paris, she repeated, crying happy tears! She dropped the phone, asking Davidson how long.

As the Gypsy Bride's navigator she already knew the answer. Davidson took up the phone, howling with laughter, telling his son and everyone listening that he would be in Paris no later than mid-October with the most beautiful woman in Europe who didn't have a spot of white on her. The teasing remark earned him a jab. Being in Paris would give them the time needed to complete minor improvements to the Gypsy Bride, provision her for the springtime South Atlantic crossing and spend Christmas with their extended family.

Lilly was a beautiful bride in a traditional Cree dress embroidered with beads and semi-precious stones. Chantal was equally lovely in her simple knee-length satin A-line dress and matching jacket, each woman nervously squeezing Davidson's arm as he walked proudly between them. He gave one woman away, and then the other, standing by Henri as Gérard took his place by his brother's side. Gabrielle was living her second happiest moment and when the two couples returned from their trips abroad Gabrielle insisted that Christmas be a frugal one: she had no more restaurants or hotels to give as gifts. Her best gift to Davidson was free. She hadn't thought of dying in seven months. Her skin still glowed with a pale tan and Davidson's remark regarding her tan and certain missing photographs had earned him a smack. To the other men she issued the threat of one if they didn't stop being stupid.

They had been together for almost two years and to each one the passage of time had seemed like days. Gabrielle's whirlwind had not slowed and she was adamant it never would. They said their goodbyes in May once again, amongst a flood of warm tears and warm embraces. The sixty thousand nautical miles would take four years to complete and she promised to call them all at least once a week. Jean-Alexandre had never shared his secret with anyone but his father. He was the only one who knew they might never see Gabrielle again, and Davidson eagerly accepted his son's proposal that those left behind spend their vacations and Christmas wherever the Gypsy Bride might be. Gabrielle was ecstatic when they told her. It made leaving them that much easier.

They sailed the western coast of Africa to Sierra Leone, where they crossed at the narrowest point to Natal, Brazil to continue southward to Bahía Blanca, Argentina, a thousand nautical miles from the tempestuous dangers of Cape Horn. They changed course to head north, to Barranquilla where Marie-Claude met them before sailing to Panama and then south to Bogotá where Henri and Lilly were next to meet them at the dock. Christmas was in Santiago de Chile and the conversation was as much about the journey as Chantal's rounded stomach.

They spent spring in Peru with Gérard who came alone with photos of their grandson, Joaquin de-Saint-Valéry. They spent summer along the western coast of Central America and autumn in Mexico with Joaquin and his parents. They wintered in California and had Christmas in San Francisco. They drove through the Rockies in the spring and saw Alaska in the summer. Their third Christmas was in Havana and they wintered in the Caribbean. They went to Mardi Gras in New Orleans where Gabrielle did what Davidson didn't believe she would do, not believing it herself, and they drove to San Antonio to stroll along the canals and visit the Alamo.

They island hopped throughout the summer with Henri and Lilly, Marie-Claude and Gérard. Jean-Alexandre and Chantal met them in Miami with Joaquin for the month of September and Christmas had already been planned for St. Simon's Island in Georgia. In the spring they did the east coast to Nova Scotia and drove to Quebec City before crossing the Gulf of St. Lawrence to Newfoundland and a north-easterly course to Greenland and Iceland, altering course to The Faroe Islands, the North Sea and home to Saint-Malo. They had been gone four and half years, more than six years after Gabrielle and first been diagnosed with congenital heart disease. She had already cheated the Grim Reaper by more than a year.

Over the winter Gabrielle fussed over Joaquin, Davidson put their home up for sale and in the spring they set sail for their new home on their perfect island: Las Palmas on the northeast coast of Grand Canary. She had learned that her green gypsy eyes were no match for Davidson once he had his mind set, particularly on matters concerning her. The Canaries had a milder climate year round, without the deathly heat of the Caribbean. The air would be fresher, the pace slower and Paris was no farther than a four-hour flight. She would see her family and friends often, he had made certain of it, and by mid-summer they had moved into the private oceanfront villa in time for his birthday and everyone was in attendance, save Antoinette who had passed away in her sleep several weeks earlier. Argue as she might, Gabrielle had not been allowed to attend the funeral service. Davidson had been adamant: she would no longer fly.

He was back home within twenty-four hours. They became liked by the locals, they perfected their Spanish and Gabrielle opened a small café which soon became the island's finest. They made new friends, they constantly had visitors and year after year they discovered something new to look forward to or remember. Life was perfect and the summer of '83 was no exception as they prepared to leave the island for two weeks along the African coast.

They had slept onboard the eve of their departure, both of them wanting to set sail into the rising sun. They made love and Gabrielle told him a hundred times how much she loved him, how much she had always loved him and always would. When they awoke she made coffee and sat drinking it in the open cockpit, staring into the warm sun as Davidson made ready to cast off, insisting as he always did that a man's work was to be done by men, really meaning he didn't want her to exert herself.

He called out to her from amidships that he was nearly done, that he would have another cup of coffee, and he went closer to her thinking she hadn't heard. He smiled down at her from the deck, leaning with an arm outstretched to the boom and thinking how lovely she was, how much he loved her and how peaceful she looked with her hands clasped together as a pillow against her cheek.

He called her name and when there was no answer he sprang down into the cockpit, smiling, leaning forward to kiss her awake, not expecting her hands to fall limply away from her face. He whispered her name, choking, until quiet tears became uncontrolled sobbing. Her eyes stayed closed and her body, still warm from the sun, felt strangely more vulnerable in his arms. He kissed her face and her eyes, her nose and her arms. He held her close and cried out to Big Earl, begging his friend to never let anything else happen to her.

By late afternoon Gabrielle lay in their berth, the half-bottle of scotch had not dulled his pain and he had asked one of the dockhands to deliver a message to the post office for furtherance to Jean-Alexandre and Gérard. The telegram read: Arriving Honfleur Friday 1200. Stop. Come alone. Stop. Worst has happened. Stop. No pain. Stop. Signed: From the deck of the Gypsy Angel. As far as anyone would know, Gabrielle de-Saint-Valéry had died at sea and her husband had taken her home.

At Honfleur they would unstep the masts and the Gypsy Bride would travel the Seine to Paris with her sons onboard. She would be buried as she had always wanted, beside Jean-Philippe and one day Davidson would be with them. Throughout the four-day journey he could not bring himself to cover her with more than a light cotton sheet, constantly looking down at her tiny frame illuminated with the red glow of the ship's navigation station.

The funeral was simple, the way she had lived her life and when she was laid to rest Davidson returned to Las Palmas with his sons onboard. Once in the marina the masts were unstepped for the final time and the ship was emptied of all its possessions and equipment until only a shell remained. Early the next morning, in the dim light of predawn, the Gypsy Bride cruised for the last time with Jean-Alexandre at the helm of the motor yacht that followed closely behind.

Twenty miles offshore they toasted Gabrielle and the Gypsy Bride as the scuttled vessel listed in a lethargic roll before disappearing beneath the gurgling surface. They waited no longer than they knew it would take the sailing yacht to come to rest on the bottom. There was nothing to say. They steered a course to Las Palmas where the men said their goodbyes. They both wanted to stay longer, to help their father through his grief, disappointed by Davidson's refusal.

He made frail promises to visit them soon, promises

neither son believed and he returned to an empty home.

39

Emily was sixty-three and had not thought of Davidson once in ten years, though her deep hatred towards him was an integral part of her. She never remarried and was generally thought of by her pretentiously haughty seaside neighbours in Charleston, South Carolina as eccentric. She could often be seen giving hundred-dollar bills to vacationing couples who strolled along the beach in front of her home, paying the restaurant bills of absolute strangers or preceding the town's meter maid with her pockets full of quarters. She donated large sums to the arts and not all her investments had been particularly wise.

She had spent her first year alone after the divorce, each day creating yet another believable excuse not to call Noëlyn, knowing perfectly well certain emotional accusations would follow the initial and obvious questions. She had lived a lie, never understanding the deception had been hers alone. The first year apart she had not stopped resenting Davidson for his weakness, or his French whore for conspiring with his bastard son to ruin her status quo. She spent her time being bitter. She tracked down the man who was Noëlyn's biological father and had lunch with his wife. She showed the distraught woman the candid photographs Davidson had left with her of Noëlyn and had fabricated every detail of how she had been raped by the woman's husband one Christmas Eve so long ago, how he had then fired her from her position and left her to fend for herself.

She discovered where the man worked as production manager in a small ceramics firm and went to see him. She threatened the owner with competition that would undersell him into bankruptcy unless the man she claimed had raped her was dismissed and his record altered to make his life difficult. She found their children and told each one of their half-sister in New York. Content to have ruined the man's life and marriage, she gave away all that Davidson had left her and she moved to South Carolina.

It was early into the second year that she called her daughter, and the conversation went as badly as she had expected. She told Noëlyn who she was, that she was sorry she had waited so long and how she needed desperately to know her daughter and granddaughter Jodie were well, to know if they needed anything at all. Moments after, the line went dead. The next day she called and left a message, and again the day after. On the fourth day Noëlyn's husband, John Gupman, answered the call. The entire conversation was terse and uneasy. He asked specific questions and she gave the answers she thought best. Less than a week later she understood from her neighbours and banker that someone had become quite interested in her. A man had been knocking on their doors asking personal questions about her and they all thought she should know.

Of course the banker had been discreet and the neighbours had said more of what they didn't know of Emily than what little they did know, and some weeks later a timid Noëlyn returned what Emily had promised would be her final call. Her daughter needed to know why her real parents had given her away. Her adoptive parents had never told her of the adoption and the only mother she had ever known had become too flustered to discuss the matter when Noëlyn had confronted her, placing the blame entirely on her deceased husband who had never thought it appropriate to reveal the truth. What purpose would the truth have served? Noëlyn was their daughter. So what did the truth matter after so many years? Still, Noëlyn needed to know why Davidson had abandoned his wife and a daughter he had never wanted to know, when they had first known about little Jodie and why Emily had waited so long to call.

Emily cried, and Noëlyn cried as her husband sat by her side ready to intercede. After Emily had told her daughter the truth, Noëlyn agreed to meet with her mother in Charleston, alone. Perhaps Emily would see Jodie at a later time, but certainly not until mother and daughter bridged the thirty-year gap between them.

They met in a restaurant overlooking the Cooper River and Patriots Point and strolled to Waterfront Park where the conversation turned from Noëlyn and Jodie to the man Noëlyn now believed was her real father. He had been one of the first of his friends to enlist in '39. Three years into the war he had been so severely wounded that the army had discharged him and sent him home. The government had promised benefits and assistance, which weren't enough to cover never-ending medical bills and, when they discovered to their complete surprise they were to have a child, they did their best to plan for its future and to put their own concerns aside.

However after two years of struggling on one salary to make ends meet, between Davidson's medical bills and caring for their daughter, and seeing no light at the end of the tunnel, they did what they knew would be best for little Noëlyn. There was a middle-aged couple of means who had desperately wanted a child of their own, but couldn't, who had heard of the Alexander's difficult situation. Knowing how much better the baby's life and future would be with them, the couple offered to adopt the little girl and Emily had never stopped regretting it.

Despite their modest success, mostly due to her long hours of work and her personal finances, Davidson had never entirely recovered from his mental and physical battle scars. He would drink excessively most days, often striking out at Emily to vent his frustration and lack of esteem. Finally he had left home one morning, not far from a year earlier, threatening never to come back and he never did. Emily was left to close the business that was only as successful as it was because of her inheritance from her mother: money derived from her father's arduous years as a gold digger in the Klondike before his death. She had not seen Davidson since. He had abandoned her the same way his father had abandoned Davidson's mother when he was no more than a young boy.

Noëlyn listened to the creative story, despising Davidson more with each word. She liked Emily, as anyone would like an aunt or a neighbour's mother, though she felt no immediate mother-daughter emotion. Noëlyn had lived the previous ten years of her life in New York City. She was far from naive and even farther from being gulled into a new relationship when her current mother filled that position well enough. Neither did Jodie need a third grandmother. The two she had served their purpose and that was the best Emily could hope for in the short term.

The evening of their first encounter Noëlyn dined with her husband. She told him of the cheque Emily had written at the restaurant table in the amount of one million dollars, which she was to deposit in trust for Jodie on the condition that Emily would see her grandchild at least twice each year for one week until the age of twenty-one. The decision was an easy one and Noëlyn had agreed to meet with Emily's lawyer the next day to sign the agreement. From then on Emily and Noëlyn grew closer, Jodie came to know her new grandmother as Emmie and Noëlyn's husband was rarely seen. There was something about Emily he didn't like, though he wouldn't ignore a million dollars.

He had tried every conceivable means to convince Emily to deposit with his firm, once she had been investigated yet again to confirm her financial standing. The intrusion into Emily's affairs had been a serious mistake. Gupman's manager had never stopped haranguing him to acquire the management of Emily's fortune and Gupman had never stopped harassing his wife to influence Emily on his behalf.

Emily's favourite time to spend with her daughters was the spring and fall, before and after summer's oppressive heat. She loved to sit by the edge of the rocky beach and to paint sailboats tacking through the glittering water or to look at them through the telescope that soon became Jodie's favourite pastime when she wasn't running ahead of meter maids.

Each year they grew closer and, when the grandmothers who Jodie had known first passed away, Emily became all the more important to her. By the age of thirteen Jodie's one million dollar trust fund had become two million and still she had been told nothing about it. Noëlyn's husband still saw no reason to pretend the slightest affection towards Emily and Noëlyn had long since stopped trying her best to bring them together. They had never shared Christmas and never would until John Gupman died, and Emily found herself hoping the happy event would take place sooner rather than later. He was an obstruction to all that mattered to her, sadly the happy phone call would not come for several more years and she would resent him until the joyous day.

It was a constant point of contention for Gupman to know of Emily's staggering wealth and how she was squandering the fortune without any legal right to stop her. He often argued with Noëlyn, asserting it was ridiculous for both parents to be working to support a lifestyle when their own daughter was a millionaire.

Emily told herself it was enough that Jodie was spending more time with her. Jodie was spending her summer vacations at the luxurious South Carolina oceanfront home as her parents travelled abroad with tickets and spending money given to Noëlyn as gifts from Emily who knew all too well how her benevolence belittled her son-in-law. And, as she grew older, the young girl began to know more about her family, her mother and the father who had never adopted her as his own after marrying Noëlyn. It was something her mother had never told Jodie, and certainly never would. Now that she did know, Jodie promised Emily she would never reveal her newfound knowledge. She would never hurt her mother, and her father had always been just that, a father: there to pay the bills, to work late, and to miss most of her special occasions. What did it matter, if keeping a secret meant another million at graduation? Emily could not help herself, smiling widely with self-satisfaction as she told Jodie of her trust fund. The girl should know how wealthy she would soon be and how to manage the wealth, which also meant learning with whom not to share it.

By '83 those long hot summers had become a tradition and Emily had become the greater influence in her impressionable granddaughter's life, worlds apart from another's deep grief she would have scorned. Noëlyn was more than content to send her adolescent daughter away from the drug-rampant summers in the Hamptons and happier each year to see her bond more with Emily whose wealth had never been an issue the way it had evolved from an obsession into a deep disdain on the part of her husband. Noëlyn was content to know Jodie's future was secure, that she would be independent and in control of her destiny. She wouldn't have to marry the first man who came along because she had been tainted by another whose name Noëlyn had never revealed to Emily the many times her mother demanded to know.

The happy year Emily had been awaiting arrived in 1991, when John Gupman died at the age of sixty-two, one day before Jodie's twenty-first birthday and the release of her five million dollars. Life was also good for Emily, and getting better. Life also became decidedly better for Noëlyn with what Emily referred to at the funeral as her five million-dollar Merry Widow's Allowance, payable immediately. She was old and she didn't need the money. What she needed was for her daughters not to leave her.

PART FIVE

1999

40

Davidson sat reflectively on the veranda of his villa, looking out across a calm late day sea as he sipped his second snifter of his favourite malt scotch. As much as he felt he should, he was too weary and disheartened to cry only a day after his return from an unexpected trip to France and a subsequent phone call that morning which he had not expected at all.

Throughout the eighties and nineties Davidson's wealth had more than quadrupled as his life grew inversely less meaningful. He had lived alone for the sixteen years since the morning Gabrielle had gone to sleep forever and had since limited his travels to three annual trips to France. He travelled to be with his family at Christmas and October 28th to lament the day he had first left her. July 28th had become the most important, when he would sit alone by her grave to ask her forgiveness for not being with her for their son's birth and to tell her how deeply sorry he would always be for having left her. This year there would be five trips and, despite what was left of his family, he felt entirely alone.

Each year had become a more difficult reminder for him

of the many wasted years he had lived without her, and he had made clear to Jean-Alexandre where he was to one day be laid to rest. Each Christmas had become less meaningful to him and more a time to remember those taken from him as old Henri had been the next to die after Gabrielle. Now he wondered what purpose he had in life or if he had ever had one.

After Henri's death Lilly had moved in with Marie-Claude who had never married. They lived on an expansive estate overlooking the French countryside and had their every need attended to by a personal staff who reported to Jean-Alexandre as the administrator of the endowment given to them by Davidson. He had refused to listen to any protest from the two women. Gabrielle's wish would have been to see her friends living together in luxury, not in a home for the aged or the infirm, and, despite their combined resources and protests, he wrote the cheque for a gift of several million as easily as though it had been pocket change.

Jean-Alexandre had become a magistrate of the court who, with Chantal, doted over Marie-Claude and Lilly. Gérard, the eternal bachelor, was kept busy running the ever quaint La Plus Belle, two hotels and a restaurant whose reputation had become well-known beyond the borders of France. Accustomed to the deliverance of bad news, Jean-Alexandre had been the one to call Davidson, to tell him of Marie-Claude's passing. Lilly had insisted that Davidson stay with her on the estate until after the funeral. She would not tolerate him staying anywhere else. She needed to be with her Little Brother. Her summer visits in Las Palmas and his infrequent visits to Paris had always been too fleeting. At times she slipped into her native Cree, using simple words she knew he would understand. They remembered Big Earl, and she thanked Davidson again for the time so many years ago he had taken her with Gabrielle to see the exact spot where her brother had died and where he had been laid to rest.

He wanted her to accompany him to Las Palmas, to live at the villa with him and she refused. The estate had become her home with fond memories of Marie-Claude, and loving memories of Henri. It's where she belonged and, when the time had come for Davidson to leave her, she kissed his cheeks and hugged him with surprising emotion.

Three days after the funeral he awoke to a sunny morning and walked the beach to absorb the curative warmth of early spring and to speak with Gabrielle as he did every morning. When he arrived back at the villa the red light was flashing on his phone. Jean-Alexandre had left an urgent request for Davidson to return his call as soon as possible. Lilly had passed away peacefully in her sleep the night before.

By mid-afternoon the bottle was empty and his misery of self-pity had disappeared into a weightless slumber. By early the next morning he was at the airport en route to bury Shimmering Moon, the sister of the one man he had ever thought of as a true friend and brother.

Jean-Alexandre had insisted his father remain in Paris with him and Chantal after the funeral, to live with them. The couple was sincere, and sincerely thanked before being graciously and summarily turned down. Davidson would live the rest of his life where he had spent too few years with Gabrielle and there would be no further discussion about the matter, as much as he loved them and Joaquin whom he had not seen since the young man's decision to discontinue his studies in favour of travelling abroad.

The latter had been the cause of Davidson's first stern warning to Joaquin in front of his father and mother: He was not to rely on the possibility of any future inheritance. Joaquin had not yet been included into Davidson's current will and would not be until his graduation from university, whenever Joaquin determined that would be. Everyone in the family had worked hard for their individual successes, he had chastised. Joaquin would be no different, other than by his failure to succeed on his own. He was not to expect that Davidson would one day provide an easy life to a village idiot. It was the last time he had seen his grandson who had departed France not too many weeks later to travel Europe and Asia.

Back in Las Palmas Davidson stood alone on the veranda, looking up at a midnight sky sprinkled with flickering silver stars and a moon that shimmered through eyes blurred with tears. He needed to cry. He knew Gabrielle would forgive him the uncharacteristic lapse, he knew she would understand the pain of losing all his friends. He filled his snifter halfway and held it to the stars before bringing it to his lips. When the glass was empty, he sat down, wiped his eyes and began to write the first of several drafts of a letter he would soon have delivered to Jean-Alexandre.

When he finished he put it aside and made a call to his Paris-based lawyer and to each of his bankers in Paris and Montreal. He poured another scotch before writing the next letter to Emily, whom he had never forgiven for her deceit. Yet he could not do what was now uppermost on his mind without her and that was his only assuagement. He wrote impassively, letting his emotion show in the thickness of the written words and their impression on the paper. Though Emily was now seventy-nine and he doubted she would notice.

His lawyer and both bankers would arrive in Las Palmas in two days. Mike DuFour would arrive two days later, Saturday, May 01, for their meeting on the Sunday.

41

"Thank you for coming so expeditiously, Monsieur DuFour. It is appreciated in the extreme as I feel time is of the utmost importance."

"Monsieur, it is I who must thank you for selecting my firm from so far away. I don't often take on projects personally, monsieur. However I felt the need to be involved in this particular case, in the event I take it on once I am more acquainted with the particulars."

Davidson casually waved an arm, indicating for DuFour to be seated. "You will take it on, monsieur. You have already decided that you will, otherwise a simple e-mail or phone call would have sufficed."

DuFour acquiesced graciously. "I must say you did make it all sound all very intriguing. I also must tell you that I have made certain inquiries about Davidson Alexander, which is one of the reasons I'm here."

Davidson smiled. "That you did so, monsieur, confirms the wisdom of my choice. I have no doubt you will accept the challenge. Now, if you don't mind, I will explain in greater detail why you are here, what is expected of you and in what timeframe, though the greater part of your undertaking is contained in a more complete file which I have prepared for you. May I serve you a refreshment?"

DuFour put up a hand, refusing. Davidson poured a scotch for himself and took a seat across from the detective. Mike DuFour was early fifties, his face and hands were weathered more than tanned, he had no wedding ring and his hair was a yellowish-white. His best suit was made-to-measure, his tie and pocket hanky were Italian silk and his shoes were polished to a dull gloss. He was a head shorter than Davidson, the easy manner in which he carried himself eradicating the difference and when he sat he did so with equal self-assuredness. Davidson knew instinctively that DuFour would get the job done and dispelled from his mind any thought of being disappointed, confident in his decision.

"Your job will be to find my family, Monsieur DuFour, in particular my daughter and my son. My fondest wish to see them, to meet with them," Davidson sipped from his snifter, "for the first time. I assume those few unforgivable words alone will tell you much about the journey upon which we are about to embark together. Some of them, however, I will tell you quite forthrightly, I have no particular interest in seeing. They are merely a vehicle to ensure that I do see the ones who are important to me." Davidson picked up the briefcase beside him and passed it to the detective. "As mentioned, you will find all pertinent information inside: birthdates, names, possible locations and photographs which were taken almost thirty years ago. I apologize for giving you much less than what I expect from you in return, although I have done my best to be thorough. My first wife, Emily Ashton, and I had two children, Katherine and Theodore. I am very certain that without Emily's participation I will not succeed in seeing either of the two who are now fifty-three. I want the most complete information possible on them: their spouses, their children, their education, everything. You might begin your search on the west coast, though on my part that is speculation based on very old data. In any event, I want to know as much about them from your investigation as I would have had I not given them up for adoption."

DuFour listened without taking notes, reading Davidson

as much as hearing his words.

"Emily's daughter, by another man, a woman whose name was then Noëlyn Daniels, I care nothing about, though I do want to know about her and her own daughter, Jodie, who may or may not be married. If she is, I want all those details as well. Better that I have details at the outset, than disappointments later on. The Daniels woman once lived in New York, she may still. Emily's home is in Charleston." Davidson swirled his scotch and sipped a small quantity. "My grandson, Joaquin, has been gone for quite a few years, in search of himself, I suspect, despite anything else he might believe. He writes to his father infrequently, my son Jean-Alexandre, and his letters are vague at best with little reference to his future plans or current relationships. I want to know where he is, what he is doing and who he's with. Other than my twins, Joaquin is the one I care most about with regard to this investigation."

"Do you wish me to begin with your son and daughter, and then Joaquin before your ex-wife and her side?"

"I wish you to be finished in three months. I believe the easiest to accomplish would be her side, as you put it. The most difficult to track will undoubtedly be Joaquin who could be anywhere across Europe or Asia, and I would not discount Africa, Monsieur DuFour." Davidson leaned forward. "Spare no expense. Do what you must to find them. You have carte blanche."

DuFour nodded. "Of course, thank you."

"I also want to know if there are others involved, such as grandchildren, adopted or otherwise, illegitimate baggage or any other dirty laundry…any and all dirty laundry."

The detective nodded again, not changing his expression. "You will have complete and timely information."

"I have every confidence in that statement. However, having said that, you have no more than three months after which I will engage another firm to replace you, a firm I have already selected. I want detailed reports and I want absolute secrecy. They are not to know of your investigation. I want to know everything about them, everything, good or bad. There is, of course, an incentive: Do what I ask inside of the three months and you'll spend the rest of your life doing whatever it is you wish to do. You will be a wealthy man, sir, overnight, and there is no limitation attached to your investigation. You will have whatever you need. There is a substantial cheque in the envelope. Should you need more, please advise me with supporting documents. I want these people found, and found quickly. The only exceptions are my sons, Jean-Alexandre and Gérard."

DuFour opened the envelope. He stood and walked to the edge of veranda to scan through the information. "I don't see, based on this information, that any particular complication should arise, Monsieur Alexander. Three months should be more than adequate time and I can't see where I won't have funds to return to you."

"I expect you'll be a very busy and very tired man when all is said and done, which is when I will expect to see you back here at Las Palmas anytime other than the end of July. Plan to stay for a few days. I'll make the arrangements. At that time I will give you letters to deliver to each of the persons you will have investigated. The interim will allow me adequate time to reflect on the contradictions that exist between what I intend to do and the essence of my reasoning for doing it." Davidson finished what was left in his glass. "At the risk of repeating myself, they are not to be aware of your investigation."

"I understand."

"You come highly recommended, sir. I expect results quickly. Do you have questions?"

"No, sir, I do not. Your information is complete. Should there be a need to contact you, I will. Barring any unforeseen eventualities we will meet again within three months."

"I want your full attention. I want your exclusive attention. Do you understand?"

"I do. You will have regular updates."

"Don't waste your time. Be here within the stated timeframe, or call me to tell me I have selected the wrong firm."

"You have not, Monsieur Alexander. I assure you."

"Then I will bid you a good day. My car will take you back to your hotel. Enjoy the island until your departure tomorrow. I look forward to our next meeting." Davidson put down the empty glass. "My sons, Jean-Alexandre and Gérard, are being apprised of my intentions as we speak, Monsieur DuFour. Should I be unavailable to you for any reason in the future, you are to communicate directly with Maître d'Avignon as indicated in the file. In any such case he will be expecting you."

"Sir?" DuFour questioned, seeing Davidson's face light up with a bright smile.

"I am eighty-one, Monsieur DuFour. Please, do not take two days to do what can easily be accomplished in one. Good day, sir."

42

The winding road in front of the carriage house was a tree-lined cul-de-sac and never heavily travelled, sparsely dotted on either side with stately mansions and security was never an issue. The locals called it La Colline, and those at the bottom of the hill knew not to be curious. A black vehicle with dark tinted windows was always parked by the side of the gatehouse at the narrow entrance which was seldom barred. On those occasions when there was a reason for the vehicle or the gendarmes not to be there, the gates were closed and a plethora of hidden cameras directly linked to the roaming vehicle continued their surveillance.

The driver of the limousine knew to stop and identify his passenger and the intended destination. Jean-Alexandre had known to expect the visit from Davidson's attorney, Maître Karl d'Avignon and had called Gérard the day before to request that his brother arrive his home sometime earlier than noon on the Sunday. In his own inimitable fashion he excused himself for not being able to elaborate as to why. He did not know himself. Although he did know of the letter and the dossier that would accompany the attorney who was acting on behalf of their father, he was not yet privy to their contents. The need for secrecy was a formality, of course, and as a longstanding officer of the court he could certainly interpret the reason for diplomacy. He had learned years earlier that his father did nothing without good reason.

He had never known the extent of his father's vast resources. He had always known Davidson was rich, even very wealthy, though not for a moment had he imagined how wealthy and had never considered it his business to enquire. When his mother passed away she had bequeathed nothing to Davidson other than his ring, which he had left on her finger. Everything else she had not already transferred to them had gone to their sons and Marie-Claude. Davidson had been in full agreement. To have done otherwise would have been to drop grains of sand onto a vast beach.

Jean-Alexandre and Gérard went to the door together. Sunday was the one day Chantal had always insisted there be no personal staff in their home, and no business conducted. She acquiesced this one time for Davidson and had excused herself after greeting Gérard.

"Thank you for seeing me at such an unusual time, Messieurs de-Saint-Valéry. Your father and I concurred that it would be best if we were to meet before the opening of business tomorrow for reasons that will soon become clear to both of you. I trust that I have not inconvenienced either of you."

"Not in the least, Maître d'Avignon." Jean-Alexandre extended his hand. "It is a pleasure, of course. Anything concerning our father is our first priority. Please, do come in."

D'Avignon stepped into the expansive entranceway. "Monsieur, if I may say so, this matter concerns you and your brother more than it does your father. Though I have no doubt whatsoever that his thoughts are with us at this very moment."

Gérard shook the attorney's hand, speaking with a hint of good humour in his voice. "I have always known him to be a man of surprises, Maître d'Avignon."

"That may soon prove to be the greatest understatement of your life, monsieur."

Jean-Alexandre led the way. "May I suggest a cognac in the study, gentlemen? The lady of the house is nowhere to be seen and I do not believe the hour is too early."

The three men grinned at the polite jibe. When they had toasted Davidson's health d'Avignon began smoothly, passing each of the two men a blank envelope.

"These are letters to each of you from your father, gentlemen. Please read them as a prelude to this meeting."

"They are not addressed, monsieur," Jean-Alexandre questioned.

"They are identical, sir. You may exchange them at any time. Each of the letters is addressed to both of you, as you will see. Please take your time." D'Avignon raised the snifter to his nose. "I commend you on your excellent choice of cognac, sir."

As he read the letter, Jean-Alexandre's entire body shuddered. When he saw the cheque assigned to him he could only look to his brother who had already emptied his glass and was staring at his own cheque. Their quizzical expressions made the attorney discreetly chuckle. There were two questions to be answered and d'Avignon asked each brother in turn for their respective answers: Did they, his sons, each agree not to interfere with the d'Avignon law firm's management of the tontine as laid out in their father's request of them, in the event of Davidson Alexander's untimely demise? And did they, Jean-Alexandre and Gérard de-Saint-Valéry, both agree not to contest Davidson's intention?

"Monsieur, none of this can be true," Jean-Alexandre exclaimed. "It must be a fanciful attempt at humour on our father's part. A tontine? Although I know they exist, I have only read of them, a thing of novels and intrigue."

"It is indeed true, monsieur. I have known your father since he first arrived in France so many years ago. As you must certainly know, he is a dear and close friend more than a client. I have also enjoyed the absolute pleasure of knowing your dear mother," d'Avignon grinned with solemnity, "even though I was so much younger then. With your permission, sir, I have never forgotten her. Such women as your mother are rare and timeless. She is most certainly an angel above us. I doubt anyone who has ever met her would argue with me."

"Thank you, your very kind words bring back fond memories. But, please, sir, speak frankly. Is our father sound? Is this letter cause for worry?"

"Messieurs de-Saint-Valéry, I have never known anyone any sounder of mind. His gift to you is real, as is the one to your brother. There is nothing whimsical about either one, which is why we thought it best to meet with you together and at this particular time. Your banks have been instructed to advise you at the opening of business tomorrow. You have both been given twenty-five million dollars U.S., gentlemen, without condition. May I be the first to congratulate you? You do understand, of course, that yours, Jean-Alexandre, as stipulated in the letter, must be shared equally with Mademoiselle Chantal. He is very fond of her, as you know. The amount will be deposited separately into her account for the sake of your wife's valued independence, and not due to any misconception of your unquestionable integrity."

"I understand entirely. I would expect nothing less," replied Jean-Alexandre, his eyes alternating between the letter in his hands and following Gérard's path across the room.

Gérard plucked the crystal cork from the decanter, arbitrarily refilling each of their glasses. "Monsieur, speak to us of this tontine, and of these people. Our father was once married to another woman, this we know, but what of the others?"

D'Avignon turned to Jean-Alexandre expectantly. "With all due respect, sir, and with your father's wishes. He anticipated the question. May I ask that you be the one to respond?"

Gérard looked at his brother, his brow furrowed with curiosity at the remark. "Alex?"

"It is a very long story, Gérard. I have kept it from you because I gave Davidson my word twenty-seven years ago. It is I who found him. You know that already, and you know why. What you do not know is that I also discovered Davidson's other family. Davidson has two other children of his own, twins, and his first wife has a daughter who was fathered by another man while Davidson was fighting here in Europe. It took place one year before he met mama. That illegitimate daughter, whose name is irrelevant, also had a daughter out of wedlock. I assume those are the people who are to be invited to the tontine. Forgive me, Gérard. It was Davidson's sincerest wish. I am grateful that he has chosen to tell you and relieve me of the burden."

Gérard raised his glass, smiling mischievously. "To Davidson's health, gentlemen. As I have already said: a man of surprises."

"Was I accurate in my assessment, Monsieur d'Avignon?" Jean-Alexandre asked.

"Yes, sir, though as we speak your father is making arrangements to investigate any additional persons who we may not yet know. Your son, Joaquin is also to be included, which is to say investigated. What we do not yet know is whether Davidson's first wife's granddaughter has made additions to the equation, or whether either of his twins has made him a grandfather and so on. We expect complete information by late summer." D'Avignon's expression changed imperceptibly. "Gentlemen, there is an additional and final request your father has made of you. Please do note the word final. He asks that you not disclose your gifts to, or share your gifts with Joaquin de-Saint-Valéry at any time. He also requests that you bequeath to one another, including to Mademoiselle Chantal, what remains when the time comes and that the last of you to survive make a separate bequest to the less fortunate. He considers Joaquin to have enjoyed a gilded life and that he must now make his own way if he is to be the man his father, his uncle and his grandfather expect him to be. Your father expects your cooperation in this matter, though it is not a condition of your gifts, simply a request. Your father has no desire to impose his will or restrictions on either of you. However, that said, you are not to advise your son Joaquin of the tontine. To do so will eliminate him forthwith. He will be found in due course and given the same opportunity with the same conditions as the others."

Gérard spoke next. "Might we expect to be privy to any information gathered regarding the tontine?"

"No sir. In the event of your father's untimely passing I shall personally take over the management of it. Your father desires complete impartiality, as much as he admires and trusts each of you. He also wishes you to understand that Joaquin will not be forgotten or excluded for any reason, other than neglecting a few simple rules, and that you understand his need to see his two other children."

"Do you have any idea of the extent of the tontine?" asked Gérard."

"I presume you mean the value?" D'Avignon paused. "I do, though I am not at liberty to say specifically. It suffices to say that the amount boggles the mind and that each of you has been treated preferentially."

"Monsieur d'Avignon," returned Gérard, "I did not mean to imply…"

"I do not in any way doubt your integrity, Monsieur de-Saint-Valéry. It was a natural enquiry. I would have reacted no differently were I in your position." D'Avignon sipped his cognac. "As I have said, certain conditions precedent do exist, which will vary according to specific participants. In the case of his direct children, one of them is success, which your father recognizes as both important to the human condition and the individual. He believes people must make their own lives, as admirably demonstrated by both of you. Need I say he is equally proud of you?"

Jean-Alexandre tilted his head politely at the compliment. "Sir, what I know of the human condition has more to do with corruption and violence."

"And in my case, I am ashamed to say," Gérard broke in, "opulence and excess."

"Indeed, gentlemen. You are both correct. One set of conditions promotes the other. Let us hope this will prove to be the exception."

"How will the tontine proceed?" asked Jean-Alexandre.

"When all pertinent data has been received and reviewed by your father, personal letters will be hand-delivered to the invited individuals."

"His ex-wife will be one of them?" asked Jean-Alexandre.

"Yes."

"Monsieur d'Avignon, you know my father. Is this a matter of expunging the guilt of having rejoined my mother?"

"It is not. Such guilt has never existed in his mind, not for one moment. Simply put: she is a means to an end. The end being to see the twins he fathered, and perhaps their children. He views the tontine as a probable deterrent to any possible impediment to that end on the part of his former wife. She has no condition precedent other than her presence. He cares not at all about the presence of her daughter or granddaughter. Need I say more?" D'Avignon savoured the aroma and taste of the cognac. "On a personal note, messieurs, I recognize loneliness when I see it. And I see it in your father's eyes. There is no guilt. Be assured. There is only good intent and anticipation."

"Anticipation of what, sir, exactly?"

"He misses your mother deeply. What else is there to say?"

The brothers shared a disheartened look. "When do you

expect the letters will be sent?" Gérard asked.

"Sometime near the end of summer. Until then he would prefer that it not be a topic of conversation." D'Avignon cleared his throat.

"Is there reason for us to be concerned for his well-being?"

"No, sir, there is not. Your father is in perfect health. Nothing regrettable is to be expected and I have every expectation that his good health will continue, in which case you will receive no additional information regarding the tontine. However, what he would like to expect, he complains, are more frequent visits from his family."

"If we had only had him with us those first twenty-some years, I can't imagine the difference he would have made in our lives. I've thought about it ever since that first day he sent me into our mother's bistro. I was an orphan child of the streets and only seven. Mama gave me my first hot meal in days and a job until the fall when she sent me to school. I remember them together and to hear Henri's stories was to hear of fire and water that soon became passion's boiling cauldron. It was a passion never lost. I remember looking up at him the very first day and thinking he was a giant, I still do. I remember mama telling me to go to him, warning me sternly not to say she had told me to do so. I still have the coins he tossed to me." Gérard fought his emotions. "So many lost days, so many lost moments."

"Nothing is lost, sir. Nothing would have changed. You are what you are, the both of you, and he is what and who he is. He is a giant to many of us, and he is proud of you, as is your mother who is still very much with you. He asked that I say that to both of you. It is what he believes. Nothing would have changed in your lives."

"Twenty five million dollars, what right do we have?" Jean-Alexandre said stupidly. "I never once imagined his resources to be so vast."

"Sir, Davidson loved your mother so much more than a

few dollars can express. In fact, he loved her more than my weak ability allows me to express. Gentlemen, I had the rare privilege to see them together, as perhaps you might not. He has lived a life of incredible and overwhelming grief since her death. Believe me, had he not come back to her, these fifty million dollars would be a virtual drop in a bucket. His wealth has meant nothing to him since the moment he saw her for the second time, as she ran to him. He is a special man, very special indeed. Certainly you know that."

"Years ago I hated him," said Jean-Alexandre. "There was no one I hated more for years. The more I researched him, the more I hated him. It was what drove me. Then I met him, man to man, and I loved him immediately and hated myself. The most difficult moment of my life, sir, was telling him of my mother's desperate prognosis, and when I saw his reaction that morning at the airport I knew I was right to feel about him the way that I did, and still do. I know my father. He is a man who is cautious about most people around him. He loves very few. Those few are fortunate and I see that we are amongst those privileged ranks."

"Indeed. Monsieur, secrecy is uppermost. May I ask if your father might rely on you and your brother?"

"Yes, sir, on my word, he may count on both of us."

Gérard concurred. "I give you and our father our word. I also speak for both of us. Be assured."

Maître d'Avignon looked at each brother in turn. "Messieurs, if there is nothing else, I believe our business is concluded and I will leave you to envision, if not enjoy your relaxed and respective retirements." He stood, extending his hand. "Please convey my respects to Mademoiselle Chantal. I daresay she will be quite taken aback by all of it and not believe a word either of you will tell her. Good day, gentlemen."

43

Early May was a good time to be paroled, particularly for a parole officer. Springtime meant that by the dead of winter their case-files would either be well on the way to better lives or deservedly ensconced back in prison. Many POs, made apathetic by too many years and ineffectual careers inside an archaic system that preferred punitive reprisal to corrective rehabilitation, couldn't care less about the first and least likely scenario. The second and most likely would make their winter much more relaxed and most secretly hoped for it.

The man's feet were shackled. His orange overalls were evenly creased along the sleeves and pant legs, his white tee-shirt was very white, his face was clean-shaven and his head showed a course outline where a thick mass of dark brown hair could have been.

"Take a seat, Philips, over there."

"Go," said the guard behind him, "and sit."

Dexter Philips ignored the guard's inconspicuously sharp pressure into the small of his back, maintaining eye contact with the warden of New York's Attica maximum-security correctional facility. "Thank you. Thank you, warden. Thank you, sir."

Philips pulled the chair away from the steel-grey table with his hands cuffed, not letting the legs touch the floor, not wanting to draw any attention to himself that wasn't completely positive. This was his last chance. The appeal was his third in front of the parole board. Next time they wouldn't bother with him. If he didn't succeed this time he never would.

He had just turned twenty-seven, though he looked more like forty-seven. He was slim at the waist and broad at the shoulders with no excess weight on his six-foot-five frame that was well-defined and muscular. He had no scars or tattoos, and he had never fit in. What had kept him safe for eight years was pure attitude: he didn't care about anything or anyone and if he ever had he had long since forgotten who, when or what. But today was different, today he had to care, or at the very least make them believe he did.

He had left his parents' home at fifteen, not so much dropping out from high school as never going back. His parents had loved him as much or as little as any other kid on the block had been loved by his parents, the honest and introspective ones at any rate: by degree. They adored him when he was new, and then as a baby. They loved him when he was a little boy wanting to please his mommy and to be like his daddy. And then they wondered why they ever had loved him as he entered into his turbulent teens and they looked forward to the day when they could love him again. Although the love never came back and the gap between them widened the more he stood out, not for what he was, rather for what he was not.

His parents could not afford hockey or football equipment, he was the wrong build for basketball and he had no proclivity for music. Parents of girls who might have been girlfriends thought he was older than he was and that he wanted only one thing from their daughters. He couldn't dance, he was never invited to parties and he looked more like his teachers than the other students. There was only one subject in which he excelled: getting into trouble whether he wanted to or not. He took the path of least resistance, which was also the path of greatest temptation and what he saw as the greatest freedom.

For two years he lived on the street and slept wherever he could: sometimes in the park, sometimes in open doorways or at the Y when he had the money. Mostly he stayed at the mission. Often he would share the back seat of abandoned cars with girls his age or younger who were also searching for a life that was better than the one they had managed to escape. He liked the parks the most, and summertime. Winter was the harshest, when he needed more money for a warm bed or a furnished by-the-week apartment to share with whoever, or however many could come up with their portion of the rent money. Unless they were girls, which is what led to his first crime.

He'd been a squeegee for most of those two years and when he wasn't washing car windows he was collecting returnable bottles and delivering fliers, but the winter of '90 was severe and the mission was full most nights with the older or sicklier of Montreal's burgeoning homeless population. The girls had all agreed: None were virgins and what was the difference if they did it with Dexter or with someone else for money that would allow them to eat and stay warm through the winter. He would even let the girls find their own men, men who would make them feel mature and in charge of their own lives for once. He took fifty-percent, and by the end of the third winter, weeks from his eighteenth birthday, Dexter Philips had full pockets, a few new girls who loved him and cold steel wrapped tightly around his wrists. He was sentenced to two years less a day and got out a year later. Some of his girls had been sent home, some to parents who had never missed them, though most went through the system and back to the streets to work for someone else.

No one wanted him when he got out. He hadn't improved in any way and he had refused rehab. He said things would work out, that he didn't need them and within a few months he was back on his knees with his head hanging down as some faceless cop restrained his hands behind his back while another pointed a nine-millimetre Glock at his chest. He barely heard them. All he remembered was being jerked to his feet before they shoved him unceremoniously into the back of a cruiser.

He'd been looking for work in all the wrong places and had been given a chance to prove himself. He'd been walking out from a bar after delivering several cases of liquor when he knew the best thing to do was to lie face down on the street with his arms stretched outward. He was sentenced to three years for transporting stolen property by a judge who had taken his age into consideration and he was back out after doing little more than a year due to overcrowding. He spent most of that winter in a halfway house while working in one cheap bar after another, cleaning urinals and toilets and mopping floors until his three months at the house was up and his bed was needed by someone else. His last resort was the mission, where he spent each night sitting on his cot with his legs straight out and his back wedged into the corner, planning his future until sleep eventually overtook him.

Throughout the following summer and into autumn he tried to round up some girls to work for him, soon discovering no one wanted any part of him. He tried to get work as a bouncer in strip clubs and decided he had hit rock bottom when he was turned down by a company looking to hire a refuse collector. All that was left to him was washing dishes in late-night diners and delivering fliers during the day, jobs that paid cash, and in between he would sleep in abandoned cars or in alleys under unyielding layers of cardboard that would mould to his body when it rained.

He had taken little more than five years to ruin his life and it had sounded too good to be true when the man came up to him in the park and offered him the opportunity of a lifetime. No more than two hours each night, and he would get a thousand in cash for each delivery. He'd be told where to be, what vehicle to acquire and where to deliver it. Two hours of his time for an easy grand that would change his world. There would be no borders to cross, no highways to travel, just a few city streets under the cover of darkness to where the trailer would be waiting for him and the chance of being caught was next to nil.

He took the job, and a thousand up front. He did four and sometimes five deliveries a week. They helped him get his own car, and financed it for him. He wore suits that gave him the look he needed and he started going to nightclubs and fine restaurants. He had a girl most nights, sometimes two, and a new apartment where he could entertain them until he kicked them out at dawn. He had no illusions about whom and what he was. He knew the more he said the more someone somewhere would eventually understand how little he really did know and he never said more than was necessary. He knew his limitation, though no one ever thought to question him. He was too imposing.

He never took chances. He always drove the limit and slowed to a stop at yellow lights. He did complete stops at stop signs and always circled the block where the trailer was parked at least twice as a precaution. Late one November evening was no exception, but it had been raining torrentially and the kid who ran the light Dexter was crossing had no idea until the impact of his father's sedan into the driver's door of the stolen European import.

The car theft ring was one of the most efficient in the city's history, and Dexter had come perilously close to ruining the operation. That the court gave him three years without probation was the least of his worries. What concerned him the most was the verdict of the second court sitting in judgement of him, a court he knew could easily issue a death sentence for what he had done. They didn't. Instead they promised to be there for him when he got out. He was not to worry. No one else had been caught, the driver of the trailer had left the scene before the police arrived and they appreciated that Dexter had kept his mouth shut. No one would touch him, he had their assurances. He would be fine. Mario DiFiore was as good as his word and he never forgot family.

Dexter Philips' freedom had lasted four short months. What he had not spent of his eighty-thousand dollars the authorities had confiscated, and he cared very little whether the judge had said three or thirty. He had a job, a good one, and they would be there for him. So what if he had to do a bit of time first. He would do the time and learn from those who knew more than he did. Next time he would be much smarter and not take chances. He leaned back against the wall in his cell, his face expressionless, looking down at the rough plaster casts on his broken left leg and arm. He had already been on the inside a week.

Then a month had passed, seasons had no meaning, '93 had become '96 and Dexter Philips was standing outside, not looking back. He never would again. So much had changed in three years, he thought. He had a job, they were waiting for him, there would be no more parks or cardboard blankets, and there would be no more stupid mistakes. Mario DiFiore hugged him and kissed his cheeks. There was nothing to forgive. Business had never been better, the cops were as stupid or as crooked as ever and he hadn't forgotten how Dexter Philips had put family first.

The first day on the job would only be three weeks after his release, giving him time to adjust. First there would be girls, lots of girls, a trip to Barbados with any one of them, a new BMW and a new wardrobe. He had hit the big time. Best of all: the job was easy. It was a no-brainer, they told him, and he believed them. Why wouldn't he? He had listened and learned from the best for three years. He could tell the smart ones from the losers, and he was no loser. The sky was the limit. He finally fit in, he was finally someone. He had family and that had to count for something.

Like the man had said: the job would be easy. Cars acquired from Montreal would be delivered to La Guardia,

JFK or Logan, those from Toronto would go to Detroit's Wayne County or Chicago's O'Hare where other cars would be waiting for transference to Canada. It was simple and profitable with zero chance of failure. He would do a minimum of two trips per week for an easy three grand per trip and easy women. That's all he would ever know and who deserved the good life more than Dexter Philips? Absolutely no one, that's what he knew. He had paid his dues and his time had come to collect. It was time for payback. Fuck the cops. All that mattered to him was his new family.

By Christmas he had put his three years of incarceration and intensive study in criminal affairs behind him. He had gifts to open, girls to entertain him and a new career. He was twenty-three and the sky was the limit, they said. And he believed them. That's the way it had to be, that's the way it would be.

In early April of '96 Dexter crossed the border at New York. He felt good, everything was coming together. The voluptuous Cindy was waiting for him back home and by noon the next day he would be back with her. That's what he thought until he pulled into the Niagara US Customs and Immigration who asked him politely to pull over to the side and pop the trunk. He smiled confidently and kept that face despite the tension until the Border Patrol pulled up behind him and agents approached from the four corners of his car. He sighed deeply with both hands on the steering wheel and let the senior officer open his door. At the end of an afternoon of intensive questioning he knew nothing about Operation Cindy and the DA's office would tape several more interviews with Dexter Philips after agreeing to a plea bargain for a lesser charge that would save him from a life sentence. He took the ten years and told them everything he knew about Mario DiFiore and his brothers.

That was then, this was now. He looked at the two other men first, then at the middle-aged woman who was dressed to make herself look androgynous in a cramped kennel full of deprived males. He saw past it. He saw what she would look like after hours with her hair hanging down in matted wet strings as she lay naked and moaning under warm soapy suds to bathe away the pungency of sweat and disinfectant found only in prisons. He hadn't seen a woman in three years. He hadn't had one visitor, let alone a woman and the image of how she would look luxuriating in a bath with oil glistening on her naked body he would keep to himself until later.

Women knew when they were being undressed by men. He knew most of them enjoyed the lewd fantasy, secretly craving it and this woman was no different on the outside. But now she was on the inside and his eyes darted back to the warden's after relaxing his lips and face into a nondescript expression he hoped would not appear furtively submissive. Succeeding was all about relaxing, all about breathing, all about balancing regret and humility with sincerity and confidence.

"When did you first join us, Philips?"

"Three years ago, sir, less a day or two."

"And before that you did a few years in Montreal's Saint-Vincent-Paul, and before that," the warden sneered, "two one-year stints. Almost eight years all told, Philips, with not much outside time in-between. You like it on the inside?"

"No, sir. I don't. I just got in with the wrong people. Those days are finished. I proved that when I worked with the police and DA."

"You mean when you gave up DiFiore."

"Yes, sir."

"And now you want us to believe you're a model citizen and let you go, when you know full- well you're coming back to us sometime soon?"

"I won't be back, sir, with respect, sir, never again; not here, not anywhere." He looked at the woman. She was the one any con would have known would make his day or bust his balls. She was the one he would have to convince, the one who would think the worst of him. "Ma'am, I've studied every single day since I've been here. I've read more books than anyone else. I even got my high school leaving last year. I know that doesn't mean much to a lady like you, but I know things I didn't know back three years ago. I'm smarter. I've worked double shifts in the kitchen and maintenance to earn a bit and I've saved it all. I've gone for rehabilitative counselling, on my own. I didn't even know that word before I got here. I've stayed out of trouble, ma'am. I won't be back, I swear. I'm still young. I thought I might go back to school to get a college degree at night while I work. I've learned a lot about sandwiches and burgers, ma'am. I won't be back."

He let his smile disappear rather than letting her see his lips quiver under the stress. The woman remained silent. She flipped a page in her file folder and made a notation. Philips looked at one of the two other men who cleared his throat.

"Why did you say you might go back to school, and not that you would, if you're so intent on getting out?"

"I'm nervous, sir, that's all. I will go back, sir, if I can get into a school. I'll go to whichever one takes me."

"And study what exactly?"

"Don't know, sir, maybe something social. It's not like I don't know how the other half lives."

"Cure the world, be a Good Samaritan?"

"Cure myself first, sir. I'll never be a Good Samaritan, but I will be a better person. I already am as much as anyone can be in a place like this."

The warden said: "Two-thirds, Philips, that's how many of you come back. You've already proven that. What makes this time any different?" He looked at the sheet in front of him, as though he was studying each word. He wasn't. "You're out in seven years anyway, Philips, so why not save everyone the trouble. You won't have to get caught all over again, the cops and the court won't have to waste their time with you and you won't have to find someone new to keep you company."

Dexter Philips looked at the floor, squeezing his lips together before talking. "That's not how it is, sir. You know that. You know no one bothers me. I've always been a loner. I don't bother them, they don't bother me. I don't have friends here, and I don't want any."

"Not since your first day. Your fist went into the guy's face list a steel piston. You took out half his teeth and broke his jaw. He was in sickbay for a week and the second guy couldn't breathe through his nose for a month. Do you have any idea how much all that cost the state?"

The warden paused long enough for Dexter to answer.

"What happened the first day was a test. You know that, sir. I passed, they failed. They thought they were bigger or better than they were. They found out two isn't always better than one." Finally Philips smiled. "I would have done the very same to help you out of the same situation, sir. I did what I had to do to survive. You know the drill, sir. You know I didn't argue or resist on my way to solitary and those other guys didn't have much to say about it once I got out. Now we get along just fine." He looked at the woman. "It was a little misunderstanding, ma'am. They were marking their territory, like the wolves do. When they found out I was no threat they left me alone. I was protecting myself, what I had to do to survive."

"Marking territory, Philips? The warden repeated, coughing a laugh.

"There's a lady in the room, sir." He turned to her. "Ma'am, it's not something that'll happen on the outside."

She seemed unimpressed, her face devoid of any expression as though she could see through him.

"You made some pretty serious enemies three years ago, kid. Those DiFiore brothers are as bad as it gets. As much as I'm surprised you're still alive, did you ever consider you'd be better off not getting out?" the warden asked.

"I don't plan to look them up, sir. It'll be awhile before they know." He shrugged. "And most of them got more time than me. Those who didn't don't count for much."

"Still, it won't be long before they know you're out, if you do get out. News travels fast. It would be open season and you'd be the duck."

"No more than I am in here, sir. The inside's a good place to learn how to cover your back and I'm a good student."

"Do you have friends on the outside, people you can turn to?" the third man asked.

"I don't have friends inside or out, sir. I've got family, a mother and father who are more like strangers. I haven't seen them in eleven years, not since I left home."

"And got yourself into serious trouble eight years running," continued the same man.

Philips nodded. "A third of my life, yes sir. It's time for a change. Don't you think? Sixty minutes a day in a walled yard isn't much like a forest or an ocean. I'll do what I said. I'll go to school and flip burgers if I have to. Maybe one day I'll own the place. But I can't do that from in here."

The woman asked: "Will you find your parents? Will you ask them for assistance?

"No ma'am, I won't. I'll do it on my own. They were okay parents. They did their best, I suppose. They got hit hard in the pockets in the early eighties and nineties when my old man lost his job. I don't imagine they have much to spare. It's not like they're young, and they took it pretty hard the first few times I got put away. They didn't even come to court the last time and they've never been here to see me. Maybe I'll visit them when I've done something worthwhile with myself, I'm not sure. They've already said goodbye to me in their minds. They're better off."

"Where would you go?"

"I have to say Toronto at first, ma'am. Going back to Montreal would be asking for trouble. That's what they would expect me to do, and one day I'm going to see the ocean, maybe the east coast or Vancouver."

"Unfortunately, Mr. Philips, I'm not as convinced as you are that it would be in your best interest to leave here."

"Ma'am?" he questioned.

"Your release at this time, I'm not certain it would in your best interest. You are able to continue with college in here. Perhaps even get a degree before your time is up."

"And then do what with it, ma'am? If I don't get out now I won't need an education, not that kind. This isn't that kind of school, ma'am." Dexter paused long enough to swallow. There was no moisture in his throat and it showed. "It's now or never, ma'am. No one will want me after fifteen years in prison, papers or no papers and that's what it'll be by then. This way I've got a chance, a good one."

The woman made more notes and looked at Philips without feeling. "Warden, might we have a moment without the prisoner."

"Philips, get out. Guard, stand him outside the door."

Dexter Philips had no time to react or to scan their faces for the slightest indication. The guard moved him through the doorway quickly and stood him in the corridor with his back to the door's wire-reinforced glass panelling. It was like being sentenced all over again, to seven more years. He said nothing. It was pointless. There was nothing to say. He knew the guard who was watching for the warden's signal would ignore him, as though he were waiting for permission to pull the switch that would send the current through the metal skullcap and into his brain.

Then he was grabbed, turned abruptly by the shoulders and guided roughly back into the stark room with one hand at his back and another still grasping his shoulder. He sat, slowly, resisting the pressure. He studied their faces from left to right, stopping at the woman. They were all looking down, except the warden who stared back as though searching for a truth or a lie.

The woman closed her file mechanically, not looking up as she checked her cell phone. "Gentlemen, is there anything further you wish to say to this prisoner, or ask before we leave here?" There was no comment. "Warden, thank you. Gentlemen, I believe we're finished with the prisoner."

Dexter Philips felt his body go rigid. Two firm hands pushed down on his shoulders from behind. She had been the one in charge. He searched his mind for something to say, something she would believe in the few seconds left to him, something that would compel her to listen.

"Ma'am…"

"Mr. Philips, whatever you wish to say you can say to the warden. It's really not our place to say more. We're done. The decision has been made. Thank you, and good luck."

"Ma'am, please, just…"

The warden interceded. "Philips shut your damn mouth before you say something stupid to make us change our minds. You're a free man. You're going to spend the next few nights away from your block, to be sure nothing happens to you and you'll be out by the end of the week. Now get out of here." He nodded to the guard. "Philips, being in here's been a walk in the park for you and it's next to a miracle you're being released so soon. Next time there won't be a release, wherever they put you. It'll be a lifetime deal so stay clean and don't screw up."

The warden and the board looked at him with solemn faces, indifferent to Dexter Philips' wide-eyed elation as he thanked them profusely. They had seen it too often before and they each knew there was a better than even chance he'd be back. He knew otherwise and he lay awake in a segregated cell throughout the night. The formality with the warden three days later lasted a record five minutes. He left without shaking hands and he was a free man.

The State Police drove him to the border where they gave him over to his parole officer. He was advised by the border personnel that he'd be barred from entering the U.S. at any time over the next seven years, the term of his parole, and that he'd be persona non grata any time after that unless in possession of a proper visa. When he entered Canada they made him feel equally welcome.

En route to Toronto the PO explained his parole: If Dexter remained marginal with no particular highlights in his file they would be in constant communication for the duration of his sentence. If, on the other hand, he excelled in some way, the parole officer would be more than happy not to see him any more than was absolutely required by the courts. In effect, he was still in prison with more room to walk around. He would report each week by phone and twice a month in person, at least for the first year. The better he did, the more scope he'd be given. Anything else was not an option. He'd be sent back. In the meantime, temporary arrangements had been made for him at a halfway house and the PO had found him a job as a labourer on a construction crew whose boss believed in second chances.

His first paycheque came a week later, enough for a shabby by-the-week apartment, new clothes and the T-bone he had been dreaming about all week while eating sloppy mashed potatoes with canned peas and hamburgers or over-cooked sausages. What he wanted more than any of that was to find somewhere to drink a couple of beers while he looked at something soft, curvy and naked before heading to Younge Street to see what was available in any of the regular bars. Whether she had a face or not didn't matter.

44

Kitty Hawk turned twenty-two on July 17th. It was a Saturday and her busiest night. She was unusually tall for her profession and after three minutes on stage she was entirely naked. The other girls wore six-inch stilettos throughout their routines, not Kitty. Nor did she need a stainless steel pole make her body move in a way that was exotic and inviting. All the girls were model-perfect and brought in top dollar, yet beside Kitty they were clumsy and amateurish. She was inherently sexual and exotic. She was lithe and moved her body easily in ways that left nothing to the imagination. The other girls would let the front-row patrons touch their feet or do wide Vs for those they knew would later ask for a lap dance or for an hour alone in a salon where they could do more than just look at the girl. Kitty did not. What they saw was from centre stage and frequent customers all knew that anything more would cost two hundred per hour on a selective basis.

She would refuse any man who would have to look up when standing beside her, anyone who had downed one beer too many or anyone who had excessive body hair or none on his head. She would refuse anyone she considered overweight, out of shape or with bad breath, and she did no more than three singles each night. She would do couples if they were women, or when a horny husband wanted to watch his bi-curious wife get off. In either case she charged double.

She never pranced around nude between shows. She never served and she never danced at tables. When she first began her career she quickly realized the need to set herself apart. She had made herself exclusive and cleared two thousand on a slow week, four times what she had first earned as a waitress in a downtown bar and double what she had taken in as an escort for two years after.

This was so much better. There were no old men with flaccid skin panting and sweating on top of her. There were no freaks who wanted to role-play and no hotshots who thought escort was synonymous with slut or that for five hundred or a thousand a night they could do what only her father had ever done to her. That is, until that last night when she had smashed in his face with the back of a cast iron skillet. It was the night he threw her out, the night her mother stood by and said nothing, the night she had dreamed about for so long. She was fourteen at the time, though with the make-up and clothes she had bought from nearly-new stores she had passed easily for nineteen or twenty.

She had spent the night with a friend and the next morning she disappeared forever into an unforgiving adult world where she quickly found her place. She waited tables from her first day. She found a room she could afford and by the end of her first year she had gone through four or five men as much as three times her age. At first she just gave them the one thing she had to offer because they all loved her and had bought her little gifts. Then towards the end of the year, when the love seemed less real, she took more from them. The gifts became more expensive, gifts she wanted, gifts she would later return for their cash value until the love ran out.

Despite the gradual setback, by age fifteen she understood the rudiments of supply and demand. She continued waiting tables during the day, though now she was accepting dates from her regular customers, each man thinking he was the one and only. She made it very clear on the first date that sleeping with her would come at a price. It was business. By seventeen she had no boyfriend and didn't care. What she did have was a safety deposit box filled with more than forty thousand tax-free dollars. Waiting tables had become a means to an end, working fifty-hour weeks to earn less than half for what she did three or four nights a week after being wined and dined. She also had a clientele, and when she made the final decision to approach an agency she believed would best suit her and promote her, to offer her services, they took her on immediately, no questions asked. By eighteen she had her own condo, a convertible and had already taken two trips abroad.

She enjoyed what she did. She delighted in men looking at her, eager to see her naked and knowing the only way they could have her was to pay for her. Her body gave her power over them, and she enjoyed that the most. Yet she despised them, the superior male sex: men who liked to play dress-up or to be spanked, or to call her mommy as they were pounding her from behind to avoid seeing her face that was almost always grinning mockingly. What she did not like was being under them, smelling them and having to pretend each one was the best ever.

She would occasionally take on a female client and some had become regulars. Often she would stay with the younger ones through the evening and into the early morning: a reprieve, an escape not from reality, but from men. It had lasted two lucrative years and if she never saw or felt another penis again it would be too soon. Yet she still had to work, and one afternoon she let curiosity get the better of her and she went to The Booty Lounge for a drink.

The girls were all beautiful, yet she stood out as gorgeous and she knew it. She could tell the lesbians from the dykes and those from the heteros. She stayed throughout the afternoon talking with the girls, even asking one to dance for her. Then she asked to speak with the manager who had been watching her closely from the monitor in his office. She did her first dance in private for the girls, then for the boss behind closed doors. The next morning she was fitted for her costumes. She began the following day per their special arrangement: She would dance, but she would not do tables. She would service special customers, strictly those she wanted to be with and she would work exclusively at night. Her real name was Belinda Samuels, to anyone else she would be Kitty Hawk and no one in management could expect her body to be an on-call receptacle for their ejaculate, not even Abacus. That had been a one-time courtesy for her new boss and he hadn't seen her mocking grin from behind his desk. What the other girls did was their problem, for Kitty Hawk dancing would be a strictly financial arrangement.

After two years she still demanded star billing at the city's premier gentleman's lounge. She wore designer clothes and had upgraded from a Ford to a Mercedes. Her life was good and getter better each day. The one thing that would make it better was to know the man who had married her mother was dead. She never mixed business with pleasure at the lounge and only did girl-on-girl privately. On her nights off she would often be seen at a bar across town not known by the girls she worked with, and would occasionally take a girl home for the evening, preferring to be alone the rest of the week.

The male employees knew better than to try and several of the other dancers had tried and failed to be more than friends with her. She wanted no involvements, no complications. Even Abacus had kept his word not to exhort special favours, though he did continue amassing an impressive and exclusive home library of her hour-long sessions in private salons from cameras intended to spot check on the girls' well-being while entertaining customers who were not always respectful.

She knew about it, everyone did except the customer.

She liked knowing that watching her turned him on enough to record her. Kitty Hawk was a consummate actress as much as she was a methodical seductress and he had often suggested to her that she at least think about getting into the film business, certain she would be an instant hit with the porn crowd. That she enjoyed what she did showed in her face. Watching her on tape was like being invited to private screenings, each new one as hypnotic and as compelling as the one before. She had become his favourite aphrodisiac during those evenings he was at home with his wife, Leona DiFiore, who had often asked to be part of the show.

Dexter Philips was led to a table in the centre of The Booty. Sitting at the front row was always at a premium and he wanted to drink more than tip a bouncer. Ten weeks had gone by since his release. He was still living from pay to pay at twelve bucks an hour and his idea of a long-term relationship was meeting her Friday night and still seeing her at breakfast on Saturday before asking her to leave so he could move to his newest address.

He had gone back to wearing suits after hours: one blue and one black, which he had bought at fifty percent off because of the out-dated style and slight dusting at the shoulders. He allowed himself a weekly massage to reverse the three-year stress of never knowing when a shank might rip through his skin and his hair was finally at a length he could comb. He wore eyeglasses he had bought from a drugstore with the weakest possible lenses, thinking they would soften his look and he was halfway through a summer semester towards a degree in Social Sciences. He read voraciously, often aloud, trying hard to improve his diction and lose the distinctive quality of voice that comes from the school of hard knocks. That was during the week, the weekends were his.

At first there was too much to see. The girls serving tables were either totally nude or wearing sheer panties, and each one who passed his table had leaned in close to tell him that she gave the best lap dances in the club. Most every patron in the bar was male. The few who were not were with other women and much more interested in the girls dancing at their tables or on the stage than the thought of being picked up.

The girls were called Dixie and Bambi, Delightful Deloris and Heavenly Heather, whose real names were likely: Brenda, Joan, Alice and Wendy, but when he heard Kitty Hawk his eyes went to the stage and never left her. What details of her he could not clearly see, he imagined. When she finished she stepped to the bottom of the low spiral stairway where he strained to see her wrap a white satin bandeau with short tassels around her waist that fashioned an exotic skirt and a matching top which did little to conceal her breasts. As she came closer he eased himself up from a casual slouching position and smiled directly at her, holding up his empty glass.

"Sorry, sweetie, I don't do drinks," she said pleasantly with a voice that was neither husky nor feminine.

He bounced his knee. "Then come back in five minutes, after I get one, and dance for me."

"I don't do laps either, sorry. Give one of the other girls a chance. They're all super good. This place only hires the best."

"I see that." He frowned, tilting his head and looking through the upper and lower tassels. "So what do you do, Kitty, other than give everyone in the room a hard-on?"

She smiled back. "It'll cost you two hundred to find out, sweetie. It'll be the best hour of your life as long as you don't tell your girlfriend or your wife."

"Not an issue. The issue is the two hundred. I've already blown my paycheque. Now I'm the one who's sorry."

"We take cards, sweetie."

"Don't have one." He looked at her skirt that was perfectly at eye-level. "Maybe that was a mistake. Payday's not for another couple of weeks."

She found it strange he would say such a thing.

"Well, I tell you what. I don't give freebies because it's not good for business and the management guys wouldn't go for it, but how about a sneak preview." She parted the front of her skirt. "Only two hundred and it's worth every penny. You get to touch …that's all. What's your name?"

"Dex," he answered, grinning widely, mesmerized by what he was seeing. "What's yours, Sandra or Louise?" He shook his head slowly, his grin slightly wider than sly. "No, not Louise; you're definitely a Sandra."

"I'm Kitty Hawk, sweetie, and don't you forget it. I'll be here when you're ready. Saturdays are always busy, so are Sundays and I don't do the whole room so don't come too late. Mondays are a little slower with mostly out-of-town expense account types who get too drunk too fast. I leave them to the other girls, so Mondays are good. Do what you have to do. I'm off Tuesdays and Wednesdays. If you don't see me just ask for Kitty, or you can call and reserve me," she closed the skirt one side at a time, letting the tassels swing freely with the motion of her hips, "with a card."

"Two weeks is a long time. I could die thinking about it."

"What makes you think you won't die because of it? Could be I'm giving you longer to live," she said unwittingly with a grin. She leaned closer to whisper in his ear. "See you soon, Dex," and she walked away before he could answer, with her skirt swishing tauntingly to and fro across the curves of her perfectly rounded buttocks.

That night and Sunday he could not stop thinking of her. It's all he could do. He had scarcely enough money in his pockets for food, let alone an hour with a stripper. The men he worked with all knew of her and each one wanted to be there with him to see for themselves that Kitty Hawk would actually choose someone they knew, someone who didn't wear a Rolex or Armani. He thanked them, insisting that anything worth having was worth waiting for and he tried to put her out of his mind. He worked as many overtime hours as he could. If she was going to be as good as she promised, he was going to want her for two hours.

Monday night, two weeks later, Dexter Philips was front row centre, dressed in blue denim jeans and jacket, cowboy boots and a crisp white shirt he had earlier taken to the launderer to have starched and ironed while he waited. He saw her perform twice before following her into a private salon. When they were finished he sat through two more stage performances before his second private session that evening, during which he touched every inch of her gently with his fingertips as though moulding a three dimensional likeness of her in his mind.

Her body was flawless. She looked like a mythical Scandinavian goddess with long white-blonde hair, high cheekbones, chiselled features, blue deep-set eyes, full unpainted lips and a slender neck. Her breasts were firm, her nipples taut only when he pinched them and her stomach was flat with the tone of someone who took pride in how she looked. Her labia were moist to his touch, their folds delicate and surprisingly cool. Her thighs and calves were firm and her slender feet were tipped with perfect toes painted red. He enjoyed feeling the weight of her body moving over him. The sensation was euphoric and her body odour was intoxicating. When she turned to face him she wrapped her arms around his neck, letting the fullness of her breasts massage his face. Her arms were firm and when she took one away to reach down he missed the pressure, until he felt the assertive strength of her fingers acknowledging his arousal. He was going insane. He wanted to kiss her, but he knew better. It was enough she was letting him explore her body beyond what was usually expected or accepted. Her back was muscular without being hard. Her buttocks were smooth and firm, the soft flesh undulating between his probing fingers. All she knew about him was his name. She also knew he couldn't dress as well as he wanted to and that in another life she might even have liked him if it weren't for the fact he was an ex-con.

It had been worth every penny of the four hundred and when she asked him jokingly if he had any money left for a late night snack he answered no, that she would have to pay and on a sudden whim she said she would. She wanted instantly to take back the words, but she didn't, and then it was too late. He was gone.

They met away from the club. They had coffee and split a club sandwich, not saying much of anything and when they left the diner he walked her to her car where he blew too much air past his lips to whistle. She was big time, he should have known. She chuckled at his reaction to the silver sedan as she pushed two hundred dollars into his pocket.

When she offered to drive him to his car, he answered no. He preferred to walk. He would have more time to think about her and would see her the next night to give her back the two hundred.

"Sweetie, you come back for me when you're rich enough to marry me and take me away from all of this. Until then I'll only be a very expensive cheap feel you can't afford. Get a girlfriend you can feel up for free and save your money."

"But now I've got two hundred for another slice of heaven."

"Do what you have to do. Just remember that Thursday, or whatever other night, there won't be a coffee or anything else. Sorry, Dex. I didn't mean to lead you on. I'm a stripper. It's what I do, and I've got a past."

"So do I."

"Yeah, I know. You're not walking home for fresh air. You're walking to a bus stop or a taxi stand, or some piece of shit you don't want me to see. You're an ex-con, a bad boy and you're looking for someone to help you forget. There's a look: old before your time, and it's nothing creams will ever take away. It's in the eyes, Dex, and the mouth. Lips that never really smile, just curl up. All the girls know it, and you've got it. It's something to unload real fast. I'm not the only one who'll see it, though you do hide it better than most. What was it," she asked calmly, "drugs, a bank, a few stupid B & Es? It couldn't have been murder, not unless you got out on your own."

"A bit of everything: stupid kid stuff."

"Somehow I don't think so." She put an open palm to his cheek. "Goodnight, Dex, or whoever you are."

Over the next three days it was all Dexter could do to not think of her, not think of who would be seeing her naked or feeling every inch of her beautiful body. Despite his best efforts to disconnect his brain from his penis, she never went away. She was the sexiest woman he had ever touched. He also knew the kind of people she worked for and doing anything more than paying for his beer and a cheap thrill would constitute a parole violation, not to mention a broken leg or arm.

He was nothing, a loser. He had nothing going for himself, let alone for anyone else. That would change. One day he would be something, and be someone, one day. All he needed was a break. She had seen right through him. So what? She was no better. They were two of a kind. He had a dead-end job, no savings and no education. Literally all he had was on his back, with memories of a life he would never share, not even with a dancer.

Thursday night he sat along the edge of the stage. He watched her first show and when she left the stage he stood and went to the private salon he had reserved. Ten minutes later she came through the double portiere wearing garters, sheer panties that did more to highlight than conceal and a bustier. She stood there with her legs together and her arms akimbo, rolling her eyes and shaking her head as she smiled back at him. She would let him down as easily as she could, but she would let him down. She hoped he would listen.

Five minutes before his time expired she snuggled her naked body tightly against his and put her lips to his ears, grinding her pelvis gently against his in tight elliptical circles.

"Dex, do you like girl-on-girl. Do you, Dex?" she taunted.

"Sure I do. Who wouldn't?"

"You'd be surprised, Dex. Lots of guys don't like it: the freaky ones, the ones who think vaginas exist only to validate their manhood. In fact, they're the real pussies."

He looked at his watch. "We're talking minutes here. Are we expecting company?"

"No, we're not. We're done. The point is: I like it, Dex. I like girls: brunettes, reds and blonds. I don't care as long as I can kiss them without stooping. I enjoy my job and being with girls gives me balance. Without them I couldn't do this. Guys are too much trouble. They expect too much. Quite frankly, on stage, I don't even see them and that includes you. What I'm saying is: don't get too involved in coming here, or thinking you'll get anything more than one of these." She pressed both her hands into his crotch and squeezed "It's a job for me. Whatever else you do with this thing tonight won't be with me."

"You live with a woman?"

"Not your business."

"I've never beaten a woman. I've never even raised my hands to one. I'm an ex-con, so what? I'm going to college and I've read more books in the past year than in the last twenty. So maybe one day I will be back for you, to marry you. Maybe one day I will be that rich guy."

"I hope so, Dex, for you." She giggled. "Just don't wait too long. I can't do this for more than another few years."

"And then what?"

"I'll disappear from all this and live happily ever after."

"You and me?"

She shook her head. "No. Just me."

"It's a pipe dream."

She smoothed his cheek. "No, it's not. It's a business plan."

"Why do this at all? Be something else."

"I clear more in a week than other girls my age gross in a month, and I don't have to fuck anyone."

"Or make love."

"Or fuck anyone."

"You're cynical. Good for you. Just know you're not the only one with eyes. I see what I see, too." He eased her away, smiling more than he wanted and reaching into his shirt pocket. "I'm Dexter Philips, my real name. Call me sometime, because I think you like me."

She put a hand to his mouth. "Nobody has to know who you are. Nobody cares. It's the same for all of us and no one other than a complete fool uses his last name or a credit card in a place like this." Kitty Hawk sighed, taking the small slip of paper and putting it back into his pocket. "It's what I do, Dex, and the girl thing is who I am." She took up his wrist. "You have exactly two minutes left. Make the most of it and don't come back. The people who run this place don't like trouble and that's what you're looking for."

She hadn't moved. Her long legs still straddled his. Whatever she had expected had not been the smile fading from his face. Her smile evaporated with each word he spoke, as though he had heard the question she had wanted to ask.

"It's what they always say: the guards, when cons have visitors. You have exactly two minutes left. Make the best of it. For years I wanted to be able to hear those words so badly. I envied the other guys who got to hear them. They had visitors. I never did, and now that I have heard them I really wish you hadn't said them."

"Get yourself a girlfriend, Dex. Do this for free. I guarantee you'll wonder why you ever blew six hundred bucks to cop a feel."

He held her hands as she stood, absorbing one final look. "Dexter Philips. It's my real name. Don't wait too long Sandra."

He smiled back at her, letting the folded slip of paper flutter to the carpet before he swept aside the curtain and walked out.

Belinda Samuels gathered up her costume in her arms and slumped down naked and exhausted onto the soft fabric of the sofa to wait, staring down to the tiny white square. When she finally left she casually kicked it in front of her, not wanting to reach down even at the periphery of the camera's field of view. It would be late Friday night before Abacus would anxiously insert the tapes into his VCR and jump onto his bed to join his excited wife. She loved watching Kitty Hawk naked and was going to ask her husband again and again until he either brought Kitty home to her for an evening, or took her to the club. It would be an hour later that Abacus would leave his unfulfilled and disgruntled wife to take the tapes to his studio to replay them and print out an image of the man's face. Then he would call The Booty Lounge to tell Kitty Hawk not to leave. By mid-morning Saturday he would be seated face to face with a very pleased Mario DiFiore.

45

Jean-Alexandre and Gérard did have quite a bit to explain when Chantal had joined them in the study, once she had seen Maître d'Avignon's chauffeured car pull away, with not much to say. The clock in the vestibule had not yet chimed one o'clock and both men were finishing their third cognac. They were seated on the same heavy leather sofa, looking up at her with the same nonplussed expression. She looked at the decanter which she had filled herself the night before, their flushed cheeks and she chided them insouciantly for imbibing before lunch had been served.

They looked at each other and chortled, making her wonder what had gone on with their visitor that would make them act so strangely. The men's light-hearted mood was too incongruous with the seriousness of their disposition prior to the lawyer's arrival and they were at a loss for words, something she found even more peculiar given the brothers' proclivity for mischievous banter which was quite often directed at her. All Jean-Alexandre managed to say was that there would be no lunch; they would have an early dinner at L'Assiette Élégante once they had spoken with Davidson to discuss a visit: Chantal's domain. Then he stood and poured three more cognacs, suggesting to his ageless wife that she be seated before he placed the call because, as Maître d'Avignon had so eloquently forewarned, she would not believe him.

What they did tell her was a jumble of incredibly

unbelievable words. From the first day they had been introduced, Davidson had treated Chantal like the father she had always missed, the father she had once played with and talked with and played tricks on before a sudden tragedy stole him away from her only hours after her mother. She had never forgotten how Gabrielle had leapt into Davidson's arms the day he had come back to her, or how they had kissed, or how the reunited couple had hurried past her to the sanctuary of a more private place. Nor had she ever stopped remembering the two gossiping old men who had invited her to a mysterious dinner they had planned in the very same restaurant, coaxing and pulling a reluctant and argumentative Jean-Alexandre to the table without the slightest knowledge of what was happening to him or why he had an armful of roses he hadn't bought. He had fallen in love with Chantal instantly, fearing someone else would if he didn't and he had not ever stopped loving her: like father, like son. Chantal regularly spoke with Davidson two and three times during any given week and, when in Las Palmas, they were each other's favourite strolling partner.

Listening to Gérard and her husband speak to Davidson on separate phones Sunday afternoon, seeing each man choose his words so judiciously, she knew there was more to it than what they had told her. She also knew her husband. If he intended for her not to know, she never would, and she would never ask. Jean-Alexandre was adamant when he handed her the receiver: She was not to say anything more than a simple thank you, and not mention for what, before discussing their upcoming trip. She stuck out her tongue and scrunched her face, her usual response when she already knew perfectly well what to say. She just wanted to talk with Davidson.

When she had finished a long time later, Chantal joined them in the study to say they had been invited for dinner at Las Palmas the following weekend. Davidson had hoped they would stay for the week and no more than a gracious mention had been made of their gifts. She knew Davidson. All he wanted was dinner with his family and to walk along the shore with Chantal, if she would favour an old man and tolerate his rambling tales of days past. She stuck out her tongue once again and went to change, leaving the men with flushed grins and very little to say.

Chantal loved Las Palmas and she adored Davidson. She loved walking with him along the beach, holding his hand and listening to his long stories. He would always be Davidson to her: the tall, dark and secretive man with the strangely accented French whose eyes she could only look into when he was seated and she was not. She wanted him to live forever and, as usual, the week and their time together had gone too quickly. She kissed him goodbye and was inexplicably melancholic throughout the return flight to Paris.

Nothing had been mentioned of the tontine in Chantal's presence, or of the gift, though Davidson did understand the need for the men to express their feelings. He had assured them with very few words that well before their next communication with Joaquin their new wealth would seem no more important than the day's weather and he raised the palms of his hands to bring an abrupt end to the subject. By July 15th, the country's Bastille Day, not only had they forgotten his words, they had not thought to mention the windfall to Joaquin who had called them from Bahrain. He would be home very soon, he promised. His life had recently been diametrically and pleasantly altered and he was anxious to tell them all about it.

46

Mike DuFour had taken every moment of the three months to fulfill his mandate. He had travelled in excess of thirty thousand miles and had compiled paper and electronic files which had required two large briefcases to carry the information to Davidson. There were photographs, recent videotapes and copies of official documents that included birth certificates, death certificates and marriage licenses. The files included academic records, medical records, work histories, financial reports, credit checks, one diverse criminal record and one record of exemplary military service.

Mike DuFour had surpassed all expectations. The previous day, the last day of July, during their first phone conversation in three months, Davidson had asked the detective to be available on Las Palmas for the week as a well-deserved, all expense-paid vacation. There would be no business other than the preliminary report until the end of the week, which would allow Davidson the time he needed to study the files and prepare his letters. Assuming the detective's arrival, the finest accommodation of the island's premier hotel had been reserved for DuFour and an envelope addressed to him would be waiting at the front desk with sufficient funds to care for the most extravagant vacation needs.

DuFour was met at the airport by Davidson's always affable chauffeur, Jorge de la Vega, and rode quietly behind the privacy shield, thinking of what he would say and how he would say it. He was still amazed by what seemed to be the old man's unwavering confidence in him. He had on several occasions thought to call Davidson to report his findings, not doing so because his greater temptation was to believe Davison would construe any such call as a sign of indecision or his inability to perform.

Davidson stood smiling at the entrance of the villa to greet him as the limo passed through the wrought iron gate and slowed in front of the unadorned portico. They shook each other's hand and exchanged polite civilities as they walked into the cavernous main room looking out onto the Atlantic. Davidson wasted no time. He had waited three months that had seemed more like that many years and more. He called for a jug of Maria's highly reputed sangria and as the two men waited he placed a micro-cassette recorder on the table between them and Mike DuFour reached into a briefcase for a notebook and an envelope he passed to Davidson.

"The balance of the generous funds you supplied me, sir."

Davidson returned the envelope unopened. "Thank you for your integrity, Monsieur DuFour. Consider your diligence duly noted, and consider whatever is left as a partial and separate bonus. As agreed, your fee will be deposited into your account at week's end."

DuFour knew instinctively not to argue. "Thank you," was all he said.

Davidson nodded mechanically, before acknowledging Maria. "Her sangria is the finest you will taste anywhere, Monsieur DuFour: strong enough to warm the soul, yet not to weaken the tongue or dull the mind." He waited until the cheerful woman had finished filling both glasses. "Allow me to toast your good work, sir, and your health." He looked up at the younger woman, then to DuFour. "She won't leave us until you compliment her. It's what happens when they've been with you too long." The rapid slur of Spanish-accented tsks was meant to be heard, "But I don't know what I would do without her, or her husband, Jorge, for that matter. He's the best gardener on the island and there's no better driver anywhere. I'm fortunate to have them both."

DuFour took a sip, letting the flavours linger and infuse his palate. "Muy bueno, señorita Maria, muy bueno. El mejor."

Maria beamed at his Spanish. "Gracias, señor," and then she looked to Davidson.

"Como siempre, Maria. I am spoiled by having you here, and you know it." She patted his cheek and left them to speak. "She thinks I'm helpless without her, and I'll never admit that I am, except to you Monsieur DuFour, not to mention her English has been better than mine for quite some time. So beware. I suspect she also speaks French, though I've yet to catch her up." Both men took a moment to appreciate Maria's work. "Monsieur DuFour, before you explain the files which you've compiled, I would like a verbal version of your written report, hence the cassette recorder. It is important for me to hear and remember your tone as well as read your words. You have my fullest attention and we will not be disturbed."

"I will begin with your former wife and end with Joaquin de-Saint-Valéry." He leaned forward, placing his drink on the table. "Monsieur Alexander, I am truly very sorry for what you are about to hear." He looked down to the two cases Jorge had placed by his side. "There is not much in all that information to gladden your heart, monsieur; though much of it, I'm afraid, will do quite the contrary."

"I am eighty-one, as I once told you, Monsieur DuFour. The greater part of my heart stopped beating sixteen years ago. What is left of it I won't need very much longer, an eventuality towards which I am becoming increasingly indifferent. My greater interest and concern is for the twins. Tell me what you have discovered and leave out nothing. I assure you I will not crumple and I shall still be here for our meeting at the end of the week."

The detective moistened his mouth with the sangria and placed his glass on the table. "Sir, I thought it logical for my search to begin in Montreal where you lived for so many years. Miss Emily, as she prefers to be called, moved to Charleston about a year after your departure for France. She reunited with her daughter and at the beginning she made several trips to New York where Noëlyn Daniels lived with her husband who worked as an investment banker until he died in'91. Miss Emily never remarried and made herself a patron of the arts. Her own paintings never excelled beyond private parties and, as far as I can determine, she gave away far more in donations than she ever brought in as an artist. Very early on in the new mother-daughter relationship she gave her granddaughter one million in trust which grew to four, and then she added another million for an undetermined reason. Since she first arrived in Charleston she's been known in the neighbourhood as being very quirky, if I may say so. One of her idiosyncrasies is to walk into a restaurant on a whim, pick out a table and pay the bill of the persons sitting there. Or to walk into a store with no other purpose than to pay anonymously for someone else's merchandise, normally for children. Of course, she's very well known in her community and I would suggest that anonymous is a loose term at best. She's in good health. She continues to live in her own home at the shore, close to her daughter's home and, although she's far from being destitute, she has much less than three million in the bank."

"Less than three million?" questioned Davidson, shocked. "She's squandered that much? She should have a hundred, at least," Davidson exclaimed. "Have you been able to determine whether she's got all her faculties about her, Monsieur DuFour?"

"She's quite sane, and very generous to a fault. By way of example, when her daughter's husband died, a transfer of five million was made from her bank to Noëlyn's. She's also taken some bad advice over the years and apparently never trusted her money to her son-in-law's firm. My written report is much more complete."

"She always did like to live the high life. Though with a comparatively paltry three million she'd better stop being so kind." Davidson sipped his sangria. "What do you know of Noëlyn Daniels?"

"She's fifty-six, attractive, as you will see by the photographs and videos and, like Miss Emily, she never remarried. Her daughter Jodie was illegitimate. No details exist regarding her biological father and I have no idea whether or not the daughter is aware of her status. Noëlyn moved to the States where she met John Gupman months after the girl's birth. They married, though he never adopted the girl."

"Was he good to her, at least? Do you know that?"

"There's nothing on record to the contrary. As you might imagine only negative parent-child relationships are officially recorded. She worked part-time as a designer, eventually finding a full-time position and they always lived quite a bit above their means: a house in the Hamptons, European cars instead of local brands and twice-a-year offshore vacations. He was about fifteen years her senior, for what it's worth. When he died, life insurance paid off the Manhattan apartment, the Hampton home and the cars. When she sold she walked away with about four million, plus the five Miss Emily gave her. She has about two left, with zero debt load."

"Like mother, like daughter. She's pissed away seven million."

DuFour nodded for affect. "That would be a reasonable assumption, sir. She doesn't work. She travels frequently, always alone, mostly to Europe, and seems to favour the all-inclusive, hedonistic lifestyle. Once away she becomes another person and, by all appearances, she doesn't want to break any one man's heart, or his wallet. She never went to her room alone at night and, during the week our schedules coincidentally intertwined, she entertained at least three different men, one particularly young, who were able to join her for champagne breakfasts." DuFour smiled. "Our travel agendas seemed to take us both to Greece at the same time, sir. It could be Gupman held her back, or that she's trying to compensate for her daughter being a lesbian."

"So, she's a lady at home and a tramp when she's away. Is that the general idea, Monsieur DuFour?"

"Let's say she's not holding anything back, monsieur. She treats herself very well. She seems to enjoy or want the best of everything, including her beachfront property less than two miles from her mother. Sparkling wine would never be good enough and her weekly trips to the spa are a must. She likes to be noticed."

"And what of her daughter, Jodie?"

"She's twenty-nine and she also lives in Charleston. She's a lesbian with no current partner and works as a Professor of English at Charleston Southern University, which gives her fifty-five K a year. She's very close to Miss Emily." DuFour paused, reaching for his glass. Davidson did the same. "Her five million dwindled quickly to less than one, mostly due to lifestyle and possibly learning from those around her. Her credit card statements tell a fairly comprehensive story of spontaneous desire, for lack of a better word."

"By 'those around her' you mean her mother and grandmother."

DuFour nodded. "It could be she believes her mother and grandmother have greater resources than they currently do, or she just doesn't care. She possesses many of her grandmother's traits toward the frivolous and her mother's toward the good life. She owns a loft in the high-end

Market District with no mortgage, she owns a Mercedes she practically never drives and I doubt if she can boil water. She eats out almost exclusively, though she has no debt load and never travels abroad. Her two annual trips are to San Francisco and to the gay thing they do in Montreal each year. She's somewhat on the rotund side to understate her physical appearance and she is certainly not as pretty as her mother who really is quite attractive in her own way. As far as I can determine she spends most weekends at the shore with Miss Emily, and occasionally with her mother, Miss Daniels. I've seen her go into several bars that specialize in a female clientele. The one time I saw her leave with someone I actually felt sad for her."

"Certainly not for being a lesbian, Monsieur DuFour?" Davidson asked quizzically. "I've met a few in my life and, I must admit, when I was younger they were the subject of many a pleasant dream." It was Davidson's turn to smile. "I've always considered any discordant male opinion on the matter as the quintessential hypocrisy. Don't you think, Monsieur DuFour?"

"I do indeed, sir. I also presume, Monsieur Alexander, that as men of refined taste we are talking about the prettier ones?"

"We are indeed, detective, however not to the exclusion of others."

Mike DuFour shrugged his shoulders to emphasize his quandary. "We are, sir, of a like mind. I doubt whether Señorita Maria would be impressed with what comes next. What I intended by my comment was that I would have been a much prettier choice. The woman, if that's what she was, had to be at least mid-fifties and well-travelled, if you take my meaning. As an aside, it's as though Jodie Daniels is two different people. During the day she's Miss Prim and Proper, though her sexual inclinations are no secret. At night she's into leather and spikes, though from what I've ascertained none of her students or fellow alumni professors seem to know about her nocturnal side." DuFour paused. "Sir, as I have mentioned, the files are very complete, including videos with sound tracks. At the outset you said you wanted tone; you have it. She's a sad young woman, if that's the right word. It could well be resentful or hateful. The long story short is that she's carrying heavy baggage and that's never good. Her grandmother has made no further provision for her that I was able to determine. I can't say I blame her, and if her mother doesn't soon curb her own lifestyle her few million won't last her very long. Once the beach house goes, everything else will go with it. I assume her university salary won't take her very far."

"I'm sure you assume correctly. Thank you. And I assume we've come to my son and daughter."

"Yes, we have."

"Are they well?"

"They are both very well." DuFour paused. "Monsieur Alexander, I've spent the better part of three months sitting in cars, airplanes and hotel rooms. May we stand outside in the fresh air, sir? I believe it will be good for both of us and I do love the ocean."

Davidson called to Maria to bring fresh glasses, and both men walked out onto the beachfront property to wait for her. Neither one spoke during the interim, though the sudden complexity of Dufour's expression did not escape Davidson in the least.

"Monsieur Alexander, if it's your intention to meet one day with your children there are many unanswered questions you may feel the need to discuss with them. They are both well, and they are both successful in their careers. You have much to be proud of, sir. Together they have overcome many difficulties."

"So, they've come to know each other. Then they must also know they were given up for adoption."

"It's difficult territory. I would suggest…"

"Don't presume to prepare me for the worst, Monsieur

DuFour," Davidson cut in. "Simply tell me what you know."

"Your son, whose name is James Parker, endured a difficult adolescence, or so I must believe. I say that because in his mid-teens he ran away to sea for several years before joining the U.S. military to fight in Vietnam on a riverboat. Most kids will run to a ghetto until they discover it's not as glamorous as they thought, or as comfortable as their own beds; not many sail the oceans in boiler rooms. So we might assume his youth was not a very pleasant one. In any event, you will be proud of what he has accomplished since those early days, all of which is included in my files. He is well-educated with an MBA and owns a successful marketing firm. He married soon after his discharge from the military, to a woman called Helen North; they had one child together. They currently live in Nova Scotia. She's a rather successful folksinger and her paintings do very well in local galleries with several exhibitions each year. They're not rolling in it, although they live very well and don't exceed their limitations. If anything, they live more modestly than one would expect. They seem to be very much in love, they are both respected in the community and together they are a very beautiful couple."

Davidson leaned forward. "His adoptive parents?"

"Both dead."

"And my daughter Katherine?"

DuFour drank from his glass, wishing the sangria would dull his mind more than it had. He drank again before answering.

"Monsieur Alexander, Helen North, your son's wife, is your daughter Katherine."

DuFour mentally counted the seconds.

"Excuse me, sir. Do you realize you're implying that my son is married to my daughter?"

"Yes, I do, though not by implication."

Davidson dropped his arms, spilling his drink onto the tiled patio. "You're telling me that my Katie is married to my Theo."

"Yes, that is precisely what I am saying. There is no mistake. You have full and complete documentation. I don't know what else to say."

Davidson drained what little was left in his glass, letting the meaning of Dufour's words sink in.

"Do you know how?"

"No, I don't. As I have said, you will have something to talk about when and if you meet with them. All I can say is that they've been married for twenty-six years and still act like new lovers when they're together. I've tried to imagine how such a thing might possibly have happened. Helen was raised on the west coast and left home a year or so before they married. James had been back from Vietnam for about as long. It could be they don't know. Or possibly they discovered the truth after the fact and decided against convention. She was pregnant when they married. There is no doubt, sir, though any conclusion as to the origin of their life together is complete conjecture."

"It's bloody incest."

DuFour shrugged his shoulders sympathetically. "I'm very sorry. Perhaps when you see the video tape of them together you might think differently. It has weighed heavily on my mind for several weeks, Monsieur Alexander. It was a difficult discovery. Believe me when I say that I have verified every minute and difficult detail. It's all in the file. Her adoptive mother is dead; her adoptive father is in a home with an increasingly simple view of reality. He has no memory of her."

"You said they had a child."

"Yes, they did, a son." DuFour spread his hands and washed them over his sullen face. "They gave him up for adoption at birth. Helen was raised as a catholic. That might be one reason there was no abortion, if they even knew of their sibling relationship. Their son's name is Dexter Philips. He's twenty-seven, and from here the story doesn't get much better, sir. Again, I'm sorry. I know how important all this is to you and, as generous as you have been to me, I must admit to regretting that I ever took the case. I had hoped my days of giving grievous news to parents and kinfolk were over. Apparently, such is not the case."

"It's that bad?" Davidson chortled weakly. "Can anything possibly be worse than frivolous waste, hedonism, incest and lesbians, which I don't entirely disapprove of?" he added.

"Quite possibly, sir. Yes, I believe so."

"What's his story? Be frank with me. Leave nothing out."

"That he was given up at birth by the Parkers, for whatever reason, was the worst part of Philips life, as I see it. His adoptive parents were average, hardworking with more lows than highs in life. Dexter was bad at school; what you would call an underachiever. He solved many or most of his youthful problems with his fists or his mouth and he got into more than his fair share of trouble until he dropped out. No one seems to have liked him. He wasn't a bully. He just wasn't liked. Those I interviewed who remembered him said he never fit in and there was no trace of him for two or so years after he left home, which probably means he lived on the street doing drugs or whatever. It could have been a hundred different things, and probably was, but it also included pimping, which is not conjecture on my part. I'm sorry, sir. Since then he's been jailed four times for everything from drugs and prostitution to grand theft auto. Somehow he managed to get paroled a few months ago after doing three of a ten-year sentence. It's not so much that he kept his nose clean; it's more that he's a very big man, with prison smarts, and he's no one to mess with. However, having said that, and according to Attica's

353

warden, he has some very serious enemies north of the
border. At his pre-trial three years ago he traded detailed
information about the DiFiore brothers for less time. Less
time in prison, not necessarily more time to get on with his
life. His testimony shut down a very lucrative operation. I
would say it's a matter of time, and not much time, before
they find him, unless he's really smart about it. You can
also be sure some sort of advisory has been sent out and if
he screws up or gets too close to them, they'll know.
Sometimes the temptation for cons to go home is
overpowering."

"And if they find him, what then?" questioned
Davidson.

"They'll kill him, Monsieur Alexander, as certainly as
we're standing here. They're a bad bunch."

"Do you have personal knowledge of them?"

DuFour nodded mechanically. "As much as I care to
have, yes, I do. Until their arrests three years ago they knew
how to keep their noses clean and stay on the right side of
Angelo Bardollini who really runs the show, the real family
so to speak. He's high-end, strictly big business. DiFiore's a
rank amateur in the same ring and he knows it. He does the
low-end stuff: cars, prostitutes, cheap drugs. Putting
DiFiore and his thugs away has had zero impact on
Bardollini's business interests, but it crippled the DiFiore
auto ring, his mainstay, and I don't mean to insinuate he's
not dangerous. He is, although currently he's operating
from a cell and not from the back of one of his strip bars.
He's got a couple in Montreal and one in Toronto out by the
airport."

"So, at his own level, this DiFiore fellow represents
organized crime."

"He certainly wanted to, and maybe by now he could
have been part way there, but Dexter Philips was
instrumental in the demise of that eventuality according to
my contacts. If they were as organized as they once wanted

to be, monsieur, your grandson would already be dead. The two elements that have kept him alive thus far are that: he was sent to Attica and DiFiore has no contacts inside the U.S. correctional system. Simply put, they don't know where he is."

"And is this fellow Bardollini a possible consideration?" Davidson questioned.

"Bardollini's never been a gun for hire. He couldn't care less about your grandson. However DiFiore's car operation was pretty sophisticated for a local player and you can be sure not all of them were indicted. Someone's taking care of his daily business. Your grandson was a flunky. He didn't know everything that went on. In fact, he knew very little. He did what he was told to do, and when. Case closed. I doubt the cops would do much to find his killers, especially if the sanction comes from inside. It's a matter of time."

"He must know his chances are extremely slim?"

"I'm sure he does. Unfortunately for him, he's regarded by the system as a two-bit repeat offender and not important enough to warrant a new identity or relocation. So unless he finds a hole of his own to crawl into, and very soon, they will find him. In the meantime, the farther away he stays from urban areas the safer he'll be. Thus far he hasn't signed a lease or applied for bank or credit cards. The fortunate thing for him is that his driver's permit doesn't expire for another eight months so at least he can get around as long as he pays cash for everything. That said; if he's as smart as I've heard, meaning street smarts, he'll find a way."

"Is he worth saving?"

"Who knows? He's a con, and he doesn't have much reason to believe in humanity. He's had a hard life. Who hasn't? Although in his case he might not be entirely to blame. It could be more a question of genetics. In a better world he would still be inside, it's not. It's the system's way of throwing out the trash. I'm sorry, sir. I'm speaking frankly. To his credit, he hasn't crossed the line since his release, but, then again, he can't really afford to. The slightest misdemeanour would mean a mandatory life sentence, which would be no different than delivering himself to the brothers on a platter." DuFour took a deep breath. "He's worked in construction since the spring, at different job sites, which is a good thing vis à vis his longevity. Each week he moves to a different rooming house or weekly apartment in suburbia, something I don't imagine he'll be able to maintain indefinitely. The strange part is that he did enrol in university, as he told the parole board he would. It probably wasn't his smartest move, not that college would be the first place anyone would look for him. It could be he's playing games...or trying to prove something. Who's to know? In any event it wasn't a smart move."

"Do you have any prediction?"

"If you're going to meet with him, or speak with him, do so sooner rather than later. My sense is that he's surviving; the reality is that he doesn't have the means. Even with a new name, he's very recognizable, and a new face is at least ten grand, if not fifteen or twenty for good results. He's a common labourer, with no education to speak of, who likes to pretend he's somebody he's not. In short, his resources and earning potential are meagre and that means he's living on borrowed time. Eventually he'll screw up, if he hasn't already. What goes around comes around, simply put. My prediction would be that without help he's going back."

"When did you last see him?"

"A month ago, personally, but the video information in the file is as recent as a few days ago. I still have a man on him. I thought you'd want me to do that. To say the least he's remained very transient since his release. At first glance you might see on the tapes that he seems very at ease...Upon closer inspection of his facial characteristics it's clear that he's wondering."

"What do you suppose he'd be wondering about?"

"My guess would be his last breath, sir, about how it will feel when the bullet bursts into the back of his head from half a mile away." DuFour paused. "I'm sorry. It's human nature to think of death when it's chasing you. I didn't mean to be graphic or theatrical."

"So, I'm to expect that one day he will be killed?"

"Sometime soon, yes…soon being a variable. What we don't know is what they know."

Davidson took a deep breath and put down his glass. Both men stood quietly, each one unconsciously burying his hands in the pockets of his tropical slacks. DuFour eyed Davidson, studying him, seeing a man deep in complex thought. He waited for the right moment that was long in coming.

"Monsieur Alexander, there is more, one more person to report on."

"Yes, of course, my grandson Joaquin."

"Yes sir."

"And will your report on Joaquin be as difficult to hear as the others?"

"I'm not at all certain. What I've learned could be a horrible mockery of your values or a wonderful love story. I'll leave it to you to decide once you know."

"Know what."

"Your grandson, Joaquin de-Saint-Valéry is living in Bahrain. He is working at an English radio station there. He has a Muslim girlfriend and plans to remain there and marry the girl. She's very pretty and seems very devoted to him." DuFour looked at his empty glass. "It is also his intention to convert to Islam, sir."

Davidson turned slowly to face his guest, looking at the man meaningfully. "Are they fundamentalists?"

DuFour shook his head. "I take your meaning, monsieur. I believe they are not; though I cannot be certain. A stranger over there can get into trouble for asking any question, let alone the wrong one. It's not as though I looked like one of them and I had no idea who I could trust when I was amongst them. There is, of course, video footage that may help you decide. I wish I could tell you more. Unfortunately, such is not the case."

"She's educated."

"Yes, she is."

"Her family?"

"They live in Manama, the capital. They have too many children by our standards, but live comfortably according their own. They seem happy enough and also seem to embrace Joaquin. As you may already know, Bahrain is one of the more modern Islamic states."

"The lad's been promising to return with happy news to share with his family. How do I not tell his father and mother, knowing what I do?" DuFour remained silent. "Do you have photos of her and her family?"

"And videos, yes."

"How long did you stay with them?"

"One week. I last saw him less than a week ago. I required quite a bit longer to track him than the others. The news is very recent."

"And how did you discover this news of his conversion in such a foreign country?"

DuFour grinned. "Joaquin told me himself. Western foreigners are quite a common sight in Manama. It's the home port of the U.S. Fifth Fleet. It's really quite a charming place, if you can get past the excruciating heat. I approached him as I would any other tourist needing directions from one of his own. He's quite a charming young man, and his fiancée, Lydyah, is equally charming. You will see for yourself that he has done well for himself."

Davidson ignored the remark, calling out to Maria for a scotch after DuFour turned down another sangria. "Walk with me to the beach, Monsieur DuFour. Allow me to take a few more moments of your time before you begin your vacation, and I'll not bother you until the day of your departure when I will need you here for no more than two hours."

"I'll plan accordingly."

"Thank you. Now about Dexter Philips, I'd like your firm to continue keeping an eye on him until you meet with him personally. Advise me only of anything untoward until that time. As for Joaquin, I would prefer that you meet with him in France, not in Bahrain. I've no quarrel with Muslims, or with his being one if that's what he truly wishes. I do have a problem with the reaction your next meeting with him might inspire when he discovers your first encounter was less than accidental, or with funding militants. Be very certain of your information."

"It should prove to be interesting in all cases, sir. May I expect to know the contents of those letters?"

"I will disclose that in part next week, during our meeting, at which time you will be paid in full for your services, including for what remains to be done. You will have to free up the rest of the month, I'm afraid." Davidson sipped his scotch. "When I know all the letters have been delivered I will see to it that a very substantial bonus is transferred to you immediately. An envelope to cover your upcoming expenses will be here for you next week. Subsequent meetings will not be necessary. A simple phone call to update me will suffice. Thank you for your time. Enjoy your vacation, Monsieur DuFour."

DuFour shook Davidson's hand and walked away. When he turned back he stood for a moment to watch the old man sitting cross-legged in the sand and looking out to sea.

47

Mike DuFour had first met Davidson Alexander as the owner of a moderately-sized security agency. For the first twenty years of his adult life he had worked his way up to Chief Inspector of Major Crimes in the Montreal Urban Police and now, sixteen years after retiring from the force, he had more active contacts than any private cop could hope to have.

A confirmed bachelor following the financial ruin of an aggressive divorce in his late thirties, he had always come and gone as he pleased. Now he could come and go from wherever and whenever he pleased. He was a millionaire, part of the nouveau-riche and he still could not believe it; nor could he believe Davidson.

The old man had him promised a bonus beyond the two million as soon as the last letter had been delivered in France by the end of the month: invitations to a tontine that would change the lives of each person he had once followed to spy upon and would now contact in order to deliver the news. Dexter Philips would be the first one visited, then the twins followed by the Charleston women and finally de-Saint-Valéry whom his client had promised would be back in France well before that time. If he were not he would be excluded from the windfall, as would anyone else not in attendance by the specified time.

Davidson Alexander had said anyone failing to attend would never know to what extreme point they should be furious with themselves, or disappointed, or how depraved to feel for having turned down such an opportunity. Davidson had confessed a disinterest to Mike DuFour in anonymous benevolence, but there were rules to the tontine and one of them was benevolence, to the tune of fifty-percent of the each person's share before the transference of the remaining portion to a Swiss bank or any one of their choosing.

The detective shut it from his mind. Two million plus bonuses, plus lavish expenses for someone unrelated would have to mean the unimaginable for anyone about to receive a letter. Philips was about to get the surprise of his life and he would not have to wait for Wednesday, September 15th, between noon and four PM, GMT.

By 7:00 PM on August 09th the detective had arrived in Montreal, he had slept for a half dozen hours before flying to Toronto and had rented a car for the ninety-minute drive to Niagara Falls. Dexter Philips' home for the week was a two-story, white brick building with open balconies crowded with parabolic antennas, damaged bicycles, faded washing hung out to dry, and rusted lawn chairs. Torn bed sheets covered some windows; those that weren't were either left uncovered or walled over by circa '70s Formica-lined stereo cabinets.

The mailboxes in the stairwell had no names. Names weren't needed because the tenants knew exactly when to meet the mailman for the much needed weekly welfare cheques. The tiny white buttons that had once been doorbells didn't buzz and the graffiti-lined hallways smelled of every tenant's preferences or abuses. The halls were dark and dank to the point of suffocation, each doorway emitting the blare of a radio, television, the caustic exchanges between the occupants or any combination of the three.

Dexter Philips lived in 102. It would be his third evening at home and Mike DuFour found himself wondering why the young man had never thought to run away to sea like his father, or if he had. The driver's door of the sun-faded green '75 Malibu Classic was opened before the car screeched to a stop on the street, directly in line with the darkened doorway. Dexter Philips jumped out with a speed and agility that took the detective by surprise. He scanned 360°, studying each vehicle on the street, looking for one that stood out, one that was clean or new. Then he ran to the building with long strides, stopping at the entrance to look behind him. When he was satisfied, he turned to go in and stopped dead.

"Good evening, Dexter. I'm curious. Are you running to or from someone?" DuFour checked his watch. "I wasn't expecting you for another hour."

DuFour was leaning across the doorway with his arms loosely crossed. Dexter Philips tensed a few feet away from the man who was shorter than him by a head, quite a bit slimmer and completely laid-back. Both men wore dark glasses and each knew the other was scrutinizing his every move, instinctively reading the other's body language, searching for the slightest indication to react. Dexter Philips stepped back defensively and turned from the waist, searching the street and parking lot. When he spoke his voice was flat, devoid of emotion or inflection.

"I haven't missed one call, my PO knows that. What do the cops want?"

"I don't know. I'm not a cop."

"Yeah, you are. Bullshit."

"I used to be. I opted for private practice."

"Once a cop, always a cop, the badge doesn't mean shit." Dexter turned to go into the building.

"What is it, Philips? Thirteen homes in thirteen weeks? How long can you keep that up?"

"Piss off. I'm clean."

"I know you are, and you're running from DiFiore. So would I and, from what I've just seen, he's not very far behind." DuFour took his hands from his pockets. "Let's not waste time, Philips. You look like shit, you're tired and so am I. Christ, am I tired. I'm here to help you, so this is what we're going to do. First, you'll get changed. Then we'll go for dinner, in my car if you don't mind. I can't sit in that thing you just drove up in."

"I said piss off. In case you haven't noticed, I'm kind of in a hurry."

"I did notice. And I said we're going for dinner. It's the one way you're going to live as long as you want to, kid. So take me up on it. There's someone who wants to help you, and it's not me." Dexter folded a fist. "Kid, you're big, and you're scary, and I'll put you on your ass in a blink. So don't even think of it. You've got ten minutes. Take a shower and wear a suit."

"Or what?"

Mike DuFour pulled his cuff away from his watch for affect. "Or I eat alone, and very soon, possibly even tonight, I'll phone your grandfather to tell him you've been shot in the head by Mario DiFiore and his friends."

Dexter Philips pulled away his glasses and looked back onto the street. "This is bullshit."

"You've got ten minutes, and if there's anything in there with your name of on it, anything at all, you bring it with you." Mike DuFour stepped aside.

Dexter waited what he thought was long enough to save face before he turned to disappear beyond the broken door that didn't close behind him. He came back out twenty minutes later, dressed in slacks and a sports jacket, copying DuFour's style, and looked in all directions as he walked with an uneasy restraint to where the detective was leaning against his rental car.

"It won't help you to be a smartass, kid. Running for your life doesn't mean moving like you're walking past adoring fans on the red carpet. Next time I won't wait. Get in."

Dexter shrugged, pulling at the door DuFour was still

leaning on. Once inside he looked straight ahead, following DuFour as he crossed the front of the car.

"This is bullshit. I never had a grandfather."

"That you knew."

"He died before I was born, so did my grandmother."

"Yes and no. The real one is still alive. He lives in Spain, in Las Palmas. He's the father of your real parents, not the ones who adopted you, not the Philips."

Dexter's head snapped to the side. "Say what?"

"You were adopted in Halifax and your biological grandfather is still alive. He wants to meet you." DuFour chortled at his passenger's expression. "It's all for real, kid, and I hope you like steak. I don't think Italian would be appropriate given the reason for this meeting."

"So why is he looking for me now? And what about my real parents?"

"I know nothing about them," DuFour lied. "And I don't know anything about your grandmother. She never came up. Take a few moments, let it all sink in."

The ride lasted half an hour. The restaurant had the look of being expensive, even the name sounded expensive. DuFour ordered two Johnnie Walker Blue that were placed on the table a few moments after both men were seated.

"I've been waiting since yesterday to do this. I want to propose a toast, kid, if you would care to raise your glass."

"To what?"

"Not what, who: to your grandfather for my own good reasons. You're toasting him because he's going to save your life. You're about to stop running, kid. You're about to have a life you've never even imagined, with conditions. First, I have a gift for you. Second, I have a letter from him to you. The letter's an invitation to meet with him, if you agree to follow the rules as laid out in the letter."

"What rules? And why does he want to meet an ex-con after all these years?"

"That's explained in the letter and has nothing to do

with the gift, which is yours whether you accept to abide by the letter or not."

"This is bullshit."

DuFour signalled over the waiter to order and select the wine, indicating to Dexter that he should order first. When the waiter left them, he continued.

"Your gift has one condition, a very simple one: that you do your best to complete the education you began a few months ago." He paused, as much to enjoy the moment as for Dexter Philips' expression. "Yes, we know, and very soon so will others, if they don't already. Whether you did something so stupid to impress your PO or you actually want to be something more than a two-bit punk is for you to know. Either way, it was one damn big mistake, kid. Real dumb. So it's time you stopped thinking you're smart and become smart. Everyone in your family, such as it is, is well-educated. Your grandfather sees little need to have a moron in the group. His choice of words, not mine. Of course, he realizes to do so successfully will call for a new name and face." Dufour's expression stiffened, lending credence to what he was saying. "That's your gift, kid: a new face, a new name and a new start. Screw it up if you want to. It's up to you. No one cares if you don't."

Dexter laughed, almost spitting out the scotch he hadn't swallowed. "We're talking at least ten to twenty grand for a face? Is the old coot rich?" DuFour nodded. "And a new name that'll take a year or more, more like eighteen months. Meanwhile my name's in the system and my ass is grass. Tell him thanks, but no thanks."

"Let's forget for the moment that you said that. Say it once more and I'll finish my meal alone. For the right price in the right hands your name can be changed inside of a week, any name you want, along with it your SI number, your birth date, a driver's permit, a passport and a bank account, the whole nine yards. You want grades that will get you into any university? They're yours, from any school you select, anyone but Attica. What comes after is up to you. Say the word. It's as easy as 1-2-3. You'll be that person by this time next week, I guarantee you. Your surgery's been scheduled for the day after tomorrow. You could come out of it with that new name, if that's what you want. I've also arranged for a safe house during your recovery. Actually, kid, you have no choice and you know it."

Dexter looked at him, trying hard to rationalize beyond his capability. "What's in it for you?" was all he could think to say.

"I'm being well paid."

"And what's up with the old man?"

"He's only known about you for a week. Give him a break, and lose the attitude."

"And then what?"

"Anything you want. It depends what you do with the letter. The first thing is to quit your job tomorrow, by phone. Call and hang up, no explanation. They've been good to you, but good won't keep you alive if you say the wrong thing."

Dexter snapped his fingers. "Just like that, I walk away. You're forgetting my PO."

"No, I'm not. He's no different. Walk away means walk away. They'll be looking for Dexter Philips, that face and those fingerprints, not you. Walk away. With your new ID you can go anywhere you want, including the U.S."

"And what do I do for money?"

"What's left from the cost of surgery and the name change should amount to fifty K, tax free. You wouldn't make as much in two years. Anyway, it's yours, and don't go spending it on those broads at The Booty Lounge ... Save the look. Being there was your second stupid mistake. Besides, Miss Kitty Boom-Boom won't want to slip and slide all over you the way you're going to look for the next two months, which is pretty much like shit. Stay away from her. She's bad news." The detective ignored the inquisitive look, giving his full attention to his meal. "Yeah, kid, I know about her, everything about her: where she lives, what she likes, who she likes, and it isn't you. She's into women, big time, and I can't say I blame her. She's had a bad life, but that's got nothing to do with you. Eventually she'll end up in the gutter giving ten-dollar BJs through car windows."

"No, she won't. She has a plan."

"Yeah, don't we all? Get something straight. She's way out of your league, which is exactly what will put her in the gutter where there won't be enough cream, surgery, make-up or cheap booze for the derelicts to drink her pretty when her earning power dries up as quickly as she does."

"I suppose my nice new granddad knows about her too?"

"Lose the sarcasm, and no he doesn't. There was no need to tell him, since your record speaks for itself. A whore's a whore, and he knows you're well-acquainted with the profession. Your grandfather is a worldly man, kid. You've been away for three years. He would expect nothing less. Actually, she only became interesting after you had coffee with her." DuFour chuckled. "Would you like to hear the conversation?"

"No."

"But you went back anyway, and blew another two hundred on her."

"I haven't been back since."

"Not for lack of wanting, I bet. Living this far out must piss you off big time. Rule number one, kid, irrespective of what's in the letter, or anything I've said about your gift: You stay away from her. Understood?" DuFour savoured a mouthful of wine. "I asked you a question. Do you understand?"

"Yeah, I understand."

"You have a new chance at life, kid, and a family if you want one, whatever. Don't throw it all away for a whore."

"She's not a whore."

"She was, for two years, and two years before that she did her own thing screwing guys twice her age with money. Now she works for DiFiore." DuFour put down his knife and fork. "Like I said, you have no choice. You probably have a few weeks at best and, judging by the way you came running home, I wouldn't discount a few days, if not hours. You walked right into their hands, kid." DuFour looked at Dexter sitting in front of him. He was stunned and his face was drained of colour. "What?"

"Nothing. It's nothing."

"Goddamit. She knows your name." DuFour leaned over the table. "Please tell me you didn't say something stupid when she was wetting your leg. Tell me she doesn't know your name."

"No, she doesn't. I didn't tell her anything. I swear."

"You're a liar, and not a very good one. She probably does twenty jerks like you in a week and each one thinks he's going to take her home to get some free candy. Believe me, you're nothing special to her and you should know that better than anyone. Or do you forget your days as a pimp. The Booty's owned by the DiFiore family. You might just have put the gun in your own mouth, kid. So you stay away from her, or is there something about this whole thing you don't understand."

"I understand. I didn't know. I was just looking for something nice, something to make me feel good for a change, and you can stop talking to me like I'm a fucking fool. I got into university on my own, without you. I did it to learn how to talk as though I'm better than I am."

"I can see you're making great strides."

Dexter downed what was left of his scotch. "I don't need this shit, so fuck off. Understood?"

Mike DuFour roared with laughter. "Yes, understood." He reached into his inside jacket pocket. "Read your letter, and try not to pass out. By the way, you and I aren't

finished, so start cleaning up your mouth."
*

Dexter, my name is Davidson Alexander. I'm your biological grandfather. Don't think to argue with Monsieur DuFour as he has been quite tireless and exacting in his search for information and its verification. You are who he says you are, as am I.

I trust you shall accept the gift I have sent to you. Think of it as compensation for my having ignored you throughout your young life. Monsieur DuFour is of the belief that it will put an end to your current difficulties; I do fervently hope so. Life has much to offer for those who are willing and prepared to work towards achieving success. Regrettably, your preparation has heretofore been misguided and it my sincere wish to help you rectify that neglect. Please accept the gift. It is not the only one, simply the key to another.

You are the first to receive an invitation to join me at Las Palmas on September 15th, by noon and not later than four PM, GMT, by which time I trust you will have fully recovered from your surgery. The objective of the meeting is to take part in a tontine of considerable importance, and to meet with me, which I hope would not be secondary in your mind. There will be six others who will share in the value of the tontine, seven in all. Those who do not arrive by the prescribed date and time will be summarily excluded and there will be no exception. Also, you will be expected to assign fifty percent of the value of your share to a charitable or other worthwhile cause and I invite you to come prepared with the particulars.

I look forward to meeting my grandson, with best regards,

Davidson Alexander
*

"What's a tontine?"

"Look it up. Your grandfather doesn't like stupid

people." DuFour drank from his wineglass. "Just make sure you're there. Don't mess up, kid, not this time, or DiFiore won't have to worry about killing you."

"Why not?"

"You'll do it yourself." DuFour cut into his steak, not looking up. "You're weeks away from becoming very wealthy. So let's talk about you going under the knife."

"Who are the other six?"

"You'll find out when you arrive. If you don't go it's not important."

"How wealthy?"

"Wealthy, the word's in the dictionary. Look it up. You'll have to be prepped for the surgery. That'll happen tomorrow. The surgery will be on Wednesday."

"Who says I'm going?"

"You'll go."

"I've spent a third of my life in prison, I've got people who want me dead, and now I've got to fuck up my face because one of his fucked-up kids got rid of me."

"You've got that backwards. You're doing your face because you screwed with people you should never have screwed with because you were going to prison for something you chose to do. Your grandfather is doing something he doesn't have to do. He had nothing to do with your adoption."

"And what if I don't go? What if I stay as I am right now, and where I am?"

Mike DuFour shrugged. "On the first count, DiFiore will find you, if he hasn't already; on the second, the ones who do go will profit by your share of the tontine. No one will cry if you don't go, kid. They'll all be a whole lot richer without you."

Dexter Philips sat back, ignoring his meal. "And if any of them don't go, I'm richer. Right?"

"That's right: once a criminal always a criminal. Sound familiar? Isn't that your mantra?"   DuFour chuckled.

"That's why you won't know who they are until you meet. Your grandfather wants to see you, possibly to make amends. It doesn't necessarily mean he trusts you, or them. He knows money changes people, especially easy money and that much of it. So do you."

"If you're fucking with me, I'll find you."

"I'm in the book. Now, tough guy, what's your new name?"

Dexter mused, reaching for his wine "Steve Brandon ... yeah, Steve Brandon."

"Got to admit, it has a certain ring. I'll run it tomorrow morning. If there's no Steve Brandon currently in jail or with priors, that's who you'll be. Start using it, start saying it over and over again. You'll have a complete new set of papers and history within a week to ten days." He looked up. "Enjoy your meal, Stevie."

"What about the hospital? What name do I use?"

"It's a private clinic and they don't want your name. They want your money, which has already been paid. They know not to ask questions and all you have to know is not to shoot off your mouth. You'll get whatever's left over from that and the name change at the same time as your papers, including your tickets, passport, and hotel reservation. Have you ever been on a plane?"

"Once."

DuFour passed him another envelope. "Five grand in twenties and fifties. It's pocket money. Don't blow it."

Dexter Philips took the envelope as though it were a fragile relic. "Mine?"

"Yes." DuFour emptied his glass. "Listen up kid. You have six weeks. I'll be with you for most of this one. After that you won't see me. Give my regards to your grandfather. Tell him thank you."

"You won't be there?"

"No, and I won't be back to check on you. So, go or don't go. It's up to you. You know the rules, and read a few

371

fashion magazines before you leave. The old man, as you call him, is a gentleman. He won't want to see his grandson looking anything less than perfect."

"Is this all for real."

"Yes."

Dexter fanned the bills. "Somehow I think I'm going to like sleeping tonight. It's been a while."

"Nicely put. I'm glad you said that. It tells me I didn't waste my time. You're not going home, Steve Brandon. You can't. Somehow I think you already know that."

Dexter took a deep breath. "There's nothing there I need. I did what you said."

Your new life begins tonight." DuFour held up his glass. "Welcome to it, kid, and give me the keys to that thing you call a car. It's gone."

*

Dexter Philips quit his job Tuesday as DuFour was speaking to the owner of a junkyard who wanted money in his pocket more than he wanted Dexter's Malibu which took less than a minute to compact into a mangled block of twisted steel and the deal was done. Dexter Philips checked into the clinic that afternoon, Steve Brandon checked out on Thursday, the sting of new fingerprints cancelling out the searing sensation of his new face. By the following Monday he was sixty thousand richer, his brown eyes were blue, his hair was several shades lighter, he had a bank account, a newly leased car and a temporary pied à terre with concierge and maid service.

He had a lot to think about. The detective had left him with precise guidelines which were intended to be definitive instructions, making it abundantly clear Steve Brandon had but one person to thank and Davidson Alexander was not one to cry over spilt milk. Staying alive was now up to Steve Brandon. No one would lament, or even know to lament his passing.

Left alone, the one enemy he feared was his own

boredom and DuFour had warned him against it; the other was the cell phone number he had copied before following DuFour's order to discard his own phone. Consciously, all he wanted was to thank her for warning him and to be certain she was alright; her brief message had been as cryptic as she could manage before disconnecting the call without saying goodbye or good luck. Subconsciously, he just wanted her.

Friday evening Belinda Samuels had told Abacus exactly what he had wanted to know. The man in the video was indeed Dexter Philips and she had not been whispering in his ear. She had been making low, guttural sounds the other girls would never think to make. She knew nothing else about the man, other than he was a horny ex-con. Abacus believed her and it wasn't until she arrived at the club late Monday afternoon that she dialled the number she had memorized, to tell Dexter Phillips the hunt for him had begun. Her final word had been a chilling: "Run."

48

Monday evening, the sixteenth, Helen Parker was sitting on the front lawn of her Cape Cod-styled home dressed in jeans and a sweater, dabbing colours onto her canvas when her husband turned into the tree-lined driveway. She heard the crushing sound of gravel compacting under the wheels before she heard the purr of the Lexus' engine. James Parker was tanned and looked mid-forties more than mid-fifties. His starched white shirt with French cuffs, ruby-coloured links and deep-red silk tie went perfectly with his tailored blue suit. He left his attaché on the passenger seat and by the time he wrapped his arms around his wife the tie had been pulled off and the cuffs rolled up. They kissed each other passionately, and hugged each other as though they had been separated for days, not hours. Then he kicked off his loafers, put up his feet and reached for his favourite summertime beverage she had prepared for him with just the right amount of lemon.

She hadn't thought about it for the longest time. He had never broken his promise to her and was as down-to-earth as ever. He had never changed and she still loved to walk in on his bath and talk with him for hours. He had once thought of cosmetic surgery to cover his thin facial scar, but Helen had adamantly refused to let him, saying it gave him a distinctive character. Neither had success changed Helen. She had kept the beauty and live-for-the-moment qualities of her youth and was as vibrant as ever. He was the most important part of her life and she knew he felt the same way. Nothing had ever been able to tear them apart, and nothing ever would.

Just moments after James sank into his thickly cushioned chaise longue a darkly tinted SUV pulled into the driveway and continued towards them with annoying slowness. James stood before the vehicle stopped, and well before the driver stepped out. Helen stayed as she was, watching as the stern-faced man came closer. James could tell by the man's suit and his stature that he had come to the wrong home. He stood out. He was out of place where most people wore Dockers and sweaters at that time of day unless they had worked late at the office. But the man looked too refreshed for that, and too intent for someone who was not expected.

"May I help you?"

"Good evening, Theodore. Yes, you may help me, if you and your sister Katherine can spare me an hour of your time."

James' body instantly went rigid, every muscle flexing involuntarily. He knew instinctively there was no reason to pretend. He turned, seeing the frozen look on Helen's face and the sudden change in the texture of her smooth skin.

"Helen, please go into the house. I'll be there shortly."

Mike DuFour put out his exposed palms to show he meant no harm.

"No, Mr. Parker. Mrs. Parker will want to hear what I have to say, as well as read a missive of considerable importance which concerns her as directly as it does you. I have not come here to cause you embarrassment or to alarm you. I have come here representing your biological father, Mr. Davidson Alexander, the man who gave you to the Parkers in 1947 and your sister to the Norths." He looked deep into James' unblinking eyes. "I assure you, I'm not here to cause you or your wife any distress whatsoever, Mr. Parker. Believe me, it's quite the contrary, and I'll be gone within the hour. May I sit down?"

James took Helen's hand, letting her squeeze hard. "Yes."

"Mrs. Parker, good evening. My name is Mike DuFour, I'm a private detective. I work for your father."

He waited for Helen to be seated.

"What is this about?" asked Helen.

"I have a letter for you and James. It's the same letter, though you each have an original duly signed by your father. He has asked me to speak on his behalf before you see the letter, unless you would prefer that I leave."

"Not at the moment," said James. "Please continue. We'll decide as we go along. Obviously you have captured our interest after so many years, as I'm quite certain you expected to do. May we offer you something to drink, a soda or white wine?"

"No, thank you. I'll be as succinct as circumstances allow. Firstly, I know a good deal about both of you, and of your adoptive parents. Helen, your adoptive mother is dead and your father has advanced Alzheimer disease; he has no memory of you. I'm sorry. James, the people who adopted you have both passed on, though I don't believe that is very heartbreaking news."

"You believe correctly."

"I will also assume, by your reaction, you have known for some time that you are brother and sister, twins. Though I must admit you have reduced the resemblance a good deal."

"We know who and what we are, Mr. DuFour, and how we look. What exactly is the information you have come here to tell us?" asked James. "What could he possibly want after all these years?"

"Your father assumes you gave up your own child once you discovered your relationship, presumably weeks after your marriage, and why Helen went through with a tubal ligation at the time." DuFour paused long enough to look at each of them. "I'm not casting stones. Neither is your father, Mr. Alexander. He and his wife Emily gave you up because they were unable to make ends meet. They fell on hard times and they wanted you to succeed in life, which I know you have. There is very little about either of you I don't know, or your father, which is the purpose for this visit. He wishes to see both of you. That is what I have come to tell you."

"Why has he waited so many years?"

"I'm sure he'll tell you when you see him."

"Where are they?"

"He is in the Canaries, she's in South Carolina. They divorced in '72, as soon as he discovered your mother had given birth to an illegitimate girl in '43 while he was fighting in Europe, during which time he also fathered a child, your half-brother. He's never forgiven her and even before the divorce was final he went back to the woman in France whom he hadn't seen for some twenty-eight years, a woman he had known for ten short days. Imagine."

James amazement was painted on his face. "I would say it's somewhat hypocritical. Don't you think?"

"It's not my business, but no I don't. Your father was dodging German bullets for five years. He had a weak moment, go figure. Who wouldn't? Your mother was at a Christmas party. One might also say what he did is proof absolute that he knows what real love is, that they both did: he and the Frenchwoman. She never married, she missed him that much."

"And now they want a handout, some place to live."

"You know better than that, James. I tracked you and Helen for close to two weeks, and many others, including your adoptive parents. I've flown tens of thousands of miles from here to Asia and have spent a good deal of your father's money doing it, money paid out up front. Does that sound like someone who needs a handout? No. He wants you. Whether he needs you is for him to say. What I can tell you is that he wants to see you in Las Palmas, Grand Canary."

"When," asked Helen, "and why now? It's been so long." She paused, looking to James. "He knows we're married?"

"Of course he does, as well as a comprehensive dossier on your son. What we don't know is how? How did the two of you come together when weeks or months before the two of you were worlds apart?"

"It was a complete fluke," answered James. "And we've never looked back."

"I know. It's very obvious how you feel about one another. He knows that, too."

"You've seen him?" questioned Helen. "You've seen our son."

"Yes, quite recently."

"How is he? How did he turn out?"

DuFour reflected for a moment, choosing his words. "He's had a bad life, Helen, a very bad life; though he seems to want to turn himself around. He has plans for himself that would make you proud. That's all I can say, other than you did him no favour by giving him away. Please ask me no more about him."

"What's his name? Where is he?"

"I can't tell you that."

"Why not?"

"He's a man in danger, though your father has taken immediate measures to reduce that danger. Don't ask me to explain. You will know his name soon enough, when you meet him."

"We never met the ones who adopted him."

Helen's eyes began to tear.

James continued. "Does he know about us, that we gave him up?"

"To the first part of your question, no; to the second part, yes he does and so does your father."

"He's no one to talk."

DuFour ignored the barb. "As I have said, your father would like to see you in Las Palmas." DuFour reached inside his suit jacket. "Please read your letters before you decide."

*

Dear Katie and Theo, my name is Davidson Alexander and by now you know who I am. It is, of course, too late for excuses or apologies and I trust that, in your own way, you are both able empathize and concur with that statement.

This week I have seen current photos and videos of you, and I have heard your voices, though Monsieur DuFour knew when to be discreet and nothing untoward was recorded. Hearing you has made up for so much time that has been lost to us.

I was very pleased to read reports of your individual successes and would very much like to hear more about them in your own words. You are invited to my home in Las Palmas and, of course, you want to know why. The first reason is to meet with me and possibly your mother who has been estranged from me these past many years. Therefore, I can neither assure you of her attendance or her desire to meet with you, though I can attest to her name being on the guest list. I have extended seven invitations in all, hence the secondary purpose for the invitation.

There is to be a tontine, or, in other words, an amount of money I have decided upon which shall be divisible by the number of attendees. Fifty percent of your shares will be given to a charitable foundation of your choice; the balances will be transferred to separate numbered accounts which will be set up for each you prior to your departure, if that is what you wish. Should you decide not to participate, I will accept your decision as final. Should you arrive late for any reason you will be excluded from the tontine as though your decision had been to not attend. Please be here by September 15th, between noon and four PM, GMT. In your particular case, both of you must attend.

I am curious more than perplexed as to the events leading up to your marriage and the reasoning behind your rejection of my grandson. I am not a religious man. Where I once thought I might have a reason or a need to be, I have since discovered on more than one occasion that such is not the case. It is possibly because of that, that I am not dissuaded in the slightest by social doctrine to receive you as my honoured guests and, should you decide to learn the particularities of your abandonment by me and your mother, I invite you to remain longer. The choice is yours.

Best regards,

Davidson Alexander.

*

James and Helen looked at each other, mystified.

"Not the warmest letter I've ever read," said James, breaking the silence.

Helen said nothing, tears beginning to trickle down her cheeks.

"You will like him, both of you. Whether you learn to forgive him is up to each of you, though I must say he is entirely engaging. I have your tickets and hotel reservations in my other pocket."

"He's serious?"

"Just be there on time, with the name of any foundation you favour and you'll walk away better off than you are now."

"We're already well off."

"Not that well off, James." DuFour leaned forward, bracing his elbows on his knees. "Listen. He's getting on in years and despite his good health he doesn't know how much longer he might have. He's very serious about the no-show, as serious as he is about sharing the good that life has brought to him."

"A life he consciously excluded us from for all these years."

"You'll have to take that up with him, or them." DuFour took a moment to scan the lakeside property and luxury home, successfully making a point.

"What we have didn't come to us easily, Mr. DuFour. Our lives would have been a good deal less complicated, not to mention our son."

"What life would that be, James, and what son? You're brother and sister. Your history is being written because he gave you away, and your son's who never would have been. The one certainty is that your son would have been spared an unpleasant youth and a much less enviable transition into adulthood. Apart from any philosophical debate, giving him away didn't alter his chemistry, rather what might have been done about it."

"And that means what, exactly?"

"It means that when you meet him you won't like yourself."

"We've learned to live with it."

"So has he." DuFour took a deep breath. "Listen, I'm not here to argue with you, James. What you've learned is how to live without him, not how to live with knowing the kind of life you preordained for him. Take it up with him."

"That would be very awkward for everyone, particularly him."

"More likely for both of you," DuFour commiserated.

Both men turned to look at Helen, hearing her long a woeful sigh.

"Can I be mercenary for a moment?" asked James.

"No, you cannot. You need only understand he's not inviting you to Las Palmas to give you loose change."

"I'm assuming our son is one of the invited guests, and that our mother may well be there. Who are the other three?

"I can't say."

"But you know."

"Yes, I do, and I'm telling you that if you don't go you'll never know the extent to which you should regret that decision." He looked steadily at James without the slightest definable emotion in his eyes, letting his remark sink in. "Your flight leaves one day before Helen's. He doesn't believe in families flying together." DuFour smiled thinly. "Any such terrible accident, however, would not exclude the ticket holder from the tontine."

Helen broke in. "Please, Mr. DuFour. Do you know if our son will be there?"

"I wish I could tell you with any degree of certainty, Helen. Beyond your father's very explicit instructions not to disclose the names of other guests, I can tell you very honestly that I have no idea who will decide to be there."

"But you do know who will be invited."

"I know whose letters I must deliver. The decision to attend will be theirs, as it is yours."

"Does he have a letter?" she asked.

"Yes, he does."

"Is Davidson Alexander one of the five?"

"No, he is not." DuFour stood. "There's no need to reply right now, James. In fact, there's no formal RSVP. Go, or don't go, though you are expected. Your room is reserved and a welcome package awaits you."

"What is our mother's maiden name?" questioned Helen.

"None of the attendees will learn the names of the absentees; they'll just be all the happier. Read your letter once more. I understand this has all been very overwhelming. Good evening, James." He turned to Helen. "I told your father you were a charming couple. I see that I was right to do so. Your flights leave on the 11th and 12th. You have three and a half weeks to decide. Do what you think is best. Good evening, Helen."

DuFour felt their eyes following after him, thankful they could not see his smile. He liked them, he was happy for them and he was happy for Davidson. He knew the decision to meet with Davidson had already been made, one that had nothing to do with money.

49

Mike DuFour spent the night and next day down by the harbour front, not thinking about the Parkers or Brandon, but planning his first real vacation in years. He already knew what he would do with his security agency: he would give it over to his staff and walk away. He had been a cop all his life. No longer; his time had come to be with nice people, to do nice things and to think nice thoughts.

He flew from Halifax to Boston's Logan on the Tuesday evening and Wednesday morning to Philly and Charleston where he arrived late. Emily Ashton lived on the outskirts of town and Jodie Daniels lived downtown, which is where he had reserved his room, not wanting to waste time driving in circles while trying to find the Isle of Palms in the dark. Downtown was also where he wanted to spend his time between his appointments. As much as he loved the sea, he loved beautiful woman that much more.

When he arrived at the hotel in the Market District the valet parking was unavailable, which would most likely mean a ticket on the windshield in the morning. When he rang the bell a third time for service the Night Auditor came out. The dining room had closed for the evening and room service would be unavailable until breakfast.

He showered, he opened the mini-bar, he took out two micro scotch bottles and lay on the bed with a bag of chips. His new day would start in less than eight hours and when he woke he was lying over the bag of pulverized chips and the only bottle he had opened the night before had spilled onto the mattress. He showered again after ordering breakfast from room service and was gone from the room before seven-thirty, taking the parking ticket in stride.

Emily Ashton's luxurious home along Palm Boulevard on the Isle of Palms was private and gated from the front, though the gate was never closed, considered by Emily to be an unneeded inconvenience for herself and frequent guests. She also thought it completely unreasonable that her home should deprive others of a beautiful ocean view.

By the time Mike DuFour arrived Thursday morning, looking more refreshed than he felt, Emily was sitting at the back edge of her property reading and enjoying the early morning reprieve from the sweltering mid-August heat.

DuFour came in wide, not to alarm her, and waved to her from several dozen feet away. As he came closer he waved again. "Good morning, Miss Emily. May I intrude on your peaceful morning for a few moments? My name is Mike DuFour. I have come with a message for you, from a mutual acquaintance. I also have messages for your daughters, Noëlyn and Jodie."

She was still petite, still slim and her shoulders had rounded slightly with age. The little grey around her temples she insisted were silver highlights and she wore round, steel-rimmed glasses that gave her a deceptive granny look. She dressed as she always had, based on what DuFour had heard of her from Davidson: to be seen and talked about. Thursday morning was no different. She was dressed in a deep pink silk blouse and camisole, a knee-length beige linen skirt with flat leather walking shoes and a wide-brimmed straw hat with a ribbon that matched her blouse. Her few discreet pieces of jewellery were diamond earrings and a matching pendant. He assumed her wedding ring had long since been tossed into the ocean or some gutter.

The wind was calm and the ocean seemed more like an

endless plain of deep silver-blue crystal and obsidian black. There was not a single cloud in the bright sky and DuFour only realized how piercingly inquisitive her eyes were when he removed his sunglasses.

"Do I know you, sir?"

"No, Miss Emily, you do not. I have come to deliver letters to you and your family."

She brought a hand up, shielding her eyes. "Please stand between me and the sun, Mr. DuFour, or sit beside me and tell me who has sent the letter. Is it another request to help fund next year's art festival?"

He smiled inadvertently. Emily had adopted the exaggerated southern accent of the Hollywood southern belle. "No, ma'am, it is not. I have brought a letter from your ex-husband, Davidson Alexander. I am not privy to its contents, though I can tell you he is well. His letter to you does not relate to his health, which is fine."

"And is his little French whore also fine, and their spawn?"

He was taken aback by the sudden acerbic quality of her voice. "Madame de-Saint-Valéry passed away sixteen years ago, Miss Emily. I believe you might have been aware of her illness."

"Indeed."

"Regarding their family, perhaps you might enquire about them when you meet with him."

"Don't talk in riddles, sir. It has been thirty years. Why would he presume that I would allow him on my property after all that time? The bastard deserted me. Or does he forget that?"

"I can appreciate your feelings, Miss Emily. There isn't very much more I can say, other than suggesting that you read the letter. Choosing not to does not negate my obligation to contact your daughters."

"For what reason would you possibly want to see them? Has he waited this long to disrupt my life more than he has?"

"That is not his intention. I believe, when you read the letter, you will understand the reasoning behind all three letters."

DuFour pulled the envelope from his jacket.

"He ruined my life because of one little mistake. I don't suppose he told you that. I was an impressionable and lonely young girl when it happened, but it was quite fine for him to spend his time sleeping with a French whore." Emily leaned back into the large wooden beach chair that made her appear smaller than she was. "What does the old bastard want? Did she leave him penniless? Does he want to come crawling back?"

"Davidson Alexander is not a man who crawls, Miss Emily. Please read the letter. He was quite insistent that I not beg you." He put the letter across her folded hands. "Have you ever wondered about your children, Katherine and Theodore?"

Emily turned her head slowly. He could see in her eyes that her mind was churning.

"I used to, Mr. DuFour. I used to everyday, especially on their birthday. He promised he would bring them back to me ... he never did. He was always too busy, always driven by success. Our children were never as important to him as success; neither was I. He was never a very good husband, Mr. DuFour. His mind was always somewhere else." Her mouth twisted into grim smile. "I'll be sure to send him a card offering my condolences. Better late than never, isn't that what they say?"

Mike DuFour's hand reached to take back the letter. "I'm sorry to have bothered you. It wasn't my intention to stir up old emotions."

"I never said they were old, Mr. DuFour." She looked at the envelope. "I will read his letter, if you would not mind giving me a moment alone."

He stood and walked to the far side of her, turning to

look back when he felt comfortable she was sufficiently alone.

*

Emily, I will get straight to the point. There is no way to preface this message with soft words of endearment, nor would you expect them of me. I would like you and your daughters to join me at my home in Las Palmas. Naturally all expenses will be paid for the three of you, including your accommodations. The purpose of the visit is to reunite with Katie and Theo whom I have recently been in contact with through the efforts of Monsieur DuFour. They have also received an invitation and I have every reason to expect they will join us if you are here with me to greet them.

They are aware of our separate lives, as they are of my sons and your daughters. That said; they have their own son whom they have not seen for years and who has also been invited. I expect the reunion will be quite eventful. At least that is my ardent wish.

Allow me to be even more pragmatic. I am proposing a tontine, a reward, or, in your case, a bribe for being here. I am fully aware of your relatively meagre financial status and your peculiarities, as well as the questionable lifestyles of your daughters and I cannot pretend any degree of surprise.

Those who decide to attend, according to the few rules of the invitation, will share immediately in my substantial liquidity, including you and your daughters; those who choose not to will forfeit the windfall. You will have little to leave them after taxes when your time comes and, in turn, I expect whatever is left to Noëlyn will be squandered in her vain search for whatever she believes is missing in her life. The end result being that her daughter will very soon feel the tight restrictions of her relative poverty. Please understand. My motives are completely selfish, to ensure your cooperation, not for any other reason that you may be predisposed to imagine.

The two women will also hear independently of the tontine by way of Monsieur DuFour. What follows are the conditions.

Davidson Alexander

*

When she had finished reading the first page Emily crumpled the letter and threw it down between DuFour's feet.

"The bastard's been spying on me and my daughters."

"It made good sense for him to make enquiries, ma'am, to understand his chances of success or the impediments he might face."

"Meaning my cooperation, or lack of it."

"Not entirely yours alone. There are others involved, seven in all. I suppose you can speculate as to the six of them, though I'm not at liberty to disclose anyone's name."

"It's not necessary. The seventh would be the one the Frenchwoman left him and it's not important for me to remember his name, if I ever knew it. But I won't have you speaking with my daughters. I will do so myself and let you know their feelings."

"That's not an option, ma'am. I'll be seeing your daughter in a few minutes. I intend to be very discreet. What they may or may not know about your ex-husband is not my business."

"That's very true. It is not your business, although it is very much mine and I cannot allow you to meet with them."

"I will meet with them, Miss Emily. I have my instructions," he paused, "and I have letters for each of them, which they are required to read personally. I have no idea what either one contains, which is precisely why I must see them, to be fair."

"When does he want us there?"

DuFour stooped to reach for the letter. When she held up her palm with a look of loathing etched into her face, he kept it.

"That information is all in the addendum. It's been arranged for the three of you to fly in together, as a family." DuFour passed her the second envelope. "He's very adamant that you be there on time. It's all I can say without contravening his wishes."

"Is he that wealthy?"

"I have no idea, Miss Emily. What I can tell you is that he does seem to live comfortably."

"How much does he know of my daughter?"

"There is nothing he doesn't know. If I may say so, ma'am, I'm very good at what I do."

"You're the spy."

"I'm the investigator; yes, ma'am."

"And my granddaughter?"

"Her file is very comprehensive."

"She's never married. She keeps herself busy teaching at night when she should be out dancing and having fun with young men. She's a pretty girl, albeit a little too shy for her own good in social settings. I suppose my own past and her mother's life with Gupman haven't helped much. She should be more like her mother, more outgoing. She's still so young."

"Perhaps she'll no longer have to teach at night, Miss Emily. Perhaps she'll be able to travel more and be more like her mother," DuFour said, wanting to leave. "However, the decision will be hers."

There was too much for Emily to absorb, thinking back to all her lies that she knew lay in wait. She needed time.

"Let me think about it. Let me talk to my daughters, and please be circumspect in what you say to them. Please do not make this anymore difficult for me than you already have." Emily stared out to sea, making it clear DuFour was expected to leave. "I will let you know."

He stepped away. "There is no time frame, Miss Emily, other than what is mentioned in the letter. The tontine is secondary to seeing his children and he believes your presence will help them decide in favour of reuniting with him. It's a good deal. Good day, ma'am."

DuFour bowed imperceptibly from the waist and turned to walk back the way he had come. He was at Noëlyn Daniels' home within ten minutes.

50

Noëlyn's property was not as wide spread as Emily's and not as open. When Mike DuFour arrived the gate was locked. When he pressed the buzzer the call was answered immediately and he could see the camera lens focus in on him.

"Good morning, Mr. DuFour. I wasn't expecting you this quickly."

"Good morning, Miss Noëlyn. Thank you for answering your gate. May I have a moment of your time? I suspect you know my reason for being here. I assure you, I'll be brief."

"No, you may not. I have no interest in what you have to say. Perhaps after I speak with my mother and she explains to me exactly what you said to upset her so much. But for the moment I need you to leave."

"Did your mother explain the invitation to meet with her ex-husband and the tontine that will likely put a very substantial sum of money in your pockets within the coming month?"

"The old man's delirious. He's a fool and a drunk. That's what she explained a very long time ago. We don't need him. My finger is on the speed dial for 9-1-1, DuFour. You must know what southern cops are like …On the count of three."

"Your mother's ex is not a drunk, nor is he feeble minded."

"Yes, he is. What he's not is a father. He abandoned us."

DuFour paused, furrowing his brow and squinting into the lens. "I don't understand, Miss Noëlyn, Davidson Alexander has never been your father. I'm very sorry, I truly am. I told your mother I would be discreet, however it appears to me you're thinking badly of the wrong person. You were born out of wedlock. Mr. Alexander did not come home from the war until you were two years old and he had left three years before you were born. You are the result of a momentary lapse in good judgement, Miss Noëlyn. That is not my employer's fault. Please, may we speak?"

The silence was long, and uncomfortable.

"We may not. I want you to leave."

"A few moments are all I ask of you, a few moments that will secure the rest of your life, and Jodie's. What I am saying is true. It has all been substantiated and I know your mother will no longer deny the truth once she knows we've spoken somewhat more candidly than she's hoping. You have nothing to lose."

He could hear the sigh through the speaker. "I'm in the back of the house at the pool area. You can park in the front and follow the stone footpath to the rear."

The soft click ended the call and the gate swung open.

"Thank you, ma'am," he said to his car door. He had a good idea what he was in for, remembering what he had seen a few weeks earlier in Greece, and those antics had been in public.

The property would never be an estate, but was certainly enviable as an extravagant beach property. The two-story building was pink stucco with the arched doorway, upper front terrace and windows painted white. The extensive rough lawn was manicured better than most other properties in the Deep South, including a private patio and pool area designed to resemble a country club.

All he could see of Noëlyn were her darkly tanned shoulders, her face and shoulder length hair that was too blond to be real. She clung to the contoured edge of the pool's deep end, sipping a tall green and red concoction and high enough out of the water for him to see she definitely was not wearing a top. He smirked as he scanned the deck, seeing her top hanging to dry from the back of a canvas chair. No one else was with her and there were three possibilities: she would climb out using the ladder beside her, she would pull herself out of the water from where she was or she would leave her drink and swim to the concrete steps at the shallow end where he was. He waited, betting silently with himself that he would see as much of her, or more, than he did in Greece.

Noëlyn drew one last sip through her plastic straw and pulled herself out from the water in one smooth motion. He gave her credit. She wasn't slim, though far from anything remotely resembling her podgy daughter. Her stomach was even, slightly sculpted, her breasts were firm and her buttocks were as shapely and firm as her legs and arms. She wasn't a bad package, he thought, as she stood facing him with the smallest possible triangle covering her body. Towelling herself before turning sideways, she leaned forward with her arms outstretched for her robe.

"Don't just stand there, Mr. DuFour. I'm sure you've seen it all before. I'm afraid I've become overly accustomed to the lax ways of the islands and shamelessly nonchalant about myself. I hope you're not embarrassed"

She left the sheer yellow robe undone to show the smooth curvature between her breasts and the slightest swell of her abdomen above the tiny and sheer yellow triangle as she walked towards him with the hem of her robe fluttering at her hips. He already knew she had no pubic hair. Despite his dark glasses she knew what he was looking at and she smiled. She liked men paying attention to her. He returned the smile, not to would have changed the dynamics of their meeting. She might have been a turn-on, had he not seen her in Greece, but he had, and now she was just another naked broad doing her best not to grow one day older.

This time he smiled sincerely. "Your mother moves pretty quickly for a woman touching eighty."

"She used her cell. I've never seen my mother hurry."

"Sit down, Mike, and call me Noëlyn. Can I get you a drink?"

"I'm good, thank you."

She stretched out on her side on the lounge chair alongside his, baring her hips and stomach to arrange her cover-up so that her nipples were covered by the sheer fabric. She raised one leg into an arch, so he would see where the bottom of her triangle disappeared between the round curves of her tanned ass.

"So, the old guy's had us followed to find out what we're all about and he wants to give us money to make up for what he did to us. Why?"

"Miss Noëlyn, I'm not here to contradict your mother's impression of her ex-husband, or dispute whether or not he's your father. The fact of the matter is he wants to see his own two children, not you or your daughter who are indisputably not related to him. He wants to see his own children, their children, and he believes Miss Emily's presence will help to that end."

"Then who is my father?"

"A man your mother destroyed out of spite after Mr. Alexander left her. The man died alone many years ago, on the street. I've recently spoken with his ex-wife who never regretted leaving him. Your mother made certain the woman would live very comfortably, once she left him. Miss Emily can explain the details to you."

"You want me to believe that my mother lied to me, before giving me a ton of money, that her husband's not my father and that my real father is a dead prick. Do I have that about right, asshole?"

"Yes. You must also be aware that your ton of money won't last much longer." He grinned, letting his eyes travel her body. "You asked if I've seen it all before. Well, I have, in Greece, when you were more of a redhead and that's only a minute part of what we know about you, apart from the obvious." His eyes stopped at the sheer yellow triangle that was still wet and ensconced into the symmetrical folds of her labia. "In fact, Miss Noëlyn, I excluded certain details from my report which I knew even a spry octogenarian would not have to hear. Having said that, I will tell you that Mr. Alexander is nothing if not a perfectionist. He cares nothing about mediocrity or vanity."

Noëlyn sat up, closing her legs. She faced him and cinched her belt. "First off, cut the Miss crap. Call me Noëlyn. I consider myself a New Yorker more than anything else. In fact, there isn't anything else. As far as I'm concerned anything before New York doesn't exist and I'm down here as much to be with mother as I am for the climate and spending my days dressed like this. I'm no southern belle so give me the frigging letter and take a walk around the pool. I'll let you know when I'm finished reading."

*

Good day, Noëlyn. What a pretty name, and I mean not to be facetious. The name your mother gave you is lovely and celebrates one of the loveliest times of the year, does it not, and judging from the reports I've received you are just as lovely.

Let me get straight to the point. Your mother and I, when we were married, had twins, a boy and girl, who we gave up for adoption for our own regrettable reasons. I now want to reunite with my children for the first time and I see your mother as a vehicle to assist me in achieving that end. I have no reason to meet with you, or your daughter, other than to ensure your mother's cooperation. Also, please be assured that I have no ill feeling towards either of you.

For that reason I have decided to make you and Jodie part of the reunion and tontine, which may be of greater importance to you. It will compensate for, or possibly correct, your heretofore lascivious lifestyle. I would ask you to read through to the addendum for the simple rules that you must follow implicitly. The same offer and rules will soon be delivered to Jodie.

I make no apology for my motives being strictly selfish. I want to see my children at least once before my time is at an end and I am offering you and your daughter an opportunity to benefit from that need. Needless to say, this offer is conditional upon your mother's cooperation and attendance. If, for whatever reason, she decides against assisting me to achieve my objective, this invitation will be rescinded and you will be summarily excluded from the tontine.

I look forward to seeing you in Las Palmas, Grand Canaries.

Davidson Alexander.

*

Noëlyn stood, kicked off her strapless sandals and threw her cover-up casually to the side. She dived into the pristine water directly across from him and surfaced at Mike DuFour's feet.

"I'll be there, with my mother. You can tell him that."

"Just simply arrive. Further instructions and information packages will be waiting for you at your respective hotels. He wisely foresaw a need to keep his guests apart prior to the reunion."

"So, the old guy really isn't my father."

"No, he is not."

"He could have adopted me."

"He might have, possibly, if he had known about you."

"Why would she have lied to me? It's no big deal. I was thirty when she found me."

"A year younger than Jodie." He snickered. "Does your daughter know Gupman wasn't her father?"

"No, she doesn't. They were never close. He came along

at the right time and liked what he saw. It was a win-win. I got the Hamptons, he got this. If I had got the money before he croaked I would have left him. Anyway, Jodie's got enough problems dealing with being a fat dyke. Emily gave her too much too soon. It went to her head, not to mention her stomach. She's about as messed up as it gets and scraping the bottom of the barrel."

"Sensitive motherly affection."

"It's true.

"She won't hear it from me."

"Whatever."

Noëlyn smoothed her wet titanium hair and scissor-kicked at the water to propel her tanned buttocks to just below the surface before pushing herself from the edge and pulling at the ties of her thong in one easy motion. She smiled up at him, trying to appear pert as her legs and arms treaded the water with wide, slow strokes.

"How come, Mike?"

"Ma'am," he responded.

"How come you didn't flirt with me in Greece? We could have had some fun together. There's no way I would have turned you down. Don't you like what you see?"

He waited a moment before answering, watching the tiny piece of yellow fabric flail in the trailing vortex of clear bubbles. "Good day, Miss Daniels. Please, when you call your daughter, tell her to expect me about nine this evening at her home. Thank you for your time."

Mike DuFour chuckled inwardly, walking away feeling sorry for her. He wasn't looking for a Noëlyn. He wanted someone to be with for more than twenty-four hours, someone whose purse wasn't crowded with condoms and someone who would remember his name in the morning.

51

Jodie Daniels was twenty-nine. She worked as a professor of English at CSU and had created a lifestyle for herself that was fast becoming unmanageable. When she buzzed him in without speaking through the intercom, Mike DuFour was too weary to bother looking up to the ceiling of the entranceway for a camera he knew was there.

The tenth-floor condo was spacious with a panoramic view of the city and its patio looked out over the comings and goings of the Market District. The modernist décor was completely feminine with high white walls lined with small to oversized black and white photographs of female nudes or semi-nudes that contrasted with the bright red and yellows of her European-styled furnishings. Many of the vases and statuettes were as tall as DuFour and the muted lighting and music made walking on the plush carpet seem like floating on a cloud. The décor could only have been planned by someone with more talent or skill than a woman who wore plain cotton skirts and dresses during the day and studded leather skirts and metal-tipped bras at night.

She was five-nothing, tops, and her light-weight summer sweater hugged the swell of her stomach and each of the side rolls which formed an indistinguishable and shapeless annex to it. Her jean short skirt would have been a sexy tease on a more attractive woman, not so on Jodie whose thighs were dotted with tiny indentations that seemed more like numerous small bruises from her knees to the ridge caused by the tight hem. From her closed knees to her ankles, seemingly thicker than they were because of her rolled-down bobby socks, her calves were parted in an inverse V as though her body instinctively knew the proper angle required to support and stabilize the weighty sum total of its moving parts.

The freckled skin on her face was tight and her shadowed eyes had a natural squint that gave her a frustrated or confused look which DuFour could not determine. Her honey-coloured hair was cut short, deprived of curls and any trace of femininity, and DuFour knew that on any given night it would be bright red, green, purple or yellow, any colour that would match her knee-high stockings or boot laces.

"Thank you for seeing me, Miss Daniels," he began, a sudden thought of Davidson flashing across his mind. "I hope I'm not disrupting your evening."

"Earlier would have been better, Mr. DuFour. I can't imagine you had much left to do in Charleston after seeing my mother and grandmother in the Palms."

"Paperwork, I'm afraid."

"Come in. I hope this won't take long. You're not the only one with paperwork," she said caustically, turning her back to him. "Please close the door."

"I require no more time than I spent with your mother and Miss Emily."

"You upset my grandmother very much with your visit."

DuFour smirked. "I know. I'm sorry. Learning of such sudden richesse is quite often very unsettling, though I believe your mother is adapting well to the news."

"Don't be snide."

"Let me be very clear, Miss Daniels. Tracking you and your family was one thing. Having to meet with each of you is turning out to be the least pleasant part of this job. I also happen to know you and your mother have become less critical to this reunion than previously thought. So, please, be more gracious. You stand to lose a lot, one hell of a lot and right now I'm feeling very inclined towards facilitating such a loss. I assure you, a simple phone call will irrevocably remove you and your mother from the equation. So don't push it, and we both know the only paperwork you've got planned for tonight is moving your napkin from under one drink to another at one of your girl-only bars."

"Well said, detective. Bravo. I see you have also investigated me, though didn't you have so much more fun watching my mother running around naked in Greece? Sorry I can't offer you the same turn on. Did you happen to take any worthwhile pictures?"

DuFour remained silent, averting his eyes as Jodie Daniels fell back uncontrolled onto the supple leather sofa.

"Tell me, what else have you learned about the fat lesbian teacher?"

"Be assured, my findings were for Davidson Alexander's eyes only. He cares not at all about your sexual preferences or your mother's inclination towards the natural."

"To what extent."

"Suffice it to say comprehensive, and exclusively for Monsieur Alexander. If your grandmother wants to believe you work nights, it's not my place to tell her differently." DuFour sat, before being invited to do so.

"No amount has been mentioned, Mr. DuFour. My grandmother is very old and my mother is greedy and self-absorbed. I have to be a little more pragmatic. About how much are we talking?"

"I have no idea, Miss Daniels. My single purpose is to deliver a letter to you, though I can say that, as Miss Emily was squandering her money, as well as providing you and your mother with extremely generous endowments, which you have also squandered, he has not," DuFour reached into his jacket pocket, "which leaves very little for us to discuss. You will either accept the offer or you won't. Miss Emily's visit to Las Palmas is seen by him as requisite, not yours. Either she attends the reunion on her own, or all three of you go. Without your grandmother your presence will neither be expected nor acknowledged. Please read your letter. I also have flight coupons and hotel reservations for you, if you agree."

He placed the envelope on the marble coffee table and pushed it towards her.

*

Jodie, my name is Davidson Alexander. I am, as you have already been made aware, your grandmother's ex-husband. You must also know at this point that you are not part of the family my ex-wife and I began together.

More to the point, I have invited your grandmother to visit with me on Las Palmas as a means of encouraging my children to reunite with me. I believe her presence here will make all the difference in their decision to attend, and to that end I have decided to include you and your mother in a tontine that should serve to reverse the increasing fragility of your respective financial situations. This, please understand, is contingent upon your grandmother's attendance. Should your grandmother decide not to attend, though I anticipate such will not be the case, your presence will not be required or expected. I extend the invitation on this one occasion as an encouragement to you to influence your grandmother with regard to my wishes, nothing more.

Please read the addendum and respect the few rules implicitly, should you decide favourably.

Regards,

Davidson Alexander

*

"Short and sweet. Now I understand why she left him."

DuFour shrugged, pleased not to be with all three women in the same room. "Actually, he left her."

"Just because of my mother. What was the big deal? Was she that afraid of the drunk?"

"No. He's not a man to fear, he's a man to respect. He left because she sold your mother for five-hundred dollars and waited twenty-nine years to tell him."

"Yeah, right, like I believe that. Get real. Her own mother was still alive. They lived together in a mansion and were independently wealthy with gold money from the Klondike. Her father struck one of the richest veins ever. Five hundred would have been peanuts, even back then. Tell your boss to get his facts straight."

"There was no Klondike. Your great-grandmother operated a boarding house after her husband deserted her and she barely eked out a living. Your grandmother helped to clean guestrooms and cook meals when she wasn't working as a bookkeeper, until Davidson Alexander came along. The five hundred would have been a major windfall for her."

"What about the drinking and the beatings?"

"I don't have time for this, Miss Daniels. I have a very long trip ahead of me and I'd like to rest a few hours before my departure. Just know that, if not for him, your five million would have been zilch, though you would never have known the difference. It seems to me you are already greatly indebted to him. Your grandmother was average at best, Miss Daniels, if not poor before she met him. She lied to you."

Jodie's face darkened to beat red. "I love my grandmother."

"Who doesn't love their grandmother? Five million would buy anyone lots of love."

"Fuck you. She's always been there for me. Now you want to ruin my memories of her and make me despise her."

"No I don't. I have no preference whatsoever as to how you view your grandmother. Davidson and Emily made their considerable fortune together. When he left she got half, including profits from the mansion and the island retreat and, oh yeah, and the yacht." He nodded his head as though agreeing. "You're right, Miss Daniels, he is a terrible person." Then DuFour stood. "He's one of the nicest guys I've met. It could be that he would have adopted your mother, but he wasn't given the chance. I'd say the old girl has a lot to explain and I imagine her next story will be as equally entertaining as her first. I have no doubt she's working on the script as we speak."

"Five hundred dollars," Jodie's face twisted in disbelief, "she sold her baby for five hundred dollars?"

"It was a lot of money back then, more than a year's salary. We're talking about the post-depression years."

"What about their own kids?"

"As nice as any, once you factor out family."

"How many will be there?"

"You mean how many will share in the tontine: seven, including the three of you."

"And if we don't go?"

DuFour laughed openly. "Divided by four, Miss Daniels, and no one will care. You have less than four weeks to decide. Your flight departs on the twelfth. What you do upon arrival will be explained to you at time."

Jodie Daniels inhaled deeply. "I'll attend, but I wasn't expecting any of this. I have to speak with my mother and grandmother."

DuFour dropped the airline folder on the table. "I thought you might, though I don't have to know your answer. I doubt he even knows how much he paid for your tickets. Be there, or not. It's your call, but remember the old girl either goes alone, or with the two of you. Good night, Miss Daniels. I'll see myself out."

Jodie leaned forward and twisted sideways, squirming from the sofa. "One moment, detective, I have one more question."

"Yes?"

"I was never very close to my father, and when he died my mother never really grieved for him. Neither of us did, and I've never understood why. I always believed he didn't like me." She looked up at DuFour.

"Perhaps, Miss Daniels, it is you who did not like him. Talk with your mother. I believe she's expecting your questions. Good night."

52

The trip to Paris was circuitous, taking DuFour through Charlotte, Philly and New York. The journey depleted more of his energy than he had anticipated and he regretted not staying over another night in Charleston. The Alexander contract was catching up with him. He was exhausted despite the luxury of First Class flights Davidson had insisted upon.

He felt deeply sorry for Davidson who would soon be hosting a belligerent and unforgiving ex-wife and two women who would have preferred cashier cheques for whatever amount. In his mind he could see Noëlyn flipping through travel brochures and the Web, looking for hotels that suited her who-cares lifestyle. He could see Jodie planning lavish purchases, secure in the knowledge that, as much as she loved her grandmother, Emily would one day be dead and she, Jodie, would certainly not be excluded from the will after all those years of loyalty and caring. Her mother was another matter. She cared about no one but herself and DuFour had no doubt Jodie knew better than to think she would be included in any future plans, monetary or otherwise.

He felt differently about the twins, trying to imagine the inner turmoil or confusion he had left with them. He sincerely hoped all would work out for them, that Davidson would win them over and that Steve Brandon would somehow figure into that new relationship. The young man now had a real chance at life, all thanks to Davidson. Only Mike DuFour, Davidson and Steve Brandon would ever know of his true identity, that Dexter Philips no longer existed and DuFour fell asleep feeling oddly strange to be privy to that information.

When he woke to the high-pitched screeching sound of the 747's inert tires abruptly impacting with the runway's sun-heated surface he wondered for the briefest moment where he was and why. He let everyone disembark before him. Roissy-Charles de Gaulle Airport northeast of Paris was congested, teeming with irate weekend travellers whose flights were delayed. Typically unaffected parents seemed to believe their screaming offspring were adorable, there for all the world to embrace and beleaguered backpack-dependent teenagers sprawled out along both sides of the concourse walls. It was his definition of hell and he was quite certain, looking around him, that his return flight to Montreal would be his last.

He hated airports, he hated the people who worked in them, and he hated ill-mannered teenagers whose legs were blocking his path to the baggage claim area. As he came closer he looked directly down at the teen closest to him. He could the kid's eye flitter and strain to the limits of his peripheral vision behind dark glasses, another thing that annoyed DuFour greatly: kids, men, anyone wearing ridiculous caps on backwards, particularly inside with sunglasses. The teen was showing no sign of surrendering his space. Then suddenly, to his complete surprise, he was facing in the same direction as Mike DuFour who was walking away from him, leaving the kid to rub his legs to the amusement of everyone else walking past.

The only baggage he was going to carry was himself. The porter could do the rest and he was so happy he could expense a limousine rather than a taxi, not that he couldn't afford one on his own. But work was work. The Air France flight had been scheduled to depart Atlanta at 8:00AM, it had left at ten and the time was now 11:30 PM local. The drive to l'Hotel Les Fontaines would be no less than an hour and that would still not end his already fifteen hour day.

The hotel restaurant was closed, though Gérard de-Saint-Valéry had left instructions that Monsieur Alexander's visiting associate was to enjoy the best that Room Service had to offer. Mere moments after walking into his three-room suite Mike DuFour was enjoying a fine bottle of Bordeaux with exotic cheeses, pâtés, warm baguettes and fresh fruits. As travel weary as he was, the meal took precedence over his bed. When he glanced at the tray early Friday morning, it was empty.

Joaquin de-Saint-Valéry had been instructed by his grandfather to present himself precisely at noon and DuFour had no doubt that he would. That gave DuFour four hours and he suddenly reached for his keys and hurried from the room, feeling compelled in that split second to see L'Auberge-de-la-Plus-Belle-Gitane.

When the cab pulled up in front DuFour spent long minutes staring at the twin doors, the winding, hilly street and the corner where Davidson had once stood in anguish more than half a century before. Even though he had no way of knowing, nothing seemed to have changed. All he knew was the very little a lonely man had shared with him. When he went through the doors the men seated at the bar turned and looked at him. What he saw next were the well-persevered and yellowed sepia photographs lining the walls, photographs of a by-gone era. In some of the photos the woman was small, dressed like a gypsy and the soldier beside her, monolithic. In some they were young; in others they were young at heart. In others a thin, sinewy man in a white apron stood squeezed into the side of a huge, dark-skinned man who, with his other arm, held a young boy as though teaching him to fly.

DuFour looked for dates, but there was none. When the

young barman called out to him with a smile, asking what he would like, DuFour answered, "To sit for a while and think of the past, to think of what it must have been like for a young and beautiful Gabrielle, La Gitane and Davidson." That he knew Davidson began a whirlwind of chatter. The Pernod was on the house and DuFour knew better than to insult the Frenchman by refusing.

By eleven he had heard about Henri and Gérard, Big Earl and had come to know a little bit more about the reticent Davidson Alexander. He regretted having to leave the bistro, but he also felt he had somehow intruded into Davidson's personal memories. There was no need to hear more. He was content to have met the man himself.

He arrived back at Les Fontaines at 11:40, enough time to refresh himself and wait for the call. Precisely at noon the phone at his work station chimed. Moments later he was stepping out into the lobby and walking towards the private office Gérard had arranged for the meeting. Joaquin de-Saint-Valéry stood by his uncle, between them was a beautiful olive-skinned and dark-eyed young woman whom DuFour took to be no more than twenty or twenty-one.

The niceties were brief. DuFour thanked Gérard for his unparalleled hospitality and consideration, Gérard welcomed him to remain for as long as he wanted to enjoy Paris, the two men shook hands and Gérard walked away after hugging his nephew and bowing to the young man's fiancée.

DuFour leaned forward to open the door and stepped back to allow Lydyah and Joaquin to precede him. Clearly the Davidson clan had an eye for beauty. Lydyah was anything but a chador-clad subservient Muslim female. She walked straight with small, confident steps. Her hair was pulled back into a tight ponytail, her silk blouse showed a hint of the embroidered bra beneath it, her satin skirt fell to above her knees with a six-inch back slit and her shoes were two-inch Italian-leather pumps with a matching Gucci handbag. Somewhat different, DuFour thought, from the designer jeans and tee-shirts she had been wearing the last time they had met.

Joaquin was nothing like his grandfather, more a consequence of Jean-Alexandre and the predominately shorter Chantal and Gabrielle. His hair was dark. His skin was smooth and his features seemed to be sculpted. His handshake was firm, but could have been firmer and he looked as though he hadn't done a hard day's work in his life, with good reason. He was affable, from DuFour's past acquaintance with him; he was charming, already well-travelled and seemed entirely at ease as the door closed behind them.

"Mademoiselle, Monsieur de-Saint-Valéry, merci d'avoir…"

Joaquin interrupted. "If you don't mind, sir, my fiancée is more comfortable with English, though she is working diligently to correct the imperfection."

DuFour nodded to Lydyah and turned his attention to Joaquin. "Thank you for joining me this afternoon. I trust you have not been too inconvenienced."

"I had no choice in the matter. My grandfather always gets what he wants. It's very difficult to refuse him."

"You are fortunate to have such a man at the head of your family. He possesses qualities many of us regrettably lack."

"Indeed?" Joaquin grinned thinly. "Do you refer to honesty, sir?"

"Amongst others, yes."

"And how are you enjoying Paris, the City of Lights?"

"Unfortunately, my time here is limited to our meeting. I must fly out this evening."

"And how did you enjoy Bahrain?"

It was DuFour's turn to smile, looking at Lydyah.

"In fact, I enjoyed my limited time there very much, from what I saw of it: a very beautiful place with very beautiful people. The subterfuge was necessary, as you will soon discover." He paused. "On that note I must be very frank and apologize to Miss Lydyah. Mr. Alexander has expressly instructed that this meeting must be private and confidential. I am afraid I must ask for the young lady's indulgence."

"We are soon to be married. We have no secrets from one another."

DuFour looked once again at Lydyah. "Mademoiselle, without the two of us alone there will be no meeting. My instructions are very clear. Your fiancé has been called to this meeting from Bahrain. I assure you, I have not been sent here to talk about such mundane matters as tomorrow's weather."

Lydyah bowed her head ever so slightly, acknowledging DuFour before turning to Joaquin. "I shall wait for you in the lounge, my love. Give Mr. DuFour whatever time he requires of you." She held out her hand to the detective. "Thank you, sir, for your diplomacy."

DuFour stepped back to open the door. "I thank you, mademoiselle, for your understanding. I will not keep him from you very long."

When the door closed Joaquin was the first to speak. "A surreptitious encounter in Bahrain, secrecy in a Paris hotel instead of my parents' home, and yet my uncle seems not at all surprised to see me. I must confess, I'm intrigued," he said, switching to French.

"Yes, I suppose you are." DuFour responded. "Though quite to the contrary, I did not know to expect you. There has been no communication between me and your grandfather since the beginning of the month. I presume you have not yet introduced Mademoiselle Lydyah to your parents."

"I am invited for dinner this evening. I intended Lydyah to be a surprise, which I suppose she will not be. Does my grandfather know of her?"

"He does."

"When we spoke my parents mentioned nothing of this meeting, yet I sense they knew of it."

"I have no idea."

"I find that difficult to believe." Joaquin turned towards one of two leather sofas and slouched into it, crossing his legs and arms. "Now what is this all about? My grandfather said nothing other than I was to be here for my own good, as well as the good of others, and that it was time for me to come of age. What did he mean exactly?"

"He meant the time has come for you to be a man and stop living off your parents." DuFour sat into the sofa facing the young man. "First, monsieur, I will extend to you all the respect due your grandfather and your family. You will do the same for me by not sitting slumped like a dazed orang-utan while we speak."

Joaquin stayed as he was, defiant, watching DuFour slowly reaching into his pocket to produce a phone and beginning to tap in numbers with his thumb.

"I was instructed not to take any nonsense from you. We have come together for a very serious conversation, one that will affect the rest of your life. I'll let you explain to your grandfather why I have terminated the meeting." Joaquin slowly uncrossed his arms and began to ease into a straighter position as DuFour buried the inactive phone back into his pocket. "Thank you." He reached into another pocket and put the envelope on the table. "This is for you, eventually. First, there are a few questions which your grandfather feels need clarifying, information I was unable to ascertain during my trip to Bahrain. I'll be blunt in asking what he feels needs to be asked and I would appreciate honest and calm replies."

"There's nothing to clarify."

"Is Lydyah's family related in any way to any organization that might cause embarrassment to your parents or grandfather?"

"Excuse me."

"Do Lydyah or her family have anti-Western sentiments?"

Joaquin's face instantly distorted with the frustration of an inexperienced fledgling searching for the mental resources to compete with a seasoned professional who clearly had the upper hand, while trying equally hard to maintain a sophisticated decorum. DuFour waited quietly for the answer.

"No, they are peaceful and tolerant in the extreme. They are Muslims, as am I. That's my other surprise for my parents and, I suppose, for my grandfather who seems to believe my business is his."

"For the purposes of this meeting your business is his business. Don't doubt that for a moment. To do so would be a sad mistake."

"We intend to wed next spring, first in Bahrain, then in Paris. It's Lydyah's wish, not mine. She wants to respect my parents and their religion."

"You plan to live in Bahrain with her family and continue working at the radio station?"

"Yes, thus far."

"Tell me about her. But first, may I offer you wine or cognac."

Joaquin's mood seemed to lighten. "It is too early for cognac, perhaps a glass of Bordeaux."

"I see your religious conversion is not yet complete," DuFour's expression was flat, almost disinterested, "perhaps a work in progress or one of uncertainty."

"There is no uncertainty. I believe in the teachings of the Prophet Mohammed. For me the matter is one of logic: the teachings of a once physical profit versus the idolatry of an incorporeal being. I can't distinguish the slightest difference between that and a golden calf. Do you see my point?"

"No, I do not. I've lived my life as an atheist. It's hard to believe in anything but yourself when you carry a gun most times and start your day wondering if you'll be the one to kill or be killed." DuFour placed the half-full crystal goblet in front of his guest and sipped his cognac before continuing. "So you believe, thus far, and are not doing this to gain acceptance with her family."

"They have not pressured me in the least, nor has she. Truthfully, they honour their religion more than practice it. Their prayers are private and not always with regard to the direction of Mecca. You see the way she dresses. She is even more beautiful in private, if you will allow me to boast of my conquest." Joaquin took up his glass, savouring the nose of the wine before tasting the richness. "I believe my uncle has the finest wine cellar in all of Paris. I see no conflict in enjoying nature's fruit." He smiled. "Now I must apologize to you, Monsieur DuFour. I was rude: a quality that occasionally comes too easily to me, like most other things. Let me just say that you will like her very much, as will by parents."

"I liked her when I first saw you together in Bahrain, and a conquest is much better than an acquisition. If I were to ask her I believe she might tell me that you were actually the conquest. I say that kindly. All the same, your grandfather is very concerned."

"When he sees her, he will love her."

DuFour sat, swirling his drink. "He's seen her already, and he's heard her. He sends his compliments."

"What else does he know?"

"Everything from your travels to your grades and your inherent ability to spend your parents' money."

Joaquin tilted his head quizzically, looking at a stoic Mike DuFour. "What reason could he possibly have to hire a foreigner to investigate me? What is this all about?"

"It is, Joaquin, about you. Your grandfather is worried about you, as are your parents. You have enjoyed a good life, but not a life you have personally earned. You are an exception in your family. He wants that to stop. He wants you to be your own man, not a de-Saint-Valéry shadow. I would not worry about what he thinks of your young lady, I would be more concerned about what he thinks of you. You are the only grandson of his Gabrielle and he sees any lapse in your ambitions as an affront to her memory."

"And he sends a stranger to shame me, rather than tell me directly."

"No, monsieur. He sends a stranger to deliver an invitation that is part of this letter." DuFour pushed the envelope towards Joaquin. "Take your time and, if I may suggest, read the message with an open mind."

"Do you know what it says?"

"In part, yes I do. We spoke at length before he wrote it. He wanted an objective opinion. Take your time."
*

My dearest Joaquin,

I trust this letter finds you in good health. It has been too long since I have seen you and I wonder why, but that is for another time. Suffice it to say that you are missed at Las Palmas and at your parents' home, your parents' home, Joaquin, not yours, and that leads me to the purpose of this urgent communication and the reason you are sitting with Monsieur DuFour.

I lost your dear grandmother too many years ago. I spend my days thinking of her and my nights dreaming of her. What you do not know is that during my first marriage I had two children who are now twice your age.

For reasons that do not concern you, I have not seen them since their early childhood and I wish to remedy what has plagued me throughout much of my life. I also intend to see their son whom I have never seen: my other grandson. To facilitate such a reunion I have endeavoured to engage the cooperation of the woman to whom I was first married and her offspring who are in no way related to me. That assurance comes in the form of a tontine which I have extended to them, believing they will encourage one another to attend the reunion here on Las Palmas and, by now, you must be wondering how you figure in to a reunion of people who are strangers to you.

With regard to the three women of the other family, it is quite simply a bribe; my rationalization being that my children, particularly my daughter, will more likely reunite with their mother or both of us, rather than me alone. In the case of my children the tontine is a reward for their achievement. For my other grandson, two years your senior, a reward for overcoming a tragic life and not succumbing to the temptations of returning to that life. They have, in my view, earned it; though I have no doubt the tontine will factor to some large degree into their individual decisions to attend or not.

Now, my dearest Joaquin, I will address you and your inclusion. To me, and to your parents, although neither Chantal nor Jean-Alexandre will concede the point, you have become a disappointment and I wish to remedy that intolerable condition which is simply not acceptable.

Where I could have created an endowment or bequeathed to you a sum of money, you would have held your parents in contempt for the conditions I am about to impose; this way, as part of the tontine, you can blame me directly. The attendees will share equally and immediately in the portion of my estate which I have allotted to the tontine: a significant amount to say the least. Without exception, those not attending or arriving late will be excluded.

In your case, your portion of the tontine will be placed in trust until the following conditions precedent have been achieved: Firstly, I expect you to become independent forthwith and cease being a burden to those who love you. A separate and very modest fund has been arranged for you. You may reinstate your lifestyle when you have earned the privilege. Secondly, you will complete your education and do so starting immediately; thirdly, you will not marry until the conclusion of your education and the implementation of a realistic business plan. To do so will deprive you of your portion and my attorney, Monsieur d'Avignon, will oversee your compliance in the event of my passing.

All that said; I anxiously await Monsieur DuFour's feedback regarding Lydyah and her family, the fourth and final condition. What follows are my other expectations.

With love,
Davidson

*

"Do my parents know?"

"Yes."

"But they are not part of it."

"No."

"It seems unfair."

DuFour smiled and chuckled. "It has been a while since you have seen them. You will find them very happy about their exclusion. Your grandfather is very serious about d'Avignon."

"The others will walk away rich, while I must wait three or four years."

DuFour nodded. "The three he cares about have proven themselves. So why wait? Right now you have nothing to offer your young lady and very likely you never will unless you stand on your own."

"I never knew he was previously married. Will I like them?"

"I would think not. The tontine is an unexpected windfall for them. Their interest is strictly monetary."

"Will his children come?"

"Yes, I believe they will, and their son whom they've never seen. It should prove to be interesting."

"What do I tell Lydyah, and her family?"

"Tell Lydyah she's invited to Las Palmas to meet your grandfather. What happens after that is between the two of you." DuFour reached into his jacket for the other envelope.

"Inside are flight coupons for both of you. I'll be giving him another positive report on Lydyah. When the reunion is finished he will extend an invitation for the two of you to remain at the villa, so that he might acquaint himself with Lydyah. He will do the same for his children and other grandson. The three others will be leaving the island early the following morning."

"He thinks I let him down, Monsieur DuFour."

"You have let him down, kid. So do something about it. You're twenty-four. It's time for you to be a man, to make him and your parents proud of their son. Those are my words, not his. Lydyah will wait. If she doesn't you'll get over it, like the rest of us. Sometimes life sucks, but somehow I don't think that will happen. One more thing: Don't think the one-time amount he'll deposit into your account is a paltry sum. It's not. It's more than enough to support the two of you, to live well separately or together throughout your studies; proof that your grandfather is a man of vision and a romantic. That's what you'll have to tell her parents, in your own words. Good luck with that one. I wish I could seem more compassionate, but I don't see your future as very problematic and I'm sure neither will Lydyah." DuFour stood. "Unless you have further questions, Joaquin, I believe your lovely lady is waiting for you."

Joaquin stood. "I will call my grandfather immediately to apologize for disappointing him."

"No, you will not. You'll be there on time and with what he wants. It's his wish."

"Then tell him when you speak that I will apologize to my parents this evening and ask their advice about suitable lodgings for a student. Tell him I'm sorry." The young man forced a smile. "That will be the easy part. Muslims aren't necessarily always happy or polite, nor are they always very tolerant in matters concerning their daughters. I will need all of Lydyah's support."

"Good luck, kid, to both of you. Have a lunch on me, room 1218, with good wine. Think of it as a wedding gift. Now get out of here."

53

By late afternoon Davidson ended the two-hour conversation and thanked Mike DuFour for his integrity and good work. His bonus, Davidson promised, would be transferred by the start of business Monday morning. Neither man mentioned the amount, though Mike DuFour had just become a much wealthier man.

His work was finished and by the end of the following week his agency would be given over to his employees. Freedom fifty-five was a reality and his first piece of business Monday morning would be the purchase of a brand new Lincoln Town Car and a very long vacation that would not include air travel.

Davidson had been very pleased with the report, albeit indifferent to the additional information regarding Emily's daughters. It was sufficient to know, he had commented, "that the sharks had taken readily to the dangling chum."

Davidson's children were coming to him, and whether Emily had anything to do with their decision was inconsequential. They were coming, and so were Steve Brandon and Joaquin. At long last his family would come together. Monday morning he would discuss the details with Maria; he would trust no one else with the preparations and Jorge would begin his most masterful work in the garden. That evening, as Mike DuFour's flight left Europe behind, Davidson spoke with Maître Karl d'Avignon at length. Exhausted, he fell asleep to rendez-vous with

Family Lies

Gabrielle in his dreams, completely unaware that, as happened most nights, a confluence of warm tears would moisten his pillow.

54

Monday morning a new and refreshed Mike DuFour awoke not liking his home, liking it even less when he opened his computer and saw confirmation that his fee had been doubled and the balance deposited into the numbered account. He leaned over the screen in disbelief. He had never doubted Davidson's word, but this was beyond his wildest dream.

Suddenly he hated his clothes and everything else he possessed that would be constant reminders of his frugality and pitiful city pension. He wanted everything gone and promised himself it would be by the time he returned from Miami in his new Lincoln.

He was surprised to hear so soon from his accountant that his signature, and the signatures of his employees, were the two formalities remaining before he could legally disassociate himself from the agency. Something he had promised would be done by week's end. The car dealer opened at ten. He wanted the Town Car for that afternoon, and he knew which one. Then he would visit the best haberdasher in town and end his day dining at the city's finest restaurant.

He was living a dream and he wanted never to wake up. Before lunch he went to the bank. Paying cash for the car and his clothes depleted the first hundred thousand he had transferred. He wanted another hundred, just to have it, to look at it and to see his banker's reaction. When he stood at the wicket the teller looked at him the way tellers always do and asked him to wait one moment. DuFour knew why, and he did wait. A few seconds later the manager introduced himself and asked for a moment of his time; the man had never introduced himself, and had never before spoken to Monsieur Michel DuFour, even though Mike DuFour had been a client for decades. DuFour had found something else to hate in the short-term: bank managers. The man was effusive and shallow and DuFour couldn't help himself. Before he walked out he answered the man's question with a wide grin: four million.

By late Monday, after his titanium-coloured Town Car had been delivered to his modest two-storey home, one of several made-to-measure suits had been ready for a fitting and the gold Cartier was the final touch. The rest of his new wardrobe would be ready for the signing and his departure for Miami late Friday. He had never thought to wear French cuffs or even cuff links, let alone silk-lined trousers, but he would that evening and from then on. He had also become immediately addicted to supple Italian leather. Standing in front of his mirror he saw another man, a man who looked not at all like a streetwise and cynical ex-cop or someone who had spent the last sixteen years following and collecting proof positive about the worst business executives, cheating wives, suddenly out-of-the-closet husbands and crooked cops.

He was beginning a new life and he would induct himself into it appropriately with a bottle of the finest French wine. The time 7:35 when he put his empty glass on the kitchen counter, walked into the garage and stepped into the gleaming Lincoln. When he backed out from the cluttered garage he felt more like a visitor anxious to leave someone else's home and promised himself it would be put on the market the next morning.

He took the long way from suburbia to downtown, wanting to feel the car as much as be seen in it. The valets at the restaurant seemed impressed, they called him sir and he waited until one of them had taken his luxury ride from sight. The maître d' also called him sir, and showed no misgiving that Mike DuFour might not belong in his establishment. The sommelier reacted with reserved approval as Mike selected a Pomerol Chateau La Fleur-de-Gay '82 from the prestigious wine cellar; and the waiter, although completely disinterested in the choice of his à la carte dinner, timed the arrival of each course perfectly. The meal culminated with a complimentary thirty-year cognac before Mike signed the chit, bringing an ecstatic smile to the waiter's face.

He arrived home at midnight. The street was quiet; the dull amber glow emanating from the streetlamp turned the façade of his home from the yellowish-white of neglect to a lacklustre sepia tone until the piecing twin beams of his halogens instantly illuminated the garage door to a blinding blue-white reflective screen.

Mike DuFour leaned his head back against the headrest and chuckled quietly to himself as he reached up to the sun visor and squeezed the garage door remote. In the quiet of the garage he thought back to his exquisite meal and finally he understood the meaning of comfort food. He was pleased with himself. He felt good. He felt proud. His hard work had paid off by considerably more than he had ever expected. But Davidson Alexander had wanted the best and had got the best. Now Mike DuFour would have the best. Life was good. He could relax, and he could enjoy. His guns would become a thing of the past, relics to remember another era, if he would ever think or care to do so. He had thought of the past often enough. The time had come to think of the future, to let the past and future dissipate into random thoughts. He put a hand to the stainless steel lever to open the car door, telling himself out loud he would throw his camcorder into the garbage before falling into bed.

"Let's see if we can help you do that, DuFour."

55

Earlier in the evening the three men had remained in the suburbs while a fourth drove to downtown Montreal with no idea where he was going. He only knew he could not lose sight of the titanium-coloured sedan. Where he was going was unimportant, what they needed to know, what he needed to report, was when Mike DuFour would be returning home. The second car was a black four-door Chevrolet and unremarkable. Even so, the driver laughed contemptuously at the man he was following. The ominous scenario was far from the predictable intrigue portrayed on the big screen. Mike DuFour, the superlative detective, had no clue he was being followed. It was always like that: there would be no white-knuckle chase, no screeching tires and no triple rollovers. That was the stuff of Hollywood for anyone under twelve or their brain-dead parents who thought it was so cool, when it wasn't: It was someone being killed.

Earlier, when the detective had climbed out and had given over his keys to the valet the man knew his trail had come to an end. He would not go in. He would be refused and he knew why. He was a stereotype; he'd be profiled. He ate most of his meals at the lounge with girls who seldom dressed for the occasion. He noted the name of the restaurant in the Vieux-Port, and the street name he was thankful he could pronounce well enough to remember. Then he drove to the end of the block. La rue Saint-Paul was a one-way single lane of broken and uneven asphalt that was always lined with cars. The dilapidated city was enjoying the last real week of summer and the narrow road was filled with tourists who possibly felt European to stroll mindlessly amongst drivers who were arguably worse than their French counterparts. More likely, they felt safer than being with those who vied for space along broken and uneven sidewalks as they meandered in single file between orange, white and dented construction cones.

He took thirty minutes to circle the block, impeded by slow moving vehicles and the ponderous human herds, twenty minutes more the second time. He cursed pedestrians and drivers alike: Red lights meant nothing to pedestrians and pedestrians meant nothing to drivers. The city was a shambles and not the friendliest.

He was thankful the hour was late when he finally pulled into an empty spot. He had no change for the meter and anyone he approached for change had hurried away as would be expected of any desensitized city dweller. He didn't know he was in the homeless capital of North America: a town of derelicts and indigents. Nor did he know the meter maids didn't work the late-night hours. The city had no money to pay them and the cops would only patrol that part of town when everyone had gone and they could cruise the streets unimpeded.

The valet was tired and took his time to retrieve DuFour's car, who then took his time easing into the driver's seat after suitably acknowledging the valet. As Mike DuFour drove away the black four-door Chevy slowly backed to the corner and followed, ignoring the red light. The driver pressed pre-dial and spoke briefly in a matter-of-fact monotone before pressing end. His target was en route. ETA: unknown.

The three men were dressed in black slacks, sweaters, caps, dark glasses and were virtually invisible on the poorly lit street. They moved stealthily and separately from their car to the house, each one walking as quickly as possible without seeming conspicuous to the casual observer, though most of the homes had put out their lights an hour earlier. They were all large men who became obscure shadows melding with the darkness between the two towering birch trees DuFour and his neighbour had planted so conveniently many years earlier.

They said nothing. There was nothing to say. They simply waited, crouched down along the side of the house. Their backs and leg muscles soon ached and the minute hand on their watches moved with irritating slowness until a distant glow grew brighter and the grinding sound of the chain engaging with the garage door broke the silence.

They had twenty-five seconds, six seconds once the door would begin to close and when the Lincoln's taillights were parallel to the entrance the men were mere inches away. When the taillights cleared the door the dark figures were in the garage, crouched down well below the trunk lid and wondering why Mike DuFour was taking so long to bring down the door. Then, after what seemed like an eternity to the vulnerable three, Abacus stood.

"Let's see if we can help you do that, DuFour," he said, raising the nine-millimetre Glock as one man moved to the rear left panel and the other circled the car to line up with DuFour's back.

Mike pivoted from the hip with his right leg still grounded to the cockpit floor. He instinctively went for his weapon, stopping midway and feeling his shoulders slump imperceptibly. Over the past several weeks of travel he had become accustomed to not wearing a gun and he knew this was no impromptu home invasion.

"You have me at a disadvantage."

"No shit." Abacus laughed. The other two grinned, not taking their eyes off DuFour.

"You know me ... fine. So who the hell are you? What do you want?"

"Who we are doesn't matter a shit," Abacus looked at the inside door, waving to Mike DuFour with the Glock, "and what we want is you, inside. What's the code? Fuck us up and, well, I think you can imagine."

"91735."

Abacus pictured the pad keys in his mind. "Not bad." He nodded toward the man at his left and spoke to DuFour. "Toss him the keys and follow behind with your hands in your pockets."

Mike DuFour moved slowly. The man in front of him was already pushing through the door and reaching toward the control panel to alter the blinking red light to green. He nodded, releasing a breath as he stepped aside.

"Stay standing." Abacus ordered DuFour flatly. "This won't take long. We'll be gone in a few minutes, after you tell us why you were so fucking interested in Dexter Philips and why we can't find him. Who hired you, why, and where the fuck is he?"

"I don't know. I really don't. This elderly man came to my office a few weeks ago, gave me a few thousand dollars, said it was all he had and asked me to find his son. All he knew was the kid was in Attica, he was supposed to be getting out sometime soon and the old man felt bad about not being around for the trial or visiting."

Abacus leaned against a wall. "Tonight's the second time we messed up following you, DuFour. The first was when Philips screwed off from work that Monday without saying why, the night we saw you at the front door of the flophouse he was living in. We thought he'd come back for his shit; he never did and I ended up with my balls in the wringer. Like tonight, we never thought you'd be going to dinner alone on a Monday night. Go figure."

"We had dinner and I dropped him off on some street corner, a few thousand richer. Don't bother looking for him here. He knows DiFiore's still pissed with him. If anything he's probably taken a bus east or west to find work in a diner. If you know him, you also know he's not the brightest bulb." Mike looked at all three men, doing his best to appear unaffected and confident.

"Bullshit. You went to Attica after his release. His old man would have known that, and then you waited a few weeks longer before meeting with him."

"That's not the way it happened."

"Yeah, it was; so enough of this bullshit. Where is he?"

Mike shook his head. "No clue. When he left I got onto other cases. He could be anywhere."

"But he's not. He's somewhere, and you know where."

"No, I don't."

It was twelve-fifteen. Abacus pointed to one of his men, telling him to climb the stairs to the second floor. When he came to the first landing he stopped and turned. Abacus next ordered Mike to the stairs and told him to stand facing into them.

"DuFour, I don't have much time, so I'm going to ask you three questions. With each good answer you get to stay where you are, with each bad answer you get to climb one step. When you get both feet on the third step that guy's going blow off your fucking head."

"I've told you what I know."

"Why did you take so long to find him after your trip to Attica, especially with all that money from his old man? His PO would have helped you. Or didn't a smart guy like you think of that?"

"I had other business out of town. The old man knew that."

Abacus pushed him forward. "Not good enough. Take a step."

DuFour hesitated, feeling his throat beginning to hurt from dryness. He reached for the banister and Abacus swiftly pushed his arm away.

"Who wanted you to find him?"

"No one wants him, just you and DiFiore. His father

wanted to do something to help. It's all I know."

"Bullshit. Take another step. Congratulations, you're two thirds there and, by the way, if you blink or even piss yourself I'll put two in the back of your head myself. So pay attention. We know you've been out of town and out of the country. When you didn't come back to the apartment we searched everywhere for you. Then, guess what? We found you. We found you flying all over the fucking place and now you're back home, driving a Town Car in a tailor-made suit and living the good life."

DuFour's legs were trembling and he felt his insides churning with nervous tension. His step forward was uneasy but he dared not reach for the banister. "I won the lottery."

"Yeah, looks like. Did you get him out of the country? Is that it? Did you get him into the States or France?"

"You already know the answer. There was no time to get him into the States even if I had been hired to relocate him, or if he had enough money to pay for it. You know about fake paperwork. It takes time, and it costs."

"You're lying, DuFour. Where is he? Don't be stupid about this. He's nothing to you; he's nothing, period. He fucked up big time and it's payback time. What goes around comes around. He should have kept his mouth shut. He would have been out in nine or ten with a good future. Don't fuck up yours for him. We'll find him, and you know it." Abacus paused. "That was sort of your third question."

DuFour surprised himself by how calm he had become and how straight his posture had become. "A moment longer, please," he asked, serenely. He was going to die, he knew, whether he told them or not. He had always seen himself in dreams lying in some dark alleyway, bleeding, grasping his gun defiantly and dying with valour as he struggled for one last shot. Or at home in his bed, made comfortable by someone who cared for him as he reflected on all the good and bad his life had given him. Life was shit. What could have been was not to be. He would die trapped in his own stairway without dignity and his valour would go unrecognized. Steve Brandon would live, deservedly or not. In three weeks he would have the resources to both hide and protect himself. He was home free. DuFour forced Brandon from his mind. "May I ask a favour?"

"What?"

"Not in the face or head, anywhere but there."

"Sure," replied Abacus, as though responding to some mundane matter. "But you're giving it up for a punk kid who sold cheap whores and cheaper drugs. It's all he knows and we know where to find both. We'll find him. One day we'll find him. This doesn't have to happen."

"We both know differently."

"Tell us, and we walk."

DuFour took a deep breath. "Just not in the head," were his final words.

He brought one foot to the third step. To stay as he was Mike DuFour knew he would be shot in the chest and remain undiscovered until the coming Friday, the apparent victim of a home invasion. To turn he would be shot in the back, found in a downward and crumpled position, his neck askew as though running from danger, his head centred in a palette of dried blood. To lunge forward, grabbing at the feet of the man above him, the entry wounds would show otherwise and hopefully come from both directions. He would die quickly, in a matter of seconds. He lunged, while still in command of his body.

His hands contacted with the man's ankles and he pulled in with all his strength. He toppled the man backwards, losing his own footing and crashed his head into the hardwood nosing that extended out from the landing. A point-blank silent burst of nine-millimetre cartridges tore into his middle and upper back from behind, splintering his spine, exploding his heart and lungs with searing heat, but the heat dissipated quickly and all that remained was well-being.

The dazed man sprawled in front of DuFour's lifeless body cursed and crawled to his knees in the confined space. He rubbed the back of his head, grimacing, not thinking to check the wall behind him that had inflicted the damage. Still on his knees, he looked down at the tattered blue suit and the flow of thick blood slowly beginning to cascade down the stairs and he put two rounds into the back of Mike DuFour's head.

The lab would know Mike DuFour had died well, with valour. The official report would show he had died attempting to stop a crime in progress.

56

Mike DuFour died at 12:25 AM. They left him as he was, stepping around and over him with little care. They were pros. They had touched nothing with bare hands. They would soon place their clothing and shoes into separate plastic bags they would discard in unlikely places, the cartridge casings had been retrieved and the two guns would be tossed into the nearby seaway. They would leave through the back door and along the side of the house protected by dark shadows and the towering trees. They would leave in ten-minute intervals; Abacus would be the last. The first man would be met by the driver who had followed DuFour. The second would walk to the other car that would be ordinary amongst the many others parked on a neighbouring street and drive to where Abacus would be waiting.

Until then the night was still young. Abacus' two men searched every nook and cranny looking for anything that might lead them to Dexter Philips or profit while Abacus worked intently in the detective's office, telling them he was not to be disturbed. The end result would be the appearance of a home invasion gone terribly wrong: a murder with no residual traces that would later match the killer to a corpse with no wallet, no money or credit cards. But what would never be known is why an experienced cop like DuFour would have opened his door past midnight, unarmed and after deactivating his central alarm system.

The agency would confirm the theft of DuFour's

computer, two custom-made Browning Pathfinders and not much else other than a file their boss had been working on: one he had described to them as a no-brainer for a friend, an easy, end-of-the-road case file that should have been given to a junior. The real question on everyone's mind would be the two large sums of money he had transferred from Switzerland to his local bank.

None of that concerned Abacus. Alone in the house, he placed a small suitcase by DuFour's office door, filling it to capacity with a laptop, dozens of files folders, CDs and micro video cassettes. When he finished he called the man who would soon be expecting him with instructions to standby for another twenty minutes, then he meticulously inspected every inch of the office to ensure he had not overlooked the smallest piece of information on Dexter Philips or the other persons he had found stored in a separate cabinet marked: Alexander, Davidson: copies.

He left through the backdoor at precisely four-thirty. When he met his driver his blood-stained shoes were thrown into the plastic bag before he climbed into the car; the rest of his clothing would soon follow and be discarded at various pit stops along the 401 en route to Toronto. Then his first stop would be his home for a shower and he wondered how he would keep the briefcase from his wife. He considered himself as an outsider in the DiFiore family. What his wife knew her brother would soon know and Abacus knew that would not be in his immediate best interest. He was already being pressured to find Dexter Philips. He needed time and the search had become more complex with Mike DuFour's death, and much more interesting. He needed to know why Philips was in a file with six other people, certain that one of them would lead him to a more exalted position in the DiFiore family.

He arrived home at noon. He showered, changed for the second time, loaded the files into the Deville registered to Albert Sorrento and drove to the Airport Motel where he spent the next eight hours reading files and watching videos, candid videos that included footage of Dexter Philips from inside The Booty Lounge. At 10:00 PM the thought struck him for no reason that it had been too long since he had been to the lounge, finding Philips had taken up too much of his time and suddenly he had an urge to watch Kitty Hawk do her thing.

On a scale of ten Leona DiFiore was an easy eight. It's what she had between her legs that made her a nine. On good days she was a ten, but Kitty Hawk topped the chart and more often than not when he was kneeling behind his wife, watching and listening to Kitty Hawk on tape, he was with her. He wanted her. He wanted what he could never have. Anything more than doing her or any one of the other girls for a playful release would mean Mario DiFiore suddenly having to tell his sister that her husband had been brutally gunned down by some street punk. Some of the other girls didn't mind, they liked to party, but Kitty Hawk was a dream. She had made that very clear the first day as she nonchalantly let her skirt drop to her ankles before releasing the snaps on her panties, pulling her V-neck over her head and leaning over the edge of his desk.

Just thinking about that day aroused him: her long smooth legs spread apart as he sat behind her massaging the firm flesh of her bare cheeks and hips until he could wait no longer and stood to penetrate her, doing his best to delay his reaction to her moist grip on him, knowing it would be the last. Then he remembered it was Tuesday and he fell back onto the bed to make sense of the crumpled letter he had read from the Ashton, Emily file.

Who was Davidson Alexander? And what connection did he have to Dexter Philips?

By two AM Abacus was on his second bottle of wine from the Deville's trunk, a gift from a local Italian restaurant and halfway through an all-dressed pizza he had forgotten. He was beginning to understand, beginning to piece together everything but the tontine: something Alexander was holding over their heads.

57

Steve Brandon was a new man, a stranger to the man in the mirror. He practiced his name for hours each day: calling out to himself, then answering by name, or introducing himself and always to the same person. During the first two weeks he had dared to venture out only at night, for an hour each time, timid about his face, restricting himself to quiet walks and thoughts of Davidson Alexander.

The tontine was not the only gift; simply the key to another. What did the words mean? When he had questioned Mike DuFour the detective had chuckled and told him to go to Las Palmas and find out for himself, telling him that Davidson Alexander was a man of punctilious character who chose his words for the best affect and was certainly disinclined towards theatrics. There was no riddle. No one had ever given him so much as a dime, now someone he had never met, his grandfather, was going to make him rich. He wondered why. What was in it for the old man?

Nearing the end of his third week his face was still stained with the dull yellows and blues of post-op, though he began to see a difference and called the surgeon; not so much to confirm the doctor's assurances that his face would be perfect by the fifteenth, but to talk with someone. The only person Steve Brandon knew was Mike DuFour and he was out-of-country. He would have given anything to hear his cell phone ring, to hear DuFour's voice, even if it meant hearing the same answers to the same questions he had asked a hundred times during their week together.

DuFour had told him where to shop for clothes that would make him look like a man of good taste and good character, not a pimp; he had also cautioned Steve against trying to be anything other than he was: an ex-con on the road to self-motivated redemption. It was all about the future. It was who and what Davidson Alexander was expecting and he was not a man to disappoint.

Yet he did want to be more. He wanted to be Steve Brandon, smart and erudite, afraid it would never happen. What would it mean to be well-dressed and wealthy until the metamorphosis was complete and Dexter Philips lived solely in the fading memories of others? He would do just that, he determined. He would become smart and erudite one day. There was no better time to begin and Saturday was no better day to breathe fresh summer air. He would go out. He would begin that new wardrobe; he would find a café-terrace for a few mid-afternoon beers, read a newspaper, plan his future and watch the ladies. Then he would go home alone and try not to think of her spread naked over faceless men's legs and talking to them as though they were anything but pathetic as they groped and fondled her.

Saturday was Kitty Hawk's busiest day. He wondered how she would like Steve Brandon, the rich Steve Brandon who could take her away from a pointless life. But whether he could help her or not was moot, he thought dispassionately. He had made a solemn promise to DuFour who had nothing to gain or lose, and he would not break his word. There would soon be other women, countless women, fast cars and anything else he wanted, if what was happening was all true. He still was not convinced and September 15th seemed so far away.

As he strolled down the street lined with open-air bistros he wondered how those around him would see him, what they would think of him. He had never worn Dockers or soft-soled shoes and polo shirts. He liked it. His fedora was a mandatory sunshade more than a fashion accessory and felt strange to him, or strange to the part of him that was still Dexter Philips. His sunglasses were silver-coated aviators and completed one of the many looks the woman in the men's store had created for him.

He chose a bistro whose terrace seemed to be less hectic and seated himself. The waitress was young, but old enough he thought. She was petite, fragile looking with a bare midriff and a miniskirt that warranted more than a casual glance. He smiled complaisantly at her and she smiled back, asking him what he would like.

What he really wanted wasn't listed on the menu. She brought the thicker Saturday edition of the newspaper and laid it on the outer edge of the small bistro table. She smiled again and set down two Happy Hour beers she had taken from a seemingly weightless tray filled with more beer bottles, glasses and carafes of wine. He smiled and watched her walk away, thinking how effortlessly he could pick her up and not put her down until they were both satiated and exhausted.

He called her back to order dinner and tried hard to read her face, not certain whether he was unprepared or consumed with self-doubt. He wanted her. Or did he want it, or did he want both? Perhaps she was expecting it. Perhaps it's what she did, perhaps it wasn't, or perhaps it was all about him. He knew it was all about him, and he forced the image of the young woman standing naked in front of him from his mind. It was all about the future; that part of him was dead. He ordered dinner. Then he reached for the paper and his second beer. He looked down at the front page as though trying to discern the unintelligible, trying to make sense of the blatant headline until the subconscious mind met its conscious counterpart.

Ex-City Cop Brutally slain at Home
Random Incident: Say Police
Killers Still at Large
See Mike DuFour: Page three

So much that was so unreal had happened to him over the past three weeks that he doubted he was even awake. It had to be coincidence. Mike DuFour was outside the country. DuFour was a common name, so was Michel. It couldn't be real. Steve turned to page three and ignored the cold pain shooting across his new face. It was Mike DuFour, shown as he was the day he retired from the force; then shown as he lay dead, sprawled across a fountain of coagulating blood in his home.

The article took up four columns and said nothing concrete other than the police had opened an investigation with very little to go on. The second photograph explained everything: Mario DiFiore. It was too obvious, too timely to be mere coincidence.

Steve Brandon turned in his seat to scan the terrace and the street, suddenly alert, suddenly rebuking himself for becoming too lax. The luxury of his condo and his car, the new clothes and new face, his thoughts of what was to come had dulled his sense of survival. That had to change. He tried to rationalize, not to panic. His new identity had been immediate, exempted from the requisite public posting and DuFour had assured him any and all skeletons in Dexter Philips closet had been buried deep beyond any exhumation. He was safe. He knew he was, but what of the doctor? DuFour had been in surgery with him throughout the procedure to ensure anonymity and the usual documentary photographs had not been permitted. There was no paper trail, no hardcopy visual to circulate amongst those who would be looking for him in places where once he would have eventually been found. He was safe. DiFiore could not possibly know his name, what he looked like or where to look.

Steven Brandon stared down at the macabre black and white image, not realizing he had stopped breathing. He was the reason Mike DuFour had been killed. The detective had died rather than give him up and there was absolutely nothing he could do about it, now. He took up his beer and pushed his chair back; whispering his gratitude that seemed ridiculously inadequate and promising Mike he would do nothing to diminish his death and everything to make him proud. The third promise went unspoken.

When the waitress came with his meal he refused it, unaffected by her worried expression and crinkled brow. He gave her a fifty, his grim expression making his face seem all the more sallow. He stood to walk away and reached for the open paper as he explained without looking at her that he suddenly felt ill, pleased with his choice of words.

Steve Brandon would never forget Mike DuFour, or the one who killed him.

58

For the first time he gazed out over the Atlantic, enthralled by the sound of crashing waves and the glittering blue-black crystal effect of contre-jour that reached to the horizon, for the first time he smelled the heaviness of salt air and felt coarse sand shift under his feet. He was fascinated and happy to be alone to feel the warm sea breeze against his face and to feel his clothes fluttering in a wild rhythm to the whimsical whirlwinds that encircled him. He had never imagined the sensation and being there almost made him forget why he was standing at the shore. He had asked his wife to come with him, though she had always steadfastly refused to fly and South Carolina was too great a distance to drive in so short a time.

His signature style was a two-piece black suit, a conspicuous colour in the sweltering summer heat of the southeast, but he knew no better. Although his white button-down shirt compensated somewhat, anyone seeing him would unquestionably recognize him as a northerner even though his skin had the obvious olive darkness of his Mediterranean ancestry.

He felt somehow denuded and vulnerable standing there without the familiar touch of his Walther under his arm. In spite of which he was anything but defenceless: he stood a lean 6'3" he was muscular from daily weight-training and he had learned to survive on the streets at an early age. His looks were imposing more than disarming and his manners were deliberate, not inherent.

Deep lines scrawled across his otherwise smooth face, making him look older than his thirty-five years and his black hair was cut short in a military fashion to lessen the undesirable effect of what he considered a disproportionately large head.

Over the years he had trained himself to stand inertly when out in the open, to listen acutely with his hands perfectly aligned with his sides, always ready. To anyone observing him from a distance he would appear as a tall, slim column crowned with a large flat mass: an abacus.

He was glad his wife had refused the offer to join him, the answer to the impromptu ruse he had counted on. He had been in Charleston two days; he had seen Emily Ashton and Noëlyn Daniels at their homes the day before and was counting on the women not disappointing him with early morning calls of devotion. He very much doubted they would attend services, though who could know the divine needs of an aging debauchee and an embittered old women.

Jodie Daniels had been the hardest to locate and when he had finally succeeded the trail ended at a lesbian club, which he had had discovered the hard way the previous night. She also presented the most difficult logistical problem, although he presumed she would willingly assist him once she precisely understood the extent of his dilemma.

Five days had passed since the DuFour killing and not far from three weeks since he had come so close to killing Dexter Philips. He had studied the detective's files and videos all day Wednesday, intrigued by what he had read and had seen on the tapes. Thursday morning he booked a Friday flight to Charleston. He had nothing to lose. Dexter Philips had vanished and had to be found. Davidson Alexander would now conveniently help to accomplish that end.

DuFour's report had read more like a novel: lost love, a

cheating wife, lies, debauchery, incest, bastard children, a token Arab, a spoiled brat and a two-bit criminal. DuFour had done an excellent job piecing together the bizarre family puzzle. However the part that most interested Abacus was still missing and, for that, he needed the perspectives of all three women beginning with the ex-wife. He also had to eliminate any possible link between them and the tontine. He started away slowly, the deep sheen of his imported loafers covered over with salt spray and the powder of crushed shells and pebbles.

Emily was sitting as she usually did with her morning coffee and toast on her expansive veranda overlooking the sea. He waved at her from a distance, then once more as he turned inland and onto her property. She seemed not to grow in size as he came nearer and she stood to wave him away. She called out that he was trespassing and he brought a cupped hand to an ear, pretending not to understand as he waved again with his other hand. She called out again, shooing him away with both hands and clearly audible words. He smiled, not breaking his stride and reached into his jacket for an envelope. He called out: "Davidson Alexander, Miss Emily. Davidson Alexander. It won't take long."

"What does the despicable man want now?" she yelled down. "Has he changed his mind and sent you here with a coward's message?"

"No. I'm sure that's not it. He's asked me to deliver this letter and wants you to write an answer before I leave."

"Then come up, and don't dawdle. I don't have all day." Abacus climbed the two flights of weatherworn steps to the deck, amazed the view was even more breathtaking. "Well, give me the letter. Just don't stand there like an idiot."

"I'm sorry...only I've never seen the ocean before. I like it."

"How can you not have seen the ocean before if you come from him? I'm told he lives at the ocean."

Abacus cleared his throat and let the wind take the empty envelope, feigning disbelief at his own clumsiness. "Oh, man, I'm sorry."

Emily looked at him with disgust. "Well, isn't that just wonderful?" Abacus started making himself appear uncertain. "Don't think you can just run after it, not unless you can fly. Do you at least know what was written?"

"Yes, I do. Again, I'm sorry." He pointed to the wicker chair she'd been sitting in. "Please, sit down. This won't take long." He remained standing, making it uncomfortable for her to look up. "It's about the tontine. He wants to be sure you're good with it. He wants to know you'll be there to collect."

"Of course I will, with my girls. It's the least he can do for us. He had no right to do what he did to me, no right at all. It's not like he'll miss a few of his miserable millions, which should have been half mine in the first place."

"He sounds awfully generous."

"He's nothing of the sort, believe me. He gave our children away. Did you know that? Now he's buying them back, thinking he can throw his fortune around like confetti before he dies, which is years overdue. And you can tell him I said so. He's buying his final reward with ridiculous charity to absolute strangers." Abacus shook his head, not understanding. "He won't go through with the tontine unless we give half of what we get to charity. It's ludicrous, telling people what they should do with their own money."

"He means well. He wants to do some good."

"The bastard wants control, he always has. We'll be lucky if we come away with ten apiece and what of poor Jodie. Living here is so expensive for a young girl. I can tell you, and please sit down or move away. You're making my neck sore."

"I'm sorry." He moved away so that the brim of her sunhat was only slightly raised towards him. "I understand it's not mandatory for you to attend."

"Of course it's mandatory. It's a game, a silly power play and you can tell him I'm well aware of it. If we don't go, my girls get nothing and his bastard son gets what is ours. I'm not as stupid as he thinks. Now, what does he want?"

"Don't your children, Katherine and Theodore, get a share as well, and their kid. Knowing your son and daughter married each other and had a son must be hard on you."

Emily looked at him with widened eyes. "That's disgusting. I won't hear such filth."

"I'm sorry. I thought you knew." Abacus unfolded a letter he had taken from his jacket, the same letter Emily had thrown at DuFour weeks before. "It's right here in his letter to you, explaining about Katie and Theo. They have a son whom they have not seen for years and who has also been invited. He also says: I expect it will be quite a reunion." He slid the paper inside his jacket. "I suppose so, and I can't say I blame Theo. She's quite a looker at fifty-three and nowhere near as trashy as Noëlyn."

"I want you to leave, right now. I won't hear such talk."

Abacus nodded. "I will, very soon, once I've looked around your home. I need for you to show me where you put the addendum to the letter and the airplane tickets?"

Emily turned quickly in her seat and reached out for her cell phone. The huge hand clamping over hers made her wince. She struck out with her free hand and kicked with her feet, yelling at him to leave. To struggle was useless. He carried her from the deck to the house with as much effort as he would a down-filled pillow and set her down inside.

"The addendum and the tickets, old lady, and don't think to fuck with me."

"You're vile. If he wanted them back you might simply have asked. I'm not surprised. It's his way." Emily walked to her Victorian escritoire and pulled at one of the drawers. "Here, satisfied. Now leave my home."

"Thank you. You've been a great help, and I'm sorry

for the inconvenience. I'll be sure to give Dexter Philips your regards."

"Who?"

He smiled. "Your grandson, that's who." He looked at his watch and pointed to the door. "Please, walk ahead of me."

Emily's feet came away from the floor in an instant with her arms trapped and no way to break free from the smothering grip covering her mouth and nose. In less than a minute her heart gave out from the attack and he laid her on a quilted daybed by the open veranda doors while he went for his rented SUV.

59

Arriving back at moments past noon, and with his hands still gloved, Abacus took the opportunity to make up a sandwich and enjoy a beer before closing up the house and driving Emily over to Noëlyn's. He wanted to be at her home near two and planned to spend no more than a couple of hours with her, depending on how she cooperated, and another hour or so at the seashore before driving into town.

The seaside temperature was 95° Fahrenheit. In the city the mercury was reading a scorching 105 and heavy rains were promised for the evening hours. At this point he had no real idea how or when he was going to meet with the granddaughter, short of running her over. However Jodie Daniels was not the real problem. Uppermost on his mind was what to do with close to four million dollars in DuFour's Swiss bank account for which he now had the access code. How would he possibly explain the sudden fortune to his wife and expect to hide the truth from DiFiore, he worried? He would find and kill Dexter Philips, that was a given. The real issues were how long he could stall Mario DiFiore, what to do with his wife and where he could hide.

Dexter Philips seemed to be worth more alive than dead and Abacus was anxious for the fifteenth when he would know the full extent of Philips newfound worth. It was the minimum reprieve he was willing to give Dexter Philips.

The beer was refreshing and he opened another to help pass the time.

Noëlyn Daniels car was still parked at the main entrance to her home and there had been no movement at the front of her property thirty minutes earlier when he had driven by in a convoy of worshippers returning home from a morning of prayer, fellowship and a collective promise to live a moral existence. He parked the nondescript SUV amongst others whose owners had stopped to gaze out to sea from the makeshift lookout at the end of the quiet cul-de-sac and walked back without his jacket, leaving Emily alone in the cargo compartment under a blanket and privacy shield.

He manoeuvred himself over the gate in less than five seconds and walked towards the house as though strolling across his own property. The time was 2:10 He climbed the few stairs from the patio to the pool deck on his toes, though he made no attempt to conceal himself. Noëlyn Daniels was at the far end, lounging completely au naturel on a chaise-longue with the wide brim of her hat pulled down over her face and a tall drink resting in her hand. Her nudity did nothing to arouse him or give him motive. Working at The Booty Lounge had dulled his appetite for anything that wasn't a nine and ten. She was a six or seven at best and old enough to be his mother.

He removed his shoes, not wanting her to inadvertently see him tiptoeing. Then, when he spoke her name, jolting her from her reverie, her drink smashed onto the concrete deck as she jerked upright and her arms and legs flailed wide apart in a confused effort to balance herself.

He put an index finger to his lips as a warning. "Don't get up, Noëlyn. In fact, stay exactly as you are and stay quiet. I won't tell you twice. I'm not here for what you might be thinking." Her wide eyes scanned the pool deck and she swept the hat from her head to cover her front. "Though I would be less than a gentleman if I did not comment on how lovely you're looking today." He smiled.

"Isn't that how gentlemen down here talk to their women?"

"Who are you?" she asked, sounding more annoyed than afraid.

"You don't really expect an answer, do you? I'm here regarding your trip to Las Palmas and to ask a few questions about you and your daughter. Then I'll be gone." He pulled over another pool chair and sat beside her. Then he reached for her hat and flung it backwards into the pool. "It's not the first time I've seen you enjoying the sun, Noëlyn. I know you like men looking at you. So bring your feet back up, put your arms by your side and lay back so I can do that."

She did. "How do you know about Las Palmas?"

Abacus ignored the question. "This is what I need from you. First, I need your letter, the addendum and your airline tickets. Second, I need to know where your security system is located, specifically the tape from the camera at the front gate and don't lie to me. Then I think we should have a few cool drinks while we're talking."

"The letter and tickets are at the bank, for safe keeping."

He leaned forward to pick up a shard of glass, pressing the serrated edge gently into her bare thigh. "You're a good looking woman. There's barely a line on you, so let's not take all day. Or would you prefer that I change your looks before I tear your home apart and then go visit your mother?"

"They're in my bedroom."

"Good. He nodded approvingly. "Stand, on this side," he pushed his chair back, "and walk in front me."

Noëlyn swept both legs to one side. She slipped her feet into her stiletto slippers and stood. She padded away slowly, without looking back and not feeling the least bit self-conscious. "The bedroom's upstairs, the security system is in the pantry."

"Good. The bedroom's first." He followed her up the spiral stairway. "You have a nice, tight ass, Noëlyn. Let's not do anything to change that. Don't do anything stupid."

She led Abacus to the dresser and opened the top drawer, letting him reach in for the documents. He verified the contents cursorily and stuffed them into his shirt pocket. He looked around the eclectically-styled room that was neither feminine nor masculine without commenting when she reached for a clip and put her hair into a ponytail. When she asked if she could cover herself with a robe he told her to select a bathing suit and she pulled out another drawer filled with a tangled mess of coloured strings and triangles.

"Find one that'll cover your ass and your tits and keep it off till we're outside."

She shrugged her shoulders and opened another drawer, reaching in for a brand new micro-fibre one-piece with a Rio bottom and décolleté front that had been intended for après-swim at the bar of the hotel in Las Palmas. It was her most modest. He closed the drawer with his hip and took her by the arm, telling her to take him to the kitchen where he deactivated the camera and removed the tape. Meanwhile she prepared a tall gin and tonic for herself with emphasis on the gin and a generous vodka on the rocks for him.

"Now can I get dressed," she asked, once she had placed the drinks on a patio table by the lounge chairs, "since you're not going to rape me? Or are you?"

He looked at her vagina and reached out to work a fingertip between the moist folds. "I didn't come here to rape you, but I suppose I could stay a while longer. In the meantime, get dressed."

Noëlyn pulled away from him and sat at the edge of her chair. She put one foot into the suit, then the other, standing again before she pulled one strap to her shoulder, then the other. She had guts, he thought. She was a tease, as though she wanted him to rape her, or to at least come on to her. He raised his eyebrows and pursed his lips, showing his approval as she stood there unperturbed. The suit hugged her like a sheer second skin, highlighting and detailing every mound, ridge and curve of her body.

"Now what?" she asked.

"Now I'll finish my drink and leave, unless you'd prefer me to stay for another one." His lips curved into a thin smile. "Really, I'm here for the letter and tickets. Questions won't do much good. It's also what I want from your daughter. I plan to see her this evening."

"Try me." He said nothing, goading her. "So he's changed his mind, that old guy Alexander? There won't be a tontine? All this was bullshit?"

"Not quite …your mother's the problem. She's changed her mind." She watched him take the letter from his pocket and peruse it. "It's not very complicated. It's all here in black and white. She went against his wishes by refusing to attend. She called him a few days ago." He put back the letter. "Actually, I've already seen her this morning, to take back her tickets and addendum. She didn't even keep her copy of the letter. She gave it to DuFour."

Noëlyn looked stunned. "I don't believe you. She told us we'd be getting millions."

"Did she happen say how many?"

"Probably fifteen or twenty each and she told us she'd do it because she hates the old shit."

Abacus shrugged, showing his disappointment for her. "I'm sorry. This morning she seemed very bitter and very adamant. She was very upset when I left her, really pissed."

"Who gives a fuck if she's upset? She didn't say a goddamn word to me or Jodie about changing her mind, the senile old bitch. Is it too late? If we get her to change her mind, is it too late?"

He raised his shoulders again, slowly. "I don't know. Perhaps, if it's possible for the two of you to convince her by the time I leave. I've got a 10:00 PM flight," he lied. "That's how long you've got if your daughter's not out doing her girl thing."

"I'll call her right now. Don't worry, she'll be here."

Noëlyn reached out to touch his arm. "I promise. She'll stop whatever she's doing. She needs money more than any of us and she's not about to let a little pussy get in the way of so much money."

"She'll come by?" He looked at his watch to underline his seriousness. The time was ten minutes shy of two o'clock. "I need to be gone by five, the latest, if she doesn't come. And if that's the case, tell her to expect me."

"She'll be here."

"I'm glad, for both of you. I didn't like having to come here like this. Mr. Alexander is a tough nut to crack once he's made up his mind. It might help if I'm relaxed when I'm talking with him. Why don't you call her and tell her to be here around four. That way we can talk about the best way to handle this crisis and maybe have a few more drinks before she gets here."

Noëlyn was too eager and too distraught to smile. Her body was so tense she could barely walk over to where her cell phone lay under a parasol and press speed-dial. Her language was succinct and her tone left no doubt that she wanted her daughter at her home at four sharp, that she should bring the Alexander letter and tickets and that she should dress appropriately to meet her grandmother, not like a desperate and lonely dyke.

She snapped the phone closed and turned to her visitor. "It's done. She'll be here at four. So what about a few more drinks?"

Abacus followed her into the kitchen, apologizing all the way for how he had acted so rudely. She forgave him and when she went to pour the drinks he laughed and grabbed the necks of the gin and vodka bottles between his fingers, telling her to bring the soda. They walked back out together. He poured the drinks as she began pulling off her suit. He stopped her. He found her sexier dressed that way, more provocative, he said, and definitely more exciting. Besides, he questioned, why should she have all the fun? She agreed, looking down at herself and running her hands over her front.

She dived in, confusing relief with exhilaration, and surfaced at the other side. She inched her way back to him with a slow dogpaddle, looking up at him, watching him undress. Naked, he stepped to the edge of the pool where he lowered himself onto the edge to pass her the tall gin and tonic. She sipped and giggled softly, drinking a bit more before resting an arm on his thigh and openly admiring his still flaccid penis.

"We'll have to take care of that. Just promise not to kill me with it. God!"

"Yes, we will. Whatever the lady wants," he chuckled, "and I suppose you could call it a lady killer."

He slid down beside her and took her in his arms, letting her linger with her drink as he pushed their bodies through the warm, seductive surge. Not long after he frowned convincingly at seeing the empty glasses and left her to climb out for refills. She was proud of herself, proud she could still attract such younger men and she watched his every move as he played bartender and came back to her, gliding into the water with outstretched arms.

She clung to his neck and listened to what he had to say about Alexander and how he proposed to convince his employer to reinstate her into the tontine. The warmth of the water and the heaviness of the gin aroused her and she began letting the water swirling around them control how their bodies touched and swayed against each other. The combined sensations worked quickly and without ardour for both of them and she brought her knees up high against his side as he took her glass to put it by his on the deck.

He let her explore, smiling as her expert hands found more of him to control. He wanted her. He turned her around and pressed his hands against her breasts, feeling her chest heave and her nipples respond before moving his hands urgently down to intently heighten her arousal. He felt her body stiffen and shudder in unison and heard deep, wanton groans emanating from her throat as he brought his hands up to her waist, letting her ease slightly forward with her arms free to tug at her flimsy suit with one hand and guide him into her with the other.

She let him take control, suspended as though free falling through space, her ecstasy mounting with every violent thrust and the swirling caresses of the cool water. He felt her body reaching its climax, she felt her body lifting imperceptibly, frustrated at losing her grasp on him and feeling his engorged rigidness pull away from her as water rushed in over her head.

His legs closed against her sides like pillars, holding her firmly in place without hurting or bruising. Her forearms held in his hands with enough pressure to restrain her without marking her with tell-tale signs of a struggle. Her eyes opened wide with fright, seeing the muted blue of her pool. She tried to scream, losing what breath she had and sucked warm water into her nose and her mouth, convulsing as she filled her depleted lungs. She tried in vain to twist free. Her legs and feet thrashed wildly below the surface, exerting and expending all her strength to propel herself away from him. Soon he held only her head underwater as he watched her relaxed body sputter air randomly in tiny bubbles from under her suit and from her mouth. He left her and climbed from the pool to pour a generous straight vodka. He swallowed half and took the gin bottle into the pool where he turned her over and emptied most of the contents down her throat, noting the time at 3:15

He let the sun dry him as he pulled on his gloves, rearranged the furniture around the broken glass, wiped his glass clean and threw hers into the deep end of the pool. When he was dry he went into the kitchen to replace his glass in the cupboard and the vodka in the bar. Then he made a pitcher of lemonade which he took to the deck and poured half over the broken glass before placing the pitcher on the patio table under the parasol.

He dressed, checked his pocket for the documents he had come for and left through the front gates, taking Noëlyn's remote from her car. Fifteen minutes later he returned, driving to the side of the house and calmly climbing the steps to the pool with Emily in his arms.

She weighed nothing at all as he held her at the edge of the pool and let her body crumple to the deck at the foot of her chaise-longue before placing one of her arms so that it floated in the water. At 3:50 he went through the house to the front entrance to wait for Jodie Daniels. When the Mercedes drove through the open gate he was leaning against the side of his SUV with his shirt sleeves rolled up and his hands buried in his pockets.

Not laughing as she pulled up alongside him and began wriggling and pushing herself out from behind the steering wheel required a concerted effort. He could have done better with hundred-pound weights tied to his feet, he thought, very happy at the moment he had worn glasses dark enough to hide his disgust as she waddled towards him. He took his hands from his pockets, hoping she would not extend hers. She looked spongy and her face was coated with a thin layer of perspiration.

"You must be Jodie Daniels."

"Of course I'm Jodie Daniels. Where is she?"

"At the pool, sunbathing. I'm not accustomed to talking business with nude women, so I thought we could talk out here first," he looked back towards the pool, "unless you would prefer being with your mother. She does seem very comfortable with her body."

"The last thing I need to see is my mother's bare anything. We're fine right here. So what's all this bullshit about? First we're getting money, now we're not because my grandmother's had second thoughts. Is that about right?"

"Yes, but first I have to see your letter, the addendum

and the tickets. If your grandmother comes across for you, I'll call Mr. Alexander for permission to return them and it'll be like none of this ever happened." He took the envelope from her hands and read the letter, smiling when he finished. "I'm sure he'll reconsider if you and your mother can convince her to change her mind. We are talking millions for each of you."

Jodie Daniels wiped her brow, wetting the back of her hand. "She'll listen to me. I get along with her better than my mother. I know what buttons to push."

Abacus heard words, with no idea what she was saying. He was wondering how he would get her to the pool and to end the meeting with the least amount of effort. DuFour's video footage had been overly kind in its imagery of her, if not purely deceptive: she had to weigh 220 if she weighed a pound.

"Why don't we take a walk around the grounds, in the shade under the oaks? You can tell me how you think you'll convince her. Understand, I won't be with you and I'm leaving Charleston this evening. You have very little time and, as you already know, Mr. Alexander has no particular desire to see you."

"I don't enjoy walking. I prefer sitting, so let's go get Miss Nude '99 off her bare ass and get on with this. I'm sure seeing a pair of tits won't be too painful for you."

Abacus chuckled. "I saw a bit more than her tits. I think she was actually coming on to me. Thing is, I'm married." Jodie rolled her eyes and turned towards the front entrance. "She told me to have you use the side entrance to the pool."

At the side entrance there would be forty feet to travel from the steps to the pool, perhaps thirty once her mind was able to process the murder scene, though going through the house and kitchen would mean complete awareness before they reached the patio doors and he could not allow that to happen. He walked silently beside her, studying her peripherally. Doing her wouldn't be a walk in the park. She was wearing laced granny boots, nylons he guessed were pantyhose, a mid-calf peasant skirt, a cotton sweater that told him too much about the double D armature that lay beneath and she sported twin rolls of hideous fat that hung over a wide leather belt. The belt would help him, he hoped.

Just as Jodie placed a foot onto the patio at right angles to her grandmother's body, Abacus tore her purse from her shoulder, simultaneously grabbing her belt with his right hand and placing his open left hand at the nape of her neck. He ran with her to the very edge of the pool, heaving her away from him with all the strength his adrenalin would produce, but the effort was nowhere near Herculean enough. She went no farther than a few feet out before plunging below the surface in a clumsy mass of flailing arm and legs. A circular wall of water framed her before closing in over her as he hurried to pull his shirt over his head and kick off his shoes. His pants, socks and underwear followed rapidly and he jumped in on top of her as she surfaced, lashing out blindly as she gasped for new air and spit bitter chlorinated water from her mouth. His heart was racing from the exertion and heat. His weight pushed her down, manoeuvring backwards to trap her wildly flapping arms in his. He pushed her forward with tremendous effort into chest-deep water, waiting until her feet stopped thrashing and the bubbles around the small islet of floating hair subsided.

When he felt the body relax he pulled it to the steps and examined the arms and fingernails for signs of a struggle, also checking his own skin for scratches or cuts. He was clean and he guided the body back towards the deep end with a final shove to propel it farther away. Only then did he burst into a laugh at the thought of how the whole episode must have looked.

Once again the oppressive sun dried him as he went for his gloves and her purse. He took her phone and went to where Noëlyn's still lay on the table. He called one with the other, answering Jodie's immediately and he counted to thirty before pressing end: long enough for Jodie to have listened to her distraught grandmother's desperate plea. He dropped Noëlyn's phone to the deck at Emily's feet and returned Jodie's to her purse. He took four of the 500 dollars he found in her wallet, closed the purse and threw it from his hip towards the stairs as though frantically flung by a shorter person.

When he was dressed he walked twice around the pool, satisfied with the careless drowning of an intoxicated woman who had caused her aging mother's grievous heart attack and the pursuant death by drowning of her daughter who had arrived too late to save her.

Before leaving he opened the door to Jodie's Mercedes to check whether she would have had a remote for the gate and dropped her keys onto the passenger's seat. When the SUV was running, alongside the open door of the Mercedes, he activated her remote giving himself twenty seconds to clear the gate. The tontine membership had been reduced by three and he was that much closer to meeting Dexter Philips.

60

Ready for dinner, feeling relaxed and revitalized, Albert Sorrento had already disposed of some of his day's clothing. By flight time the following morning the few remaining articles would also be safely and separately discarded. He was famished and opted for a taxi rather than navigate his way through an unfamiliar city to a decent Italian restaurant. He had forgotten he hadn't eaten since breakfast and thinking back over the day it seemed like an eternity since he had left the hotel to visit with Emily Ashton. The trip had been successful. He was pleased and made a mental note to call his wife later that evening.

He had thought to go somewhere to see the ocean at night, until the clear sky had changed to black rolling clouds and he doubted whether he would see very much. The taxi driver explained the ferocity of summer thunderstorms brought on by the clash of rising midday heat and humidity with higher, cooler evening air and nature's electrical light show that most often accompanied them. The forecast had held and the deluge began well before his return to the hotel.

The taxi's windshield wipers worked hard as the driver struggled to keep pace with traffic inside a kaleidoscope of eerie streaks of bright white and muted patches of red. Looking out from the blurred side window there was nothing to see but blackness dotted with distant harbour lights. The storm would have made driving in a strange town next to impossible for him. He nodded subconsciously, feeling content, knowing the rain would certainly impose the impossible for those first on the scene of a bizarre triple death which the county medical examiner would eventually conclude had been an unfortunate chain of events.

His morning flight from Charleston to Philly left on time, as did his connecting flight to Boston. The evening flight from Logan to Halifax departed two hours late due to continuing bad weather along the eastern seaboard and he arrived well after dark, still wondering whether the pilot had pissed his pants somewhere over the turbulent Gulf of Maine.

Tuesday morning brought no relief from the storm and he was certain he would have to postpone his visit with the Parkers until Wednesday or Thursday: The parcel he had couriered to himself from Toronto hadn't yet arrived. The east coast of Nova Scotia on the last day of August was painted in ominous tones of grey and black. High winds bent trees and a slicing rain seemed to come directly from the white-tipped angry ocean rather than a low ceiling of pregnant black clouds that spit out endless jagged streaks of intense white light.

The coastal storm was menacing and violent, unlike any storm he had seen. He was enthralled, exhilarated. The taxi driver thought nothing of it, or of him. He was just another businessman in a fancy black suit who had left his raincoat at home. The driver waited with fifty U.S. dollars in his pocket while Abacus dashed into the chandlery, scratching his head when his fare came out wearing bright orange foul weather gear and asking to see the nearest ocean view.

Abacus was in another place and time. The air was cold on his face, the harsh rain chapping and stinging his reddened skin. The wind made his eyes water with strain and he covered his nose to facilitate breathing. He had never felt so good, so alive or liberated, and suddenly he was not questioning whether he had missed much in life, he knew he had.

He had the entire morning and most of the afternoon to enjoy doing nothing, to embrace new sensations. There would be time enough in the evening for the Parkers, assuming everything would fall into place. For the time being he wanted to be someone else. He was good at killing. He didn't particularly enjoy taking a life; it was just something he did well. DuFour and the three women had not been his first, though he doubted he would miss the darker side of his job after doing Dexter Philips. Strangely, he was one of the few in the DiFiore family without a rap sheet, though he was known to the police and it was only a matter of time. He now had 3.8 million and something had to change. He had no intention of spending anymore of his life looking at brain-dead naked women, laundering money and breaking the occasional arm or leg for Mario DiFiore. But he had a wife who was also a DiFiore and his boss would have him killed on a whim, despite Leona.

Philips was going to be killed, whether he pulled the trigger or someone else, which was not the question. The question was how much wealthier he could become if he let Philips live past the tontine. So what could he do? He leaned back against a brick wall and stared out to sea.

By late afternoon he had returned to hotel and had checked at the Front Desk, visibly disappointed when clerk responded that no package had been delivered. In his room he showered, changed his suit and called the Parker residence, too anxious to wait. Using a name he thought sounded credible, he left a message: he would call again at 7:00 PM sharp regarding their son, he advised, and the tontine. What he had to tell them was important, he insisted without sounding overly affected, and would appreciate a few moments of their time in person later that evening. He had come to think of the storm as an expedient ally.

When he dropped the receiver into its cradle the phone's

tiny domed light instantly flickered red. The concierge had called up to the room advising Sorrento the package he'd been expecting had arrived. Moments later the uniformed gentleman knocked at the door.

Abacus anxiously opened the box and pulled out the two high-power Pathfinders he had taken from Mike DuFour. He manoeuvred expertly into the shoulder straps, securing the bottom strap of the holster to his belt. He checked the clip, the action and eased in the gun. The second weapon attached to his ankle. He had taken them into the country on the Thursday before and had emptied the clips to make sure they worked well. The only gun he trusted was his Walther, though any thought of using it would have been unforgivably reckless. These lacked the familiar feel and sleek contours of the Walther though they made him feel whole all the same.

He went for an early dinner and tried to free his mind. At one minute past seven James Parker answered the call and agreed, after a brief conversation, to meet with him. Abacus arrived at the Parker's home precisely at eight o'clock.

In the country, without the amber glow of city lights to illuminate the dark, rumbling clouds still shooting out spears of electric light, Sorrento imagined he was driving through a black swaying tunnel and not a beautifully tree-lined country road. He saw nothing beautiful, green or inviting. What enveloped him was forbidding and haunting. The rain had not relented at all and Abacus drove with his face instinctively closer to the windshield, not wanting to miss the marker to the Parker's private off-road entrance. He drove with his high beams on, which made no difference at all apart from startling and transfixing the wide and curious yellow eyes of forlorn wild cats and other sodden forest life.

Hundred watt spotlights surrounded the Parker's home while smaller decorative lights highlighted the façade and the winding stone path leading to the entrance. The landscaping was charming and picturesque and made the house stand out like an iridescent jewel in the dark, the absolute last thing he would have wanted.

Through the plate-glass windows Abacus saw James Parker stand from his seat in the living room, reacting to the graduated intensity of the car's headlights. A few moments later the front door opened inward and James Parker stepped out onto the porch to greet the visitor.

"Mr. Randolph, I take it. Good evening, sir."

"Good evening. Yes, I'm Randolph. I was taking a moment to admire your home. I'm sorry to have disrupted your evening." They shook hands. "What I have to tell you won't take long. I appreciate your time."

"To say the least, our son has been a current topic of conversation. The more we know about him the better before we meet." James led Abacus into the house. "May I take your coat?"

Abacus pulled at the bright orange jacket. "I came unprepared for the weather. This is all I could find on short notice."

"And not out of place. Easterners are casual folk." James hung the raingear on the stylized coat rack that was not eastern. "My wife, Helen, is waiting for us in the living room."

Abacus studied the man preceding him. The kill would have to be quick, with no screw up. The man first, then the woman, he thought.

"Good evening, Mr. Randolph."

"Good evening, Mrs. Parker. My business here this evening is to tell you about your son and talk about the Alexander tontine the three of you will be participating in. I won't take much of your time."

"We understand," began James, "that we won't see him until the fifteenth. Being so near to him, possibly in the same hotel and not knowing him, will certainly be strange."

"Perhaps I can help you with that. May I sit?"

"Yes, of course. Excuse my rudeness."

"Can I bring you a coffee, Mr. Randolph, or tea?" Helen asked.

"No thank you. I'd prefer getting down to business. I'm sure you're anxious to hear what I have to say."

"Indeed we are," James sat beside Helen and took her hand, "very much so, as we are to meet with him and Davidson Alexander. Of course, it's understandable to have a few reservations."

"And to meet with your mother, Mr. and Mrs. Parker," Abacus stared at him with no expression on his face. "I'm aware of the family history. I've read DuFour's report."

"It's not a topic of conversation, not even with Davidson Alexander who, at this point, we have yet to consider as our father."

"I understand completely. I meant no disrespect."

Do you know our son, Mr. Randolph?" Helen asked.

"Yes, I do."

"We don't even know his name," she said. "Does he want to see us? Does he forgive us for what we did to him?"

"I can't tell you. DuFour didn't tell you anything about him?"

"Nothing, other than we probably won't like ourselves after we meet him."

"It seems he's had a bad life," added James, "though apparently he's back on track."

"We each do what we have to do to get by in life," continued Abacus. "I suppose you could say he's had a bad life. Who hasn't? But the only track he's on right now is a race track in a race against time that he's going to lose. His name is Dexter Philips, he's an ex-con and I wouldn't worry about meeting him in Las Palmas. That's why I'm here. Mrs. Parker. He's a criminal and not a very good one. He's been in jail or prison four times for everything from running stolen cars to teenage prostitution to drugs, and now he's running from people who want him dead. He's one bad son of a bitch, if you'll pardon my French. So, Mr. and Mrs. Parker, your kid's not going to make it past the tontine. There's a contract out on him. He's going to be killed on or soon after the fifteenth."

James and Helen looked as though they'd seen a ghost sweep past them.

"Killed," they both gasped.

"Yeah, killed."

"My God, why?" cried Helen, astonished.

"For not keeping his mouth shut, Mrs. Parker, and for not putting family first."

"What family?" James asked.

"The DiFiore family," Abacus responded, slightly changing his position. "My boss, Mario DiFiore, was sentenced to fifteen years before the possibility of parole because of your son, and now that Philips is out DiFiore wants payback. So ... I have to find your son and kill him. And I will."

"We're done. Get out of here," James said evenly, standing to put himself in front of Helen, his body tense. "There's nothing we'll say or do to help you find him and we'll be doing everything we can to warn him. Now, get out."

"I don't have to know where he is. It's enough to know where he will be, at the tontine." Abacus stood and moved behind the sofa he'd been sitting on. "I'm sorry. You seem like a very nice couple." He shrugged. "What can I say? The fewer people who show up at the tontine the easier it'll be for me to kill him. By the way, you might be interested to know I did your mother two days ago. She went easy."

Abacus reached under his jacket for the Pathfinder and fired a single 10mm round into the centre of James Parker's forehead in one seamless motion, killing him instantly, flinging the body backward onto Helen and crushing her under the dead weight. Abacus waited patiently with his arms crossed as she struggled to push away the limp corpse, groaning from the effort, not yet knowing to scream with fear, not yet knowing James was dead. When she did realize the scream was ear-piercing, until her face froze with fright and she began choking on the dryness in her throat.

She cupped his head in her hands and sobbed a low, guttural moan, completely ignoring his assailant. She kissed her husband and spoke to him in tearful whispers. Then she swung and charged over the coffee table and sofa at Abacus with amazing agility and speed, her arms outstretched. He jerked backward, startled, and she fell onto the floor, sobbing.

"I need the Alexander documents, Mrs. Parker. Show me where they are."

"No."

"You're understandably upset. I understand, but I don't have much time. Please show me, right now." When she refused to move he grabbed a length of her hair in his free hand and pulled her to her knees. "If you don't, I'll put a round into each arm and leg until you do. Believe me, you won't like it. Now get me what I want and don't test me."

"Everything's in my husband's desk. It's not locked," she murmured, numb with shock.

"Get up. I need you to come with me."

He stepped back, letting her use the sofa for leverage. James' eyes were open with disbelief, his lips slightly parted. A single thin trickle of blood crossed over his left eye and cheek, the expression on his face indifferent like the perfect mannequin and not the man who had been teasing and laughing with her moments earlier. She straightened mechanically, as though working her arms and legs against invisible restraints, and stood there looking over to him, not wanting to take her eyes from him.

"Right now, Mrs. Parker. He's not going anywhere. Or would you like me to put another one in him to make sure?" Abacus waited no longer than a single breath. "He'll be here when we get back. Move."

He pushed her forward with a hand at the small of her back. Once in the office he stood in the doorway while she found the papers and laid them on the desk. She was told to sit away from the desk, and she did. He read the letter and the addendum, and verified that both tickets. Then he told Helen to walk into the living room and as she passed through the doorway he put a round into the back of her head, obliterating her occipital bone and crashing her into the opposite wall of the hallway.

He dropped into the seat behind James' desk and looked at the papers once more. Then he looked for a briefcase, emptied the contents neatly and went into the bedroom where he found James' wallet and Helen's purse, adding her jewels for affect. Once again in the office he searched through James' computer calendar and paper agenda, pleased when he discovered September 11 through to the seventeenth highlighted in both. He put both in the briefcase, then went into the living room and removed took James' watch.

He had touched nothing, save what he was taking and he mentally reviewed his every move since arriving. Before leaving he closed all the lights and zippered his coat against the rain that had not abated. He looked out from the porch into a total blackness. A veritable flood of raindrops was splashing down so hard against the mirror-like flagstone path that each stone seemed fitted with hundreds of miniature fountain heads and the tall trees swayed with a violence that brought them to life in an uneasy mind.

He regretted having turned out the lights. As he walked to the car the Pathfinder was firmly gripped in his hand.

61

September 04th had been insignificant for Davidson. His guests would not begin arriving before the following Saturday and he would not officially receive them at the estate for another eleven days. However the previous weeks since Mike DuFour's departure had taken their toll. Maria had scolded him more than once, insisting she was more than capable of preparing for such a small group and that he should occupy himself with the affairs of men and stop nagging her. He loved her almost as much as Jorge and she knew he enjoyed being a nuisance. The sentiment was mutual: they were family.

The Atlantic Ocean was unusually calm near midnight. The moon was a faint aura behind wisps of high, thin clouds, an ideal evening for young lovers to be together and for the young at heart to remember. Maria and Jorge's own villa-styled home seemed small in the distance and the dark, despite being one of the finest homes on the island. Davidson had maintained what he considered an important credo throughout his life: treat those close to you the way they should be treated and expect the same in return. He had seldom been disappointed.

They had been with him since he and Gabrielle first moved to the island and a young out-of-work Jorge had walked onto the construction site of the estate that was already the talk of the island to apply for work. The grounds had been his responsibility since that day. The following day Maria had brought her husband a fine picnic lunch of fruits, bread, cheese and one cold beer she had bought with Jorge's cash advance on his first paycheque. She had prepared a feast to behold, spread out on a chequered tablecloth and a very beautiful Maria pampered Jorge to the envy and good-humour of the dozen other workers who sat around them unfolding their own simpler fare and jugs of ice-cold water. Maria had brought too much and went to each one, many of whom she knew, with slices of cheese and bread as Gabrielle and Davidson came to join them with their own sandwiches. Maria shared with them as well, not thinking twice about the man and women in coveralls and sweat-covered faces.

Davidson looked down at the beer in Jorge's hand and grimaced, appearing quite put out. He looked once more at the young man then once again at the beer before walking away. Jorge whispered to Maria that the man was El Jefe, the man who had hired him and perhaps the beer had been a mistake. He tried to gain Gabrielle's attention; however she was talking and laughing with the others. Jorge put his hand on Maria's knee, looking despondent, telling her he would apologize to Señor Alexander as soon as he came back. When Davidson did return he was in the jeep, not on foot, with a ten-gallon keg of cold beer mounted in the back. For the remainder of the construction project the one-beer lunch had become a tradition and, Maria, a frequent visitor.

The estate was expansive and Davidson had worried the demands would prove too much for Gabrielle to manage along with her restaurant. He was afraid it would be too exhausting for her alone and one day he asked Maria if he might have a moment of her time. He wanted someone to help Gabrielle manage the estate, not be a servant. He was very adamant that she understand the distinction. Soon after Gabrielle died Davidson had asked the couple where they would live on the island, given the choice, and they had both pointed to the very place Gabrielle had predicted they would select at the far end of the estate. The next week construction began on their home overlooking the ocean. Gabrielle's final gift to them would have made her happy to know the couple would always be with Davidson.

Davidson sat on the veranda, as he did most evenings, looking out over the sea. He thought of the time when he and his sons had scuttled the Gypsy Bride, lamenting the years onboard with Gabrielle had seemed like days, even then. He hated the thought of going to an empty bed and beginning each new day without her. Many nights he would fall asleep on the veranda as vivid memories of their times together turned to tangible dreams that made waking painful. He was still so filled with regret for those lost years.

He sipped his scotch and stared down into snifter. He had spoken at length with Gérard, Chantal and Jean-Alexandre earlier in the day, all three promising to visit with him after the tontine. They had met Lydyah and had liked her immediately. The girl fully agreed Joaquin should finish his education and begin a career before contemplating marriage. When they had questioned her as to how she felt regarding the tontine, she responded that she was not opposed Joaquin's good fortune, or his grandfather's generosity, as long as their life together would not be adversely affected. Precisely the answers Davidson had hoped to hear.

He had told Gérard how proud Gabrielle would be of him and he said goodbye, not his usual à bientôt. When he spoke with Jean-Alexandre he thanked his son for 1972, his voice quivering with emotion when saying how deeply he continued to miss her. He loved his son and told him so, then he said goodbye and asked to speak with Chantal. When their long conversation had ended she went to her room with tears welling in her eyes. When her husband followed closely behind asking what was amiss, she could only answer: "We must be with him as soon as possible.

Call your brother and charter a plane if you must." And she began packing.

Davidson savoured another warming sip of his scotch and closed his eyes. Gabrielle had been as beautiful that first day in 1972 as when he had abandoned her in 1944.

"And you were no less beautiful the day you left me, my darling. I miss those gypsy green eyes that made my knees weak and my heart pound." She looked at him, quizzically, her eyes sparking like emerald stars and a soft smile came to his lips. How he had loved those green eyes, how he had more than once been a willing slave to them. "I love you," he whispered.

"And I love you, my darling, with all my heart. I will never stop loving you."

Davidson nodded, pursing the smile from his lips, suddenly saddened. "I long to be with you, I long to leave this emptiness in my heart and feel the way we once did."

Gabrielle was by his side. He could feel her. She was more than imagination or the perfection of dreams. She was there with him, as though one with him. A mild shiver ran through his body and he opened his eyes, reaching out to her. He could see her and he wanted to go to her, to be with her.

"Close your eyes, my darling." She said tenderly. "There is no emptiness in peaceful sleep and only joy in the dreams we share. Sleep my darling."

Davidson's eyes closed stubbornly and his head drooped onto his chest. His hands loosened and his glass rolled to his knees and smashed silently into shards on the tiled floor beneath him.

"Little Brother, it has been too long since I have had to carry your heavy weight upon my back. I have missed our good times together."

"Earl, what wonderful dream is this, my friend. It's been a while since you've come to me in my dreams, though you've never been far from my thoughts."

"I know it well, Little Brother, but this is no dream. We are here with you: Gabrielle, whom you have missed for so many years; Lilly, who misses her pale-skinned brother; Henri, who still complains of his sore head; and look, your mothers Antoinette and Bonnie wait for you with another whom you have never seen."

"It is true, Davidson," said Lilly. "My poor Henri complains still, without our compassion for now we know the truth of that evening and we share no pity with him. We have all missed you, even though we have never left you. We have always been with you, Davidson, as you have been with us."

"If only it were true, Lilly, if only it were true."

"My darling, you want to open your eyes, to see us. Do not." Gabrielle said with a voice so comforting. "There is no need, my darling. Soon your senses will be as one. We will be as one."

"Misère de Brest, mon ami. Must I pull you back to her once more, as I did that horrible rainy day so long ago? Come to her, you big, stupid man. I see nothing has changed much in our time apart."

"Henri, my dear friend, I have missed you greatly. You are remembered by many, my friend. You and your stories of the big Indian live on. It is a good legacy."

"I would pound his back, Little Brother, if he had one big enough. Why do you resist? You have found your time to be with us. Come, do not falter. Your time has come. We have been anxious to once again be with you."

"Yes, come, my darling. All will be as before, only so much better. There is someone here who is anxious to finally meet his brother. Come, my darling, take my hand once again."

A steady, slow stream of air passed through Davidson's lips. His body twitched ever so slightly as his heartbeat slowed to a stop and he seemed to float more than stand.

"Do not look back, my darling. What you leave behind

is merely the physical and important only to those who will always miss you and remember you."

"I feel you, Gabrielle, my darling. I feel all of you."

Davidson felt no need to cry with sadness for having left one world, or joy for having crossed into another. He simply felt inexplicably at peace. He had always wanted to believe he had felt the weight of Earl's hand that fateful day in the trench when the German bullet had ricocheted off the front of his helmet and to believe Lilly's reassuring words the day he succumbed to uncertainty and insecurity. When Gabrielle was taken from him he wanted to believe all the more, and now he knew. He knew he would never be far from those left behind.

62

Sundays were Maria's favourite day of the week, despite the fact she went to mass alone. She loved her husband deeply and worried that one day she would have to be very persuasive on his behalf if they were to remain together forever. Nothing short of a miracle, she often told him, would give allow him a seat in heaven.

What made the day special was cooking for Jorge and Davidson who had never been permitted to miss Sunday dinner after Gabrielle had passed away. He had become a father to them. Every Sunday he would stroll along the same narrow path at noon as Maria was arriving home, and always with a bottle of Spanish red wine for Jorge and a bouquet of flowers plucked from his garden and tied with a ribbon for Maria.

At fifteen past the hour Maria peered across to the stately villa from her front patio and called to her husband who hurried along the path to see what might be wrong. He called out to Davidson from the front of the villa and circled to the back where he saw his friend asleep on the veranda. He smiled with relief and went closer to call his name, not wanting to startle Davidson. Then he saw the shattered glass and realized the complete stillness of the body, bounding over the railing with a single effort. He bellowed out his wife's name across the vast estate and within minutes he was consoling a frantic and sobbing Maria in his arms.

When finally she stopped she kneeled by Davidson's

side. She brought a cold hand to the warmth of her damp cheek and prayed that his one wish had come true. As she went to the phone to begin a difficult message she knew would alarm Chantal and Jean-Alexandre, Jorge carried Davidson to his bed and gave him dignity.

Chantal had been beside herself since Davidson had not answered her call from the airport Sunday morning and Jean-Alexandre could do nothing to calm her as the pilot did his best to expedite the process of filing his flight plan and verifying the readiness of the aircraft. The flight lasted an excruciating four and a half hours at near maximum speed, touching down at twelve thirty. Taxiing to the private gate seemed interminable despite Gérard's and Jean-Alexandre's repeated assurances that all was well; neither quite convinced they were right. They had called Davidson several more times during the flight, hearing the same message. Finally, when Chantal insisted on calling once again from outside the Customs area, a sombre Jorge answered. Both men ran to her as she dropped the phone and wailed. There was no need for them to ask. They arrived thirty minutes later.

Chantal and Maria embraced as they stood outside the doorway to Davidson's bedroom, not arguing Jean-Alexandre's reasoning that Davidson would not want to be seen by them as he was. He had always insisted that his casket would be closed. Jorge and Gérard stood solemnly by the body and Jean-Alexandre phoned the police. Davidson was taken away by late afternoon and Maria would not hear of his family staying anywhere but with her and Jorge for as long as required to arrange for Davidson's return to France.

The day had become Maria's most special Sunday of all.

63

That night, in the solitary quiet of Davidson's study, and as executor of the estate, Jean- Alexandre went through papers he had taken from Davidson's vault. To his sons, Chantal and Joaquin, Davidson had left handwritten letters expressing his warm feelings. A separate and more formal missive recently written, signed by Davidson and witnessed by Maître d'Avignon, instructed Jean-Alexandre to contact Maître d'Avignon regarding the lawyer's mandate to assume full responsibility for the tontine. He did so without the slightest hesitation, placing the call to a shocked and shaken d'Avignon who promised to arrive on the first flight out from Paris the next morning. Also in the vault was a large steel briefcase, locked with a combination and marked: For the eyes of Karl d'Avignon only. Do not open.

Jean-Alexandre put the case aside and smiled contentedly as he leaned into his father's worn leather chair, nodding approvingly as he read the final clauses regarding the disbursement of his wealth. One he would have to keep to himself until after the funeral, the other perhaps not. His father had indeed been a man of surprises.

Maître Karl d'Avignon arrived mid-afternoon Monday and was met at the airport by Jorge who assured him Davidson had passed on peacefully in his sleep with no sign of torment or discomfort. Maria and Chantal had prepared a lunch for him and when he finished he thanked them graciously and joined Jean-Alexandre for the remainder of the afternoon in Davidson's study.

"I intend, sir, to formally read my father's last will and testament the day following his funeral. I feel to do so before would be inappropriate. Of course, you are invited to attend as his long-time friend and as a beneficiary of the will." Jean-Alexandre handed the lawyer the folded document. "However, given your close relationship with Davidson, and that you shall likely be preoccupied in the coming days, I doubt he would mind my extending an expedient courtesy to you. I would draw your attention to the second to last clause."

D'Avignon read the brief clause looking across the desk with a stunned expression. "Never once did such an occurrence enter my mind, not for a moment."

"He thought very highly of you. I trust you will enjoy your retirement, sir. Our courts will certainly be disappointed by their loss."

"His gift to me is beyond words, words he will never hear."

"He knew you, monsieur, which is sufficient for men like him. I assure you, he knows." Jean-Alexandre walked away from the desk, coming back with the briefcase. "If you wish, I can wait outside until you are finished reviewing the contents."

"There is no need. I am aware of the contents, which relate to the tontine. I will review everything in depth this evening at the hotel. Your father foresaw the need to provide me with the combination."

"I will make myself available to help you in any way you deem appropriate."

"Thank you. The timing of Davidson's death could not have been more inopportune. The tontine is to take place in nine days and must proceed per his wishes, though I am saddened to know he will never see his other grandson. His name is Dexter Philips. Your father and I spoke at some

479

length about the tontine and Monsieur Philips as his investigation of all those concerned came to an end two weeks ago." Maître d'Avignon sighed deeply. "I have much to do and very little time. The time restraint has become significant, I fear. I will remain on the island until your father's conveyance to France, unless affairs of the tontine call me away. Of course, my first wish would be to accompany him home to your mother, though not my first duty."

"Understood and appreciated. He would be honoured either way." Jean-Alexandre took a moment before continuing. "Will you dine with us this evening at the home of the de la Vega? I have been asked by our exceedingly kind hostess to extend the invitation. I'm learning quickly that she is a most difficult woman to refuse."

D'Avignon smiled weakly. "I would be delighted to share your company and theirs, and to remember your father. However" he glanced at the briefcase, "I believe my dear friend has planned my evening for me, in absentia as it were. Please extend my gratitude and my excuses to the ladies."

Jean-Alexandre drove d'Avignon to his hotel, extending an invitation for the lawyer to use Davidson's study as his workplace for the duration of his stay. He accepted and returned the next morning, perplexed over what he had read and seen in the file, terrified by what he had heard in subsequent conversations. He had read the DuFour reports in their entirety the night before, he had reviewed the videos and photographs of the participants and he carefully read copies of Davidson's letters several times to understand their tone and the extent of his responsibility. The information was disturbing and he felt a deep sense of grief for his dead friend, though by midnight his grief had turned to overwhelming apprehension that ruled out any thought of sleep.

He had tried several times to communicate with the

participants of the tontine. The only one to return his call was Joaquin who was already on route to Las Palmas to join his family. The Ashton woman's phone had been disconnected, so had the phones of the Daniels women and when he had called the Parker's residence the phone had been answered by the police. James Parker and his wife had been found Thursday evening by worried colleagues. When queried as to the purpose of the call d'Avignon had, in true lawyer fashion, not been too forthcoming: The Parkers had been expected at a reunion of friends in Spain, unfortunately one of those friends had passed away unexpectedly and the others considered important that the Parkers be informed. Identifying himself as an officer of the French court he had inquired as to the nature of the killings. The detached response made him feel faint. He hung up and tried Dexter Philips in a dozen more cities without success. The man would not be found and d'Avignon knew precisely why. Though what he didn't know bothered him and he dialled the number of the one man who might possibly know Dexter Philips' whereabouts: Mike DuFour.

Jean-Alexander made no comment as to the hour of the call. Karl d'Avignon had waited as long as he could. The time was 6:00 AM in Las Palmas, one AM in Montreal, giving them time to worry as well as formulate. Murder was beyond the scope of Maître d'Avignon's realm of expertise. He had no option. He was compelled to go against Davidson's wishes and share the information with Jean-Alexandre who sat spellbound listening to the details d'Avignon had learned. Three murders and three women considered missing. Jean-Alexandre immediately called his son who had just arrived back in France with late-day flights to Madrid and Las Palmas. His instructions were terse, precluding any glibness from the young man: He was not to leave home or open the door unless to uniformed officers. He was to proceed with caution, talk to no one including Lydyah and arrive as quickly as possible. He would be met by airport security and was to follow their instructions implicitly. When Joaquin naturally asked what had happened to cause such concern, his father answered. "Do what is expected of you and do not disappoint your mother by arriving late."

When he disconnected the call he phoned his private office in Paris and was transferred to Police Headquarters. He spoke at length with the Chief Inspector of the Sûreté who called back three hours later. Mike DuFour had indeed been brutally murdered and the Charleston Police had confirmed the deaths of Emily Ashton, Noëlyn and Jodie Daniels by natural cause and drowning, respectively. The Chief Inspector also confirmed both calls had provoked new interest in the two cases and that he had linked them to the Halifax killings of Helen and James Parker, with Jean-Alexandre's previous knowledge. What the Chief Inspector had chosen not to reveal to his foreign counterparts was the creation of that link, and that Dexter Philips was not a scheduled passenger on any flight between Canada and Las Palmas, via Paris or Madrid. In fact, no reservation existed for a man travelling alone from Canada whose final destination was Las Palmas between the eleventh and fifteenth.

By the time the call had ended, uniformed gendarmes were escorting a bewildered Joaquin de-Saint-Valéry to the Roissy-Charles de Gaulle Airport and the two men in Las Palmas were no closer to understanding what had happened, or was about to happen as Maître d'Avignon handed Davidson's steel briefcase to Jean-Alexandre.

"We must now act in the best interest of the living, sir. Your father would have wanted it no other way. Six murders in two weeks are no coincidence. We need to find Dexter Philips. I fear for your son's life. He is the only one remaining. It is more than probable in my estimation that Philips has taken the essence of the tontine to heart."

"Your meaning?"

"Your father stated clearly that any acknowledgement or acceptance of the tontine was neither requisite nor wanted. According to the provisions of the tontine anyone not present between noon and four PM on the fifteenth must be summarily excluded and their share divided equally amongst those attending. As it stands, with two participants remaining, your son and Philips each stands to inherit seventy million dollars. Though, should it happen that only one person attends that one person would, in theory, inherit one hundred and forty million dollars. That, monsieur, is my meaning."

"You suspect Philips of being the killer, and you are implying my son's vulnerability."

"I am not implying, monsieur. Take all measures necessary to protect him. Your father did not envision murderous intrigue and Monsieur DuFour was the first victim. He died immediately after closing the dossier with a phone call to your father. The time has come for you to read the entire file." D'Avignon looked down at the steel case Jean-Alexandre was now holding. "I warn you. The details are less than pleasant. Two hours should suffice. With your permission, I shall leave you to the task and employ the time to contemplate how best to proceed. Personally, I have no desire to revisit the file."

Jean-Alexandre felt physically ill. As he read the reports, the letters, and reviewed the videos, he thought back to the day he had first met his father and wondered what might have been had Davidson gone back to Paris after the war. There would have been no James Parker or Helen North, and there would have been no Dexter Philips whose life read like a poorly written script for a B-rated TV movie. Nor would there have been a need for a tontine to bribe a hateful old woman or to compel the children he had once abandoned to come home, if only for a day. He and Gérard might have had another brother or a sister and perhaps his mother might not have been taken away from him so soon. Yet he felt equally guilty: What if he hadn't waited so long to find his father? When d'Avignon offered him a cognac from the bar in Davidson's dining room he gladly accepted.

"To your father and mother, Alex, and might I suggest we forego often tiresome formalities."

"I concur, by all means." Jean-Alexandre raised his glass. "To their happiness, Karl, and to our success along the perilous road which lies ahead." He looked down at the light lunch Chantal had prepared for them. "I have no appetite for food."

"Nor will you for sleep this evening, I daresay."

"There is no link other than Dexter Philips and the man Monsieur DuFour referred to as DiFiore who is currently incarcerated and will be for some time, although that may have no significance whatsoever. Even the best prisons are, at times, a convenient alibi more than a punishment. I see two possibilities, Karl: Dexter Philips has either attempted to orchestrate a series of perfect crimes, ironically in order to escape his past, and has relied on the provisions of the tontine to do so. Or, he has not escaped this DiFiore fellow and he is not the one, or the only one, who is doing the killing. As you well know, the mean intelligence of any society's criminal element is far below that of the society itself and Dexter Philips seems to be far from a stellar performer. In any event, he is on the run. Further attempts to contact him will certainly prove fruitless."

"I agree, of course. We must then prepare for his arrival, in the event your speculations are correct. Still," the lawyer pondered, massaging his chin "they were all provided with First Class flight arrangements. His was the only one not issued from here and he appears on no passenger roster."

Jean-Alexandre refilled his glass and sat quietly behind his father's desk. He reached for a ledger and perused pages of recent bank transfers and expenditures as Maître d'Avignon paced the floor in silence. Long moments later:

"Karl, it would appear that Dexter Philips may not exist. He may have been killed with complete efficacy, which would explain why there is no trace of him and quite possibly never will be. He may be quite dead."

The lawyer turned, openly distraught. "My God, not a seventh victim? We must do our utmost to protect your son, Alex."

"Not a victim, Karl, more likely the possible beneficiary of a new life who may have been killed with the stroke of a pen and reborn with this very ink," he took up Davidson's Mont Blanc between his fingers, "my father's."

"He has a new identity."

"Yes, we must presume so, and possibly a new face to go with it. The man in these photographs and videos may not be joining us, at least not as Dexter Philips. I can think of no other reason Davidson would have authorized a transfer of one hundred thousand to Monsieur DuFour with surgery annotated in the margin of the ledger. The greater question may well be: if he has undergone surgery, how will we know whether he was once Dexter Philips?" Jean-Alexandre slumped into the chair. "That would certainly seem to suggest the absence of an accomplice and that Philips is indeed running from his past with ill intent. The most probable scenario in my view is that he killed DuFour, the very one who was trying to help him, for the information previously gathered on the other participants: a despicable crime indeed, and virtually infallible, until now. We know DuFour maintained precise files on his cases, yet his agency has no record whatsoever of the work he was doing for Davidson, nor was there any mention of it by the local police who searched his home. We would be foolish in the extreme not to assume Philips has that detailed information and has used the better part it to murder his own parents and grandmother, to whom he clearly felt no attachment. To imagine the shock and the terror of their final few moments chills my blood, if indeed he revealed himself them, not to mention the Daniels women." Jean-Alexandre reached for a family photo at the edge of the desk. "We must also assume he is either currently in search of Joaquin or content to lose that portion of the tontine."

D'Avignon stood with his arms folded across his chest. "Assume the worst. I believe Monsieur DuFour died silently and bravely. His several wounds were issued from two different guns and from opposite positions, which might be explained by the fact that neither gun registered to him has been found, but to shoot a man who is already dead is unfathomable."

"I wish I had known him, Karl. He died a very rich man with a vital secret, the very secret that caused his death."

"It is a certainty that we will soon meet this Philips. His presence is a key stipulation. He knows that. As for your son, who has demonstrated good faith and has expressed his good intentions to follow his grandfather's wishes, I will exempt him from that stipulation. He need not attend."

"His mother will certainly want to show her affection to you for that kind consideration."

"D'Avignon smiled for the first time in twenty-four hours, his face haggard with exhaustion and stress.

"And with your kind permission, I will let her." The smile faded. "We still must not overlook the possibility of an accomplice. As you have noted, Monsieur DuFour died a very rich man. Knowing your father as I do, I take that to mean substantially so. He recently transferred two hundred thousand into his local account, a matter of some concern to the local police until I advised them of its being a fee for services rendered to Davidson and unquestionably ethical."

"It was a good deal more than that," Jean-Alexandre added.

"It seems his killer also took the time to examine DuFour's personal affairs. Nothing much remained, including his computer. We must assume that Philips has access to the account."

"Meaning to say, he has resources."

"Yes, sufficient I would think to involve an accomplice."

"That would be an understatement, Karl. We must be vigilant. Speculation and conjecture do nothing to serve justice, as you well know. Yet at the moment we are left with little else in the absence of solid proof. Until the fifteenth has come and gone I will see to my son's temporary protection in Las Palmas and following his return to France for the funeral. I would suggest in the strongest possible language that my brother and I also meet Monsieur Philips with you, in the name of prudence."

"Agreed, Alex. Your company would be most welcome."

"Now, perhaps you will indulge me as a concerned father." D'Avignon nodded. "Twenty million, ten million after mandatory consideration of the less fortunate, is more than anyone could have been expected. Thirty-five million is preposterous in the extreme and I am certain not what my father had in mind given the number of intended participants. Joaquin will one day inherit hotels, restaurants, our property and his uncle's. He has no need of additional excess, which I fear will be his ruin."

Karl d'Avignon's face grimaced with obvious concern. "What do you propose?"

"I must presume that none of the participants was aware of the total value of the tontine."

"They were not."

"Then I propose a flat ten million to each grandson, the precise amount seemingly intended by my father, unless the other happens to be a murderer."

"That would leave a very considerable balance of one hundred and twenty million, and would undeniably constitute a serious contravention of your father's express written wishes?"

"Indeed. Yet I know my father's purpose was never to

turn decency into decadence. This undoubtedly would. If they want more, let them do well in life."

"Am I then to assume you have considered an alternative proposition which your father would have been inclined to embrace unreservedly?"

"I believe so. He was not a man given to squander and strongly disinclined towards donating large sums to the various causes which regularly pursued him. He was never satisfied that the greater good would be achieved by top-heavy administrations, bottom-heavy incompetence, and a widespread laisser-faire attitude. In short: he feared waste. I propose that we administer the remaining funds with a social conscience and our ability to do what Davidson had intended the others to do: the most amount of good, albeit more effectively in my view. My wife will embrace the idea eagerly and we will jointly agree to a substantial future contribution to a foundation which I propose creating with your collaboration. As for Gérard, I am confident my brother would consider his exclusion as an inexcusable affront. You have my word."

Maître d'Avignon took time to ponder the question. Jean-Alexandre waited patiently, appreciating the lawyer's dilemma of conscience and professional propriety.

"I must concur wholeheartedly once again. Your word, Alex, is your well-known and foregone signature. I believe your father would agree, were he here with us."

"In that case he would fill your glass, Karl, and thank you wholeheartedly."

"To the Davidson Alexander Foundation, Alex," Karl d'Avignon raised his refilled glass and tapped the rim against Jean-Alexandre's, "and to his son who has most certainly made Davidson very proud."

64

The day Steve Brandon went home from the restaurant he felt as though he had been transported back into the netherworld from which he had just escaped. Mike DuFour had been killed by DiFiore, there was no doubt. Nervous house-invasion-assholes would more likely shoot at a wall or a ceiling than a victim. He knew as much and so did the cops. Mike DuFour had been executed.

Saturday evening he lay restlessly awake, waiting for morning and for the moment he hoped she would likely be awake to answer the phone. He went over in his mind a hundred times what Mike DuFour had tried to drill into his head. He would be smart one day. He would be the best he could be and he would succeed at whatever he would finally decide to do. Above all he would be a man of his word. He was a man of his word. There was no honour amongst thieves. The strong survived on the backs of those who paid the higher price. So where was the honour, and where was the honour in letting a man die for absolutely no reason other than to kill another? He knew Mike would understand. Hell, if anything, Steve Brandon knew DuFour would want it. Who wanted to die for no reason? He swallowed the two fingers of scotch he had been saving for hours and dialled the number. Before she answered he said. "This is for you, Mike. If I screw up I'll be in good company with you. But don't expect me anytime soon."

"Hello," she answered as though she hadn't just crawled

from her bed.

"Sandra, don't hang up." He blurted. "I won't take long, I promise."

"Wrong number, sweetie. This isn't Sandra. Sorry."

"Yes, you are, because you're not a Louise."

There was a long pause. "Oh my God, you frigging idiot. What the hell are you doing?"

"I'm talking with the girl of my dreams: Sandra Somebody who doesn't want me to know her real name. Listen, Sandra, there was a killing here last week. The man's name was Mike DuFour. He was an ex-cop and he died because of me. I'm the reason he's dead. I already know DiFiore sanctioned the hit. What I need to know is who pulled the trigger and who's on my ass."

"Why would they kill a cop because of you?"

"To get to me for something I did. I gave up DiFiore a few years ago as part of a plea bargain. It's a long story. I had my reasons. Believe me, they would have killed him anyway, whether he talked or not."

"Shit."

"So who is it? "Who got the contract?"

"No fucking way. Are you out of your mind? You fucked up big time with all that bullshit your last night in the salon, trying to be such a big man with your name and all that other bravado bullshit crap. Why Dex? You got some sort of a death wish?"

"Really?" he asked.

"Yeah, and really fast. Your time's up"

"Because I think we could work out. I wanted to see you again, I still do. I can't stop thinking about you. That's why. That's all she wrote. You said you'd let me take you away from all of it when I'm rich. So, did you mean it?"

She sighed into the phone. "Jesus, it was just words, something to say at the time to make you, I don't know, happy or something. No, I didn't mean it. Fucking H, I have my own plans, Dex, and so far they're working out just fine.

I don't need or want you or your bullshit. All I can tell you is that Abacus, the guy who runs the lounge, saw the tape of you feeling me up that night. We were being videoed, Dex, complete with audio."

"No shit, the big guy with a flat head. He looks like an ex-marine with too much shell shock?"

"You know him?"

"Yeah, I know him. I've had the pleasure, once or twice. He's done a lot of DiFiore's dirty work and I'm not talking broken legs. He had a reputation for being real clean at the worksite, so to speak. I guess he still does. I don't think he's even had a parking ticket." He paused. "I had no clue he ran the club. Shit."

"He didn't until about two years ago, maybe a bit longer. Running the club was a wedding gift. He doesn't do much apart taping me and the other girls, so he can watch them while he does his wife."

"Sick fuck."

"The next day he came to the bar. He asked me straight out if your name was Dexter Philips, like he had to be sure, and I said yes. I had no choice. He already knew, Dex. Then he left with a couple of guys and that's when I called you. I've hardly seen him since."

"Because he's looking for me."

"If it is him, his real name is Albert Sorrento and he's not someone to piss off. He won't let go, Dex. He's family. You know family ... like in Di-fucking-Fiore.

"So was I."

"Not like this. His wife is DiFiore's sister. That's how come he's got the club. You're in deep shit, Dex. I'm sorry. This was a real bad idea. Goodbye."

"Please, don't hang up." He pleaded. "It could be they're the ones in shit, all of them. They killed someone who went out of his way to help me. They're going to pay for that, and I don't think talking with you is a bad idea. I've wanted to for weeks, to say thanks. You saved my life

Sandra. The bad idea is doing what you do for a living, and doing it for DiFiore. I can change all that."

"Yeah, sure you can. You're my guardian angel."

"I can be. All I need is for you to believe in me the way DuFour did. He died because of it, because of me. I must be worth something if a man's willing to die for me."

"That doesn't mean I have to die with him, Dex. Listen, if I'm really super lucky, someone finding out about this conversation would put me in a wheelchair for life with a fucked-up face instead of at the bottom of a river somewhere."

"I know, and the last thing I need is for him to know we've been speaking, but don't think I'd ever let him hurt you."

"My hero ... like he'd phone you first to tell you."

"Actually, right now, if he has what I really hope he doesn't, he would call me first. Believe me. When is he expected back at the club?"

"I don't know." Belinda waited a moment, finally taking a deep breath. "You're on your own, Dex. If you want him so badly he's in the book under Albert Sorrento. He's not even unlisted. Guess he thinks it makes him look legit."

"All that would do is get me killed. What I need is a recent picture of him. I need to know who I'm running from until it's time for him to run."

"You're insane."

"No, I'm not. Listen, DiFiore wants me dead, but there's a real good chance this Abacus guy knows something about me now that DiFiore doesn't, something that will stop him from killing me for at least a few weeks."

"Like what, you're a nice guy and he feels bad about killing you? Dream on."

"Not quite. He knows I'm rich, or soon will be, really rich. Abacus killed DuFour to get at me, to kill me. That was then. Now bets are that he knows I'm about to become very freaking wealthy. It's also why he's not going to kill me, even if he does find me. He needs me alive at least until I've got the money."

"Wealthy?" She giggled. "I suppose some rich uncle you never knew just kicked the bucket and thought of you, his favourite nephew," she said, scornfully. "And I'm a virgin nun."

"Laugh if you want. It's complicated, storybook bullshit, only it's real. That's why I need to know what he looks like. I need to know if he's going to be somewhere I have to be. Whether he is or not doesn't matter, as long as I know."

"The answer is still no."

"Here's the deal, Sandra: "You get me that picture and you'll get one million in cash. I was going to give it to you anyway, if you stopped lapping, but, if that's what it takes, the picture has to be part of the deal."

"This is bullshit."

"No, it's not. Try me. It's one million for getting me a picture and keeping your clothes on and your legs together until I come for you. That's all, nothing else unless you get to like me."

"Like you? I don't even know you."

"Yeah, you do, and you like me. One million and you can leave with me to go anywhere you want. That happens and I'll give you half of everything I've got if you stay with me at least until I'm eighty. Or, you don't stay with me, and I'll still give you the one million the next time we meet as long as you've stopped lapping. That's the deal. If you're in the bar tonight for any reason besides getting me what I need, or any time after, the deal's off."

She laughed spontaneously from her gut. "Whenever you wake up from your ridiculous dream, Dex, if they let you live that long, I'll still be what I am: an expensive feel. I've already told you."

"You're wrong." He insisted, the change in his voice surprising her. "When all this is over I'm taking you out for dinner and when we're together I'm going hold your hand. I'm going to tell you that you're the most beautiful woman in the world, that I can't stop thinking about you. And I don't mean your gorgeous ass and tits, I mean you. Then I'm going to kiss you and you will want to leave with me," he intoned, "to go anywhere we want because I'm worth a try and you're going to know it."

"Aren't you forgetting something?"

"Like what?"

"Like my preference for girls."

"I can't say I blame you, and I didn't say you had to change completely. Did I?" He snorted. "Think about it. All I'm asking is to give me a chance. We can talk about the girls later."

"What's the time frame?" She laughed. "Not that I believe any of this crap."

"I can't say right now,"

The laugh turned derisive. "No shit. Goodbye, Dex."

"No," he yelled, "don't hang up. Listen, I can prove what I'm saying. Your name is Belinda Samuels. I know you worked as a waitress and had friends, and I know you were an escort. I don't care about any of that shit you did in the past. That's your past, like my past."

"Oh, shit," was all she could say, her mind racing. He knew her name. "What are you doing, Dex? You and I aren't going to happen. This is all bullshit."

"No, it isn't. Just give it a chance, Belinda, that's all I'm asking. If it doesn't work you've got a million."

"A million, just like that?"

"Yes."

"I can't tell you where I live."

"I already know. Listen, October 02nd is a Saturday. I'll make reservations at The Crystal Chandelier in Toronto. Be there dressed in something hot and sexy and looking out for the best looking guy. That'll be me in a blue suit, silver tie and holding a million-dollar briefcase." The line went silent. "You're thinking. That's good. It means you want to believe me. How does eight o'clock sound?"

"So I wait a month to find out you're dead. And then what?"

"You still get the million. I promise."

"Yeah, right, because I squirmed naked on your knees a couple of times before and after a hundred other guys I don't remember."

"No. Because when you did you weren't Kitty Hawk to me. You were Sandra and now you're Belinda. Besides, I owe you for the coffee and I know you like me. Why else would you have saved my ass?"

"This is stupid."

"No, it's not." Neither one spoke for a moment. "So you do like me. I can tell because you're not saying anything."

"No, I like the thought of a million dollars. Be careful, Dex. You're small compared to them."

"That's where you're wrong. They're small compared to me. They murdered someone I was too afraid and too late to call a friend. It's payback time and I intend to collect." He waited a moment, they both did. "So Sandra, what's the answer?"

"You're serious, aren't you?"

"Very serious, and I want you out of the club. I don't want you going back, ever."

She sighed deeply, sweeping an open hand through her hair and down the nape of her neck, wanting to punch the wall. "Don't turn out to be another prick, Dex. I can kill you worse than Sorrento."

"You'll do it?" Steve Brandon asked anxiously.

"I don't have the slightest reason to, because I don't believe a single word you're saying. Yeah, I do have a picture of him taken at the last Christmas party. I'll cut him out. You can have it enlarged at a drugstore." She paused. "Remember Dex, he's big and he's in good shape. He's no pussycat."

"Neither am I. What about the job? "He asked, bluntly, wanting an answer. "I'm coming back for you and I would really appreciate it if, in the meantime, you'd stop getting off on showing yourself to drunken assholes. I'm not the same guy, Belinda. Believe me. You're in for a surprise and I love your name."

"I'll get to the club at three this afternoon. My car will be at the entrance facing the street with the envelope under the wiper. You'd better fucking be there two seconds after and I don't mean to hang around."

Steve looked at his watch. He had five hours, nowhere near enough time to drive. He would have to fly. "I'll be there, and you won't see me." He hesitated. When he did speak he sounded unsure. "You haven't answered my question. What about the job?"

"Okay, no more slipping and sliding. But if you're bullshitting me, which I think you are, the next guy I do will be Abacus and I'll do him all the way for free and send you the video."

"Not funny."

"Okay, I'll be there this afternoon, long enough to get some of my things and leave, a couple of minutes. You've got until October 02nd Dexter Philips and I can't believe I'm even saying any of this. Until then Belinda Samuels needs a long-awaited and well-deserved vacation, maybe a Caribbean cruise," she replied. "And you'd better not be a shithead," she added, pretending to sound annoyed before she pressed end.

That afternoon he sat in the rental and watched her lean against her car, seemingly disinterested until she pulled up the hem of her already very short skirt and adjusted both front garters before looking in both directions with a smile and walking into The Booty Lounge. He smiled. She had been waiting for the street to clear. She did like him. The love would come later, if he lived.

The envelope was taken within a few seconds and ten minutes later Belinda Samuels came back out. With no one insight she raised one foot onto her front bumper and toyed again with her garter before turning and raising her other foot to do the same with a wide smile. Then she climbed behind the wheel and drove away, looking straight forward, content to know he had seen her leave. He hadn't.

The next day Steve Brandon boarded a return flight to London's Heathrow and from there to Rome where he stayed for a week before flying to Madrid and onto Santa Cruz de Tenerife. Mike DuFour had told him to start being smart and that's exactly what he intended to do. DuFour had also given his word that only he and Davidson Alexander knew of his new identity. He hoped so, though he wondered how much Sorrento knew of the others. He arrived on Tenerife Monday, September 06th, nine days and sixty miles of ocean from Las Palmas.

65

Davidson was laid to rest beside Gabrielle on Thursday, September 09th, under a simple granite stone. Maria and Jorge flew in for the unpretentious ceremony which Davidson had wanted restricted to family and his close legal counsel and friend. Chantal reciprocated the Spanish couple's earlier hospitality and Jean-Alexandre asked that they remain an extra night before flying home.

On the tenth they showed the couple the highlights of Paris, the quaint auberge and bistro where his parents had met, and Gérard insisted everyone be his dinner guests at L'Assiette Élégante along with Maître d'Avignon. As the after-dinner drinks were being served Jean-Alexandre told Maria and Jorge that Davidson had bequeathed to them, to the exclusion of personal items intended for his sons, the entire Las Palmas estate, its contents and ten million dollars. He then quickly offered to buy an agitated Maria a new dress to replace the one suddenly and irreparably splashed with wine. The transfer of title, free and clear, had been completed that afternoon by Maître d'Avignon's office and the intimate entourage congratulated them discreetly as the lawyer handed Jorge the title deed. The moment was as sad as it was happy.

Jean-Alexandre had one request to make of them. Davidson had planned a very private meeting for the fifteenth and contacting the person to inform him of the change of venue had been impossible, which they had intended. The meeting was as imperative and would be brief, he assured the de la Vega couple. And every effort would be made not to disrupt their day if they would allow this one and final request on behalf of Davidson.

Still flushed and flustered, Maria looked to her husband who felt as strange as she did being asked whether Davidson's home might be used for his own meeting. The couple nodded wordlessly in unison, until a moment later when Maria asked what she should prepare as food and drink for the meeting, not quite knowing how to react when all but her husband broke into wide grins and chuckles.

On the Saturday the de la Vegas left Paris to return to Las Palmas. Jean-Alexandre asked Jorge how he would feel chauffeuring his wife to their home and he got more than the expected reply. Maria burst into tears and hugged him tightly, telling him the estate would always be Davidson's home and that his family would always be expected to visit. Jorge hugged Chantal before exchanging a firm handshake with Jean-Alexandre as the women embraced one another and cried happy tears together. Each one had seen another part of Davidson's life.

A change of venue would have been ideal. Unfortunately Philips hadn't cooperated and the men agreed they could hardly be expected to approach every arriving passenger to ask if he had once been Dexter Philips, or unfold a banner showing his name. They were certain he would come, secure in the knowledge no one knew of his abominable crimes. Jean-Alexandre, Gérard, and Karl d'Avignon arrived on the island Monday, the thirteenth, unbeknownst to the de la Vegas. Joaquin de-Saint-Valéry remained in Paris under police protection and Steve Brandon relaxed on the shores of Tenerife hoping Belinda Samuels would never again be Kitty Hawk.

By late in the day, after a week of sunning and girl watching on South Beach, wondering what the hell she had done, Belinda Samuels boarded a cruise ship scheduled to make fourteen ports of call. Albert Sorrento arrived in Madrid and was standing at the Iberian counter to book a flight to Las Palmas early on the Wednesday, which he told the ticket agent was impromptu.

66

From their suites at the Hotel Las Olas the three men used what was left of Monday and all day Tuesday to visit the island's other hotels, making enquiries and showing photographs of Dexter Philips to the concierges and front desk personnel without results. Wednesday morning they arrived early to the de la Vega estate and made ready for a long day of nervous tension and uncertain resolve.

Steve Brandon was climbing aboard the fifty-three foot Marlow he had chartered to take him across the sixty miles of open water to Las Palmas in two hours and Albert Sorrento boarded an early flight from Madrid that would land at 10:45. He'd be in place by twelve-fifteen. By 10:00 the Las Palmas police were stationed at various parts of the property, dressed as Jean-Alexandre had expressly requested and looking very much like domestic staff working idly at their chores. The phone rang at eleven-fifty taking all three men by surprise.

"Digáme," said Jean-Alexandre. "¿Quien es?"

"I'm sorry, I don't speak Spanish. If this is the home of Davidson Alexander I would like to speak with him."

"Who may I say is calling?"

"Steve Brandon."

"I am terribly sorry, Mr. Brandon. Mr. Alexander is unavailable today. May I take a message and ask him to return your call?"

"No, tell him Steve Brandon. He'll talk with me. He

knows who I am. Tell him Steve Brandon and Mike DuFour."

Jean-Alexandre felt his stomach constrict. His mouth dried instantly and his skin reacted to the cold coursing through his body. "I enjoy Mr. Alexander's confidence, Mr. Brandon. I take it you would have been known at one time as…"

"I'm his grandson."

"Ah, yes. Mr. Alexander is expecting you, of course, Mr. Brandon. However, per the prerequisites of the tontine, there is no need to call in advance of your arrival between noon and four this afternoon. Mr. Davidson is not taking calls this morning."

"I need to speak with him before I arrive. There's something he has to know."

"I would be pleased to convey any message. His instructions are never to be questioned. He is not taking calls."

Steve Brandon squeezed the phone and cursed to himself. "Listen, I know he has information on me that includes old photographs and videos. He knows about the surgery and the new name. He paid for it, for Christ sake. Just tell him I have no way to prove who I am other than to say Mike DuFour, the detective who tried to help me, is dead."

"I will convey the message, sir. When may we expect you?"

"Between noon and four," was the dry answer. Steve Brandon hung up and walked toward the solitary cab at the marina. When he told the driver the address and mentioned Davidson's name the man crossed himself and murmured words his passenger did not understand.

The police were put on alert, the readiness of the concealed camcorder was verified and the three men did their best to compose themselves. When the taxi drove onto the estate at one-ten not a single worker looked up.

Jean-Alexandre filled the powerful scope from a mile away until one of the two visitors Abacus knew to expect climbed from the car. The man's frame was tall and broad, so was Dexter Philips. This one had much lighter hair and lacked the tense body language common to all ex-cons. Instead he seemed confident as he disappeared under the portico of the villa and spoke with the other man as though walking into an international summit. When he looked back from the top of the steps for the briefest moment the sun glistened off his silver-coated sunglasses. His face was smooth, years younger than Philips, without the stony-face expression and deep lines of prison life etched into his face over time from the constant preoccupation with survival. This man was no ex-con. Whoever he was, he was not Dexter Philips or de-Saint-Valéry and Abacus lowered the scope to wait for the next car that would deliver Dexter Philips, certain he had not yet arrived.

"Good afternoon, sir. May I have your name?" Jean-Alexandre began.

"Steve Brandon, I'm expected."

"Of course, we spoke earlier. I apologize for any misconstrued ill-feeling. One must exercise extreme caution at such times. I do hope you understand."

"Of course," Steve said simply. "Are the others here?"

"They are expected to arrive shortly, sir. May I assist you with any luggage you might have brought? We were not quite certain as to where you would be staying. We happily would have sent the car for you."

"I have no luggage."

"Then would you please follow me." Jean-Alexandre pursed his lips and nodded, doing his best to conceal his curiosity. He paid the fare, dismissed the driver and escorted Steve Brandon inside. "Mr. Brandon, first may I introduce Monsieur Gérard de-Saint-Valéry, Davidson's son and Maître d'Avignon, Davidson's legal counsel. I am his other son, Jean-Alexandre de-Saint-Valéry."

Their guest nodded to each one in turn. Intuitively no one thought to shake hands.

"Please, do sit down, Mr. Brandon."

"It's an impressive place," Steve remarked casually, taking in the room as he sat. "I thought you were his butler."

"Unfortunately not. I am a magistrate of the French court."

"You're a judge?"

"To the dismay of many, yes."

"Criminal court?" Steve asked indifferently.

"Yes."

He looked at d'Avignon. "And I suppose your specialty is criminal law."

"No, nothing so exciting, I'm afraid. I represent Monsieur Alexander's financial interests, which, I assure you, is quite more mundane."

Steve looked at Jean-Alexandre. "I wasn't expecting you to be French. Why de-Saint-Valéry if you're his sons, and not Alexander? Are my parents French as well?"

"Davidson had two wives: my mother and a naturalized Canadian woman. She was your biological grandmother and, from what little I know of her, very British in most respects. No, your parents were raised in English, though neither by their mother or Davidson. They were both given up for adoption at an early age, as you were by them." Steve Brandon showed his confusion. "It is assumed that when they married they were unaware of any sibling relationship."

"They're brother and sister, is that what you're telling me?"

"Yes, twins, in fact." Jean-Alexandre's trained eyes searched for the slightest variance in Steve Brandon's voice, eyes and expression. Nothing.

"Isn't that illegal?"

"Yes, in most civilized countries, though we possess

insufficient information at this time to either criticize or condone their choice."

Steve's lips twitched into a tight, fleeting curl, yet his eyes remained expressionless and unblinking. "I guess that answers a few questions about me. Is that why they dumped me, because they thought I'd turn into a circus act or a retard?"

Gérard remained silent, studying the young man's face for the slightest resemblance to Davidson. There was none other than his stature. Jean-Alexandre continued. "Most assuredly not," he insisted with no real conviction in his voice, "more likely was their intention to make your life easier."

"Then they screwed up big time."

"I dare say, though perhaps the blame for any subsequent misfortune to befall you should be more equitably distributed."

"You keep thinking that. And, if it's all the same to you, I'll stay with what I know…and remember." Steve leaned back into the sofa, crossing one leg over the other as he looked at Gérard. "So, what about you guys?"

"A much longer story: one of sadness as much as romance everlasting and perhaps better saved for a later time," answered Jean-Alexandre. "It suffices to say we proudly carry our mother's name."

"You call him by his first name?"

"Yes we do, as a matter of habit and personal preference. The manner in which a person is addressed matters more than the particular appellation one chooses."

Steve scanned the room. "It's been my experience that sometimes both matter. Is he waiting for the others to arrive before he comes in?"

Jean-Alexandre remained standing. "Davidson will not be joining us today, a fact we all deeply regret. He passed away ten days ago." Steve remained as he was, his face revealing no surprise at all. "You seem not too taken aback by the news, Mr. Brandon."

"I'm not. I never met him or spoke to him, and all I know about him is that he paid for my new face and id to help keep me stay alive. So far it's working out pretty good. I'm sorry for your loss, I am, but it's difficult to mourn a stranger. I don't mean to be disrespectful."

"I understand, Mr. Brandon. Please, tell us what you know of Monsieur DuFour's tragic death."

Steve looked at all three men in turn, his expression still showing no emotion. "He was murdered in his home about a week after I last saw him. He took a few nine mm rounds in the back and a couple more to the head. He was executed, plain and simple."

"And you know this how?" questioned Jean-Alexandre.

Steve jabbed a straightened index finger lightly against his chin. "He was murdered because certain people are looking for this, the new and improved me. They want Dexter Philips dead. "

"The police at first seemed not to agree with you about the execution, now they do since new evidence has very recently been introduced to them. Thus far, however, they know absolutely nothing of Dexter Philips or the tontine." He looked down at Gérard and d'Avignon, pausing for affect. "Strangely, Mr. Brandon, and of particular interest to us, is that when the authorities searched Monsieur DuFour's residence they discovered no documentation whatsoever pertaining to the tontine or his investigation of you and the six other participants. The same is true of his agency's office records, which might lead those of a more suspicious nature to believe Dexter Philips, who wanted and needed to disappear completely, saw the need to ensure the highest degree of anonymity by attending decisively to certain unwelcome impediments to that objective. Is that what should be interpreted from your last statement, Mr. Brandon?"

"There was no statement, only a direct answer to a direct

question. There were no impediments. Only DuFour and your father knew about me. Let's get one thing straight: I don't need the money badly enough not to put you on your fancy French ass if you're implying I killed DuFour." Steve replied evenly and calmly. "He was killed because of me and for some reason he kept the tontine information at home. Go figure. My guess is they killed him first, then found the information by fluke while they were trying to make the killing look like a home invasion. Mike and your old man were supposed to be the only ones who knew the details of my new life. If there was anything in those files about the surgery or my new identity it's a matter of time before they find me. That good enough for you, judge?"

"The men you saw on the estate grounds are police officers, Mr. Brandon. They are currently positioned much closer to the villa. No, it's not good enough." Jean-Alexandre sat beside his brother. "The basis of a tontine, Mr. Brandon is one of survival: one must live in order to finally succeed. My father modified his so that one's absence would, in effect, be tantamount to one's death, those remaining, or in this case present, in effect succeeding? Do you follow?"

"Is there going to test after this class?"

"No, sir, though you might expect quite a lengthy detention."

Steve uncrossed his legs and leaned forward. "I know the guy who did DuFour as well as the one who sanctioned it, and there's a good chance I'll be seeing the killer pretty soon. The guy's a pro. Not even a hair would have been left at the scene, and he was there. I wasn't, so what do you think the cops can do with that? There's no gun, no fingerprints and no DNA. There's also no international warrant out on me and this is Spain. So you've got squat, your honour."

Jean-Alexandre remained composed. "And how do you know them?"

"I used to work for them. The last time I messed up I was going away for twenty to life. I plea-bargained for ten and got out in three. They didn't, and they're a little pissed with me. Shit happens."

"You sold them out."

"I traded information to my advantage."

"And Monsieur DuFour is very regrettably dead as a result. And he's not the only one."

"He is the only one. I would have heard if there had been another killing."

"There are two possible rebuttals to your statement: one is that you most certainly could not have known; the other is that you did indeed know. As I have previously mentioned, new evidence exists, albeit in the form of coincidence. Emily Ashton, Davidson's first wife and participant in the tontine, is suspected of having suffered a heart attack while witnessing the drowning death of her illegitimate daughter in South Carolina. The younger woman had also been invited to attend as a participant, as part of the greater scheme of things. Apparently she had been drinking rather heavily and her daughter, Emily Ashton's granddaughter, also drowned while attempting to save her. The granddaughter had also been expected in Las Palmas for the same reason as her mother. In a word: self-serving. Strangely, when we inquired of the police, there was no reference whatsoever to the tontine in any of their homes: no tickets, no hotel reservations and no letters. Anyone possessing those letters, Mr. Brandon, in conjunction with Monsieur DuFour's information, would certainly understand the benefit inherent in the rules as drawn up by Davidson, specifically the one discouraging communication in advance of today. Or, dare I presume that anyone envisioning such a benefit might think to acquire that information and, in so doing, reduce the number of participants while significantly increasing his or her share of the tontine."

Steve laughed. "Do you have anything to drink? A scotch will do."

Gérard stood, speaking for the first time. "One the rocks?"

"Sure. I need something to wash down all this bullshit." Gérard brought the drink with three others on the tray. Steve took a sip, seemingly unruffled. "People drown all the time and what was the old lady anyway, eighty, eighty-five?" Steve raised his glass before taking another sip. "Here's to the granddaughter. Sounds like she had balls and you can check the rosters. You won't see any record of Dexter Philips or Steve Brandon flying into the States."

Jean-Alexandre looked into his snifter, swirling the contents. "That's quite true, with regard to Dexter Philips." Karl d'Avignon stood quietly and walked from the room. "I trust the scotch is satisfactory, Mr. Brandon."

"Yes, it is." Steve turned his head to the side and spoke to the lawyer's back. "While you're checking I would suggest you try Albert Sorrento, that's Sorrento with two rs." He turned back to the two men facing him. "So now there's only three others coming, if this tontine thing's going to happen at all. Or was it all pure bullshit?"

"Not in the least. The tontine is most certainly remains in effect."

"Then, let's get something straight. I'm not expecting any more than I was supposed to get in the first place. That help you any?"

"Your intended share was to have been twenty-million, which has been arbitrarily reduced by us to ten million. However, you have been exempted from naming a favourite cause. The net result is unchanged. There is, however, one condition of singular importance which was heretofore unnecessary to consider."

"Which is?"

"That you have not killed any one of the other participants, Mr. Brandon. You are not merely a prime suspect. You are, in fact, the only suspect and will, of course, become a person of interest to the authorities once your name is made known to them."

"Do what you have to do. There's no evidence and no proof. We call it burden of proof back home, including stateside. You might be familiar with the concept. And let's not forget your son could have been the one who killed them for that matter, or the other two, but I can see where it's easier to look at the ex-con. You've got until four o'clock, judge. That's when I walk, whether the others show or not."

"My son will not be attending. He has been kindly excused by Monsieur d'Avignon for obvious reasons. As well, his whereabouts at the time of all six deaths have been accounted for and are formally documented. That leaves the other two, your parents: Helen and James Parker. They were murdered within a week of Monsieur DuFour and the three women. Your father was shot once in the forehead, your mother's injury was inflicted to the back of her head. They were found a few days later, apparent victims of another home invasion. There was nothing at all in their home relating to the tontine. However, as you yourself have implied, such low-level criminals would certainly have no interest in letters and travel reservations. So, Mr. Brandon, despite the difficulty of mourning strangers as you put it, you see the necessity for our concern. You are the one possible suspect with a great deal of motive."

"I told you I meant no disrespect. I never knew them. I wanted to, and was even looking forward to the reunion. It's too bad. Still, I don't think I could have handled the brother-sister thing. How would they expect a kid go through life with that monkey on his back?" Steve swirled his drink, his thoughts momentarily distant. "But, that doesn't mean I killed them."

"There are videos of them in my father's office, should you be interested."

"Your father wanting them here was all I knew about this whole thing. I knew nothing about the women or your kid and I only cared about the money because it was going to keep me alive. I never knew the amount. Ten million's a bit of brain twist, no shit, and it doesn't mean squat if they know who I am."

"My son will benefit from the same amount and not from favouritism. The balance will finance a foundation to support a variety of causes. I can also assure you in the most irrefutable terms that neither my father nor Monsieur DuFour maintained any data, whether textual, visual or otherwise, regarding your new identity. Think what you want of what Monsieur DuFour may or may not have confessed prior to his death. You knew him. We did not."

"Your son's safe. There's no reason to worry about him. They want me, no one else."

"He is now, Mr. Brandon. We have adequately addressed that concern."

"Tell him he can relax. It's all over as soon as I walk out your door and they know it. Whatever interest they had in him before is finished as of today. There'd be no point. They ran out of time."

"You will understand that I am not entirely convinced, Mr. Brandon."

Karl d'Avignon came back into room, his expression morose. "There is no record with any airline of a Steve Brandon flying into the States at any time, strictly to and from Toronto on August 29th and to Rome and Madrid over the past two weeks." He looked down at Steve. "There is, however, a record of an Albert Sorrento flying to Charleston prior to the drownings and then from Charleston to Halifax the day before the Parker murders. He returned to Toronto the following day."

Jean-Alexandre's disbelief was apparent, his eyes making no secret of the turmoil in his mind. "We must notify the authorities at once, Karl," he said, turning back to

Steve and letting his gaze trail to the floor.

"I have already been in contact with the Toronto police, Alex. One of the division heads is to return my call."

"They call him Abacus," Steve interjected soberly, "and not because he can't add one plus one. He works for the DiFiore family. He's married to Mario DiFiore's sister."

D'Avignon appeared put off with the interruption. "Alex, they are sending additional officers to the estate as we speak, merely as a precaution."

Jean-Alexandre and Gérard looked up with the same quizzical expression. "What do they anticipate, Karl, a precaution against what exactly? It would seem more likely that apologies are in order."

"Quite possibly, as well as the need for extreme caution. This Sorrento fellow appears to have broadened his travel itinerary." He looked down again at Steve who was sitting nonchalantly and looking very satisfied with himself. "Mr. Brandon, your nemesis, this Albert Sorrento, is here in Las Palmas. He arrived this morning."

Steve stood and held out his empty glass to Gérard, telling him to forget the ice.

"I was expecting him. He's been after me since the day I met Mike DuFour." He seemed suddenly pensive. "He told me ten minutes. I took twenty."

"We don't follow," said Jean-Alexandre.

"It's not important. Let's just say it's the last time I'll ever fuc…." He took the drink from Gérard, noting the depth and tilting his head appreciatively. "Never mind. He's killed six people to get to me and you can be sure he doesn't want me dead, at least not right away. He wants the ten million. He's got all the letters. He has to know Mr. Alexander wasn't going through all that trouble for peanuts."

"We believe he has access to Monsieur DuFour's Swiss account," said d'Avignon.

"How much?" Steve asked.

"Approximately four million."

"Thanks, for making me feel like pure shit. Mike was a good guy. He taught me more in a week than I thought I could learn in a year." He looked at all three men. "If he's got access to Mike's account he's got the four million. The question is: what's he going to do with it?"

"Tell us about him," asked Gérard. "Please be candid."

"He's DiFiore's go-boy and brother-in-law. He's real bad news. He smiles when he breaks bones and can kill someone with as little emotion as when you tie your shoes. He runs a strip bar for the family, he likes the girls and he likes to watch them with customers while he does his wife."

"Pardon me," said Gérard.

"He watches the strippers on video while he fucks his wife." Steve shrugged. "Who knows? Maybe she's dog-faced and it's better than a bag."

Gérard grimaced, bringing the faintest smiles to d'Avigon's and Jean-Alexandre's faces.

"Do we know what he looks like?" he asked.

"We don't, I do, and if you don't mind I'd like to get back to the business of the tontine. We're having a smaller party than originally planned here and your guest would like to leave, with his party gift."

"You can't leave, not now," insisted Gérard. "My God, he's here. You're in peril of being killed."

"Not to mention," Jean-Alexandre was quick to insert, "that we do not possess a briefcase suitable for carrying ten million dollars. I doubt anyone does. We had intended to use a more business-like way, such as a bank transfer." He looked at his brother and d'Avignon. "In any event it's entirely beyond reason that you intend to leave. My brother is quiet correct."

"I'll have to learn to talk like that someday. Listen, the three of you have nothing to worry about, neither does your kid. It's me. I'm what they want, and now I'm good till I get back home. Besides, he has no gun. Why do you think he shot DuFour and twins and not the women in Charleston?" None of the three answered. "He flew into the States, which means airport security and clearing Customs, which means no gun and he couldn't line up a contact to get one because he couldn't take a chance on DiFiore finding out. He probably made the old lady have a heart attack before he dumped her at the pool, or maybe he gagged her and made her watch."

"He sounds positively brutal," commented Gérard. "What do you plan?"

"To find him first," Steve answered unemotionally, "but not today."

"You intend to leave Las Palmas today?" questioned d'Avignon.

"No, sir, I intend to leave this evening when it's dark. He's somewhere outside and he's probably seen that only one car has arrived since noon. He'll know it wasn't me. I hope. And if your kid isn't 6'5" he's going to be expecting you to greet a couple more people at the door. He's somewhere nearby and he's watching."

"He would follow you to your hotel and..."

"And from there to the airport and he's got me: Mr. Steve Brandon seated in 2-A."

"Precisely, so where is the logic in such a weak plan?" Jean-Alexandre wanted to know, frustrated. "He would simply wait for your departure and then he would be with you throughout the entire journey."

Steve laughed and sipped the scotch, following its warmth to his stomach. "Would you care to tell them, Mr. d'Avignon?" he invited.

The lawyer crunched his brow, puzzled. "I don't follow you, Mr. Brandon."

"Didn't the airline tell you when you called?"

"Tell me what?"

"That I'm staying on Tenerife, not here. I hired a powerboat to get me here this morning. The guy who owns the thing is waiting for me at the harbour. If Sorrento does follow me that's as far as he gets. Airlines don't give out roster information to other passengers unless it's to people like you or the cops. So I could be sitting right beside him all the way to Madrid, your right. Things is, he wouldn't know. Once I'm Madrid, I disappear. The only ones who know Steve Brandon are in this room right now, gentlemen. So, how much does each of you want to keep your mouths shut?"

"Sir, your humour is ill-conceived, as is your plan," returned Jean-Alexandre with sudden harshness.

"Not really, judge. It's only part of my plan. The rest is more permanent, more reassuring as you might put it."

"Would you care to elaborate?"

"No. You wanted me arrested for six murders in three different places that I couldn't possibly have committed. Imagine knowing that someone will be killed."

"Sorrento."

"It's him or me. I have no choice, neither does Sorrento. I'm dead if he finds me; he's dead if he doesn't. DiFiore wants me taken out and if Sorrento can't get the job done he'll bring in someone who can. Then he'll find Sorrento's wife a new husband after his funeral." Steve sipped his scotch. "If I get to him first, on my terms, the most I'll get is twenty-five to life and I'll be out in fifteen with ten million. And that's if I'm caught." he chortled. "I'll send you Mike DuFour's four million for your fund, if I can," he added, losing his smile. "You gentlemen mind if I stand out on the patio? I've developed this thing about being cooped up for too long at a time." He walked to the veranda. The three others followed. "I don't have much choice, judge. There's no concrete evidence against him. He won't spend a day in prison, let alone be in a courtroom. A heart attack, a couple of drownings involving liquor, a home-invasion and each one three thousand miles apart, are you kidding me?"

"You're talking about pre-meditated murder, Mr.

Brandon."

"You're talking like a judge, judge. I'm talking about pre-meditated self-defence. That's all. The difference is: the courts don't care who lives or dies until it happens and as long as they have someone to put away for the crime. I happen to care. I happen to believe this guy Abacus should pay for killing Mike DuFour, five others, and for wanting to kill me." Steve looked out to the sea and over to the home by the edge of the cliff where a couple stood holding hands. "His servants?" he asked to no one in particular.

"No, two of his dearest friends who miss him greatly," Jean-Alexandre replied.

Steve looked at his watch, and reached into the inner pocket of his jacket. "This is the banking information Mr. Alexander requested in his addendum. It's all there." He looked at Jean-Alexandre. "I'd like you to do me a favour, since it's been established that I'm not a mass murderer. There's a girl. Her name is Belinda Samuels. I don't know much about her other than she's in her early twenties, lives in Toronto and drives a Mercedes. I'd like you to call her and send her a million dollars if I don't call you by October 01st." He reached into another pocket. "This is her number. Call her. Tell her I meant what I said. Tell her it's legit and, in the meantime, get me the other nine million ASAP."

Jean-Alexandre took the envelope and the notepaper with Belinda's phone number. Gérard and Karl d'Avignon looked on stupefied. "You insist on going through with this crusade of lunacy, Mr. Brandon?"

"A good con knows when to keep his mouth shut, judge, if you get what I mean."

Jean-Alexandre looked at the other two for help, nonplussed. "Your new identity will be very seriously compromised."

"I grew up on the wrong side of the street and didn't get too many breaks, but I've never killed anyone. That doesn't mean I don't know how or that I don't know where to go to get things done. He killed my parents, not that I can pretend to be overly sad about them, but I don't even get to attend the funeral. When he did that he also killed your father's kids, not to mention his ex-wife, her two kids and that he could have done your kid if he had had more time. Think about it, judge. You could have been burying your kid today and blaming me. I want this guy and I want him real bad. First I have to get off this island. Remember, I know what he looks like, where he lives and where he works. There's only a fifty percent chance he knows my name and nothing else."

"He might already have passed this information on to this DiFiore."

"Not without giving up a lot of money, which I will get when, gentlemen?"

"Friday at noon, your local time," Karl d'Avignon answered. "I wish you the best of luck, Mr. Brandon."

"I guess the three of you are going back to France."

Jean-Alexandre was still looking at Karl d'Avignon incredulously. "We leave on the first flight tomorrow, from our hotel. The estate is no longer ours to use. We will leave when you do."

Gérard cleared his throat. "Alex, should we not advise our staff?"

"Indeed, Gérard, thank you. Mr. Brandon, you may leave when you wish, although it would be a simple matter for the men outside to capture and cage this rabid animal Sorrento until you depart safely from the Canaries."

"I need him with me, judge, on the same flight from Madrid. It's the one sure way I'll know if he recognizes me, if only by seat number. That alone will tell me what comes next."

"You mean whether you stay in Europe or return home?"

"I mean whether or not, after Sorrento finds himself in hell, DiFiore and his brother may do their best to follow him. Prison is a dangerous place. I bet you if I counted I could come up with nine million ways someone could do it." Jean-Alexandre's face sagged and his pallor darkened. Gérard and Karl d'Avignon could only listen, intrigued.

"Judge, do you believe in the afterlife?"

"I once knew a woman, a full-blooded and very beautiful Cree woman who tried often to convince me." He looked over to Gérard, the image of Shimmering Moon coming to life for both of them.

"Did she succeed?"

"I would prefer to believe those I have loved are not entirely gone from me. Why do you ask?"

"I don't know. Maybe because I have no one to remember, or maybe because I don't feel bad about what's going to happen, either way. If it's my time, it's my time, yet somehow I don't think so. Anyway, in case I'm wrong, my PIN is on the back of that paper with her number. If it is my time, give her what's left in the account, all of it. Tell her it's from Steve Brandon and when she asks who that is, tell her he's the guy who wanted to take her to dinner and that he's real sorry that he must disappoint her, that he's indisposed, permanently." A wide grin crossed Steve's face and his eyes seemed brighter for the first time since his arrival. "See, I'm already starting to talk like you guys. Indeed."

Jean-Alexandre let himself ease against the white stucco wall of the veranda. He stared at the chair his father had been sitting in when he died and then he looked out across the ocean. He crossed his arms and squeezed his eyes closed as though squeezing away uncertainty, fear or anguish. When he stood straight he unfolded his arms and breathed deeply as he once again looked out to sea.

"Gérard, Karl, please excuse my rudeness. I need to make a phone call from Davidson's office. Mr. Brandon, perhaps you would join my brother and Maître d'Avignon for another cocktail. I believe any previous unpleasantness can be put behind us, if you care to forgive our zealous if not single-minded diligence. We do not apologize, as much as we regret our necessary suspicions. Please do not leave until I come back."

Fifteen minutes elapsed before Jean-Alexandre returned. In his arms he carried three thick manila file folders and a selection of VHS tapes. He placed the collection on the sofa beside Steve who was listening intently to d'Avignon talk about Davidson and went to the bar where Gérard was pouring his brother's drink. He seemed pensive and resolute at once, a look neither Gérard nor Maître d'Avignon had ever been privy to in the much feared courtroom of Jean-Alexandre de-Saint-Valéry: l'Impitoyable, The Merciless, as each well-considered sentence was passed down and made final by the resounding clack of his legendary mahogany and brass gavel.

Steve Brandon looked at the files, and then to d'Avignon. "Something to read on the plane?"

D'Avignon reached for the files. "These two are very complete summaries of your parents' life and achievements, Mr. Brandon. The tapes are very recent as you might expect. The other file contains your information. All three files will all be destroyed very shortly and very completely. However you may keep the tapes. Is that not correct, Alex?"

"Yes, Karl. He may take as much time as he wishes to read through them, though the documents remain our property. Steve, the video tapes are yours to keep. Given the murders it would be imprudent to treat this information as anything less than potentially injurious to you or my son." Jean-Alexandre sat facing them. "Please enjoy the privacy of Davidson's office. You will not be disturbed." He put his hand out to stop Steve from standing and turned to d'Avignon. "We shall be receiving a visitor in the coming minutes, Karl, moments prior to the four o'clock deadline. He is ostensibly Steve to anyone who may be watching. In fact he is a local official who was well known and much admired by our father. As a matter of coincidence he is not very different in physical characteristics from our young guest, who he has no particular need to see. The gentleman will join us for cocktails on the pretext of my last trip to Las Palmas together with Gérard." Jean-Alexandre looked directly at Steve. "Unfortunately, you will not join us, Steve. However, Davidson's study is amply stocked. Karl, the second contingent of officers has been dismissed and I thank you for your prudence. When our guest leaves, the remaining officers outside will also know to leave. You and Gérard will leave soon thereafter," he turned to acknowledge his brother, "each of you in separate cars.

"And what of you and Steve?" asked Gérard. "The estate may not be very safe."

"Maria and Jorge have invited us for dinner. Need I say I have put them in a rather difficult position, although they seemed not to mind? In fact, Maria was quite adamant that she meet Davidson's Canadian grandson. Once we leave them I will accompany Steve to Tenerife and on to Madrid. It has been a while since I've been aboard a boat of any description, a planing hull should be quite exciting."

"You told them?" d'Avignon wanted to know.

"Not in so many words, Karl, more of a fanciful tale that would not upset Maria or cause Jorge to be needlessly alarmed for her well-being. As you leave, Steve and I will take a path our father walked many times. By then we shall be covered by darkness, well beyond sight of the hills and the road."

"Alex, I like neither the look in your eye nor the tone of your voice," said Gérard in French. "What are you up to that you are not telling us?"

"You will know as soon as our guest leaves, not until. Simply know that I will accept no argument from either of you." He looked at Steve, switching to English. "Parisians are sometimes thought to be inconsiderate to others. This is one of those times. May I ask you to now take those files and peruse them privately?"

"Do I have anything to say about all this?"

"Not unless you want to spend a night in a Spanish jail with drunken fishermen. I can see to the arrangements without further delay, if you so wish."

Steve Brandon looked at the two others and knew immediately Jean-Alexandre was serious. "What's Maria serving for dinner?" He said, trying to fix a convincing smile on his face.

"My favourite, chicken, and thank you for understanding. Enjoy your reading. The door is the last one down the hall. Please close it behind you." As Steve stood, so did Jean-Alexandre. "Steve, please be there when our guest leaves. I have informed the men outside to be particularly vigilant on your behalf."

Steve raised his glass. "Please be assured of my gratitude, Alex."

Gérard and d'Avignon chortled despite themselves.

67

Jorge was eager to help and asked no questions when Jean-Alexandre had called to beg a favour. He explained that he required a Spanish official to arrive precisely at 3:50, that the car be parked so that no one from the road or the hills could identify the passenger and that he, Jorge, then return home to wait for a call to drive the official back to his office.

Jean-Alexandre apologized profusely, feeling somewhat embarrassed by the inconvenience he was imposing on his father's long-time friend. Jorge would hear none of it. The limo came to a full stop at the very moment Gérard and Jean-Alexandre stepped into main portico to stand where the passenger would have no choice but to step out and walk directly to them. Jorge knew to wait until the men were inside before departing. To anyone hampered by the briefest glimpse the athletic middle-aged man would have appeared half his age, well-dressed in the latest fashion and received by his hosts in a friendly yet reserved manner. In Abacus' mind the man was Dexter Philips. He cared nothing about de-Saint-Valéry.

The man stayed for two hours, paying his respects to the memory of Davidson and entertaining his hosts with humorous anecdotes of his frequent meetings with a friend he would not soon forget. When he departed the sun was low in the western sky and there was a flurry of activity as the men on the grounds left their tools and hurried to their scooters and bicycles. The limo was parked between the pillars of the portico and Jorge stood waiting by the open door. The ceiling lights remained off as bright halogen spot lamps turned monochromatic tones of pre-dusk into a blinding burst of colours behind him.

As they went out Jean-Alexandre handed the man a framed photograph that showed Davidson congratulating his promotion with slap on the back. The exchange produced the desired effect of making the man look down, and as they arrived at the car Jean-Alexandre stepped behind so the man would turn his back to the nearby hills before looking up to bid his host farewell.

Two taxis soon followed. Karl d'Avignon was the next to leave. He extended his hand without words, pleased that Steve Brandon extended his own unhesitatingly. There was nothing to say. He walked out with his head down, deep in a confusion of unfamiliar thoughts.

Gérard was next. "I won't insult you further with trite words that serve no other purpose than to alleviate my own sadness and shame for how we have mistreated you, albeit with good intention. Good luck, Steve. Miss Samuels will receive our closest attention, though my most fervent wish is for you to honour your dinner obligation with the young lady."

"Thanks, Gerard." Steve extended his hand. "By the way, I'm not the guy you read about in those files. That was Dexter Philips. Steve Brandon's not going down that road thanks to your father and Mike DuFour. I wanted you to know."

Gérard turned to his brother. "Exercise the most extreme caution in the coming days. Your use of the word rabid was not inappropriate. Call me regularly with current news."

"I will. Were I convinced of any real danger I would certainly pursue another course of action. However I see no reason for us not to arrive safely in Madrid within a day or two."

"In any event be careful, Alex." The brothers shook hands and Gérard looked at Steve as he reached for the doorknob. "I own one of the finest restaurants in Paris. Simple modesty precludes me from saying anything more superlative. Perhaps one day you might think to introduce us to your Miss Samuels."

"First I have to introduce her to Steve Brandon. If it turns out she likes the guy, I'm sure you'll like her."

"Done, and I look forward to the day. Bonne chance et sois sain et sauf." He walked out, closing the door behind him.

"What did he say?"

"He said for you to be safe, to watch out for yourself."

"Was he serious, about the restaurant?"

"Yes." Jean-Alexandre looked at his watch. "We have another hour before Maria expects us. In the meantime I invite you to attend a bonfire at the back of the villa." Steve raised an eyebrow questioningly, letting his face relax into a smile. "If you have decided against keeping the video footage and photographs of your parents, now would be the opportune time to tell me."

"I'm not sure."

"Then keep them. There are no copies other than Monsieur DuFour's. There is no need for a hasty decision. Come, the files await their destiny, as does Dexter Philips, unless you're too squeamish to see what remains of him go up in smoke."

The fire raged in a ragged crescendo of orange flames and blackened smoke fed by kerosene-soaked logs, paper, photographs, black plastic and currents of warm evening air funnelled through clay conduits at the sides of the bricked-in pit: a wordless epitaph. Both men stood solemnly, their faces warmed by the fire. For one it was an end, for the other a beginning. When they were done, and the sparking embers still glowed with searing heat, Jean-Alexandre spoke above a whisper as they walked along the well-trodden path, telling Steve of Davidson's Sunday dinners. When the young man met the de la Vegas he was amazed by their warmth and how readily they had greeted him and welcomed him into their home. Steven Brandon was learning. He was learning that it was never too late and what it was like to have somebody care.

He listened for hours as they spoke about Davidson. Jean-Alexandre watched his face crease with laughter and frown with sadness as Maria cried and Jorge wrapped his arms around her to console her when she spoke of that final day. He was learning. He was learning what it was like to be loved and for a moment he let his mind wander into a future time and place.

Maria was small beside him, yet she hugged him as tightly as she could, making him promise to visit. He looked at Jorge, uncertain, and the older man shrugged and waved him on with a smile. He leaned down and hugged her back and said "gracias." The warmth of the experience was strange to him, peculiar, and the one word was all he could think to say, all he wanted to say. When Maria asked him for what he smiled and remained silent. The time had come for him to go. It was all too overwhelming.

Jorge feigned indignation and Jean-Alexandre knew better than to test him. He drove them first to the Hotel Las Olas, waited for him to check out and drove them to the Hotel de la Marina where goodbyes were once again difficult. Steve held out his hand, thinking Jorge would do the same. Instead he waved away Steve's hand and embraced Davidson's grandson as tightly as Maria. He drove away at 10:15

"Nice people."

"They are amongst the best. Maria is an angel not yet in heaven and Jorge is one of the finest men I know."

"It's a nice hotel, judge," Steve commented looking up, "but what are we doing here? I've got a boat waiting for me."

"We'll be spending the night at this hotel, Steve, after our meeting with Albert Sorrento. I took the liberty of reserving two suites. Unfortunately none with an ocean view was available."

The young man jerked involuntarily. "You're crazy, man. We don't even know where he is."

"In fact we do. Your grandfather was a man of certain influence on the island, much respected and much remembered. I have taken advantage of his most influential friends. We do know where Sorrento is staying. I must also tell you that I spoke with the marina earlier on and asked the harbour master to discharge your transportation." Steve raised his open palms and furrowed his brow, wanting to ask a question that eluded him. "We'll arrange a flight to Tenerife after we have dealt with Sorrento and are well-rested."

"Deal with him how? This is my thing, judge. What do you think you're going to do to him, slap him?"

"Steve you have read James Parker's history, your father's history. Clearly he was a man who walked tall, melding dignity with humility, as did Davidson. Together we share an origin, you and I: a man who despised cowardice. He would have liked your father as he would have liked you. Sorrento has killed six people and might easily have killed a seventh which is of great concern to me. He killed my father's children and, despite the fact I found all three of the Charleston women to be rather distastefully mercenary, they were still murdered because of your connection to the tontine. And let us not forget that Monsieur DuFour was killed in a decidedly cruel fashion while successfully saving your life."

"Where's this going, judge?"

"In my courtroom I sit in judgement of men who have killed their wives, or the inverse, sloppy professionals, a contradiction to be sure and a host of other socially derelict individuals who believe taking another's life is quite alright. We have more stringent penalties than your own too lenient courts, yet I have no choice but to simply incarcerate those who should otherwise be put down, to coin a phrase. It is in itself an aberration of justice decided upon by bleeding heart liberal politicians. France last executed in '77, Spain in '75 and your homeland in '62. Extradited from here Sorrento will one day be back on the street, presumably with four million dollars. I won't allow such a travesty to happen. Must I say the words, or have you caught my meaning?"

Steve coughed out a spontaneous laugh. "Judge? Hello? We have no guns, nothing."

"I believe I have designed an appropriate punishment for Sorrento, one befitting the crime, one that will certainly appease both the Parkers and the Daniels women. That said, what we don't have is much time left to us. Come. It is time for you to speak with Mr. Sorrento."

They called from Jean-Alexandre's suite, once he had convinced a very bewildered Steve Brandon that Albert Sorrento was not going home. The guns were Davidson's matching chrome-plated .357s; the forty-two foot Grand Banks had been arranged earlier in the day when Jean-Alexandre had excused himself from the veranda. He regretted having deceived his brother and, although he would never be the wiser, Jean-Alexandre knew full-well that d'Avignon would categorically approve.

Steve sat by the phone, pensively staring out over the cityscape. "This is all bullshit. You're a goddamn judge for Christ sake. We're talking about killing someone here."

"That would certainly be one way of viewing the situation. The other more positive point of view would be that of preventing a killing: yours. Davidson intended to bring his family together Steve, not to have it obliterated. He checked his watch. "I believe it's time. Let us hope he has not gone gallivanting."

Steve reached for the phone mechanically, not believing any of it and punched in the numbers. Jean-Alexandre stood by the extension with his finger pressing down on the tiny disconnect nodule.

"Yeah?" was the response that came moments later.

"Sorrento, you asshole, you've fucked up big time."

"Who is this?"

"Good response. Better yet, you don't know where I am or what I look like, even if you were watching when I pulled up in the limo a few hours ago."

"Philips."

"Yeah, I'm Philips, and I need you to listen up. You did DuFour, you snuffed out the old lady before you killed the two women in the pool and you killed the two in Halifax."

Abacus chuckled. "The older broad in the pool was the most fun. She died happy. I should have played a bit with your mother. She looked pretty hot for mid-fifties."

"So she died lucky, good for her. I never knew her, but then you know that. So here's the thing, Sorrento: you fucked up, big time. I've got your flight records that coincide with five murders, a trip to Spain that coincides with a tontine where the five were expected and a shitload of fucking evidence somewhere that links you to all of them and DuFour. There's also a matter of four million in a Swiss bank that I'm pretty sure hasn't been transferred into DiFiore's account." He paused, expecting Abacus to say something. What he heard was laboured breathing from the other end. "Good. So you've got the four million. What I've got in return is solid information for the cops and contacts here that will stop you from leaving the island. To coin a phrase," he looked back to Jean-Alexandre, "you're fucked, asshole. So here's the thing: you're going to meet with me, you're going to get me half of the four million and you're going to tell DiFiore I'm dead. Hey, I'll even let you take a picture of me to show him. Then you've got two million and a happy brother-in-law who won't put a bullet in your head for fucking with him. Fuck with me and you'll be arrested by midnight, about the same time as the cops will be swarming through your nice big house in the burbs and the same time I'll be calling DiFiore to tell him you've had four million for three weeks. By the way, this call is being taped and you've just confessed to six murders... fuck-ass."

"You've got shit, Philips. You're a two-bit piece of shit."

Jean-Alexandre lowered the receiver of the extension to his mouth. "Mr. Sorrento, Mr. Philips is quite correct. This call is being monitored and the authorities have been instructed to stand by. You may have noticed their arrival at the estate this afternoon as well as an unusual number of gardeners. Thinking you can leave this island before meeting with Mr. Philips would a folly of the highest order. You would indeed be arrested forthwith."

"Who the fuck are you?"

"That is as inconsequential to you, Mr. Sorrento, as you are to me. Do as he says." Jean-Alexandre showed his satisfaction with a wide grin as he raised the receiver away from his mouth.

"Be at the Marina del Rey at eleven-thirty, slip H-14," Steve continued. "One minute later and I phone DiFiore while my friend here sends the cops to that two-star shit bag you're staying in at the airport."

"That's only fifteen minutes."

Steve ignored the remark. "Listen up. Bring DuFour's computer or the deal's off. Wear a tee-shirt, shorts and sandals."

"Say what?"

"You heard. I don't give a shit if you have to wear your underwear and come in bare feet. I want to see as much of you as I can, and nothing else except the computer and cable... no bag." He hung up and turned to Jean-Alexandre.

"Most interesting jargon, Steve. I shall have to learn to

talk like that someday."

"Be careful what you wish for, judge. You might get the chance if we mess up on this."

"One should never underestimate one's adversary. However your Mr. Sorrento does seem to be a man of dubious intelligence and more than a little gullible."

"Just don't stand too close to him. Let's set some ground rules, judge. Once he's onboard you stay away from him. Understood? He'd snap your neck in a blink and wouldn't think twice about it. You're about to meet fucking Frankenstein, just a bit dumber."

"And your neck?"

Steve pushed himself away from the desk. "Just don't get in the way."

"Understood."

Jean-Alexandre looked on with obvious interest as Steve reached for one of the two holstered guns on the coffee table and wrapped the tangle of leather straps around his shoulder as easily as though he were putting on a shirt. When Jean-Alexandre went to do the same he was much less graceful, though neither man saw humour in what had become his defining moment that would last his lifetime.

68

The marina was strangely tranquil and seemed deserted, phantasmal. The only sounds came from halyards slapping lazily against short and tall masts and fenders being squeezed against the floating docks. A light southwest breeze undulated the dark water with an erratic pattern of endless miniature waves.

H-14 was a slim finger jutting from the dock and swayed noisily under their feet. Tied to its cleats was the Grand Banks. In the moonlight the trawler loomed bigger than its forty-two feet, and whiter. The bright work was cold to the touch and the fibreglass decks were covered with dew. Jean-Alexandre boarded and went immediately to the helm to start up the twin Cummins that brought the yacht to life with a low, groaning rumble.

"This is too spooky, judge. I'll take the city anytime." Steve said.

"There's no better feeling than to cruise the ocean alone with one's thoughts under the moonlight."

"Going out is one thing. Are you sure we can get back?"

"GPS and two separate radars. Yes, we'll get back."

"How far out are we going?"

"Twenty kilometres, roughly twelve miles to the northeast and no longer than half an hour in these calm seas." He smelled the night air. "The breeze will carry any sound farther out to sea and well away from the islands."

"Calm is good. I like calm."

Jean-Alexandre cocked his head and turned in the direction of the footsteps. "I believe our passenger has arrived."

Steve walked to the transom. He signalled Abacus to stop with one hand and into silence with the other. Then he pointed to the swim platform.

"Put the computer right there, and back away." He did, slowly, not taking his eyes off Steve who clambered over the transom to retrieve it. He passed the computer to Jean-Alexandre and reached under his jacket to grip his gun. "Turn around, Sorrento. Lift your shirt, turn your pockets inside out and throw me the room key with your wallet." He did. "Now, get onboard, real slow, and pull your shirt over your head and down to your elbows."

"Nice face job, Philips. Got yourself a new name to go with it?"

"Philips will do."

Jean-Alexandre passed behind him and stepped onto the transom. He disconnected the power supply, undid the stern, bow, and spring lines and stepped back onboard barely causing a ripple as he eased the trawler away from the dock.

"Where we going?" Abacus asked, trying hard not to appear nervous.

Steve brought out the gun. "Where it's quiet. Now, shut your mouth and sit in the corner until we get out of here."

The Grand Banks pushed its way effortlessly through the water and within minutes the marina lights were no brighter than the millions of flickering stars. Jean-Alexandre stood at the helm manipulating toggles and dials as he steered into a north-easterly heading of forty degrees. When he was satisfied he stepped down to sit beside Steve and begin scrolling through Mike DuFour's stored files.

"Judge, aren't you sort of forgetting something?"

"Referencing what, exactly?"

"Oh, I don't know, like maybe the steering wheel or

something."

"The helm is quite fine. The course has been set, as well as the precise location."

"Where we going, Philips?"

Jean-Alexandre answered, reaching under his own jacket. "We are going to Davy Jones Locker, Mr. Sorrento. It's here." he looked at Steve, "Three point eight million."

"Can we get to it?"

"Without the slightest difficulty."

"Then it's yours, for that foundation thing."

"I graciously accept. Thank you, from all of us."

"Fuck that," blurted Abacus. "You said half, Philips, not the whole fucking thing."

"I lied." Steve burst into loud laughter. "You know how long I've been waiting to say that? Where are the files, Sorrento," Steve asked, chuckling," and all the information you took from the people you killed."

"What information?"

"The letters, the tickets, DuFour's files."

"I tossed that shit."

"The tickets maybe, and the letters, but not DuFour's stuff. So where is it? Don't tell me and I'll go find it myself, after I bang your wife a few times, maybe even watch a couple of videos while I'm doing her. I hear she likes that." Jean-Alexandre looked over with a worried expression, his grip tightening on the gun. "Don't hurry fate, Sorrento. It'll happen soon enough." Abacus stared out into the darkness beyond the portside gunwale, and then over the starboard side behind him looking for the shore, panic suddenly etched into his face. "That's right, Sorrento."

"Where we going?"

"I've already told you, Mr. Sorrento. We're going to Davy Jones Locker."

"Who the fuck is Davy Jones?"

Jean-Alexandre stood and stepped backwards to the helm. "You shall see for yourself in precisely five minutes."

"Tell me what I need to know, Sorrento, or I'll visit your wife. She won't walk straight for a week." Abacus jerked to his feet, visibly stunned by how swiftly both men poised their guns at his head. "Tell me, Sorrento. There's no need for her to suffer."

"Three minutes," said Jean-Alexandre.

"Fuck you."

"Sit on the edge." Steve waved the gun. "The edge, sit on it."

"Gunwale," corrected Jean-Alexandre.

"Yeah, that. Sit on it. Three minutes don't mean shit to me, man. For you it's a frigging lifetime so sit on it and keep your shirt where it is."

Abacus was trembling. The ocean which had so enthralled and mesmerized him now terrified him. There was no brilliant sun, no glittering surface or white crashing waves. What he saw was blackness, what he felt was total fear.

"You keep the money, no sweat. I'll tell you where the files are when we get back to shore. That's the deal."

"One minute," Jean-Alexandre called out from the helm.

"You need those files so bad that's the deal."

"Everyone in them is dead except me and this man's kid." Steve chuckled at Abacus' reaction. "Yeah, the one you didn't get to because you ran out of time."

A low buzz sounded from the helm. Jean-Alexandre reached for the throttle and eased into neutral, slowing the trawler to a stop. "Zero minutes," he said dispassionately, holding his gun firmly as he positioned himself by Steve.

"Sorrento, you know how these scenes always last so damn long in the movies with crying and screaming, the bad guy on his knees pissing or shitting his pants," Steve put down the gun, grabbed the metal boat hook and rammed the tip into Abacus' chest, sending him flailing backwards, "not this time, mother fucker." He took up the gun and hurried to the starboard side even before Abacus was able to surface with his arms and legs thrashing at the black salt water that had begun choking him.

"Sorrento…we're twelve miles out. Enjoy your swim."

Jean-Alexandre leaned over, taking no pleasure in the man's twisted and terrified expression. "Mr. Sorrento, you are indeed fortunate. Unlike your victims, you get to extend your life by sheer will: the ultimate test of your prowess. However, I do suggest drinking in as much water as you can to expedite matters in your favour. The longer you splash about the greater chance you have of being some shark's seafood platter. It's quite nasty. They don't eat you outright. They play with you first, with their food as it were."

"Tell me, Sorrento, right now, and I'll put one into your head, like you did to my father."

"My car, it's in my car, at the airport," he screamed.

Abacus was crying. He was clawing at the water, doing his best to look in all directions, his face a contorted death mask as Steve raised the gun.

"My friend here told me blood is sort of like a dinner bell for sharks." Steve cocked the gun, aimed and blew off most of Abacus' right hand. "That's for my mother, asshole."

With the same speed as Abacus grabbed at the fingerless stump, rising out of the water like some garish aquatic performance, Jean-Alexandre levelled his gun and blew the left hand from its wrist with precision, the force of the impact forcing the mutilated torso below the surface. Jean-Alexandre and Steve Brandon both backed away, the groan of the twin engines soon muffling the crazed hysteria behind them.

"Mine was for Monsieur DuFour, Steve. You understand, of course, that I could not allow you to carry the full burden, or wallow in the full credit."

"I'm glad, judge. I feel real good about it."

"As do I."

"So what now? What happens?"

"I will go to his hotel, vacate his room and pay cash for his stay. No airline cares about no-shows. What is of most concern to me at his juncture is whether you intend to injure his wife or spend any of your nine million to deal with DiFiore?"

"There's no need. Dexter Philips is dead. He died in a fire, remember? But there's still a question about the Canadian and U.S. cops. You opened a real can of worms."

"We will, of course, assist them with their investigations. All they need know is that Davidson passed away from natural causes and the murders obviated the need to continue the tontine which was intended strictly for the purpose of seeing his children. Dexter Philips has never once been mentioned to the authorities."

"I believe you, judge. And Sorrento?"

"He ran away to sea." Jean-Alexandre replied sombrely. "I trust you shall be able to locate his vehicle without difficulty."

"Easily." Steve pulled the parking stub from the wallet. "As soon as I get there. All I need are the car keys from his room."

"To be done this very evening, and what of his wife?"

"Not my type, judge. I didn't mean it. Steve Brandon wants someone a whole lot better."

"Excellent. On that note, I spoke earlier with my brother and Maître d'Avignon while you were more focused on Maria's congenial hospitality. We are of the shared opinion, the three of us, based on what you told me by the bonfire, that you and Miss Samuels should begin your life together on equal terms, in the event she accepts your proposal. Were it not for Miss Samuels your mission here would have been a good deal more difficult, if not a good deal worse. Despite the fact that you are indisputably in her debt, no woman would want to feel indebted to a man for a million dollars, certainly not a woman of high moral standards which we take Miss Samuels to be."

"What are you saying?"

"Simply put, you might want to advise Miss Samuels to check her bank statement sometime after noon on Friday. I am quite certain she will feel like a million dollars. The deposit will be made directly by Davidson's estate, not by you." He grinned, the glow of the radar and GPS screens bathing his face in red. "The amount of your transfer, Steve, has been increased to fifteen million. Your father was quite successful in business and one must assume the joint Parker estate would have been a considerable inheritance for Dexter Philips which is now lost to him. My son Joaquin will one day inherit substantial property and our wish is to compensate you for that imbalance. We see no reason for you not to one day meet Joaquin on equal terms."

Steve blew air from his mouth "Fifteen million. No shit."

Jean-Alexandre chuckled. "Yeah, no shit."

"Thanks, judge. It doesn't sound like much, but it's all I can say right now."

"On the contrary, it is I who must thank you. We all must." Jean-Alexandre reached into his pocket. "Steve, your grandfather would have been proud of you this day. I believe he would want you to have this," he opened his hand, "if I have not mistaken your character and I believe I have not."

"What is it, judge?"

"It once belonged to a Cree warrior, a brave man who fought and died alongside Davidson many years ago. Davidson has worn it ever since. It is a warrior's ring, Steve, a chieftain's ring. As much as I love my son, he has never been a warrior and he never will be one, which I do not intend as an aspersion against him. It's not in him. He's led too privileged a life, gilded as his grandfather recently voiced quite appropriately, and I intend to guide his life somewhat more stringently as of this very moment. He will have his own ring, one of ruby and sapphire, once he has earned the privilege. Take yours, Steve, and wear it with pride. Think of it as a talisman, for that is what it will be if you let it, and do nothing to belittle the memory of those who have worn it before you. Impose that same requirement the day you pass it to your own son. By then you will know the stories of Big Earl and Little Brother."

Steve Brandon took the silver and turquoise ring and stared at it on his finger, losing track of time. "He won't be ashamed of me, judge. It's too bad he can't be here with us now, so I could tell him myself."

"He is with us, Steve."

Steve leaned into the matching captain's seat and thought for a moment. "Judge, can you do me favour, a real easy one?"

"What, exactly?"

"Can you transfer her money on the first, October 01st?"

Jean-Alexandre looked at the young man again, raising an eyebrow at the devilish smile. "Consider it done. The first it will be."

"So I guess your back to being a judge next week."

"I believe not. I shall be announcing my resignation Friday morning, effective immediately."

"Because of him?"

"No, Steve, because of me. I am bothered not in the least to have sent that man to his well-deserved fate, which does not exonerate me completely. Enough said."

"Davidson wrote in my letter that the tontine was not my only gift, simply the key to another. What did he mean, judge?"

Jean-Alexandre considered his words for a moment and held out his open hand. "He meant that you have family yet to meet, Steve. Come back to us very soon. You have friends here now ...and family"

"Family, how weird is that?"

Jean-Alexandre chortled. "Sometimes it's very weird, as you will soon see."

"Then, can I ask one more favour?"

"Yes, of course you may."

Steve averted his eyes toward the speckled aura of marina lights beyond the helm.

"Eight years in prison kind of makes a guy forget his table manners. Know what I mean?"

69

She was tanned and sexy and tall. The men in restaurant were obvious, each one entertaining the same impossible thought. Her shoes were patent leather low-heeled pumps, her silk dress was knee-length and décolleté and her hair was swept up into an elegant French braid. She was femininity personified and becoming angrier by the moment. It was the evening of October 02nd and her new Lady Rolex showed eight-fifteen.

There was only one man in a blue suit who happened to be wearing a silver silk tie, and he certainly was not Dexter Philips. This man was tall, good-looking, his blond hair was styled and he seemed relaxed. Dexter Philips was pure attitude: wound up tight and ready to snap. The man she was looking at was a gentleman, at least from a distance and had probably never seen the inside of a strip bar, she thought. Dexter Philips was an ex-con and would never be more than an ex-con. She could see from where she was sitting that the man's nails were manicured, that he was up-and-coming. Dexter Philips was a down and out loser.

She hated herself for what she had done because of him. She hated Dexter Philips even more for making her feel she could ever be more than what she was. How could she have been so gullible, she asked herself a hundred times? The man in the blue suit had been seated when she arrived and hadn't looked at her once, nor had he once looked at his watch, yet his table was set for two. He was confident, or conceited, and she envied him. Who would stand up a guy like that, she wondered? Who was the one who had decided he was no good, that he wasn't worth the trouble, or had some woman forgotten him all together over the past month because he wasn't worth remembering? What a fool she had been.

When the waiter came closer to her table she thought to stand. She wanted desperately to leave, to get out of there. Her eyes went to the silver dome he carried and her heart sank, feeling trapped. She wanted nothing more than to smack the grin from his face when he stood by her side and leaned forward discreetly.

He placed the dome on the table in front of her.

"Madame, the gentleman across from you in the blue suit wishes to present himself. He wishes to know whether you would care to join him for dinner this evening."

Belinda Samuels bit her lips, her mind racing, too afraid to look across the room. She moved back the silver cover, her eyes locking onto the tiny red velvet box. She looked at the waiter who was poised as detachedly as he could manage.

"He sends his compliments, madame."

She opened box hesitatingly, her stomach suddenly cramped by a sickening knot. The titanium band shined so brilliantly under the dazzling hue of the diamond that the two appeared crafted from a single piece. She looked at the man in the blue suit who sat casually sipping his wine and not acknowledging her. She wanted to scream away her confusion. What she was seeing was impossible! What she was thinking was impossible.

"The gentleman also sends a note, madame, under the velvet box."

Her hands trembled in spite of her best effort to control them. She touched the envelope with reluctant fingertips and looked back at the man just as he turned to meet her gaze, as though on cue. One side of his mouth curled into a mischievous grin and for the first time she saw his eyes: They were clear and piercing, yet warm when he smiled at her. Her entire body quaked.

"Madame, the envelope," the waiter prompted, startling her.

When she opened it she gasped, sweeping an open hand to her chest. What she saw was a confirmation of a bank transfer in the amount of one million dollars. She opened the small card attached to the form. The note was handwritten: Miss Samuels, with the deepest and most sincere gratitude from the family of Davidson Alexander.

The waiter discreetly handed her a second small card which she barely managed to open. There were three handwritten lines:

Thank you for believing in me, Belinda, like they do.
If you say yes I will never hurt you and never leave you.
Steve.

She screamed.

Family Lies

Other Mystery – Suspense - Thriller Novels
By Doug Booth:

Split Verdict
The 4th Man
The Madam
Family Lies
Mother of Pearl
From Inside Her Bedroom
The Feast of Tombola
Deferred Prejudice
The Hunt for Gilligan Rose
The Fatal Diners' Club
Silent Conviction
A Christmas Killer, Comfort and Joy
Pariah In the Mirror

***

No One to Tell (Creative Non-fiction)